THREE CAN KEEP A SECRET

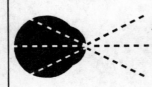

This Large Print Book carries the
Seal of Approval of N.A.V.H.

A JOE GUNTHER NOVEL

THREE CAN KEEP A SECRET

ARCHER MAYOR

THORNDIKE PRESS
A part of Gale, Cengage Learning

GALE
CENGAGE Learning

Detroit • New York • San Francisco • New Haven, Conn • Waterville, Maine • London

GALE
CENGAGE Learning®

Thorndike Press® Large Print Crime Scene.
The text of this Large Print edition is unabridged.
Other aspects of the book may vary from the original edition.
Set in 16 pt. Plantin.

LIBRARY OF CONGRESS CATALOGING-IN-PUBLICATION DATA

Mayor, Archer.
    Three can keep a secret : a Joe Gunther novel / by Archer Mayor. — Large print edition.
        pages ; cm. — (Thorndike Press large print crime scene)
        ISBN-13: 978-1-4104-6421-7 (hardcover)
        ISBN-10: 1-4104-6421-0 (hardcover)
        1. Gunther, Joe (Fictitious character)—Fiction. 2. Police—Vermont—Fiction. 3. Murderers—Fiction. 4. Burglars—Fiction. 5. Brattleboro (Vt.)—Fiction. 6. Large type books. I. Title.
PS3563.A965T47 2013b
813'.54—dc23   2013033760

Published in 2014 by arrangement with St. Martin's Press, LLC

Printed in the United States of America
1 2 3 4 5 6 7 18 17 16 15 14

To Keith Kahla, my editor, a man whose steadfast support and encouragement have been unstinting, ever-present, and welcomed. You have kept alive the best traditions of the great editors of yore by recognizing and nurturing the heart within the prose.

ACKNOWLEDGMENTS

These books are the result of my overworked imagination, true enough. They are also informed by my experiences living and working in Vermont. Each individual volume, however, is helped in its creation by the knowledge, insight, and/or assistance of a collection of special people whose generosity cannot be overpraised. In the case of *Three Can Keep a Secret,* this group consists of the following people and organizations:

Bill Phillips
Marty Hunt
Ruth Kaufmann
Ray Walker
Paul & Dana Waters
Castle Freeman
Julie Lavorgna
John Martin
Becky Smith
Margot Zalkind Mayor

Tom Stevens
Dave Emery
Rich Cogliano
John Angil
Mike Stevens
Kevin Rogers
Steve Shapiro
Scout Mayor
Greg Davis
Lulu Kline

7

Green Mountain Horse Association
Vermont Emergency Management
Office of the Chief Medical Examiner

CHAPTER ONE

Leo Gunther gingerly closed the squeaky door of his beloved and battered Ford Mustang and glanced up at the low-hanging sky. He was a butcher by trade, a collector of vintage cars from the '60s, who still lived with his mother on the family homestead. But while also the second son of a lifelong Vermont farmer, now long passed on, he wasn't any more connected to the soil or dependent upon the weather than the average bank teller. Even as a kid, he'd mostly only accompanied his taciturn father back and forth along the dry dirt runnels of the family's cornfields. But traditions remained, and his weather eye was always on the lookout, as were so many others, across this mountainous, rural, ancient New England state.

Especially today.

Leo crossed the parking lot, pulled open the door to Mitchell's Dry Goods, and exchanged the charged, gunmetal outdoors for the dimly lighted embrace of a cluttered, tight-fitting country store, jammed with cans and boxes lining bowed wooden shelves, and crowded with square-built men holding Styrofoam cups in blunt-fingered hands. Mitchell's was where local loggers, farmers, heavy equipment operators, and the town road crew met every dawn to authoritatively trade information about everything, anything, and everyone within their combined realm of knowledge.

Except that on this Sunday, no one was headed to work, and it was already long past dawn.

"Leo," one of the men called out over the noise of the TV set mounted in the corner, near the stained ceiling. "What d'ya think?"

Leo shrugged as he crossed to the magnum-sized coffeemaker and poured himself a cup. There was only one topic of conversation that morning. "I think Irene is a lousy name for a hurricane."

"Tropical storm," corrected someone, to an underswell of mutterings.

"Whatever," a third intoned, "I think it'll be a rainy day — that's it. These weather guys're just looking for better ratings."

A heavy, bearded man laughed as Leo turned to look at the TV screen. "That's no rainy day, Jesse. That reporter's in Jersey, and he looks like he's drowning."

"They said wind. There's no wind out there."

Leo quietly nursed his coffee. Mitchell, of the name above the door, had been running this store for forty years, handing out free coffee to all of them — although readily accepting donations, which were surprisingly forthcoming — and acting like both the town's radio station and newspaper, since the greater Thetford township hosted neither amenity. Located near high-profile Hanover, New Hampshire — just across the Connecticut River — Thetford had been all but eclipsed by its neighbor's ritzier reputation.

In truth, Leo's own butcher shop across the street bragged of the proximity in its advertisements, which worked to lure meat lovers from thirty miles away. It had helped propel him from homegrown boy to businessman of renown, featured in glossy travel and food magazines, and even the occasional television piece out of Boston.

"The governor made it sound pretty bad," he said softly, recalling the recently declared state of emergency.

"What the hell does she know?" someone said darkly. "Goddamn hippie New Yorker."

Leo smiled. Their chief executive had been that, first appearing in Vermont decades earlier at a commune outside Brattleboro. He knew her well. His brother, Joe, had dated her for years. But she would forever be a flatlander with this crowd. No getting around it. That was just the way it was in Vermont.

Which hadn't stopped her being elected governor. Probably helped, in fact.

Leo pointed with his chin at the screen. "I'm with Mitch — she knows enough to look at those satellite pictures. Irene's a big girl. I think we're gonna get the brunt of her."

"The National Guard's been put on alert," a voice added somberly.

"I heard the power company's doubled its crews."

"It's the wind," Mitch said from behind his counter. "That's the killer, every time."

"It's not the wind; it's the flooding," someone countered. "Always has been; always will."

"There *is* no wind," the same voice repeated from earlier.

That had struck Leo as well. He drifted over to a window overlooking the dirt parking lot, foreseeing its dull silver surface becoming pockmarked by raindrops. He'd heard that Irene had produced winds of 110 miles per hour at her peak, a few days ago, down south. Even Governor Zigman had mentioned strong winds. Winds were attention-getters. Mitch was right there. Cars, houses, power lines. The whole state could look like a pile of pick-up sticks if Irene got pissed off. Leo was old enough to have seen similar damage from tornadoes and ice storms.

But water was worse, as proven by those wet reporters. Water could make wind look like a minor irritation. Vermont was called the Green Mountain State for good reason. It was a dented, twisted, punched-out washboard from overhead, with barely a flat acre across its surface. And it featured a dinosaur-aged spinal column of mountain peaks down its middle, which forced the roads to parallel a spidery maze of waterways lining the bottoms of countless valleys, ravines, and vales. There were dams here and there, put up during the Depression after a couple of killer floods, but Vermont had grown since then, with more people, more pavement, and more communities. As far as Leo was concerned, Gail Zigman was right — they were in for something big. The water would come guttering down the slopes, accumulating in mass and strength until it became its own uncontainable force, capable of feats beyond imagining.

Leo knew that much from personal experience. He had been in and around water all his life. Fishing, swimming, canoeing, hiking along its edge. He'd come to see it as a noncompressible, shape-changing solid — heavy, forceful, and relentless. As a member of his local fire department, he'd helped extract more bodies than he could recall from one watery embrace or another, and they'd all looked the same: pale blue, limp and pruney, smeared with silt and often bruised and battered — drained of vitality in a way peculiar to drownings, as if the water had sucked the heart out of them.

He looked through the window again into the thick, laden, featureless sky, the coffee mug — ironically, to his way of thinking — warm and comforting near his chest.

He didn't feel good about any of this.

Time to head back home.

Willy Kunkle stopped in his tracks, forcing Joe to come up short behind him. "You gotta be shitting me."

Kunkle squatted down in the dim light behind the gas station. "This guy doesn't need jail time. He needs therapy."

Joe Gunther crouched beside his colleague

14

to see what had caught his attention. It was a wet, banded wad of dollar bills, still startlingly crisp, even in the rain.

"He dropped it?" he asked rhetorically.

"More like it fell out of his stupid bag." Willy looked over his shoulder and gestured for Ron Klesczewski, head of Brattleboro's detective squad.

Joe stood back up, as much to ease his knees as to minimize the amount of water soaking his pants. It had been raining for several hours by now, from well before sunup, and was slated to get worse. He stepped out of the way to let Ron in. They were working a gas station robbery together — the PD and Joe's own Brattleboro-based Vermont Bureau of Investigation squad. Normally, the locals would have handled it on their own, but Ron was alone this morning, his small team having worked late into the night, trying to coax people away from the trailers and affordable housing units that were located — as they were commonly across the country — among the lower-cost floodplains.

Klesczewski also had considerable exposure to this specific type of crime — Brattleboro had suffered a rash of them recently. But despite Joe's VBI being a statewide, exclusively major crimes unit, such distinctions seemed trivial in the face of what was bearing down on them. Besides, most of this particular VBI crew had worked for the PD once, before jumping ship for a better offer a few years back. Both the PD and the VBI's one-room office were even located in the same building. In the light of all that, opportunities like this robbery felt more like reunions.

Willy was correct with his scorn for this crime's complexity. They'd known who did it upon first glance at the store's surveillance tape. Caspar Luard was a twenty-something half-wit repeat offender who'd found flipping burgers a challenge and so took up crime as a fallback. This time, with predictable forethought, he'd approached a gas station, put a paper bag on his head in full view of the exterior camera, walked inside to relieve the counterman of the register's cash, and then exited — to again pose for the camera as he removed the now half-torn bag and filled it with money before taking his leave.

Not all police work was a brainteaser.

"Boss?" Willy addressed him.

Gunther's cell phone buzzed at the same time. An older-generation cop, Joe frequently remained surprised by the notion of a phone going off in his pants. He pulled it

16

out and said, "Hang on a sec," while he turned toward Willy, his eyebrows raised in inquiry.

Kunkle was holding his own phone aloft. "It's Sam," he explained. "She was waiting for Caspar when he got home. He can't believe we figured this out."

"He still have the rest of the money?" Joe asked.

"Less than half of it. He lost the rest. We take this route to his apartment, we'll probably find it scattered like rice at a wedding, assuming some other loser isn't already buying beer with it."

Joe nodded and returned to his own phone. "Sorry. Hi."

"Hey, Joe. It's Harry. You knee-deep or can you come over to the command center?"

"Sure. 'Bout five minutes."

Gunther took his leave, crossed the gas station apron to Main Street, and stood at the curb, waiting for the crosswalk light to favor him. It was a quasi-idiotic gesture, he knew, given that the town appeared as empty as a movie set awaiting a crew. There were no cars in motion, a couple of people barely visible two blocks in the distance, and very few vehicles parked by the meters. Even for a Sunday morning, it had an eerie, abandoned air to it, and — with the lowering, rain-sodden sky feeling fifty feet off the ground — it also looked like a black-and-white photograph, set off here and there with hand-applied painterly touches, like the brilliant yellow slickers of those far-off pedestrians.

His caller, Harry Benoit, was the town's fire chief and the head of emergency operations. Over the years, Harry had made it his business to figure out how to manage chaos, from major fires to natural mishaps to protesters thronging the streets for assorted causes. And, through a combination of grant money, political arm-twisting, equipment acquisitions, and training involving a network of like-minded agency heads, he had succeeded in building a pretty solid organization across Windham County.

Joe tilted his head back and let the rain wash his face under the brim of his hat.

There was no wind to speak of; no lightning or thunder. Tropical Storm Irene, now that she'd arrived, was feeling like a summer shower.

But with something more malevolent lurking within her.

Joe took his hat off briefly and let the rain hit him fully. It was a farm boy's variation on a cook's dipping his finger into the sauce to finalize his appraisal of it.

This was no summer shower, Joe concluded, at last crossing the street to the signal's steady chirping. There was a steadiness to this rain, and a weight — a sense of permanence that foretold it would be with them for a long time. It was the kind of rain that he'd loved in 1930s melodramas, supplied by pipes and sprayers kept just out of the frame.

Harry's command post was in the basement of the town's municipal building, which also housed the town offices, the police, and — on the second floor — the VBI's cramped quarters. It looked like a structure that the Addams Family might have called home, and had begun as the local high school, before being steadily and repeatedly remodeled from the 1800s onward. Through the decades, every tenant had groused about its inefficiencies, its layout, and its temperature fluctuations. Joe had always enjoyed the antiquity of the place, and sympathized with a cranky old behemoth that, like him, had quietly endured the finicky technology forever being thrust upon it. In that way, he was reminded of the entire state's dilemma, struggling to keep current in an ever-more-modern world while touting tourist-friendly images of photogenic cows, tasty syrup, crusty locals, and hot spot ski resorts.

The Emergency Operations Center, or EOC, like so many of its ilk across the nation, was located out of sight in a windowless, subterranean corner enclave. Joe had found it a curiously common habit of government bureaucracies to locate such centers in the heart of structures most likely to suffer from damage or pointed attack. Typical had been New York City's, located on the twenty-third floor of the World Trade Center, *after* the 1993 bombing of the parking garage had revealed the building's appeal as a target.

Joe had once mentioned all this to Harry, but all he'd found was a kindred spirit equipped with a gallows sense of humor, resigned to following directives from politicians far away and far removed.

And so they made do with the basement, with fingers crossed.

Joe climbed the steep approach of broad, uneven granite steps leading up to the municipal building's entrance. They were set into a hill overlooking Main Street and the district court across the way — admittedly a location that alleviated most concerns about water doing much more than flatten the grass to both sides of him.

Still, as he well knew, water had a way of

doing as it liked. Just ask New Orleans.

He paused in the old building's lobby, shaking off the rain and slapping his damp hat against his leg, before descending a nearby staircase made of much-painted, scarred, and splintered wood, massive and old enough that it might have been pried off the Ark for reuse. There was a fitting thought, Joe mused.

The basement was normally a somber, tomblike place, relegated to storage, an officers' rarely used gym, a *Titanic*-sized furnace, miles of awkward overhead wiring, and the usually darkened EOC.

But not today. Joe entered a beehive of activity, with people milling about and the smell of coffee strong. The air was electric with talk, ringing phones, buzzing printers, and the background chatter of TV weather stations and news programs.

He stopped on the threshold of the Emergency Operations Center itself and took it in. He recognized over three-quarters of the people there. He'd lived his entire adult life in this town, and knew most of the cops, firefighters, EMTs, social service folks, and politicians by name. But there were more than those here now. The room was packed with people typing, talking on phones, and conferring over wall maps covered with pins, overlays, and grease pencil scribblings. It was a low-ceilinged, cramped version of a war room.

"Kinda cool, huh?"

Joe turned at the voice by his shoulder and took in Harry Benoit, a steaming mug of coffee in his hand. An affable, disarmingly funny man in normal times, he'd been in the fire service from high school onward. He'd made crisis a primary food group.

But despite his opening one-liner, he didn't seem to be enjoying himself right now.

"You look like hell, Harry," Joe told him.

Benoit smiled tiredly. "Thanks. Been up most of the night. Not smart, considering what we're facing today. This wasn't supposed to hit till late morning. It's six hours early. Now is when I was figuring for some shut-eye." He paused to drink from his mug before adding, "Best-laid schemes."

Joe caught his implication. "This really going to be bad?"

Harry gave him a serious look before suggesting, "They call these things 'Hundred Year Storms' for good reason, Joe. We're on the verge of a world of hurt."

Bonnie Swift looked out one of the windows of what had been evasively retitled the

Vermont State Hospital. Built in the 1890s in Waterbury as the Vermont Hospital for the Insane, and chartered to address "the care, custody, and treatment of insane criminals of the state," it was now a kinder, gentler place, in both name and practice. Bonnie had been an RN here for twelve years, and despite the ribbing she got from her outsider friends, she enjoyed both patients and coworkers.

Not that there weren't times — frequently — when the two contributed to a Kafkaesque nightmare. Still, she had always enjoyed the offbeat, and what better place for that than a now politically correct loony bin?

Today, however, the tensions were coming from the outside, and the entire facility had been injected with an unusual camaraderie, as if the certifiably sane and those aspiring to that status had come together against some ominous threat.

Bonnie Swift leaned in close to the windowpane, blocking out the light behind her to better see into the surrounding gloom. It was midmorning, and yet as dark as dusk, with the sky uniformly heavy. She didn't need a forecaster's warning to know a natural train wreck when she saw it coming.

It wasn't just the wind and rain she was

23

considering. The remnants of the hospital were located at the rear of a sprawling state-office complex that had slowly overtaken the old hospital buildings as the patient population retreated from its 1,700 heyday to about 50 now. The campus — housing dozens of agencies as diverse as hers and the Department of Public Safety, across the driveway — even bragged of the totally renovated State Emergency Operations Center — one of the few in the country to be located above ground level. The upper-floor placement struck her as propitious, since the SEOC not only acted as the go-to place for all of the EOCs across Vermont, but the entire campus was situated on a floodplain.

She wiped the pane free of the mist from her breath. She couldn't actually see the Winooski River. An earthen berm had been built alongside the lowermost parking lot, in a mainly psychological effort to keep the water contained. To her mind, it served the same purpose as drawing a thin curtain against the sight of a raging fire.

Waterbury, being so close to the capital, Montpelier, had been an overflow parking place for state facilities for decades — dependent on the fact for its financial vigor. But it bordered Vermont's second-longest

24

river, and despite the Winooski's having overflowed multiple times — drowning twenty people in 1927 — the town, along with the building Bonnie Swift was in, had slowly expanded to the river's edge.

One of the doctors stepped into the hallway from his office and noticed her by the window. He had arrived from Boston a year ago.

"How's it looking?" he asked. "We going to float away?"

She glanced at his smiling face. "I can't say we won't," she said seriously. "The river surrounds us on three sides. Where we are hangs down like the udder on a cow."

He turned to study her, struck by her tone of voice. "You don't make that sound good."

"I just hope our evacuation plan works," she concluded, breaking away to return to her rounds. "Or that we even know where we filed it."

CHAPTER TWO

"Leo? It's me."

Leo heard the tension in his older brother's voice, and immediately tried putting him at ease. "It's all good up here, Joey. Just rain. No bullshit. You wanna talk to Ma?"

He handed the phone to his wheelchair-bound mother, who was already reaching for it, a slight frown on her face because of his language. Not just the one crude word, he knew. Funnily, she had less of a problem with that than with his use of poor grammar.

"Joe," she said in place of a greeting. "Leo's correct. We are absolutely fine, up here on our little hill. Even the electricity's still on."

"And I checked the generator." Leo shouted. "A-OK."

"How are you faring down there?" Joe's mother asked him.

"Personally? Fine," he reassured her. "The

house is out of harm's way, and I've been keeping myself busy and mostly dry. That may be about to change, though."

"Flooding?" she asked.

"Yeah. It started with a few basements a couple of hours ago. Now we're getting whole neighborhoods underwater that haven't seen that in half a century. West Brattleboro is getting really creamed — all those low-lying housing developments. The Whetstone has turned into the Colorado, and quite a few residents have refused to move."

"That's terrible," she said with feeling. "Will you be able to help?"

"I think so," he told her honestly. "There are swiftwater rescue teams here from as far away as Colchester. They never even got to staging — just went straight to their first assignments. So far, no deaths have been reported. But it's early yet," he added grimly, "and we're hearing that, closer to the Green Mountains, towards Wilmington, Wardsboro, and places like that, they're getting hit much harder. Route 9 is cut in a couple of spots. Roads and bridges are going out all over. What are you hearing from around you?"

"Much the same," she answered. "Mostly, it's been just wait-and-see — or listen, in our case."

"Leo's store is okay?"

"As far as we know."

She heard some noise on Joe's end, in the distance, and he said in a slightly more rushed tone of voice, "Gotta go, Mom. Take care of each other and I'll try to call later."

"Don't worry about us, Joe. Be careful out there."

"Love you," he said, a fraction of a second before the line went dead.

She merely smiled sadly and pushed the disconnect button.

Caspar Luard looked glumly out the window of the cruiser's backseat, uncaring of the watery sheets greatly limiting visibility. He was too lost in his own misery to give a damn about some rain. Rained too god-damn much in this state anyhow. That was one of the reasons he'd tried to rob that gas station — to get the hell out of Vermont. Assuming he'd had enough left over after buying himself a little peace of mind. That's what he liked to call the various substances he put into his system to distract himself: peace of mind.

He glanced at his lap and squirmed a little, trying to get comfortable on the hard plastic seat. They could've put him in a regular car, or even the van they normally used for prisoner transports. It's not like he was going to throw up. He'd never done that in a cop car yet. He adjusted the chain that ran around his waist and interconnected with his handcuffs. At least they hadn't locked his hands behind his back. That hurt like hell.

In the front seat, beyond the plastic and metal mesh divider, the two transport deputies weren't so distracted. Nor were they ignoring the weather.

"You wanna tell me why we're out here?" said the passenger, a deputy sheriff for five months by now.

"Give it a rest, Al," said the driver, not receptive to casual chatter. The windshield wipers were on their highest setting, and yet at split-second intervals, he lost sight of the end of the car's hood, along with the road ahead. On average, it wasn't as bad as that, but they had a good half hour to go before they reached the prison in Springfield — their customer's home away from home. And then they'd have to go back out into this mess, probably to guard some washed-out bridge.

"I'd like to," Al continued complaining, waving his hands around, "except here we are, right? Why couldn't they've just put this

29

jerk in holding overnight? Answer me that."

"Don't know, Al."

"The PD just didn't want to be bothered. That's why. All hands on deck; can't spare the manpower; special circumstances. Like the Sheriff's Department's not busy, too? We got guys all over the county, right in the middle of this shit storm, drowning right where they're standing, and the great Bratt PD can't house a single loser in their nice, dry basement? Please."

The driver didn't answer. The wheel between his hands was growing mushy, as the puddles they hydroplaned through grew in depth and number. He slowed down further. He was already taking back roads, instead of the interstate, from Brattleboro to Springfield, in the hopes that visibility would improve and the chances of skidding decline. Now he was beginning to doubt that any choice would have made a difference.

"Al," he said shortly. "I need you to shut up."

Al looked at what was going on through the windshield as if for the first time, and then stared at his colleague. "Jesus, Tom. Are we gonna make it?"

Bonnie Swift stood at the halfway point on

the stairs, speaking gently and clearly to each passing patient. "It's okay. Just a bit of water. The second floor is fine. Turn right at the top. Stay calm. Stay calm."

One of her favorites came into view, Carolyn Barber, nicknamed "the Governor" by her own preference. She was, as usual, looking stunned and wide-eyed, as if having just been startled awake.

"Hi, Governor. Everything's okay. Just take a right at the top, keep with the others."

But Barber stopped and studied her closely, from about four inches too close for comfort — a habit Bonnie was used to. "It's wet down there."

"Yes, it is," Bonnie said quietly, taking her elbow and steering her toward the next step up. "It's raining very hard and some of the water is getting inside. Nothing to worry about. That's why we're going upstairs."

Carolyn Barber paused a bit longer, watching her, before finally nodding. "It's wet," she repeated, but allowed herself to be directed.

One of Bonnie's colleagues appeared from below after five more patients filed past.

"Everyone out?" Bonnie asked.

"All the patients are," the other woman confirmed. "Maintenance is wrestling with the utility panels and computer servers. They said the automatic door locks might short out, so we should keep an eye open. They said Richardson better distribute some keys and man the doors so we can override the system if necessary. Also, we should start distributing flashlights."

Bonnie made a face. "Good luck with the keys. He may not even know where they are. It's been years."

The two of them walked up the rest of the stairs and followed the patients down the hallway. The lights flickered, switching to the eerie backup units placed along the ceiling, and suddenly the fire alarms all went off, accompanied by a woman's gentle and deliberate voice intoning, "Code Red. Code Red. Please proceed to the nearest emergency exit," again and again, in an endless loop.

"Damn," Bonnie muttered, covering her ringing ears. "This'll make things better."

Ahead, the line had stopped at one of the electronic doors. She sidled along the wall to get to it quickly and keep the group moving, but when she reached it, she found that it had automatically locked after allowing several patients through, separating them from their handlers.

"Shit," she whispered to herself, her head

beginning to pound from the bells and horns. She quickly slid her pass card through the lock.

Nothing happened.

She looked back and called out. "Jenn. Did the maintenance guys say they'd be fooling with the locks?"

"No. Like I said, just that there might be glitches," Jenn shouted over the noise from the rear.

"That was really rude, what you said," a woman nearby told her severely.

Bonnie ignored her and tried the lock again, to no avail. She peered through the mesh-wired glass door into the hall's extension. Amid the pulsing red lights, she could just make out three people wandering away, including the Governor.

She pounded on the door to get their attention, wondering where the staffers were at that end of the building. Two of the three patients turned around, and she gestured to them to return. However, Carolyn Barber only stiffened slightly, as if caught in the midst of some mischief, before cutting left and vanishing through a doorway.

It was the back staircase.

Bonnie yelled back at Jenn. "Punch in the alarm. One of them's in the stairwell."

It wasn't an actual alarm — which

wouldn't have been heard in any case —
but a series of red phones located throughout the facility, programmed to trigger a
complete lockdown, just in case one of the
patients made a break for it.

Bonnie expected to hear the sound of the
alarm — a mechanical clicking, echoing
throughout the building like oversized
dominoes striking each other in turn.

But there was only silence from the door
beside her.

"You do it?" she asked in a loud voice.
The line between them was becoming res-
tive with people covering their ears, shouting, and beginning to react to the wall-to-
wall wailing. Bonnie didn't like how things
were developing.

"It won't take the code," Jenn announced.
"It's dead."

Bonnie hit the intercom button on the box
beside the frozen door — a backup system
to connect her to security.

There, too, nothing happened.

She looked back at Jenn and put up her
hands, trying to keep her expression mildly
bemused for everyone's sake.

But she was closer to panic than that.
Controlling a bunch of patients in a locked
corridor was not a great challenge. But
they'd just abandoned a rapidly flooding

basement — which was where she suspected Carolyn Barber was now headed, no doubt seeking the familiarity of her room amid the confusion. And the people down there had no idea who she was or what to do with her. There was any amount of trouble she could get into, including finding a way outside through the suddenly compromised security system.

Bonnie began struggling to get back from where she'd come, hoping the other stairwell was still open.

"You're up, Joe," Harry told him as Joe hung up the phone on Leo and his mother.

"What've we got?" Joe asked, relieved to be put to use at last. Almost everyone else had been chest-deep in this mess for hours by now — handling washouts, accidents, calls for heavy equipment, stranded people, failed wires, fallen trees, and more. He and the rest of his team had been all but sitting on their hands, at most helping with computers, manning the phones, or keeping the coffee coming.

Benoit was still holding a phone at his ear. "West Bratt. Report of looters breaking into an abandoned trailer." He handed Joe a slip of paper with the address.

Joe took the slip, looked over at Sammie

35

Martens, who merely said, "I'll get Les and Willy," and headed toward the door.

"Meet you at the parking lot entrance," he told her.

Two minutes later, the four of them paused at the glass doors, watching a deluge so complete that it seemed to be pouring from a battery of fire hoses.

"Damn," Lester Spinney said quietly. "That's really coming down."

"That the best you can do?" Willy groused.

"I think it's cool," Sammie said wondrously.

Joe glanced back at them. It was rare that they all four set out on a job together. They were an independent bunch, paid to be so, divvying up the workload to get it done efficiently and thoroughly. They were veteran specialists and considered among the best in the state.

Joe had also known them for a very long time — certainly Sam and Willy, who'd been his detectives when he headed the Brattleboro squad. Lester came from the state police, whose erstwhile investigators populated most of the VBI's ranks nowadays. But with Lester, too, Joe had undergone an arc of experiences that few other coworkers got to share with their colleagues. This was a team forged by fire, who'd literally worked to save each other's lives on occasion. Sam and Willy even lived together, and she'd recently given birth to a baby girl — a miracle to most who knew them, if only because so few could believe that any woman would get that close to Willy Kunkle.

"We're not gonna drown any less if we stand around here," Willy commented now, pushing against the door's handle. "Might as well get it over."

He preceded them into the rain as the others adjusted their raincoats. Willy, typically, hadn't bothered donning one, knowing that there was no true protection in these conditions, and not wanting to add another layer of wet clothing to his burden.

Joe realized he was right, of course; he was about so many practical matters. Once a sniper in the military, Willy had learned to live with discomfort, and as a recovering alcoholic with a crippled left arm and an attitude problem, he'd also learned to cope with adversity — if not hypocrisy, dishonesty, or laziness. The man had the zealotry of a convert there, and cut nobody slack — especially himself.

They sloshed over to the SUV parked fifteen feet away, the weight of the water heavy on their shoulders. Spinney, true to his generally upbeat demeanor, began laughing — his head back like Joe earlier — standing tall and frighteningly skinny. "Geez Louise, why not just wear swimsuits? This is crazy."

He had a point. By the time they slammed the doors from the inside, the windows were fogged with their own humidity. Joe fired up the engine and adjusted the air-conditioning to improve their visibility.

Slowly, they left the parking lot, entered Grove Street, and began driving toward West Brattleboro, beyond Interstate 91.

"Tell me we're not heading for a cat up a tree," Willy said sourly, sitting in the front seat and staring beyond the ineffective windshield wipers, the vehicle feeling more like a boat than a car.

Joe took Sammie in with a quick look over his shoulder. "You didn't tell him?"

"Oh, great," Willy muttered as Sam conceded, "I said we had police work." She addressed her companion: "You were having that much fun answering phones?"

"Convince me I wasn't," he said without twisting around.

"Report of a break-in at one of the West B trailer homes," Joe updated him.

Lester laughed again, having been just as ignorant as Willy about their outing. "You're kidding. Who cares if it's thieves or the flood that takes your junk? It's all going down-stream anyhow."

Surprisingly, Willy countered, "That 'junk' matters if it's yours. Just 'cause they're trailers doesn't mean they're not homes."

There was an embarrassed silence before Willy himself changed course by addressing Sam unexpectedly. "Did you call about Emma?"

She nodded. "High and dry. I even had Louise look out her window and describe what things looked like."

"How long ago?"

"Fifteen minutes."

He pressed his lips together, clearly not satisfied. "Things could change in two. You know that."

"I know that we discussed it," she said patiently. "And that we agreed I'd keep calling throughout to check on her."

The other two in the car kept silent, knowing of Willy's twin obsessions about his daughter's welfare and every possible misfortune awaiting her. She was currently in the care of the aforementioned Louise, whom they'd all had to meet as part of Willy's vetting process, and who must have felt afterwards worthy of national security clearance.

Joe reached the interstate overpass, and

Sammie redirected the conversation by pointing out her side window. "Oh, God. I hate that. Look at those stupid kids."

They watched as two teenaged boys in bathing trunks rode a large inner tube down the middle of the grassy median strip between I-91's two lanes, which at the moment was a roaring, whitewater brook.

"They're gonna love the drop-off between the bridges around the corner," Willy said. He reached into his pocket with his one good hand and pulled out a cell phone. "I'll tell the state police to either pick 'em up or scrape 'em off Williams Street below."

Joe kept driving, knowing that Willy was right. In the time it would take him to swing around and access the interstate, the two boys would have either had the ride of their thoughtless lives, or been mangled at the bottom of where I-91's twin bridges leaped over Williams.

Assuming that Williams hadn't become a torrent itself, he continued thinking as they passed a couple of shuttered gas stations and entered West Brattleboro — a row of stores, restaurants, a church, a service station, and a post office, all paralleling the racing Whetstone Brook. Here the water was making a shallow river of Route 9. They all knew what this meant, even before they got there: Farther west, the topography flattened, spread out, and became more level with the brook, meaning that what was a passable sheet of water here was most likely a cascade beyond.

As Willy talked into his phone, Joe said to the rest of them, "Take your seat belts off, people. If we need to move fast, you don't want them in your way."

All became silent in the car, aside from the deep-throated thrumming on the roof.

The mood in the car carrying Caspar Luard had worsened. Tom, his driver, had committed a fundamental blunder. Somewhere between Rockingham and Springfield, on Route 5, he'd rounded a corner, calculated the dimensions of the lake swamping the road ahead, and despite Al's growing apprehension, white-knuckled the wheel and gunned the engine.

"Holy Jesus." Al yelled out in fear as the car plowed into the water, twin plumes sprouting like wings to both sides. For an instant, they were fine. Tom felt the bite of the road beneath him, and thought he glimpsed its emergence beyond.

But it didn't last. There was a lurch from underneath, the engine suddenly roared as the tires left the road, and the entire vehicle

41

sloughed and twisted on its axis as it was transformed from car into raft.

"Damn," Tom almost whispered as the cruiser began listing, first slowly, and then with increasing speed, as it found a downward embankment and slid into deeper water.

"It's coming in." Luard shouted, kicking at the seat before him, fighting against the chain around his waist. "Hey, you assholes, it's coming in through the doors. Come on, guys. Come on. Make it stop."

But there was no stopping anything now, Tom knew, his hands glued to the wheel while they slid like a newly christened ship into the middle of a bounding, curling, mad rush of earth-brown water. Now it was just a matter of finding out where they'd end up.

Until Al changed the dynamics by opening his door.

"I'm getting out," he yelled, oblivious of the idiocy of both gesture and statement.

Tom stared at him in astonishment as Al put his weight against the door and was instantly sucked from the car, the current having reacted to the sudden appearance of what amounted to a large oar by snapping them around like a leaf in a torrent.

There was no time to respond. The cruiser

flipped, Caspar's screaming from the back was overwhelmed by the symphonic blending of rushing water, the tearing of metal as the door vanished altogether, and — most ominously to Tom, who heard it all in distinct detail — the deep, throaty rumbling of thousands of unseen boulders tumbling in the heart of the river into which they'd been delivered.

It was that primordial growl, above all else, that caught his attention, as dreadful to him as watching footage of lava flows and eruptions of molten rock — a childhood terror he'd never been able to handle.

"Hang on," he shouted to his hysterical passenger, finding himself gripped by a cold and calculating understanding of their situation, their odds, and their options.

Hearing the engine still roaring, he seized upon what he assumed were the car's death throes to reach out and hit the automatic door locks, lower the windows, put the transmission into park, and unhook his seat belt. The last gesture popped him free of his seat and pressed him up against the steering wheel, since right then, the car was riding the river nose down, its engine acting as an anchor.

Caspar looked around in panic as the water poured in through both windows and shot through the partition like a geyser. "Holy fuck, man. You're killin' us."

Tom didn't answer. The surrounding water had a smothering menace to it — opaque with mud and filled with grit. It entered from all sides, weighing him down and lunging for his throat. He spat out a mouthful and took a deep breath before sliding through the gaping door opening like a porpoise as the car caught on a boulder and twisted, driver's side down. His prisoner's screaming was swallowed by the roar and tumult around them.

Tom hooked onto the door post between front and back and reached into the window to grab Caspar's seat belt, following it underwater to the buckle, doing his best to avoid the other man's thrashing upper body as he fought his restraints in a burst of fading energy.

The car shuddered again, almost throwing Tom free, but not before he'd slipped the buckle loose and grabbed Caspar's shirt, pulling him halfway out of the window to where he could breathe.

Caspar coughed and spat and threw his head back, gasping for air, as Tom continued extracting him from the tossing car.

"Oh, my God. Thanks, man. Holy Mother of Mary."

The two of them were finally thrown free in one final, explosive encounter with a boulder, Tom clinging to his prisoner as to a long-sought-after lover.

Now separated from the vehicle, but weighed down by his gun belt and his manacled companion, Tom slipped an arm around Caspar's chest in a lifeguard's grip and struck out in a clumsy stroke for a passing tree, catching one of its limbs like the baton at a relay race.

In itself, it was no solution, but the tree caught something along the edge of the bounding river, and swung them around into a small island of more vegetation, bobbing within the relative calm of a temporary eddy.

Tom clawed them farther into the tangle, away from the water's grasping embrace, dragging Caspar Luard as if he were a duffle bag filled with rocks. He cursed all the way, as Luard's clothing and chains got caught in the branches, or as Tom's feet slipped through holes on the shifting matting beneath them.

"Who're you yelling at?" Caspar complained. "You got us into this."

"Shut up," Tom ordered him. "Or I'll throw you back. Use your feet."

Slowly, they worked their way to the top

of what appeared to be a makeshift hum-
mock of debris, perhaps crowning firm
ground but surrounded by the fast-snaking
tendrils of the caramel-colored river they'd
just left.

At the far end of it was Al, Tom saw,
stretched out like a beached whale, bleeding
and torn, but alive enough to offer a feeble
wave. Too tired to resent his abandonment
of them earlier, Tom merely returned the
gesture.

"Hey, Chief?" Caspar's plaintive voice
brought him back.

"What?" he asked almost peevishly.

Caspar jangled his chains. "Do I still have
to wear these?"

CHAPTER THREE

Joe rolled to a stop in the middle of the road. Ahead, the Whetstone Brook was arcing over the Route 9 bridge, the railing no longer retaining errant vehicles, but instead acting as a launching ramp for a continuous rooster tail of liquid mud fountaining through the sodden, gray air like a broken water main spewing across the road.

"Gee, boss," Willy commented. "Not gonna go for it?"

Joe didn't respond, craning to see to their right through the streaming water on the glass. "The address is over there. We might be able to get closer to the trailer park using the back feeder road, instead of the main entrance."

"We putting a lot of effort into this?" Lester asked from the back. "I mean, not to be coldhearted . . ."

Joe held up his hand. "I know, I know. They had no idea what was out here when they assigned us." He put the car in reverse and began turning around. "Let's just give it a vague look around. We may not even get out."

They'd barely engaged the road in question when Sam announced, "There, to the left. Two guys in a tree."

The rest of them turned to stare.

"Idiots," Willy said.

Joe cast him a look. "You don't know that's them."

"Yeah I do," the old sniper assured him. "The one on the upper branch is Zach Neeley. Worthless piece of crap. This is totally his style. I don't know the other one."

"Thank God for that," Sam muttered.

"It's gotta be one of his new recruits," Willy finished. "Nobody's dumb enough to do more than one job with Zach."

"They look comfortable enough," Lester said hopefully.

"They look half dead," Joe stated, reaching for the radio. He gave their location and an update to Dispatch, adding that the priority of the call should be pretty high, as the situation looked "fluid."

"You did actually say that," Willy challenged him after he finished.

Joe shook his head and flipped on the car's blue lights, to indicate their location to

48

responders. This wasn't going to be easy, he knew. Plucking these two morons from their perch would involve many skilled people trying their best not to get killed in the process.

"Now you did it," Willy said.

Joe looked back at the men in the distant tree. One of them was pointing and waving at them, attracted by their flashing strobes.

"Oh, for Christ's sake," Sammie said, and without further comment, opened her door and stepped out into the storm, Les sliding out right behind her.

Joe immediately followed. The treed men had reacted to the sight of them by jumping into the water in obvious hopes of swimming across.

"That's about right," Willy groused, joining them in the downpour. "Trust a moron to think he can walk on water."

Joe gestured to the rear of the SUV. "Get whatever you can find — ropes, vests, whatever makes sense. Maybe we can snag 'em on the way by." He began jogging toward where the swollen brook crossed the road ahead, his eye on a long branch he'd spotted lying along the impromptu bank.

To his left, he could barely make out the two bobbing heads amid the trees, building fragments, furniture, and personal belongings, all careening toward him at high speed. With the sound of the water obliterating all chances of being heard, he began waving at them to swim toward his side of the river.

"They might as well be tennis balls," Willy shouted beside him as Lester and Sam began rigging a coil of rope to the branch Joe had spotted earlier, hoping to extend a hanging lasso to the two men as they swept by.

It didn't take long, but it only half worked. With the four of them as a counterbalance, they got the branch well in position, but only the man they didn't know managed to snag the loop. Neeley took a swing at it and missed.

"I knew he wouldn't let me down," Willy said as he dropped the branch, took off at a sprint alongside the churning water — trailing a second coil of rope that he'd unobtrusively tied around his waist — and leaped almost on top of the flailing Zach Neeley.

Sam and Joe threw themselves onto the quickly vanishing rope as Lester kept pulling the unnamed man ashore.

"Willy, you son of a bitch," Joe heard Sammie grunting as she struggled for a foothold against the dead weight of the two in the water. "I will kill you if you survive this."

50

■ ■ ■ ■

In Waterbury, Bonnie Swift — her ears stuffed with toilet paper against the incessant, malfunctioning fire alarm — finally managed to use a fire extinguisher to smash the handle off the locked door to the Brooks Rehab unit in the basement, only to be pushed back by a four-foot wall of dammed-up water and a stationery store's worth of papers, files, books, plastic trash cans, and, incongruously, one poster featuring surfing off Hawaii. She stumbled against the stairs behind her, fell on her back, and felt the tidal wave wash over her, smelling of diesel fuel and oil, among other things she didn't want to know.

Spitting and rubbing her mouth, she staggered back to her feet, swearing and looking into the murky water for the flashlight that she'd dropped. In her search for the wandering Carolyn Barber, she'd found several people feverishly trying to rectify the building's electrical problems, but no sign of the Governor.

And by now, what little light had been supplied by the heavily masked sun was all but gone, and the normally long summer day was shortened by the weather to resemble its briefest winter kin.

She followed a faint glow to her submerged waterproof flashlight, near the bottom step, and sloshed through the open door ahead, into a maze of shadowy corridors.

Carolyn Barber had blundered into the state hospital's famed tunnels. Unperturbed, even smiling at the novelty of her surroundings, she walked slowly ahead, hands outstretched, along the narrow corridors. The state office complex sat atop a honeycomb of such passages, some large enough to house offices to either side; others so cramped as to qualify as crawl spaces. The purposes of these tunnels had varied over the decades, as had access to them, depending on the overhead building's function. The state hospital and the public safety headquarters had been considered drum-tight, for instance. Others were pretty much common areas.

Until the water had altered all such distinctions.

Carolyn hadn't been looking to escape. She hadn't even known about the tunnels. She'd just wanted to return to her room. The tunnels — by the doors, defaulting to unlock instead of to lock — had simply been delivered to her. With the ebbing light, the disorienting noise, and her desire for peace and quiet, they'd appeared to offer solace.

She was beginning to fret, however. The water, for one thing, had deepened. Initially reminding her of when she'd enjoyed wading as a child, it had now reached her waist, and was not smelling good, either.

She stopped, working her perpetually fogged brain for a clear thought. She had memories of being able to do that. She remembered a time, long ago, when she hadn't felt trapped in a daydream. But she couldn't swear to it. After all, she also vaguely recalled having been called a leader once, although none of her listeners seemed to know of it, which made her doubtful. They did honor the title she'd insisted upon, the Governor, which sounded right to her, if again tempered by their bemused expressions.

She looked ahead. There was the tiniest sliver of light, perhaps from a small window, itself out of sight. It was enough for her to see that the water level and the low ceiling almost met as the floor ramped down beneath her. It didn't seem like a good idea to keep going.

She turned to retrace her steps and let out a startled cry. Something large had appeared right behind her, floating up without a sound and wedging itself into the tight passage. She tentatively tried determining what it was, and what to do with it, her terror heightening. In fact, it was a large wooden desk, liberated from a nearby office by the rising water, and set free to float like a clumsy crate.

However, Carolyn didn't know that. She just felt hemmed in, which was a bad thing for her in particular. She therefore opted for her original route — away from the hard, large, slightly bobbing threat and into the deeper water.

Jenn stared openmouthed at her colleague. "Oh, my God. Bonnie. What happened to you? Are you all right?"

Bonnie Swift was drenched, covered with filth, and appeared exhausted. Jenn gently moved one of the patients from a nearby chair and steered Bonnie toward it. They were all on the second floor, the lights were back on, the alarms had been stilled, and, other than the staffers keeping a perpetually keen eye open for any mishaps or sudden movements, things had become relatively boring.

"I lost the Governor," Bonnie admitted, dropping into the seat.

Jenn's eyes widened. "She's dead?"

But Bonnie shook her head and shrugged. "No. I don't know. Maybe. I lost her in the tunnels. She's gone."

"She still pissed at me?"

Joe smiled as he applied a Band-Aid over Willy's left eye. "She mentioned something about a newborn's father risking his life for the sake of a dirtbag who didn't have the brains of a urinal cake."

Willy burst out laughing. "She said that?"

Joe sat back, his task completed. "Almost a direct quote — the last part, anyhow."

"I love it."

"So, yes, she is still pissed at you," Joe concluded, just so the point wasn't missed.

Willy made a face. "I know."

Joe put away the first aid kit. They'd moved to a small staging area not far from their river rescue site, recently established for unrelated reasons. There were several trucks from various fire departments surrounding them, an assortment of vehicles from FEMA and the National Guard — places aplenty for Sam to get out of the rain, have a hot drink, maybe find some dry clothes, and cool off far from Willy. Lights on tripods had been rigged around the periphery, which — given the comings and goings of strobe-equipped vehicles and the people milling about in electric-colored slickers — lent the entire scene the look of an alien landing site.

Joe understood both sides — the impulse that made Willy dive in after a man who was now claiming Willy had hit him on purpose in the process; and Sam's maternal outrage. It spoke to the passion and decency of each of them, as far as Joe was concerned. One of the graces he'd valued during his career was that for as long as he could still show up at the office, he'd get to work with people whom he'd have happily selected as his own kids.

Even if, on occasion, they were ready to kill each other.

Lester Spinney ducked under the raised hatch door of the SUV that Willy and Joe were using as a rain tent.

"All patched up?" he asked.

"They take care of our two burglars-in-training?" Joe countered.

Lester nodded. "Took 'em out back and executed 'em. Beat 'em to death — didn't want to waste bullets."

Willy laughed as Joe just gave him a look.

"Yeah, boss," Spinney conceded. "They're under lock and key. No trip to Springfield, though. You hear what happened to the last transport detail that headed that way? Got swept up in the river. Lost the EQ; damn near lost the crew."

"Everyone okay?" Joe asked.

"Wet and embarrassed, but fine. We're gonna hear a thousand stories like that before this is done. Guaranteed."

"Got anything for us?" Willy asked, already getting restless and, Joe suspected, wanting some more time between now and when he and Sam reconvened at home.

"Oh," Lester said, "Yeah. We've been called up north. It's a little vague, since communication is falling apart, but we should be able to make it. We're supposed to hitch a ride with some other folks on a Humvee to a spot somewhere in Newfane. They say we can still reach it, at least for now. You hear they're talking about evacuating the state EOC? The whole Waterbury complex flooded and it's threatening their computers and power."

"You're full of good news," Joe told him. "What're we supposed to check out?"

"That part's a little jumbled. The emergency coordinator in the area — don't ask me who or what — said he didn't have time to go into detail. Apparently, most of South Newfane is being washed into the Rock River and beyond. But he said first that he needed cops, and then that they should be detectives — he was specific. 'We got a missing person up here,' or something to that effect. Sorry I don't have more. I did ask."

Willy was not in a mood to argue. "I'm in," he said, sliding out of the SUV's back.

Joe addressed Spinney. "They need a full crew?"

"Not our choice," Les responded. "The Hummer only has room for two more. Pretty packed as it is. This is more the incident commander's call than ours."

Joe glanced at Willy. "You and me?"

Willy gave him a crooked smile. "Me and anyone 'cept you-know-who."

The drive north was made in darkness, the Humvee's roof, spot, and headlights all ablaze and, Joe thought, working as much against them as for them, the way the white light bounced off the prisms of a million falling raindrops. He imagined that from the air, they must have looked like a grounded cloud of fireflies, winding through the woods.

It was slow going. They avoided the pavement, since it was prone to caving in. They also had to double back a couple of times, their information being dated by a critical few hours. Conversation was minimal; a few actually dozed off. It was cramped, uncomfortable, damp, and clammy because of the partially open windows. Nevertheless, they made headway.

Where they ended up, hours after what would have been a twenty-minute drive — and after dropping off most of the other passengers along the way — was a cemetery tucked in amid a copse of ancient trees. It was high on a hill above a narrow, sylvan valley and normally solely populated by a small scattering of headstones.

But not tonight.

Joe and Willy eased themselves out of the vehicle and stretched in the fading rain, which was at long last reducing to a steady drizzle. A young man dressed in a yellow coat labeled EMS approached them, looking wet, unshaven, grim, and beyond haggard.

"You the police?" he asked hoarsely.

They merely nodded, perhaps sensing the inanity of displaying their shields in a place and time like this.

"I'm Joe," Gunther thought to say. "He's Willy."

The man didn't introduce himself, turning on his heel instead and leading them across the small cemetery's uneven surface. Usually, trees are planted in such a setting to add grace and peacefulness. Here, the graves had come later, dug among the trees so that the huge trunks and gnarled roots appeared to have grudgingly made room.

"It's over here," their host said, speaking straight ahead in a loud voice, no doubt finding it less taxing than turning his head. Around them, small clusters of men and women, mostly dressed in fire department gear, watched them walk toward the very edge of the burial ground.

"There's no river or creek to speak of up here," the EMT was saying. "But once Irene let loose this morning, pretty much everything that could run water did." His right arm flapped out to his side as he added, "And we have about two hundred feet of elevation above us here, so a lot of water ended up coming along this western boundary."

He stopped near a roaring generator attached to three lights that his team had hung from an assortment of nearby branches.

Now he was shouting over the engine to be heard, and Joe and Willy leaned in close. "This is a small local cemetery. I don't even know its name, and I've lived here all my life. But it's still used, if not much. Anyhow, people take care of it and watch out for the stones, and mow it in the summer. It was the caretaker who got worried about what the runoff might be doing, and came up to see what was happening."

He took a few steps toward where the light was focused, and his two guests finally saw the custodian's source for concern — the water had indeed sliced alongside the lot, and created what looked like a six-foot-deep archeological trench, exposing the sides of several coffins in the process. There remained a trickle along the bottom, but the evidence spoke of a far more destructive cataract earlier.

"That's dust to dust with a vengeance," Joe heard Willy say softly to himself, adding, "Or mud to mud."

The young man jumped down into the ditch and pointed at the row of more or less exposed boxes. He looked up at them, still shouting. "Pretty much speaks for itself, and no big deal when you get down to it. Not like anybody was actually carried away. That would really suck."

Joe nodded to show his agreement, although he was beginning to question why they'd been called here.

Their host beckoned tiredly. "I'm real sorry, but you're gonna have to come down here. I guess it's not the first time you've gotten wet today, though."

That having been said, they complied, slithering down the side of the ditch and joining him as he squatted down and played his flashlight along the side panel of the centermost coffin.

"Don't know if it was a cheap box, or the passage of time, or maybe both, combined with the force of water, but you can see right here how the side caved in."

Joe shifted around so that his sight line followed the light, dreading the macabre nature of what he was about to see.

"First time I saw it," the EMT explained, "I thought it was just rubble that had piled up against the damn thing. But it's not."

He moved, handing the flashlight over. Joe lowered himself to his knees, feeling the water curl around his thighs. He pointed the shaft of light into the gash of splintered wood as Willy slid in next to him.

"Far out," Willy said. "We got ourselves a mystery, boss."

The stones and rocks weren't piled against the coffin. They were spilling out. There was no body within.

Chapter Four

It was a beautiful day the next morning — sunny, cloudless, pleasant. From the tree-tops, and above, the scene was what brought poets and artists to New England in droves. But below that lay the weather's onslaught and the disjointed distribution of its destruction. Across the entire region, riverbeds were gouged and scoured as by passing glaciers, and left shimmering in the sun, bone white and raw, looking like the cast-away skeletons of a geological rampage. They were strewn with rocks and boulders that had blended in harmony with the interstitial soil and vegetation for generations, to the delight of fishermen, boaters, and mere lovers of nature — soil that was now gone, wide and deep, and with it the substance that had made the rivers whole and vibrant.

What remained were hundreds of miles of hard, broken, shattered water channels, bereft of life and looking like smashed concrete. The vegetation had been stripped from the banks, the fish and frogs swept away, and the rest made to seem poor and exhausted and humiliated in the falsely cheerful sunlight.

The soil had not simply vanished, of course. It had been removed, as if by scientific process, down to its smallest granules and redistributed by the water across fields, lawns, streets, and into cellars — water that had then retreated almost as quickly as it had arrived.

Homes and garages were full of the resulting muck, cars were axle-deep in it, inventories from bookstores to machine shops to groceries were cemented in place by it. And artifacts like furniture, clothing, toys, and kitchen appliances had been scattered far and wide, later to be found as half-buried, crooked talismans — like pseudo Easter Island totems — stamped with logos reading GE and Frigidaire.

Joe Gunther toured his southern Vermont world in the company of a survey team composed of variously initialed agencies, and saw mile after mile of crumpled homes shifted from their foundations, roads returned to their dirt origins, and bridges caved in or missing altogether.

And yet, people resembling Bedouins in a desert, incongruously alive and active against a desolate backdrop, were at work everywhere they went. Farmers, equipment operators, National Guardsmen, common citizens with pickup trucks — some sanctioned by FEMA and its state-based counterparts, others in defiance of such organizations and the regulations they tried to impose — all were reclaiming their homes, their roads, their bridges, and their other infrastructure, sometimes using the very same, rock-clotted streambeds as sources of raw material.

It wasn't pretty or easy. In the fine language of the law, it often wasn't legal. But within hours of that ironically cheerful sun's first appearance, it was already beginning to make a difference. By the end of Joe's limited tour, done to show support and to satisfy his own curiosity, he couldn't shake the conviction that — the extent of damage notwithstanding — the worst of it would be dealt with quickly and practically.

Just as clearly, the same was not going to be true for some of the problems that his VBI had picked up overnight. Phones were down, cell towers damaged, electricity was out, e-mail was affected — not all of it universally, some of it not even badly — but simply getting around was already a problem. Statewide, thirteen entire communities had been effectively sealed off from the surrounding world, with all roads and bridges cut. And some, like Wilmington, Waterbury, Halifax, Killington, Rochester, and others, had suffered devastating damage to the hearts of their downtowns.

For the short term, at least, pursuing police work was going to be a challenge. Standard operations were about to be made "flexible," in the words of one memo.

For example, while the Vermont Bureau of Investigation was designed to operate with five interlinked squads — one in each of the four corners, and a headquarters unit at the Department of Public Safety in Waterbury — for a while, that neatly diagrammed command structure had been abruptly rendered more free-flowing.

As the residents of the state hospital had discovered overnight, that entire campus, housing some fifteen hundred state workers — including the VBI administration — had abruptly become an abandoned, soggy ghost town. Fortunately, the DPS building had suffered the least, and was likely to be reoccupied soon, but that lay in the future. In the meantime, the VBI office there was empty, and they'd all just received news —

very quietly delivered — that one of the hospital's patients had gone missing.

As Joe found out upon returning from his field trip.

"Did he just wander off into the rain?" he asked Lester after hearing of it, sitting at his desk and struggling to replace his rubber boots with a pair of shoes.

"She," Lester corrected. "And yeah, in a sense. Found a way into the tunnels and basically evaporated. Search and rescue did their thing, but no luck so far."

"So far?" Joe looked up. "That mean they've kicked it to us, or are they still looking?"

Lester gave him a crooked smile. "Little of each, I guess. I don't think we're in the world of hard-and-fast right now."

Joe tied his second shoe and straightened. "Great. So, now we've got two missing persons cases."

Willy was sitting at his corner desk, his feet, as usual, propped up on its surface. "Better'n a couple of dumb floaters," he said.

"You got another?" Lester asked, not having been updated on Joe and Willy's nighttime escapade.

Willy shrugged with his right shoulder. "Coffin filled with rocks. Might mean somebody faked his own death; might mean something more complicated."

Sammie laughed as she filled her coffee cup at the side counter they used as a kitchenette. "You'd love that, wouldn't you?"

"Totally," he agreed, unconsciously touching the Band-Aid over his eye, happy to have survived his impromptu swim in the river, and her accompanying wrath.

"Well, brace yourselves," Joe told them all. "We may get more MIAs as people sort out who's where and who's not, but for us, and for the time being, there's no doubt that a live, roaming mental patient takes priority over a coffin filled with rocks." He looked at Spinney. "Give us what you got."

Lester consulted his notes. "Carolyn Barber. One of the few longtimers. Right now, with all the computers down, the building evacuated, and the staff scattered, it's a little tough getting particulars, but I was told she'd been there for decades, which is super rare, and that she was a peaceful soul, kept to herself, never caused trouble. That was one of the things that surprised them when she went missing. They get some over-the-top funny farm candidates there, and they watch those like hawks, but not Barber. The guy I spoke with said she was like a shadow, just drifting around. Kinda poetic."

"Great," Willy snorted. "We'll lure her out playing sitar music on a loudspeaker."

"If she was so laid back," Sammie asked, "then why wasn't she put into a halfway house or something? I thought that's what they did nowadays."

"They do," Les agreed. "But she was a special case. My source didn't know why. Maybe it was money or connections. He said he didn't think she had any family — hadn't had a visitor as far back as he could remember."

"How old?" Joe asked.

"Seventies," Lester continued. "They nicknamed her the Governor. I guess she was delusional or something. Claimed she'd actually been governor once."

"Huh," Joe let out, tapping his forehead. "She was."

"The Governor?" Lester asked him. "Really? I asked this guy. He said they checked, just so they wouldn't get a nasty surprise someday. There was no record of Carolyn Barber being head of state."

"It wasn't official," Joe explained. "I don't remember the date, or any of the circumstances, but it was either a publicity stunt or a political slap in the face, or who knows

69

what — maybe half a century ago. At the time, they made it out to be a show of democracy in action — to take an ordinary citizen and make her Governor-for-a-Day. Who knows what they were thinking? But the shit hit the fan as a result — some people saying the real guy should take the hint; others saying it was a sham and an outrage. Nobody thought it was a good idea, and it was never done again. Those were times of big transition — when the state was shifting from being one of the most conservative in the country to what it is today, so all sorts of fur was flying back then. Even so, this stood out in my mind. It was pretty crazy when you think of it." He paused and smiled, adding, "She was pretty cute, too. I remember seeing a picture. That probably added to it being all the rage around the dinner table."

"Our dinner table conversation was all sports, all the time," Spinney commented.

"Mine was dead silence," Sammie said reactively, before looking around as if wishing she'd kept quiet.

Willy wasn't sharing. He asked, "Who was she? The governor's secretary or something?"

Joe shook his head. "I don't think so. I'm drawing a blank. Maybe an additional point was that she had no affiliation. Anyhow, the punch line here is that she's not totally nuts, claiming to have been the governor."

"Well," said Lester, bringing them back on track, "she's a missing person now."

A generalized pause greeted that comment, as they all reflected on the difficulties of a run-of-the-mill missing person case — never easy at the best of times — now superimposed onto a state infrastructure in serious disrepair.

Joe broke the silence first. "Okay, let's start with the basics. Les, you and I can travel to Waterbury and check out where she was last seen and what possible routes she took. Sam and Willy, why don't you two hold the fort, find out what you can about her background, and if you have time, start looking into who was supposed to be in that coffin?"

Joe's choice of Lester to accompany him to Waterbury had not been arbitrary. During his tour of Windham County early that morning, he'd learned that the damage had exceeded the visible. Along with the roads and bridges and houses, the floodwaters had also stirred up petroleum deposits, sewage treatment plants, farm manure storage facilities, and carried them far and wide.

One of his co-travelers had commented that he'd heard of a Vermont-stamped propane tank found floating in the Hudson River, and another had told of a virulent computer image making the rounds of a mobile home surrounded by a bright red pond of spilled fuel. More directly, when they'd stopped to examine Brattleboro's Flat Street — in part, so named for its proximity to the Whetstone Brook — they'd found it under several feet of dark brown water, shimmering with an oily sheen from untold hundreds of polluted sources.

Joe knew that Waterbury would be similar, and that Sam was still breast-feeding her daughter, Emma. He had no kids himself, and Lester's were both teenagers. So, his choice of companion was at once protective and practical. Not that he bothered explaining it to anyone.

It became an expedition traveling the normally two-hour journey. I-91 and I-89 were in fact largely open, but given that they'd been told they wouldn't be allowed into the tunnels until the next day, Joe and Lester agreed that the drive should double as an exploration. The two therefore switched from dirt roads to highways to occasionally the interstate, sometimes backtracking, often using the phone — assuming there was coverage — to get and give road-closure updates as they went. All along, they found people outside, sometimes forlornly poking through belongings spread out in the sun, but for the most part working hard to address the damage. On the radio, they heard about the governor commandeering one of the few National Guard helicopters for an overview of the damage, and about FEMA, the Red Cross, the Salvation Army, and others setting up command centers and shelters to help the dispossessed, the homeless, and the simply stunned.

But what they saw as they crisscrossed toward Waterbury was less organized relief efforts, and more individual evidence of that older, less official, rural New England code that tended to respond to catastrophe stoically. Things were what they were, such a philosophy dictated. And then you got on with it.

It was close to the end of day when they reached their destination, and Joe was happy that he'd called ahead instead of relying on serendipity to supply them with room and board for the night. On the map, the town's main street was ruler straight for over a mile, with the Winooski River hanging like a droopy clothesline from each end, outlining a half-oval parcel containing the

office complex, a large field, and one per-
pendicular street with its bridge at the bottom. By and large, that whole section of
land, roughly seven thousand feet long by
two thousand at its widest, had been
plunged underwater.

Waterbury had received the proverbial
shellacking.

"Damn," Spinney said as they crested the
hill heading down into the floodplain at the
center of it all. "I'm impressed they're only
missing one person."

Traces of recovery were plentiful, as they
had been all the way here, along with defi-
ant hand-lettered signs adorning mud-
clogged front yards and semi-destroyed
homes, but the brutality of what had occurred lingered in the faces they saw as they
drove by. This was a community funeral of
sorts, and there was no amount of
thumbs-up or spirit-rousing rallying that
could alter it.

The man Joe had phoned was Bill Allard,
the director of the VBI, who — along with
the squad that handled this portion of the
state — had been evacuated from the public
safety building while inspectors checked it
out. This made Allard at once a busy guy,
making sure that his other units were up
and running smoothly — by whatever

means they could muster — and someone with time on his hands. He'd been the one to ask Joe to handle this missing person case.

Bill lived on Winooski Street — located within that flood-prone bulge between Main Street and the river. Fortunately for him, his address was near Main, and thus on higher ground. Those closer to its far end had run the gamut from getting their basements flooded to having their homes washed away. Turning right to reach Allard's house, Joe was again reminded of his family's good fortune. A second call to Thetford had recently revealed that Leo and their mom had suffered nothing beyond being cooped up indoors on a terrifically rainy day.

As Joe and Lester emerged stretching from their vehicle in the driveway at last, a square-built, muscular man approached from the adjacent Greek Revival home.

"Rough trip?" he asked, extending a hand in greeting. "I didn't have a clue when you'd get here."

"Would've been sooner," Joe told him. "We rubbernecked some on the way. Wanted to check out the damage."

Bill shook his head sorrowfully. "I wish I'd had to do that to see worse than what we got here. But this was about as bad as it

75

gets. They're saying over two hundred homes have been either badly hit or totally destroyed." He waved a hand down the street, adding, "Including a couple almost within sight of here. My own backyard was flooded. It stopped just shy of the place." He indicated his home. "It feels so random, you know? Fluky. I've been watching the news. They've got footage of a streamside house that looks so good, even the garden's okay, but the next-door neighbor — not a hundred yards away — is off his foundation and sitting in a field of mud. Makes me feel guilty, almost. You got more bags?"

The three of them entered Allard's home and settled in the kitchen as he prepared them something hot to drink. His wife came down to meet them and offered to cook dinner, which they gratefully accepted. Bill therefore shifted them to his office off the living room to give her space.

Joe glanced around at the signs of upheaval — piles of folders and files and scattered paperwork, covering every flat surface. "All the conveniences of your real office?" he asked with a sympathetic smile.

Bill was clearing seating space and groaned. "Yeah — right. I have no idea how people work at home." He then looked up and added, "Thank God, we run a pretty autonomous outfit with the VBI. Can you imagine if we were more traditionally top-down? Other agencies are in a real pickle right now."

They settled down with their coffee, making themselves comfortable.

"How is the public safety building?" Joe asked.

"It would've been fine, except for the damned tunnels," Allard explained. "The water never reached the walls, pretty much like this house. But no one thought to rig the tunnels with watertight doors, so that's how it got in. So stupid," he added. "It's always the things you don't think of."

"Those the same tunnels that Carolyn Barber used?" Lester asked. "They sound like a rabbit warren, going everywhere."

"Pretty much," Bill agreed.

"I take it there's still no news about her?" Joe asked.

Their host shook his head once more. "Nope. Vanished into thin air."

"Or drowned," Lester added glumly. "From the looks of downtown, she may be fifty feet from the hospital, caught in a flooded passageway. When will we be able to get in there to check? I had no idea the whole campus was still six feet under." He looked at Joe for confirmation. "We thought search and rescue had already gone through the tunnels."

"They did what they could," Bill hedged. "Not an easy job." He raised a finger for emphasis as he answered Lester's question. "If the estimates are correct, you might get in tomorrow. The water's draining fast. It'll be a mess, but it should be accessible."

"You have hazmat suits for us?" Joe asked. "I could smell the pollutants as soon as we hit town."

Lester shot him another glance, clearly not having considered the issue.

"Yeah," Allard said airily. "We've got you covered. You're not only facing all the crap you can guess, but there's asbestos, too, from the leftover underground pipes and conduits, dating back to the bad ol' days. It should be a real blast, poking around down there."

"Great," Lester murmured.

"Not to worry," Allard reassured them. "You'll have people with you who know their stuff. I'm not sending you in there alone."

Lester did his best to fake a pleasantly surprised smile. "Ah," he said. "That makes all the difference."

CHAPTER FIVE

"How're you holding up?" she asked.

"Better than most," Joe admitted. "I can think of ten other professions right now that've been working harder than us from the start. The uniformed cops are mostly making sure people don't get into trouble, and we fancy guys in suits are being called on to do even less."

She laughed knowledgeably. "Unless they're Willy Kunkle, diving into the floodwaters to save the brain-dead."

He was impressed. "You heard about that?"

"I'm the governor, Joe. I have *people.*"

He smiled at the phone in his hand. She was, and she did. And Gail Zigman also made it her business to be better informed than most of her recent predecessors. Her early years as a selectman and prosecutor had sensitized her to the old rule that all politics are local. Among the backroom organizations that she'd created before her first day at work was a team of phone and e-mail workers whose sole duty was to keep in touch with handpicked human listening posts all across the state. These were mostly people whom Gail had wooed and won during her years of ascension, ranging from small-town politicos to fire chiefs, town clerks, church leaders, and almost anyone else who was engaged, informed, and/or just plain nosy. It had served her more than once in sensing an upswelling before it became a tidal wave.

"How're your people serving you in the middle of this mess?" he asked.

"Pretty well, up to now," she said confidently. "But we're so early into it, I wouldn't even call it the end of the beginning. I'm just happy we have only three dead, so far. States below us did much worse in that department. On the flip side, our infrastructure got hammered — thousands of road breaks, hundreds of miles of pavement, rail, and power lines lost. God knows how many houses and businesses damaged and destroyed and people ruined. It staggers the mind."

It could have been a political pitch, of course — a sympathetic sound bite — except that it was near midnight, they were alone, if in different parts of the state, and they knew each other with the intimacy of an old married couple. They had once been virtually that, a few years ago, before her ambitions and the risky nature of his job had pulled them apart. And they'd been that couple for well over a decade — albeit living in separate houses, pursuing divergent careers, and keeping different friends. The physical part may have passed, he understood, but what they'd forged afterwards had struck him as a dependable, valuable, and cherished friendship, nurtured by a trust he'd once thought unlikely.

He had been sensing a change in her, however. She'd been ambitious and hard-working when they first met. But, born wealthy and urban, and having escaped to the allures of communal living in Vermont, she'd settled for a selection of pursuits — hippie, Realtor, small-town leader. A brutal rape had changed all that, creating a crucible from which she'd emerged shaken, hungry, and in need of a higher purpose — striving to build something in a life that he'd previously felt she'd mostly toyed with. Sadly, it had also made her a bit reckless with the people she once held dear. In truth, there were times toward the end when Joe, for all his sympathy for and understanding of her demons, had wished they'd call it quits.

Lately, though, now that Gail had been governor for half a year, he'd begun to notice small indications of her earlier, gentler yearnings. He sensed in her an element of loneliness, perhaps, or maybe something subtler, akin to regret, if not so definable. But whatever its nature, it had resulted in a series of phone calls and a visit or two, in which she appeared to be reaching out to him. That having been said, he'd undergone his own emotional journey to get to where he was, and he wasn't entirely sure that he wanted or needed any new developments.

"What have you been seeing out there?" she asked him practically, if in a tone of personal concern.

"Stamina," he answered. "Stubbornness. Also frustration with high-visibility targets like FEMA and anyone in a jumpsuit carrying a clipboard. Probably to be expected. I'm just hoping word gets out for everyone to cut each other a little slack."

"I think they will," she stated. "I'm getting good vibes from most legislators right now. They'll run out of Kool-Aid eventually, but I'll do what I can to stretch them out as long as possible."

"You're kind of a student of Vermont politics," Joe said suddenly, his own duties for tomorrow looming in his mind. "You ever hear of Carolyn Barber?"

There was a pause. "In what context?"

Joe shifted the phone from one ear to the other and adjusted how he was sitting. He was in an upstairs guest room of Bill Allard's house, using an armchair he'd placed by the room's one window. The scene outside, normally overlooking a quiet, partially darkened rural town, was instead pulsing with the lights of stationary fire trucks, police cars, and yellow highway signs telling of dangers ahead. It felt as if the entire community had been transformed into a hospital ICU.

"I'm working a case in Waterbury," he explained. "A woman who went missing from the state hospital. They nicknamed her the Governor because she claimed she'd been one a long time ago. They thought it was a delusion, but I remembered she really was governor, for a single day back in the '60s, as part of some PR thing. Her name rang a bell."

"Not with me," Gail admitted. He could hear her moving about, presumably searching for a pad or a pen. He imagined her in her pajamas. The image wasn't a stretch —

he'd seen her dozens of times, having turned her bed into an office.

"How do you spell her name?" she asked him. "I'll look into it. The whole thing sounds weird, having a governor nobody knows confined to the state hospital? It's got to be something else."

Joe slowly pegged on what she was implying, and felt a little slow for not having considered it earlier. Governors — even sham ones — were not regular folks from off the sidewalk. Along with creating a gimmick like Governor-for-a-Day, consideration had to have been given to the individual chosen. It wouldn't have been a random selection. That would have been too politically risky.

Carolyn Barber's status was abruptly bumped up the ladder in his mind.

"Thanks, Gail," he told her. "I appreciate it."

"How many people know about this?" she asked.

An interesting, slightly paranoid question, he thought, probably typical of any politician. "Only a few," he reassured her. "We want to find out what we've got first. The tunnels they think she used should be accessible tomorrow. For all I know, we'll find her drowned right there, and that'll be the end of it."

"It's never that easy, Joe," Gail said with a conviction born of knowledge.

He didn't doubt the truth of that. But the source of the prophecy was interesting. Did Gail suspect something she wasn't admitting to? Or was she simply being watchful?

"Let me know as soon as you get anything, okay?" he asked. "It might really help me in locating her."

Their point of departure was a large, unmarked white truck, parked just outside the former admissions entrance to the state hospital. As Joe, Lester, and the two HazMat technicians they'd been assigned clumsily emerged from the back and stepped cautiously onto the slippery mud coating the parking lot, Joe couldn't help thinking of so many postapocalyptic movies, where the irradiated remnants of buildings, streets, and playgrounds lay abandoned and eerily silent. All around him, he could see only a wet and soiled urban wilderness, bereft of movement or sound.

He flexed and moved his limbs, adjusting to the bulky Tyvek outfit, rubber boots and gloves, and mostly, the tight-fitting respirator and confining helmet.

"Comfy?" the senior tech asked in a

muffled voice, a man named Kevin Teater.

"I feel like I'm inside a body bag."

Teater's laughter sounded odd, unaccompanied by any visual clues beyond a slight crinkling around his eyes. "You'll get used to it fast," he reassured the two cops. "It's the same for all of us."

They proceeded toward the building's front door in a shambling herd, churning up the slime beneath their treaded feet and feeling the weight of it clinging to their boots.

"You can see how high it got," Teater pointed out with one gloved hand, waving at a distinct waterline some seven feet off the ground. "The whole first floor was wiped out."

Knowing of the devastation and seeing the dampness still glistening attractively in the morning sun, however, Joe was struck by how normal everything looked.

It didn't last. As they filed deeper inside, even the respirator couldn't block the smell of dampness, chemicals, and something more primordial — something hinting at the earth's very fundament.

The walls were stained and smeared, the furniture moved helter-skelter, and the whole littered with a madcap tossing of files, papers, documents, and books, along with dozens of less recognizable items, making it look like the soggy remains of a tornado's passage.

Kevin Teater slowly led them down a dark hallway, the sun outside having little influence in this grottolike environment.

"The entrance to the tunnels is this way — at least the one we're thinking she used." He twisted around stiffly to address them directly. "You hear what happened to the doors' electronics?"

The cops nodded, not bothering to shout against their shrouds.

However, at the door in question, separating the facility's inner core from access to the underground passages, Joe asked in a loud voice, "Why is this even available to people in this building?"

"Convenience, laziness, habit. You name it. The tunnels went in when the complex was built. They've ended up serving every purpose you can name, from supplying overflow office space to giving people a shortcut to the cafeteria in winter. Not to mention plumbing, electricity, the Internet, heating pipes, and whatever else. To a certain extent, I don't think anyone's ever thought about the security aspects." He pushed open the unlocked door and ushered them through. "And I never heard of anyone

87

ever escaping this way, either, until now."

Joe understood that the power was out and the place trashed by recent events, but even so, he found what lay ahead to be dark and threatening, and could only imagine that someone whose paranoia or mental illness was already in high gear wouldn't want to venture too far down these earthbound corridors.

Teater switched on the lamp attached to his hard hat, prompting them all to do likewise. The sudden darting of lights suggested a mixture of fanciful images: a mud-floored, buried passageway to some long-forgotten burial chamber; a battlefield-blasted building interior, redecorated with the detritus of a full-fledged firefight. The reality amounted to a dank, stagnant, gluey obstacle course, blocked by office furniture and the same stationer's fodder they'd encountered in the lobby.

"This should be fun," Lester said with false cheer. "Like a boot camp obstacle course for astronauts."

Already, Teater was setting the pace, scrambling over the tangle with the ease of years of practice. Joe followed next, feeling clumsy and amateurish, aware of Lester and the utterly silent fourth member of their party standing patiently in line. It was during situations like this that Joe felt his age the most, and was reminded of the decades that he'd spent in this physically challenging job, at first as enthralled by the challenges as were his three younger colleagues right now. He rued the toll it had all taken on his body.

Still, as Teater had promised, it didn't take long to get used to the awkward suit and forget its restrictions, in the face of simply trying to keep moving.

The piled barriers weren't the only challenge. They had a double mission here: to find Carolyn Barber's dead body, and if not that, any evidence that might tell of her fate. The first demanded the shifting of heavy objects and mucking through any slime deep enough to hide a body. The second called for an opposite set of skills — more delicate and interpretive, less disruptive. Here, Joe or Les would briefly stop one of the techs from tackling a desk or file cabinet, in order to quickly read the scene before them.

Like a single blue slipper, shaped for a small left foot, found about an hour into their expedition.

Joe held it up before Teater's lamplight. "You're familiar with the hospital's workings," he said. "This look like something the

89

patients wear?"

"Sure does," was the answer. "Standard issue."

Joe reached into the kit he had slung over his shoulder and extracted an evidence bag into which he placed his discovery.

To their frustration, that single slipper marked their only success for another three hours, during which they covered about half the campus, often traveling down routes that either ended at sealed doors or simply dwindled in diameter to make further progress impossible. More than once, Joe made a point of thanking Teater for his guidance — without which he became convinced that he and Spinney would have gone missing as well.

Finally, mirroring the topography overhead, they began seeing signs of the ground ramping up and the water having leveled off, to the point where the damage became reduced to a thin sloshing underfoot.

It was there, at a Y-shaped juncture — with one shaft leading upstairs — that Lester made their second and final discovery. A single bare left footprint was clearly stamped in drying mud, matching the slipper in size, two steps above the high-water mark. Then, nothing.

"Didn't Robinson Crusoe find something

like this?" Lester asked, readying his camera. They worked together to light their finding properly, placing a ruler beside it as reference, before straightening and looking up the steps, as if anticipating the appearance of a celebrity.

"Where's that lead to?" Joe asked.

"Out," Teater said simply. "That's the bad news, I'm afraid. Above us is one of the least occupied and most open buildings in the whole complex. Anyone can just come and go."

They headed up, their eyes on the treads before them, hoping to catch another telltale sign, but Teater's implication was well taken. Assuming that Barber's feet had dried quickly upon leaving the water, and that she'd met no opposition from either locked door or human being, there remained nothing to pursue. When the four of them stepped into the fresh air, outside a door a few feet from the staircase's apex, they found themselves in a huge, flat expanse — not far from Main Street — with unlimited access in any direction.

Kevin Teater removed his helmet and peeled off his mask before radioing their location to the command truck. He then rubbed his face with his open palm and raised his eyebrows at Joe. "What d'ya think?" he asked.

"I think it would be a stretch to say that footprint didn't belong to Carolyn Barber," Joe answered indirectly.

"Which brings us," Lester suggested, "from Robinson Crusoe to Cinderella."

"Or the Hunting of the Snark," Teater suggested.

His three companions each gave him a blank look.

Willy Kunkle killed the engine and observed his home, located defensively at the top of a horseshoe-shaped street in West Brattleboro. His neighborhood hadn't suffered from the flooding, being situated on a slope above the otherwise devastated Whetstone Brook valley. There had been at most a damp cellar on the block or an old tree toppled because of overly saturated soil. But Willy's house had suffered nothing, in part because of his own preparedness.

And not in advance of just this storm. It wasn't Willy's style to yield to a single threat. To him, there was nothing but peril all around — and all the time — which was why his house had been chosen for its strategic location, why his property's trees and shrubs allowed for clear sight lines down both streets, why he had two sump pumps in the basement and a backup generator, and why his locks and doors and windows were all high security-rated.

The coming of Irene had been no more for Willy Kunkle than a confirmation of his everyday fears, and his survival of her passing mere proof that you can never be too cautious or too prepared.

But it wasn't the condition of the house that he was contemplating. His thoughts were on its occupants, as Sam had left the office early to relieve Louise from her babysitting.

Sam had been steady from the start of their union, seeing beyond his paranoia to identify the love he held for her and now their daughter. For him, predictably, that had only added to his worries. Sam gave so much with her forbearance, her patience, and her generosity. When was that going to run out? When was she, like everyone else in his life — including him — going to realize that he was a lost cause?

Willy watched his large right hand, resting on the bottom of the steering wheel — powerful, capable, a veritable weapon to so many who'd suffered from its strength. But what did it represent? A surrogate for its useless left companion perpetually stuffed into his pants pocket; a reminder that he was a cripple in fact and in function. The arm had been destroyed by a bullet years ago, taken in the line of duty, and despite the handicap, Willy — with Joe's urging and to everyone's amazement — had battled back to requalify as a fully certified police officer. He'd done as well over time combating alcoholism, Post Traumatic Stress Disorder, depression, a broken marriage, and the social isolation caused by a complete lack of diplomacy.

He closed the hand into a fist, acknowledging none of those victories. What he believed instead was that someday he'd wear out his welcome with the very family he'd traveled so far and worked so hard to create.

As if activated by his thoughts, the front door of the house opened and Sammie stepped out with Emma in her arms. Smiling a little sadly, she crossed the lawn as Willy rolled down his window, and handed the little girl in to him, murmuring, "Here you go, sweetie. I think Daddy needs a hug."

Willy looked into his partner's eyes as he took the child to his chest and cradled her there, his earlier concerns struggling against the warmth and sincerity he saw in Sam's face.

"How did you know?" he asked, kissing

his daughter's feather-fine hair.

"We watch each other's back," she answered simply, and opened his door. "Come on in."

Willy swung out with surprising grace, given his handicap and his bundle, closed the car door with a foot, and fell in behind Sam on the way to the house.

"Hear from the boss yet?" he asked as the baby snuggled into his neck.

"Yup. He and Les spent hours making like moles and came up with a single footprint. They're thinking Barber made it out alive, if minus one shoe."

Willy took that at face value, knowing the rest would come later and in more detail. "What about her? Barber?" he asked next, referring to the assignment they'd been left by Joe. "You find out anything?"

Sam held open the front door to let him by, stroking his shoulder as he passed. "Not much yet. I wanted to clear off some other stuff on my desk first. I found out she worked for the state about forty years ago, and that she was the same Carolyn Barber Joe was talking about — the Governor-for-a-Day. He was also right about that being a one-shot wonder, never repeated. My gut tells me I'll get more from talking with people than digging through files. Right now, she just looks like she was a clerk or a secretary or something almost invisible. How 'bout you?"

Willy had taken on what he was calling the "box of rocks" from the cemetery near Newfane. He turned into the living room and carefully slid into the rocking chair by the window, seeing that Emma had nodded off.

"Herb Rozanski," he said in a soothing voice as Sam sat on the arm of the nearby sofa. "Only son of Bud and Dreama Rozanski. Brother of Eileen Rozanski Ranslow. Died twenty-seven years ago at the age of eighteen of an industrial accident at the family's logging and lumber operation. The accident was witnessed by the father, the body checked out by the authorities, and all the paperwork signed, sealed, and delivered."

Sammie smiled at the domestic scene and the tone of Willy's voice. "They must've really loved those rocks," she said.

Willy laughed gently. "Yeah. Well, you got that right. Guess I'll be doing a little up-close-and-personal interviewing, too."

CHAPTER SIX

Lester Spinney settled into the corner of
one of the Waterbury fire department's
empty back offices and extracted his smartphone. Joe and he had ended up here to
conclude the HazMat aspect of their day —
returning the equipment and filing a report
with the police chief about the state of the
tunnels. The police department had been
evacuated, forcing the chief to catch his
meetings wherever he could for the time
being, including in his cruiser.

None of which was Lester's concern. He
was more than content to leave that conversation to his boss, and to instead reach out
quickly for home. Lester's was the unit's
lightest heart — a family man, a Springfield
resident, born and bred, married to the
same woman he'd first met in community
college. Stayovers like the one he'd just
spent at Allard's house were not his idea of

a good time. He preferred going home every night.

"You out there, babe?" he texted.

"Hi," came the near-instant response from his wife, Sue, a nurse at Springfield Hospital.

"What ya doin'?" he typed. His daughter, Wendy, had tried to educate him on the protocols and practices of proper text-speak, but he and Sue preferred their own version.

"Good timing," she wrote back. "Babysitting a pt. in ICU. U?"

"Waterbury. Just went thru the tunnels here. Creepy."

"Dangerous?" was the immediate reply.

"Nope. HazMat suits. Town a mess. Missed U last nite."

"U2."

"Dave do OK on test?"

"Thinks so."

Spinney heard Joe calling out for him from somewhere in the building. "Gotta go, honey. Luv U."

He was reading "Luv U2" when Joe poked his head through the open doorway and smiled. "Tell her I said hi."

Les laughed and dutifully followed orders, reading aloud to Joe, "Tell him to give you back to me in one piece."

"I promise," Joe said, and crooked his

98

finger. "I found a girl who knows a guy who knew our missing person — a nurse at the hospital. Maybe she'll tell us Carolyn's couch surfing in her living room."

Gail Zigman stepped into the small back office on the top floor of the Pavilion building in Montpelier, located beside the statehouse, and closed the door behind her. Vermont governors were paid a little over $150,000 per year; were issued a security detail, complete with vehicle; and had a staff. They were also the chief executive, with all the attending perks. On the other hand, they still headed up one of the least populated states in the Union, which translated into Gail's living in her own condo just outside Montpelier, although having access to an admittedly spacious combination office/apartment in this building, and another ceremonial office in the statehouse, equipped with a chandelier. There was no governor's mansion, no stretch limo, no executive helicopter, and no palace guard to snap her a salute when she showed up for work every morning. Vermonters had other expectations of their leaders than their appearing like foreign potentates or overindulged chiefs of industry.

Not surprisingly, Gail had also quickly

discovered, governors had virtually no privacy and little time to themselves. Which explained why she was standing here with her back to the door. After six months of agreeing to everyone's requests of her to do what they wanted and to be where they directed, she'd finally demanded ninety minutes of complete solitude, every afternoon. It was impractical, and honored only about 30 percent of the time, but it beat what had preceded it. And she cherished every minute.

She wasn't getting that now, however — not with the post-Irene mess demanding that she be in all places at all times. But when she'd announced five minutes ago that she was going to grab a little time for herself, her staff's reaction hadn't been stunned disbelief.

The downtime wasn't so she could watch TV, do crosswords, or read a book. In general, it was to help her address the private daily duties that she set herself, for herself, outside the demands of her job, her constituents, and her omnipresent staffers.

This time, for example, it was to call Susan Raffner.

Politicians — even small state ones — are surrounded by a hierarchy of friends. Some are heartfelt associations, others practical,

still others obligatory and occasionally onerous, as with party chairmen, committee
heads, key lobbyists, and the like, with
whom one is pretty much stuck whether one
likes them or not.

For Gail, Susan Raffner was something
else entirely — a fellow resident of Brattleboro, a friend and advisor for decades, a
sounding board, an ally, a defender, and a
fellow feminist of the old school, Raffner
had early seen in her friend the potential
that Gail had achieved in the last election.
When Gail had first toyed with becoming a
selectman, Raffner had been by her side,
giving advice, fielding problems, and handling many of the logistical headaches,
especially as the stakes had grown along
with Gail's successes. Beyond that, when
Gail had been raped — and Joe almost
killed — Susan had been beyond supportive, offering counsel and challenge during Gail's struggle for balance.

Unusually — if typically for this woman
— Raffner's only request in exchange for all
of this had not been a cabinet appointment
or the leadership of some agency. It had
been to request an endorsement from Gail
in Susan's run for one of the two Windham
County state senate seats.

And it had worked, if controversially. Winning as a Democrat hadn't been much of a reach in Vermont's southeast corner; but Gail's stirring of the pot by backing Susan against the Democratic incumbent had caused a real hornet's swarm. The man in question had been popular, if only mildly competent, and had been serving for sixteen years before Candidate Zigman had vouched for Susan on the stump. The two women broke the rules and outraged their own party bosses, and created an effective if inaccurate image of Raffner's stunned opponent as a chauvinist, do-nothing male who was probably harboring malicious intentions toward women, children, farmers, gun owners, and the American Way. The poor bastard never knew what hit him, and on election night, Gail and Susan had briefly retreated amid the hoopla to raise a private glass to their dual success.

It wasn't just the victory they were toasting. On various levels, they were angry women, fed up with the status quo, tired of waiting for change, and happy with the turmoil they'd stirred up. The fallout afterwards would be predictable, of course, and was already starting. Both women winning by popular landslides while thumbing their noses at the Old Guard — including Vermont's Washington delegation, nicknamed the DC-Three — had prompted a chorus of angry muttering from the back rooms that guaranteed an untold number of future headaches for each of them. But in the short term, as for so many idealists preceding them, that hadn't mattered. They were flush with success, and presumed that the spirit that had carried them here would sustain them while in office.

It was a miscalculation common to many a dreamer.

In the meantime, Gail now had her best friend in the senate. However, she'd also lost her closest advisor as a result, and Susan had already twice taken opposing views to a couple of the new governor's pet projects, but such was the rigor of their mutual honesty that details like that mattered little. In an ironic homage to much of the politics predating modern extremism, they embodied the older tradition suggesting that close friends could be politically opposed while still finding enlightenment in each other's insight.

As with right now. Gail pulled out her cell phone and dialed the number she knew better than her parents'.

"Nice interview on VPR," Susan answered without preamble. "I might not have gone on so much about that funding issue. Uncle

103

Sam always sounds more generous on the heels of a disaster than he does a year later when the checks need to be written."

Gail knew better than to be sidetracked by someone else's issue. It was a lesson that Susan herself had taught her early on. Instead, she ignored the comment and got straight to the reason for her call. "Stretching back into Vermont political history," she asked her friend, "what can you tell me about Carolyn Barber? Governor-for-a-Day a long time ago?"

Raffner didn't mind and didn't hesitate. "Wow — that's a name from the past. Like bringing up the Black Dahlia in Los Angeles."

Gail raised her eyebrows at the obscure reference, but stayed silent, knowing Susan's process.

"One of the most famous unsolved murder cases in U.S. history," came the follow-up.

"And relevant how?"

"Okay — a stretch, I'll grant you. But just like you had no clue about the Black Dahlia, most Vermonters have never heard of Carolyn Barber. At the time, it was seen as a publicity strategy run amok, since most of the coverage made fun of it. But there were rumors that some kind of deal was responsible."

Gail frowned at the phone. "A deal? What was the point? Did money change hands?"

But here, Susan proved less helpful. "Not that I know of. Barber was a nobody, and as far as I know, nothing happened as a result except for the bad press. Of course, I wasn't there, and it wasn't like it was news even a month later. I only know about it because I love this stuff, and I went to school with a girl named Carole Barber — no relation, I think — and it stuck in my head."

Gail considered what she might be missing. Susan interrupted her thoughts. "Why do you want to know about her?"

She opened her mouth to pass on Joe's news from the state hospital, but then shut it again, reconsidering. She had lived for years in Joe's company, often serving as his sounding board on complicated cases. Discretion had become ingrained over time, and she felt its tug upon her now, if for no discernible reason. "Her name came up in conversation," she answered truthfully enough. "It didn't mean anything to me, but it sounded odd. I just wondered if you knew anything."

"I can dig into it, if you want," Susan volunteered. "You are the governor, after all."

Gail laughed. "Right — like you have

nothing better to do. I wouldn't even put my own staff on this."

They chatted about other matters for a few minutes, mostly the flooding and its impact and implications. There was little else being discussed anywhere in the state, and probably wouldn't be for some time.

Nevertheless, once the call ended, Gail remained thoughtful about what had stimulated it. She still wanted to know how a governor — even a bogus one — could have ended up in a mental facility, and then gone missing.

As for Susan Raffner, she wasn't the least misled by her friend's dismissal of Carolyn Barber's importance. As she pocketed her phone and set out for her next meeting, she made a mental note to dig into Barber's moment of fame — and why the chief executive had thought it worthy of special inquiry.

Willy negotiated the washed-out road gingerly, pausing occasionally to figure out where to point the SUV next, sometimes opting for the field alongside.

"Might be faster if we walk," Sammie suggested, clinging to the handhold by the doorframe.

"Might be," Willy agreed, to her surprise, "but I like having the radio nearby."

She raised her eyebrows at him. "You expecting trouble?"

"I'm expecting a half-wit Li'l Abner," he countered. "We don't show up in some official-looking vehicle, he'll shoot our asses off for sure. Probably will anyhow."

Willy had been born and bred in New York City — a place that he'd clearly left only in body. "It's a rural state," she instructed him defensively. "Not a backward one."

He laughed and jutted his chin straight ahead to indicate the road. "Right — clearly."

"That's the flood, you moron," she remonstrated.

"It is *now*," he suggested. "You ask me, it was no better before."

The large vehicle gave a lurch and there was a grinding, scraping sound from underneath that made them both wince. They'd borrowed it from the Brattleboro police, and while Willy clearly didn't care about its condition later, Sammie was less sure about how they'd gotten hold of it in the first place.

"You sure you got the chief to sign this over?" she asked, settling herself more securely after the jostling.

"It's gotta be over the next hill," Willy

avoided answering, adding unexpectedly, "You call Louise?"

Sam cut him a look. "You know I did."

"Emma okay?"

A sarcastic comeback offered itself, but not about this. Emma was sacred ground for them, if for divergent reasons. While each was a wounded survivor of childhood, their own child represented a different type of hope. To Sammie, Emma was a reward to be cherished and protected; to Willy, she was more like the cross between a miracle and a mirage — the latter image being one that could wake him up in a cold sweat and make him visit her bedroom just to confirm her existence.

Instead, therefore, Sam merely said, "She's great," and changed the subject. "What's the name again? Rozanski?"

"That's what's on the headstone," he told her. "Herbert Rozanski. But this woodchuck empire belongs to somebody named Jeff MacQuarrie — Jeffrey, according to the records; Jeff on the phone. He's supposedly a relative."

"You talked to him?" she asked, startled.

"Kind of. I didn't really say who I was, and he didn't do much more than grunt. You know . . ."

She did. When you went to interview

someone who might have something interesting to say, you didn't want to show more cards than you had to.

"What did you say?" she asked.

"Just that we'd found the grave exposed and needed to know about next of kin for legal reasons. I told him I had a form to fill out — made it sound boring as hell."

"He's related how?"

Willy gave a shrug as they edged over the top of the rise and finally saw a farmhouse ahead, nestled against the forest behind it like a newborn tucked up against its mother.

"Beats me," he said. "That's why we're here."

The road was slightly better on the other side, so they closed in on the house in a couple of minutes. Nevertheless, they paused in the dooryard with the engine running, respecting the rural protocol of giving homeowners time to take notice — and to call in any near-feral dogs that might be prowling about.

But it didn't apply here. The peeling front door to the battered house yawned open, and a large bearded man stepped out and waved to them.

"Gee," Sammie muttered as she slid out of the SUV. "Not a blood-dripping sickle in sight. Bummer."

"Next time," Willy assured her.

They approached, still watching the terrain before them, if this time for chunks of wood, randomly scattered tools and farm equipment, and assorted other lumps and clumps that had acquired a thin skin of earth and weeds over the years.

"You Jeff?" Willy asked, drawing near.

The man nodded. "Yup."

He stepped free of the threshold, leaving the door open, took two steps forward, and waited for them, the sun to his back. There was no shaking of hands or other formalities. Jeff simply waited, his hands hanging loosely, for his guests to speak their piece.

"Jeffrey MacQuarrie?" Willy repeated. "Just for the record."

MacQuarrie acknowledged with a single, silent tuck of his chin, his eyes steadily on Willy's.

"We're from the Vermont Bureau of Investigation," Sam announced, showing her credentials, which MacQuarrie ignored, his gaze unshifting. "We're here about the grave of Herbert Rozanski," she finished.

"So I heard," was MacQuarrie's response.

"From me?" Willy asked, who'd neither introduced himself nor shown his badge. "Or someone else?"

"Both."

110

"What did they tell you?"

"The water opened up the grave." Mac-Quarrie's voice was deep and friendly in tone, although his body language remained neutral.

"That all?"

"Pretty much."

"They tell you what they found inside?" Sammie asked bluntly.

"Yup."

"What do you make of that?"

The hint of a smile lurked within the heavy beard, and MacQuarrie's eyes narrowed with humor. "The grave was missing something?"

Sam laughed while Willy grunted, "Very funny."

MacQuarrie tilted his head to one side. "You gotta admit."

"Okay, okay," Willy conceded. He looked around at the disheveled front yard. A rusty pickup was parked nearby, and he walked over to it to sit on the lowered tailgate, using the trailing edge of the truck bed as a backrest. The move also allowed him to shift from where the sun had been hitting him in the face — a position he wasn't convinced that MacQuarrie, presumably a seasoned hunter, hadn't calculated.

"Now that we got the country hick bullshit

111

out of the way," he told their host, "you want to tell us how you connect to Herb Rozanski?"

"You found me," MacQuarrie told him. "Don't you know?"

Willy just stared at him.

"Cousins," MacQuarrie yielded as Sam crossed over to join Willy, at the opposite end of the tailgate. MacQuarrie followed suit by settling onto a large, leveled-off tree stump whose scars attested to its use as a wood-splitting station.

"My mother was Herb's father's sister," he explained.

"Herb's father being Bud Rozanski," Willy suggested.

"And his mom being Dreama. They died, so I got the place."

"Just like that?" Willy asked. "They didn't have other kids?"

"A couple more," Jeff said.

Willy chuckled and shook his head. "You must really like us."

In the silence following, Jeff shifted his attention from one to the other of them. "Pardon?"

"The 'yup-nope' treatment," Willy expanded. "We actually get overtime for sitting around listening to this crap. I can do it all day."

112

Jeff MacQuarrie appeared to consider that. "Another son named Nate, and a daughter — Eileen Ranslow," he stated, thereby announcing his choice to be more communicative. "Nate pretty much took off. Eileen got married and never liked living here anyhow. We all talked it over when Bud was about to pass. I was starting a family, and Bud didn't see just letting the place go; Eileen was cool about it, and Dreama was long dead. So, I got it."

"For future reference," Willy said, "we'll need a list of relatives, complete with contact information and how they fit into the family tree. You good with that?"

MacQuarrie nodded.

"Okay," Willy kept talking. "Tell us about Herb. And don't hold back."

The bearded man smiled again. "Not much *to* tell. Bud was the eldest. My mom was the youngest; about twelve years apart, and Mom had her kids later in life — just the opposite of Bud. So, Nate, Herb, Eileen, and me didn't mess much. I was a kid when Herb died. All I know was that he got caught up in some equipment and was killed. Used to happen all the time, back when."

Willy waved his hand around vaguely. "Here?"

113

Jeff pointed into the distance. "They had a lumber mill set up in an old barn, out that way. A big shed, really. 'Bout ten years ago, I had the fire department come out and burn it down as a training exercise. Wasn't much left to it. Bud had sold all the equipment long before, and Mother Nature had done the rest." He contemplated his comments briefly before adding, "Anyhow, that's about it. Like I said, Herb got tangled up somehow. It ran off a truck PTO, with open pulleys and leather belts running every which way, and no guards or safeties on the saw blades. I seen pictures — crazy dangerous. One wrong move . . ." His voice trailed off, as if surprised by its own sound.

"He was working the mill alone?" Sammie asked, speaking almost for the first time.

Jeff shrugged. "You wouldn't think so, but I don't know. It got to Bud pretty bad, I can tell you that. But he was a stoical man. Dreama? Family stories have it that it killed her. I guess Herb was like her favorite, or something. She died soon afterwards, people said of a broken heart."

"So why did they bury a box of rocks?" Willy asked.

MacQuarrie spread his hands. "I didn't know they had — not till old Irene brought it up to light. That's what the Bible says,

114

right? About the cleansing power of water?"

Willy pushed out his lower lip thought-fully, not having the slightest clue about MacQuarrie's allusion. "You a big church-goer?"

The other man laughed gently. "Not hardly. My wife would like me to be. I just stick to weddings and funerals."

Sam read Willy's body language and hopped off the truck bed. "Okay, Jeff, could we get that family tree off you?"

MacQuarrie rose more awkwardly and led the way back toward the house. "More like a shrub. I got most of it stuck to the fridge, near the phone," he said.

"What about people who might have a better memory about when Herb died?" Sam asked. Willy was already wandering around the yard, as if exploring the more obscure piles of junk.

"Oh, sure," MacQuarrie said without looking back. "I mean, it may've been almost thirty years ago, but people remem-ber. Shit, it's all they got to do. I figure every screwup I've ever pulled, from childhood on, is like carved in stone with some of the people around here. It's crazy."

"You think there're any other coffins filled with rocks?" Willy asked from twenty feet away, having not indicated he'd even been listening.

MacQuarrie let out a deep laugh and faced Willy with his arms spread wide — the innocent bear, incarnate. "Hell," he said. "Could be. I wouldn't put it past one or two of them. But you're the police, eh?"

CHAPTER SEVEN

Bonnie Swift lived in the Waitsfield–Warren area, about fourteen miles south of Waterbury — if also, some argued, on a whole different planet. There, they'd be speaking economically, although the geography was tellingly different as well. But where Waterbury was dominated by the state office complex and the Winooski River, Waitsfield–Warren was best known for the Sugarbush ski resort — among the state's largest — and the far more picturesquely labeled Mad River, which had clearly lived up to its name on Sunday.

Lester Spinney's attention was more given to the neighborhood's economic reputation. "This is where they tow your car away if it's last year's model, isn't it?" he commented, observing a large spread, anchored by a mansion standing regally at the back of a manicured if soggy field.

Joe laughed, negotiating a tight curve

between traffic cones. Also unlike Waterbury, this was mountainous terrain, which
in parts had made traveling the washed-out
roads even tougher. "That's Manchester.
Get your prejudices right."

"Right," Lester said, jerking a thumb at
the big house. "Makes me a believer."

"That's more like Warren than Waitsfield,"
Joe said. "Back in the old days, which for
me stretches pretty far, Waitsfield was for
the regular crowd, and Warren was where
the rich skiers hung out. Things have
changed, though." He slowed to a crawl to
show his badge to a flagman, "Especially
now.

"We get through?" he asked. It was another blessedly beautiful, dry summer day.

The flagman spoke into his portable radio
and eventually waved them past. "Stick far
to the right. You goin' beyond Waitsfield
proper?"

"Nope."

"You should be okay, then. They're still
not sure about the covered bridge in town."

Spinney shook his head. "What d'ya want
to bet even the rich guys don't have flood
insurance?"

Joe slowed down before cutting onto a
side road and heading uphill. Immediately,
the road was in perfect condition. "I heard

the water reached seven feet above flood level in spots, including parts of Waitsfield."

They continued for another half mile, gaining height, before seeing a mailbox labeled SWIFT on the left. Joe took the dirt driveway, rutted and narrow, and drove them another five hundred feet to the parking lot of a well-kept double-wide trailer with another of Vermont's ubiquitous, partially rusted-out, older Subaru station wagons out front.

"Ah," said Spinney, swinging his long legs out of their four-wheel-drive SUV. "This is more what I'm used to."

A woman appeared on the deck at the top of a short flight of wooden steps. "Are you the ones who called?" she asked.

The two men pulled out their IDs as they climbed. Joe spoke for them. "I'm Joe Gunther. This is Lester Spinney. Really appreciate your agreeing to meet with us."

She gave him a rueful expression. "Bonnie Swift — and it's not like I have much to do right now."

They reached the top and shook hands. "No, I guess not," Joe said. "What *is* the latest about the hospital?"

"Too early to say," she told him, heading toward a picnic table that was set up at the far end of the deck. "Right now, we're just hearing rumors and waiting around, none of which is doing anybody any good. You want some iced tea or coffee or something?"

They demurred and took places at the wooden table overlooking the parking area and the woods beyond. There was a shrouded gas grill off to one side. Joe imagined this spot saw more than a few pleasant weekend gatherings.

"You lived here for long?" he asked, stretching his legs and pulling out a pad to take notes if necessary.

"Fourteen years," she said. "Brad owned the property before we married — he works on the road crew and does jobs on the side. We lived closer to town for about five years, and then took the plunge, moving this monster in. That was a neat trick, coming up the drive. I thought the whole damn thing was going to end up at the bottom of the mountain. But Brad and his pals know what they're doing." She laughed. "They just scare the bejesus out of you while they're doing it."

"You got kids?" Lester asked.

"Two," she answered. "One of each."

"How did you all make out in the storm?"

She looked around. "Here, thank God, no problem. Good thing, since I was stuck in Waterbury and Brad was out in the middle of it for two days straight. The kids helped out at the town shelter, so we knew where they were. All in all, we got off without a scratch, assuming I still have a job."

Joe took advantage of the segue. "Which brings us to why we're here, of course. I heard that you were pretty close to Carolyn Barber. Is that correct?"

Swift showed some reservation at Joe's choice of words. "I wouldn't put it that way. I think she probably tolerated me better than most, but we weren't buddy-buddy. She was too lost in her own world for that. Did you get a lead on where she is?"

"No," he said bluntly, and then hedged his response. "We're working on the premise that she got out alive, but that's mostly because we haven't found a body yet."

Swift looked disappointed. "I really liked her," she explained. "She was out of it, but in a good way, you know? I mean, we can get some real crazies in there, but she was never like that. And she was a lifer, too, which is really rare. The way things go nowadays, it's kind of a turnstile operation — they check in, they get their papers, they do their contract, and they leave. They may keep coming back — I'm not saying that — but the Governor was one of the only ones I know of who stayed put."

"Why was that?" Joe asked. "If she was calm and no threat to anybody, shouldn't she have been placed elsewhere?"

" 'Ours is not to reason why,' " Swift quoted. "I did ask a couple of times, but I just got a runaround. I always figured it was because nobody else knew the answer, either."

"Who would know?" Joe asked.

"That would've been Matt Larson," she told them without hesitation, "but he died last year. I can give you the current guy's name, but he's gonna be pretty useless."

"An on-the-job-retirement type?" Spinney tried commiserating.

Her face opened in laughter. "Oh — ouch. That is how that sounded, isn't it? No, no. I didn't mean it that way. He's a good guy. I was talking literally. He'd only be useless because of *Larson.*" She tapped a temple with her finger. "Matt kept most of the records in his head — at least the older ones. He was lousy at organizing files, even worse with computers, and never shared anything with anyone. The man was a disaster and none of us knew it. We all thought he was just a sweet old throwback who remembered everybody's name and was super nice to work with. I have no idea how he got away with it for so long, but after he died, it was one of the Big Dark Secrets, especially whenever the federal regulators came sniffing around."

She suddenly looked a little shamefaced. "Which means I just screwed the pooch. Is this gonna get out? I don't need that on top of everything else, if I'm going to get my job back. Matt was like a god to some people."

The two cops exchanged looks.

"We won't tell if you won't," Joe told her, more or less truthfully. "Still, even if Barber got lost in the system, surely her medical records and her financials were kept separate. Who paid for her upkeep all these years?"

But Swift was already shaking her head. "No clue. Totally not my department. I'm not saying somebody doesn't know. I mean, I assume they do — like you said. But I never had anything to do with who was paying what and how, and I never really knew anyone in the business office, either. They were like a world apart from us. Maybe if you talk to the commissioner or something . . ."

Joe pretended to note that in his pad, to show his support of the suggestion, and then redirected her toward what he hoped was more useful territory.

"The Governor," he said. "How did she become known by that? Was it something she said?"

Swift raised her eyebrows. "Just that she'd been governor once. We didn't take it at face value. That's a little hard to fake, you know? Plus, somebody checked on it, just to make sure. We've only had the one female governor — Madeleine Kunin. I know 'cause I voted for her."

She added upon reflection, "Maybe Carolyn was related to a governor, or slept with one, for all I know, and felt close to the office. Some of the more delusional patients have all sorts of associations like that."

"Did she ever go into detail?" Joe persisted.

But Bonnie Swift wasn't going to be able to give him that. She shook her head again sadly and then just as quickly turned the tables by saying, "She could've had a sister, though. She might know something."

Joe and Lester became still. In their business, this was a classic "Oh, by the way" comment, which in the newspaper trade was referred to as "burying the lead."

Joe returned to Bonnie and smiled politely. "Really?" he said. "A sister?"

She held up her hand and wobbled it from side to side. "Maybe. It's so vague, it almost

124

slipped my mind. It was more like I wondered at the time if it might be a sister."

"Go on."

"It was years ago — back when I first came on at the hospital. I was going through some paperwork, familiarizing myself with the patients. I saw that Carolyn had someone listed named Barb Barber under next of kin. It stuck with me, I think because of how it sounds, you know? Barb Barber. Kind of musical."

"Any address?"

"Nope. No nothing. And no Barb Barber, either. She never contacted us, never visited, never existed as far as I know. I saw her name that one time, on the form, and that was it. That's why I didn't remember her." She laughed then and pointed at them in mock accusation. "I saw that look. You thought I was holding back. That's not it. I liked Carolyn. She may've been ditzy and thought she was governor, but she was sweet and never caused problems. It's sad that someone like that had a relative who never got in touch. Maybe Barb's dead. You think?"

Joe closed his pad and slipped it back into his pocket. "I think we'll do our best to find out," he assured her.

■ ■ ■ ■

Gorden Marshall had just settled into his armchair with the newspaper, adjusted his reading glasses, and checked to make sure that his ever-ready scotch-and-water was within reach, when the phone rang in his office next door.

"For Christ's sake," he muttered. "Every fucking time."

He struggled to rise, pushing on the chair's arms and dropping his paper in the process, scattering its pages. Standing at last, he tilted forward, caught the rails of his aluminum walker, and began shuffling toward the incessant ringing. His daughter had nagged him to get a portable phone, or at least a long extension cord, but he'd refused, in large part to deprive her of the victory. But times like these were reminders that she was right.

He got to the phone at last, half expecting to hear a dial tone at the far end, given his long delay, but there was no sound whatsoever.

"What?" he asked petulantly.

"You know who this is, Gorden?"

He sighed and looked around, trying to strategize how to place the walker, find a seat, and not drop the phone all at once. They'd given him the walker just a week ago, and he hated it with a passion. But the choice had been clear: Either accept the recommendation, or they'd move him out of his apartment to the Level One maintenance unit on the ground floor. Everyone here knew what that meant. "LOM," as they called it, was the next step to the hospital wing. And from there, it was the loading dock for the hearse. The Woods of Windsor may have been the state's fanciest so-called retirement home, but pragmatists like Gorden knew it for what it was — a gold-plated conveyor belt bridging his present life to an eventual hole in the ground. He was a practical man, though — he'd not only recognized early on that this situation was inevitable, but he'd also played a pivotal role in getting The Woods funded and permitted by the state.

"Of course I know," he grumbled. "Wait a second. I have to sort myself out."

He put down the phone. One of his friends' grandchildren had supposedly entertained him for what had seemed hours last Thanksgiving, detailing the story of Harry Potter to him. He'd hated the obligation and disliked the child, but the reference to Voldemort, whose name was never to be uttered aloud, had made him laugh.

The voice on the phone belonged to such a person.

Paranoid prick.

Gorden got himself situated in his desk chair without mishap, blew out a sigh, and picked up the phone again.

"Sorry. The sons of bitches saddled me with a damn walker. Guaranteed to make me break my neck, if you ask me."

"Sorry to hear that, Gorden."

"No, you're not. What the hell are you calling me for? I can't do you any good anymore. My smoke-filled-room days are long gone. You going soft in the head, too? Want a reference to get into this place? I recommend it. When they give you the lethal injection here, it's by a pretty girl with a big smile. We cater to your needs at The Woods of Windsor. That's what we say."

"Are you done, Gorden?"

That voice. Patient, calm, slightly modulated to sound friendly. Gorden had been listening to it for fifty years. Never seemed to change. Never aged, never rose in volume, never showed undue emotion. In time, Gorden and his political cronies had called its owner Hal, as in the movie.

Except that Hal the computer had been a menace. This Hal — for the likes of Gorden and his ilk — had been more like a sci-fi commingling of Mary Poppins and Rasputin. A combination of financial support, strategic advice, and the sense that, with his backing, you could have the world by the tail. Or, without it, a world of hurt.

"Okay," Gorden conceded. "I'm done. Let me tell you one thing, though, 'cause I know you're a couple of years younger than me. Don't get old. They're right about it not being for sissies."

"I'll keep that in mind. Speaking of the past, since you bring it up, do you remember Carolyn Barber?"

Gorden Marshall laughed. "That crazy bitch. She finally die?"

"Actually, quite the opposite. We have a bit of a problem."

CHAPTER EIGHT

Given that Vermont's major roads to the north had suffered less at Irene's hands, Joe and Lester, instead of returning home, went back to the interstate after meeting with Bonnie Swift for a quick trip to Montpelier and access to one of the local police department's computers. The off chance that their missing person had a sister was too good not to act on immediately.

They weren't holding their breath, however. The reference had been oblique; there'd been no implication that Barb Barber lived in the area, was still alive, or even existed. And, even if they found her, she'd still never visited Carolyn at the hospital or made an effort to reach out. Would she be likely to help now?

Those caveats made Lester's satisfaction all the sweeter when he dropped his hands from the computer's keyboard and announced, "There you have it. I'll be a son of a gun."

Joe circled around to peer at the screen. Lester had typed in the name Barbara Barber, gotten a hit straight off, and then opened up her involvements. There, listed under a traffic accident, he'd found where she'd recently been the passenger in a minor crash outside of Burlington. The officer called to the scene had taken the appropriate but often ignored extra step of recording the identities and birth dates of all the people in both vehicles. Finding Barb Barber's name now was a textbook example of how such diligence could pay off.

"How long ago was that?" Joe asked.

"Two years."

"She list an address?"

"Yup. Shelburne. From what it says here, she lives with her son. He was the driver."

Joe patted his shoulder. That was a town just below Burlington, not more than sixty minutes from where they were now. "It's getting late. Want to knock on her door tonight or in the morning?"

Lester twisted around in his seat. "You kidding?"

It was just dark by the time Lester rolled to a stop on Hillside Terrace, in the middle of Shelburne Village, opposite a modest, rectangular box of a house with an anemic interior light smudging a pair of heavy curtains. Through the car's open windows, they could hear the constant rumble of the heavy Route 7 traffic a block to the west.

They walked up the cracked driveway and cut across the patchy lawn to the front door, where Joe rang the bell. The house's siding had started life as white vinyl, but its color and integrity had faded over time, becoming yellowed and marred by chips and fissures, making the entire house look like an old and sleeping dinosaur.

The door opened to reveal a turnip-shaped man in baggy shorts and an untucked, faded Hawaiian shirt. He wore thick glasses and had a hank of thinning gray hair draped across his forehead, as if a once carefully applied comb-over had undergone a landslide.

"Yes?"

Spinney spoke first, having read the old traffic report. "William Friel?"

The man's voice was a monotone, devoid of curiosity. "Yes." Behind him, a television was spilling a game show into the room.

"Son of Barb Barber?"

Even then, he didn't flicker. "Yes."

"I'm Special Agent Spinney, of the Vermont Bureau of Investigation. This is Special Agent Gunther. We were wondering if we could come in and chat with you a bit. Would that be all right?"

Friel finally registered a small modicum of emotion by responding unexpectedly. "Wait a minute, okay? I gotta prepare my mother." Without further ceremony, he shut the door in their faces.

"Okay," Spinney said slowly. "That was weird."

A minute later, however, Friel was back, pulling open the door and ushering them in, muttering, "Sorry 'bout that. I don't like her surprised."

Unsure of what to expect, Lester crossed the threshold, looking around. Joe followed him into a living room with little furniture, shabby wall-to-wall carpeting, a cheap and garishly bright overhead light, and an old woman in a wheelchair, staring at the TV set, her legs covered with a thin blanket. The walls were bare, the only bookshelf had some clothes and a pile of old newspapers in it, and the air smelled stale.

Spinney straightened slightly at the sight of the woman. "Hi," he said with artificial brightness. "Sorry to barge in on you like this."

She didn't so much as blink. Friel said nothing.

"Is this Barb Barber?" Joe asked softly.

"Yes. My mother," Friel explained. "That's what I meant."

Joe cast her a quick glance from across the room before asking, "How long's she been afflicted?"

Friel's eyes seemed to settle on him for the first time. He hesitated and then answered, "Three years."

"So it came on fast?"

Her son pressed his lips together, blinked once, and conceded, "Pretty quick."

Joe reached out and touched his arm. "That's a shame. Hard to bear."

Friel nodded without comment.

"Is she reachable at all?" Joe asked. "We were hoping to ask her a couple of questions."

He hesitated before saying; "No. She's gone. I still talk to her, like just now when you were at the door, but it's mostly out of habit. She doesn't really need warning anymore."

Friel didn't seem even vaguely curious about why two cops would be standing in his house, wanting to speak to his mother. As it was, they were still standing as they'd entered, awkwardly in the middle of the room.

"Maybe we could ask you, instead," Joe

suggested. "You have a place where we could talk and not bother her? A kitchen, perhaps?"

Friel considered that before admitting, "Yeah."

Joe had by now understood the implicit rules of engagement with this man. "Great," he said, taking their host's elbow and pointing him toward the back hallway. "Lead the way."

They trooped toward the rear of the small house, passing two bedrooms and a bathroom, and entered a dingy, worn kitchen with rusting appliances, including a stacked washer/dryer. A small metal table with two chairs was shoved against one wall, a cluster of medications corralled in its middle. Joe pulled out a chair and positioned Friel to sit in it. He took the one opposite while Spinney leaned against the counter near a sink piled with dirty dishes.

"Is this your house or your mother's, William?" Joe asked first, following an instinct.

He had it right. "Hers," Friel answered.

"And you've lived here how long?"

Friel seemed a little confused by the question. "All my life," he eventually replied, adding, "Almost."

Joe nodded. His own brother could have made the same claim, the dynamics there being admittedly much different. Still, he had often wondered how Leo would fare once their mother died — just as he now wondered about this man, given the same inevitability. His bets were on Leo coming out of it far better than William.

Joe rubbed his forehead, as if chasing away such distractions. "Good to know," he said. "That probably means you knew Carolyn Barber. Is that correct?"

Friel's eyes widened a fraction as he stopped staring at the table's surface and looked at his questioner. "Aunt Carolyn?"

"Right. She and your mother were sisters, weren't they?"

"Yeah." He paused before asking, "Did she die?"

It was asked without affect, as if read from a script.

"No. I'm sorry. I didn't mean to put that in the past tense." Joe expanded his response by adding, "I've actually never met her. That's all I meant."

Friel nodded slightly. "Oh."

"Would that mean anything? If she had died?" Joe asked.

"Mean anything?" Friel replied question-ingly, a furrow between his eyes.

"Yeah. You know. Inheritance, maybe? Or just the passing of the family's black sheep.

I don't know. Anything — like I said. I don't know the woman."

"Is that why you're here? Aunt Carolyn?"

Joe sidestepped answering. "You haven't seen her mentioned on the news, on TV? We just released a bulletin on her — should be all over."

He responded. "We don't watch the news. Too depressing. Why is she on TV, if she's okay?"

"I didn't say she was okay. When did you last see her?"

Friel was shaking his head. "When I was a kid. She's been in the nuthouse most of my life. What happened to her?"

"Why was she put there?"

Friel scowled. "I don't know. She was off her rocker."

Again, his voice was flat.

"Did your mom ever talk about that? Why it happened?"

"Not really. She had other things to worry about."

Joe didn't speak. The silence grew heavy in the small, battered room. Finally, as hoped, Friel sighed and added, "My dad was a drunk. Kicked us around pretty good. Aunt Carolyn was the least of our problems."

This was sadly familiar to the two detectives.

"I'm sorry to hear it," Joe said gently.

Friel sat back in his chair and gave Joe the most direct eye-to-eye contact he'd delivered so far. His half smile was rueful and heartbroken.

"I got married once," he volunteered. "Didn't last long. Lucky we didn't have kids. It was a mess." He glanced at the hallway door, toward the sound of the distant TV set, and murmured, "So I came back. Figured what the hell."

He straightened, ran his fingers through what was left of his hair, and addressed them in an artificially stronger tone. "Look, I know squat about Aunt Carolyn, but Mom kept some items in an album. Maybe they'll be useful."

His and Joe's chairs screeched on the scarred linoleum as they stood, and Friel led the way back toward the hallway and one of the bedrooms.

It was pitch black until he switched on the overhead light, revealing as in a flash photograph what looked like a crime scene, barring a body. The bed was large, old, unmade, and surrounded by several fold-up tray tables cluttered with half-empty glasses, a stained pizza box, crumpled tissues, bags of

138

candy, and assorted junk. The floor was populated by small tepees of piled clothing. The furniture consisted of a single dresser and a makeup table so covered with belongings that only its spindly legs gave it an identity.

Friel crossed to the dresser, wrestled open one of its top drawers, making about a dozen dusty figurines grouped haphazardly across its surface tremble and rattle, and dug around until he extracted a cheap, pink plastic photo album stamped in gold with the logo, MEMORIES OF YOU.

This he handed to Joe. "Ton of crap in there — me, the old lady, my dad, Aunt Carolyn, bunch of other people. Postcards, too, newspaper clippings. Like I said . . ."

Joe took it from him and looked around. "Mind if I take this back to the kitchen?"

Friel shrugged. "Knock yourself out. I'll go keep Mom company."

"Before you go," Joe asked him, "what's the story behind your name being different from your mother's and Carolyn's?"

"Friel was my dad's. After he left, Mom went back to her maiden name."

Joe nodded. "Thanks. Just wanted to confirm my assumption."

He and Lester returned to the kitchen and sat at the small table, Joe imagining Friel and his mother sharing meals here in total silence every night, whether they actually did so or not. It was a Norman Rockwell nightmare.

William Friel had been accurate in his description of the album's contents. There were no labels to help them decipher the assortment, but in most cases, none were needed. The shots of small, stiff groupings facing the camera didn't call for more elaboration than the body language in evidence. Plus, having met Barb Barber and her son, Les and Joe could easily decipher not just those two, if younger and occasionally more animated, but they could also see elements of the son's features in the face of the brutal-looking man often posing with them.

"Fun bunch," Lester nevertheless murmured, leafing slowly through the book.

Joe stopped him with an extended finger. "That must be Carolyn," he commented, tapping on a smiling young woman standing beside Barb, their arms interlinked. "She's cute."

"Like a slimmed-down, brightened-up version of her sister," Les agreed.

Joe pointed to another shot. "She's certainly the only one who smiles any."

Les came to a page with a folded news

clipping, which he gingerly opened until it was about twice the size of the page to which it was attached. The glue had darkened a quarter of it, but it was still legible, and the grainy photograph of a beaming young Carolyn spoke for itself. She was waving at the camera next to a straitlaced man in a business suit, under the headline, GOVERNOR-FOR-A-DAY! The date at the top was just under fifty years ago.

"Who's the guy?" Les asked, squinting at the caption.

" 'Young Caroline Barber,' " Joe read, adding as an aside, "they misspelled her name, 'had her time in the spotlight as Governor-for-a-Day on Thursday, when Senator Gorden Marshall, R-Chittenden, introduced her to a joint session of the legislature as part of the Administration's newly launched effort to bring the people closer to state government's inner workings.' "

"Who in their right mind came up with that one?" Lester asked, peering at the picture. "Sure doesn't look like Gorden Marshall thought much of it."

"Is there an article that goes with it?" Joe asked, peeling the page back a bit to study the flip side.

"Doesn't look like it," Lester confirmed.

"Guess the caption did it all."

Joe took in the image for another few seconds before refolding the clipping and sitting back so that his colleague could resume turning pages.

"Oh, here you go," Spinney said. "Maybe."

He'd uncovered a pale blue envelope, mounted squarely in the middle of the page. It was addressed to Barb, with a return address of Carolyn's. He eased it open and extracted a single sheet covered with small, childish writing. He handed this over to his boss.

Joe positioned it under the overhead light, the sound of the distant TV still filtering back like a thin fog. Lester sat quietly and watched him work through the letter's contents.

Finally, Joe placed it flat on the table, next to the album, and rested his fingertips on it as if to monitor its pulse.

"Sounds like a sweet girl," he said thoughtfully.

"She talk about her big day?" Lester asked.

Joe sat more comfortably and crossed his arms, looking at the letter. "Yeah. You can really feel her happiness with it all — like a kid at a birthday party. Really like a kid."

Lester kept quiet, knowing when Joe was

mulling things over. He took a stab at interpreting what was on the older man's mind. "You want me to ask William back in here?" he asked, standing.

Joe glanced up at him in surprise. "Huh? Yeah — good idea."

Smiling, Lester stepped down the short hall and fetched their host. Friel stood in the doorway as Lester resumed his position by the counter.

"Mr. Friel," Joe asked, "did you know your aunt at all? You said that you last saw her when you were little."

"Sure — before they put her away."

"How would you have described her personality?"

Friel frowned at him. "Her personality? I don't get you."

"I don't want to put words in your mouth," Joe explained. "But what I'm looking for is how you might've described her to someone who'd never met her, like us, for example."

Friel tilted his head slightly. "Nice," he said. "She was always real friendly. Talked a lot, too. And laughed. I mean, she was simple, so that's not too surprising. She wasn't much given to serious thinking."

Joe nodded, as if hearing a confirmation. "How do you mean, 'simple'?"

Friel's voice dropped, as if his mother could hear them from the front room. "Just that. Not too bright. That's why she was fun company for a kid, I guess. She was still one herself."

"What did she do for a living, back when she was made Governor-for-a-Day?"

For the first time, Friel smiled. "Was that in there?" He pointed at the closed album on the table. "The governor thing?"

"Yeah. What can you tell us about it?"

"It was the biggest thing that ever happened to her, but I don't know much about it. I remember her saying to everybody, 'I was governor once,' again and again. It drove my mom crazy. She used to yell at Carolyn that it was just a publicity stunt, but Aunt Carolyn didn't care."

"How did it happen? Do you know? Or did your mom tell you afterwards, maybe?"

"Nah. Mom didn't talk about it at all. Like I said, she hated it. Maybe she hated that Carolyn got the attention, when all she got was me and Dad. I don't know."

Joe returned to his original question. "So, what was Carolyn doing when she was put in the limelight?"

"Working in Montpelier. That's all I know. I would hear them talking about it. But it was like when somebody says, 'He works in

Washington,' you know? It means the government. That's what I always thought. I can't swear to it, though. What would they find for her to do, you know what I mean — given how sharp she was?"

"Right," Joe said without conviction, thinking that there were plenty of things a pretty young woman might be asked to do in government, especially back then.

"Did Barb and Carolyn get along? You make it sound like they didn't," Joe asked, almost as an afterthought.

Friel surprised him with his answer. "Mom loved her. Same way I did. There was no getting Carolyn down. With all the bullshit my dad pulled, we needed every laugh we could get, and Carolyn was good for it. She may've been a loony, but she was fun. My mom and her were like joined at the hip. Maybe that's part of what got to Mom about that governor thing — it split them apart a little."

A softness had settled on his face with the reminiscence.

Joe picked up the album and asked, "Do you think we could borrow this for a while? We'll get it back to you."

"I don't care," William Friel said, sad once more. "You can keep it. That's all done and buried."

Joe understood the sentiment, although he felt in his bones that it was utterly inaccurate.

CHAPTER NINE

After their interview with William Friel, Joe and Lester decided to stay in Burlington overnight instead of heading back to Brattleboro. This, as it turned out, was a good thing, given what Sammie Martens had to say the following morning. Earlier, Joe had asked her to check on the whereabouts and activities of ex–State Senator Gorden Marshall — the unhappy politician who'd been photographed beside Carolyn Barber on her big day.

"Good news, bad news, boss," Sam reported on the phone.

"I hate that," he said, wiping the last of the shaving cream from his face and entering the motel's bedroom. Lester was doing push-ups next to the far bed, in front of the flat-screen TV. He paused to quickly hit the MUTE button on CNN.

"All right," she continued, ignoring him. "The good news is that I found Gorden

Marshall. He's parked at a place called The Woods of Windsor. It's one of those over-the-top old folks' homes where, in exchange for a small fortune, you get three squares a day, a pull alarm beside the toilet, and a one-way ticket to the terminal ward so your kids never have to worry about you when you go ga-ga."

"Ouch," Joe responded, sitting on the edge of his bed. "Do we have issues with this?"

"We do not," she said, adding, "At least, not personally. There are a few things about it, though, that bother me in principle. I think it has something to do with the money involved, but I haven't given it enough thought to know for sure."

Joe laughed. "Geez, Sam — that's very philosophical of you. You already wondering what Emma might be thinking when you and Willy get too old to use that toilet?"

"That's gross."

"That's life, kiddo. What's the bad news?"

"He's dead."

It had the right effect. Joe hesitated, reworking the conversation in his head. "Marshall's dead?"

"As the proverbial doornail. Last night."

Joe turned the phone aside to tell Spinney, "Sam says Gorden Marshall died last night."

Lester turned off the TV. "No way."

"How?" Joe asked Sammie, putting his cell on speakerphone.

"Natural causes, according to the facility. I called as soon as I read about it during my records search on the guy, and whoever it was in administration at The Woods told me that their medical director was signing it off as a natural."

"The hell he is," Joe blurted out.

This time, it was Sam who paused before asking, "Who was Marshall, anyhow? You didn't go into detail last night. I mean, I know the political part. . . ."

"That's about it so far," Joe admitted. "We found him posing in a photograph next to Carolyn Barber when she was made Governor-for-a-Day. It was just a lead I wanted to follow." He reconsidered that and added, "Or it was before this piece of unlikely coincidence. Where's the body right now?"

"Probably at the funeral home. Maybe still at The Woods of Windsor. It was dumb luck that I stumbled over this. I was running all state databases, as usual with missing persons, and there he was in the death registry. I couldn't believe it. If the Internet used ink, it wouldn't have even been dry."

Joe was gesturing to Lester to start packing. "Sam," he said, "call them back, and the local police. Tell them to freeze everything till we get there. And call the SA — that's Roger Carbine for that county — and tell him that I'll be calling him for a big favor and will phone him from the road, right after you let me know you've chased him down. We got to get Gorden Marshall an autopsy, but I want to look at him first."

Sam knew better than to prolong the conversation. Any and all discussion about this could wait until later, especially if some family member was impatiently hoping to get Mr. Marshall cremated.

"You got it," she said, and gave him the address for The Woods.

As might befit a place of self-proclaimed high standards, The Woods of Windsor was located near Woodstock, Vermont — one of the few towns in the state wealthy enough to have had its downtown utility lines buried and its streetlamps replaced with wannabe nineteenth-century gaslights.

The Woods itself appeared as a vast country estate, with rolling green lawns, a central pond complete with two fountains, and a driveway more deserving of a castle than a retirement home.

Not that The Woods of Windsor described

itself as such. While Lester had driven here, Joe had struggled using the younger man's smartphone to check out the place and get a feel for what he was about to encounter. By the time motion sickness had gotten the upper hand, he'd become all but convinced that The Woods would be an ample reward for his having lived all these years — if only he had the 400,000 nonrefundable bucks it took to secure a small two-bedroom apartment there.

"Jesus," he'd said, returning Lester's phone. "It's God's waiting room and J.P. Morgan's in one package."

Now, as they passed through the main entrance, feeling a little diminished for not being in a horse-drawn coach, they experienced firsthand the aura of what true money could buy.

They parked, entered the lobby, tactfully introduced themselves to the white-haired receptionist, and were immediately pointed to an unmarked door, halfway down the hall. As they approached it, the door swung open to reveal a tight-faced, balding man in a suit and glasses, with a harried, unpleasant expression.

"You the police?" he asked without preamble, ushering them inside and quickly closing the door behind them, as if to contain a bad smell.

Joe and Lester displayed their credentials as Joe asked, "And you are?"

"I'm Mr. Whitby, assistant to the director. What seems to be the problem? You're here about Mr. Marshall, aren't you?"

The cops exchanged glances, instinctively disliking this lemonish man.

"We are," Joe confirmed. "Is the body still here?"

"It is, thanks to you," Whitby said testily, "and my phone's been ringing as a result ever since. What you've done has pissed people off."

"We'll probably want all their names," Joe told him levelly. "So if you could keep a log from now on, we'd appreciate it."

Whitby's face closed down even more, which didn't seem possible. "I don't know about that. I don't know about any of this. I haven't been told what's going on here. As far as I know, one of our tenants passed away of natural causes," he emphasized pointedly, "and now you people are crawling all over the place as if we'd had a terrorist attack."

"We just got here," Lester reminded him.

"I think he means the local police," Joe suggested, asking Whitby, "Where are they?

We probably ought to coordinate with them."

"They're causing a stir, guarding the apartment," Whitby sneered, "as if it would fly off or something. I hope you realize what this could do to a place like this." He snapped his fingers. "One wrong move, one small piece of bad publicity, and we've had it — people'll be out of here like rats leaving a ship."

"I've got it, George," said a soothing female voice from behind, entering via the hallway door. "Thanks for your help. Sorry I was late."

A woman with no-nonsense eyes and practical, short gray hair rounded to the front of them, waited for George Whitby to disentangle himself and fade away, and then extended her hand in greeting. "Hannah Eastridge," she began. "I'm the director. I apologize for not greeting you personally. Your colleague called, of course, as has the state's attorney, and the local police have sealed off the apartment, as you heard. I hope that we've set everything up to your satisfaction."

Joe had no clue what she meant by that, but he already liked her style, especially compared to her colleague. He was also pleased by her mention of the SA. Roger

Carbine had evidently made an effort to smooth the way, even without knowing much about their interest in Mr. Marshall. Joe made a mental note to send the man a gift of thanks. However, all he said was, "Whitby also told us that Marshall's still here. We appreciate that, and thank you for your cooperation. I do apologize if we've ruffled any feathers."

"Of course," she said, and gestured to them to follow her down a short corridor to her office, where she waved them into guest chairs and offered them coffee, which they each turned down.

"You have to understand that communities like ours run as much on rumor and gossip as on cash," she explained. "And bad news travels the fastest of all. I know you may not be willing to tell me what's going on, but I was told that Mr. Marshall's death was completely natural. That's what my medical director told me when he was about to sign the death certificate."

"It may be," Joe admitted. "But there are circumstances beyond his death that caught our interest, along with the SA's. It happens sometimes that the usual protocols have to be tweaked a bit. I didn't realize we'd cause such a ruckus."

Hannah Eastridge shooed that away with

her hand. "Oh, George. He was exaggerating slightly. Death at The Woods is sadly an almost weekly disturbance. So, the appearance of the police this time will guarantee some extra chatter over dinner tonight."

She settled down behind her modest desk in an office remarkable mostly for its small size and self-effacement. "That having been said," she continued, "I can't deny that my cell phone has come alive since the first squad car pulled up, and I've already heard back from a family member of Mr. Marshall's."

A large white cat suddenly appeared on the desk between them like a magic trick, startling the cops and making Eastridge laugh as she reached out to pull the animal toward her.

"I am sorry," she said. "Meet Echo, the true boss of the operation. She's only allowed free rein in this suite of offices, but she rules the roost."

They exchanged a few comments about Echo before Lester asked politely, "Who was Marshall's family member that you mentioned?"

"His daughter," Eastridge said. "Michelle Mahoney, who also has power of attorney. She's it, when it comes to relatives. She was automatically informed of her father's passing, soon after he was found. She lives in Connecticut and is making travel plans. When she called back, I told her pretty much what you just said, that sometimes the police get involved for vaguely related reasons, and occasionally order an autopsy. I stressed that there's usually nothing to it. Purely procedural, is how I phrased it. I also mentioned to her that since this is all so vague, the police might want to access her father's apartment, and would that be all right? For the record, she told me you could if need be, but she wanted to be informed if anything was removed."

"Thank you," Joe said. "That was exactly right. You are clearly a practiced hand at this."

"Twenty-eight years in the business," she stated, absentmindedly stroking the happy cat. "Thirteen of them right here."

"And Gorden Marshall? How long was he here?"

"Eight years," she answered quickly.

"Just him?"

"Yes. He arrived as a widower, which is not the norm, since the women generally outlive the men, and to be blunt, he was never in great shape."

"How was he discovered?" Joe asked. "I take it he lived alone."

"He did," she replied. "But he also had an early breakfast routine with some buddies. He didn't show up, they made a phone call he didn't answer, and they sounded the alarm."

"How was he as a tenant?" Joe asked. "Or whatever you call them."

"We prefer 'resident,' " she instructed him. "And he could be a bear. The Woods of Windsor is pretty high on the social ladder, as you probably noticed. It attracts some leadership personalities."

Joe smiled. "Very diplomatic."

"That's the first thing you learn here."

"He was a politician?" Joe asked disingenuously. "Agent Spinney and I were called in pretty abruptly, so we didn't get a chance to dig into his past."

"A Vermont senator," Eastridge replied. "Although I got the sense that it was more than that."

"A mover and a shaker?" Lester asked.

"That's what I was led to believe," she agreed, "although I never knew the details. I understood that he was the epitome of the glad-handing good ol' boy. He certainly handled himself like that. He joined a bunch of committees early on and tended to make more of his responsibilities than perhaps they deserved."

"In other words, a real jerk," Lester said flatly.

Eastridge burst out laughing, making Echo look up at her. "I hope I can trust you not to get me in trouble, but of course you're right."

Joe was smiling when he suggested, "Sounds like he could've been pretty unpopular."

But she raised her eyebrows in surprise. "It does, doesn't it? But with this group, things are often not what they appear. We've got more ex-CEOs and company presidents and retired chairmen than this county has horses, which is saying something. The type A's among our residents tend to consider someone like Gorden Marshall as one of their own. For you or me, they can be pretty unpleasant, but in context, he was no nastier than a competitive tennis player on the pro tour. Half the time, what I might write off as pure orneriness is seen here as game playing. Just strolling the hallways, I witness as much combative psychology as I've heard they have in the Marines."

"Sounds charming," Joe said softly.

She leaned forward slightly in her chair, finally making Echo jump from her lap in search of quieter quarters. "That's the interesting part. It mostly is. I'm no glutton for punishment. I get paid well, but if the job didn't have its perks, I'd leave. I don't come from the same world they do — the real extremists, I'm talking about — but because of my title, they pretty much treat me as an equal. All the stuff I've been telling you is what I see, not what I suffer at their hands. And the truth is, they can also be generous, supportive, and incredibly helpful at times — most of the time, in fact, if you know how to handle them."

She stood up and moved to the door. "Speaking of which, I've got to head off to one of the forty or so committee meetings I regularly attend. I've arranged for someone — not George" — she smiled — "to take you to see Mr. Marshall's body and then to the apartment, if you're so inclined."

They joined her at the door, where they shook hands once more.

Hannah Eastridge held on to Joe's hand for a split second longer, in order to say, "So we're clear, the people I just told you about represent twenty-five percent of our population — the equivalent of maybe one percent out there in the real world. That means seventy-five percent of The Woods of Windsor is made up of rich people — true enough — but who're pretty regular, too. This is a nice place, filled with overwhelm-

159

ingly decent people. Some of them just have too much time on their hands."

"Okay," Joe said, touching her shoulder to emphasize that he did get the point. "We'll keep that in mind. Thanks again for your help."

She gave him a rueful smile. "It goes with the territory."

Gorden Marshall was currently residing as far away from the rest of the facility as geography and architecture would allow. Eastridge's guide took Joe and Lester on an impressive hike through the complex's nether reaches until they arrived at last at a large refrigerated room to the rear of the terminal care unit — and one door shy of the loading dock.

"Kind of says it all, don't it?" Spinney said appreciatively, looking around. "The high-end, industrial-housing version of ashes to ashes."

Joe didn't challenge him there, and headed to the one shrouded occupant of the room, now adorning a steel gurney and draped with a white sheet. On the way, he thanked their Sherpa and promised to find their own way back — although how, he wasn't exactly sure.

He peeled off the sheet and folded it

160

neatly, revealing a white-haired, oddly angry-looking man dressed in a pair of pajamas.

"Whoa," Lester said, drawing near. "Not a man to piss off, even now. Want me to poke him with a stick first?"

Joe shook his head, but with a slight smile. "Who wound you up this morning?"

Lester didn't answer, bending over to better scrutinize Marshall's face. "He doesn't look all that different from how he did in the old newspaper photo. Just older."

Joe agreed. He reached for a convenient dispenser of latex gloves and sheathed his hands in electric blue rubber. Lester did likewise, in case Joe needed help.

"What're we looking for?" he asked, positioning himself on the other side of the gurney.

Joe barely murmured, "Don't know yet," as he unbuttoned the pajama jacket.

It was cold in the room, but the body had obviously begun cooling before being moved here. The limbs and jaw were stiff, the anterior part of the body pale and its posterior mottled with pooled and congealed blood. Joe pressed his thumb firmly into a section of dark red skin and saw no blanching, indicating that livor mortis had already set in. On TV, fictional pathologists

161

were always setting the time of death as if it were stamped on the body's forehead. Joe and Lester knew better. Time of death was an elusive standard, camouflaged by the whims of temperature and circumstance, among others, and best established by someone reliable having seen the person die. Nevertheless, estimates could be reasonably assumed, as Joe demonstrated by saying, "Well, he didn't die ten minutes ago."

Lester glanced at his watch, taking a more serious stab at it. "Last night sometime? The pj's suggest after he went to bed. If we find his sheets messed up when we check his apartment, that would support it."

"He could've been a Hugh Hefner fan," Joe said distractedly, his face inches above the body and his hands running along the man's arms, checking for defects or abnormalities. He studied the fingernails for any signs of a struggle. Lester started doing the same thing from his side.

Slowly, they proceeded from scalp to toes, sometimes comparing notes, scrutinizing the body's anatomy inch by inch and then flipping it over carefully to do the same along the discolored dorsal side.

Finally, not having found anything out of place, they returned Marshall to his original position, and Joe moved to his face. There, he delicately lifted up an eyelid.

"Any petechial hemorrhaging?" Lester asked, inquiring after the tiny blood bursts that often accompanied strangulation or asphyxia.

Joe shook his head. "Nope. It's not always there, though."

His fingers felt at the lips, barely working to pry them open. But they were frozen shut, by rigor and the bonding effect of dried saliva, and he desisted immediately, muttering, "I'll let the ME mess with that."

"We're definitely going for an autopsy?"

Joe looked up. "The guy dies just as we're about to interview him? I don't care if he was diagnosed with triple cancer. That's a coincidence I want looked at. Besides, after what it took to convince Roger Carbine, I'm not about to back down now. He was already wary of messing with a famous ex-politician, complete with a doc standing by, ready to sign a death certificate."

There was a knock at the door, and a uniformed police officer with sergeant's stripes walked in, looking irritated. "There you are. We heard you hit the premises an hour ago."

Joe walked up to him, stripping off his gloves and extending a hand in greeting, which the other man had to accept.

"I am so sorry, Sergeant —" Joe quickly checked the man's name tag. "— Carrier. That was unprofessional and uncalled for. Got carried away when I heard the body was still here." He stepped aside to introduce Lester. "This is Lester Spinney. I get like a dog with a bone. The apartment okay, by the way?"

Carrier was unimpressed by the apology. His mouth curled as he said, "Wouldn't know. Your colleague on the phone made it pretty clear there was no search warrant yet and we were to bar the door and not mess up the playground. You might tell her to brush up on her manners if you expect any help in the future."

Joe could feel Spinney tensing beside him. For all Lester's joking around, he was a loyalist, and perfectly ready to defend the unit's honor.

"We're flying on instinct here," Joe tried mollifying Carrier. "Not on hard evidence. But consider the odds: We're running an interview on the far side of the state, this guy's name comes up — out of the blue — and I immediately get notified that he's dead. I don't know about you, but I had to check it out. We're all working on so little sleep by now — just like you guys — that we're getting a little punchy. No offense intended."

Joe paused for half a breath and asked, "How bad did Irene hammer you?"

Carrier paused, caught off guard. "Bad enough — like everybody, I guess."

"Yeah. We're based out of the Brattleboro–Wilmington area," Joe said.

The reference to Wilmington softened the sergeant's demeanor, even though Joe hadn't actually been to the town.

"Shit," Carrier said sympathetically. "What's left of it?"

"Not much," Joe stated vaguely. "They pretty much got clocked. The whole downtown."

"Yeah. I saw the footage on YouTube. Amazing."

Joe took advantage to pat Carrier's upper arm lightly, as a peace gesture. "Anyhow, I do apologize. None of us needed a death investigation, and you sure as hell didn't need us getting under your skin."

Carrier took the hint and moved on, casting a glance at the exposed body. "You find anything?"

Joe raised an eyebrow. "Wish I knew. We'll send him up for a closer look, but nothing obvious so far. You want to help me with the apartment? I'll get a team up here later, but I'd love to take a quick look-see. We got permission from the next of kin."

Carrier hardly jumped with joy, but he did give a grudging nod. "I suppose. Sure."

CHAPTER TEN

Gail Zigman lived in a condominium overlooking Montpelier. It was a nice place,
modern, with two floors, three bedrooms,
and two full baths — part of a complex
stretching out to either side. All the units
had views of the capitol building's shimmering gold dome, the crooked Winooski
River — now looking benign despite its
savagery earlier — and the town's scattering
of lights, cradled in the valley's lowlands, as
if delivered by an avalanche of lightbulbs
from the surrounding hills.

Of course, there was security — plain-
clothed state troopers placed inconspicu-
ously about. The neighbors only appreciated the extra protection and enjoyed the
fact that their governor lived among them.

Gail did live alone, however, as she had
ever since winning one of the more bitter
gubernatorial contests in recent history.
She'd had a lawyer companion before then,

complete with a BMW, who'd looked good on her arm and performed adequately in bed. But he'd become a casualty of practical thinking and her career, along with a rueful, late-blooming realization that she was less sentimental than she'd previously believed.

She could admit that now, much as she might have denied it earlier. And as she sat alone in the darkness of her spare and immaculate home, sipping wine in the comfort of a Marcel Breuer Wassily armchair and facing the darkened panorama through a wall-to-ceiling picture window, she could also admit that it wasn't the rape that was to blame, or her breakup with Joe. More fundamentally, despite occasionally expressing a degree of self-pity, she'd come to accept that she alone had abandoned her early communal life, not ever wanted a child, avoided settling down with Joe, and grown tired of being a local municipal politician. She had a hardness within her, she'd realized, mixed with a drive that the rape might have laid bare, but which had been hard-wired within her all along.

The doorbell rang, and she reluctantly rose from her clifflike aerie, in exchange for the gloom near the front door. It was almost midnight, she'd been up since six, and yet she approached whoever this was with more curiosity than irritation. A late-night encounter was as good a way to wrap up the day as staring into the darkness.

Still, she was pleasantly surprised at who was standing before her and happily gave the thumbs-up to the cop a half step behind Susan Raffner.

She hugged her old friend in the darkness and reached for the hallway light switch, offering to fix something for Susan to drink, but Raffner stopped her by laying her hand on her forearm. "No. Leave it dark. I like it. It's kind of wonderful."

Gail turned in the direction of Susan's gaze and saw that she'd noticed the view filling the far end of the distant living room, whose faint glitter touched the pale walls even back here.

"I've got a bottle of wine open," Gail suggested, taking Susan's hand.

"That would be perfect."

They walked together into the lofty space, and Raffner sat as at a stage play before the wall-to-wall scene while Gail fetched another glass.

Susan let out a sigh and toed off her shoes, one by one, enjoying the massage of the thick carpeting on her soles.

Gail resumed her seat and filled the glass

before handing it over. "Tough day?"

Susan took a sip. "Interesting," she said afterwards. "I know we're not supposed to gloat or poke a stick at others' misfortunes, but I think, so far, that we're doing better with this mess than they did with Katrina in Louisiana."

Gail snorted. "Well, yeah. We had three deaths and have just over half a million people in the whole state. What's Louisiana got? Four and a half million? Plus, they got an ocean surge on top of the rain."

Susan took a second sip, unruffled. "You know what I mean. Pat yourself on the back, girl. You've been out in the towns, standing in the muck, talking to people in food lines, you've been shown meeting with FEMA and the Corps of Engineers. You're like the goddamn Energizer Bunny. That's good stuff, and you know it. And we've been just as good in our districts" — she pointed out the window — "working the phones and backing you up. There's no shame in taking pride in work well done."

In response, Gail simply held up her glass so that Susan could clink it against her own.

After they'd both taken swallows, however, Gail asked, "So that's it? Rah-rah for the home team?"

"That's a bad thing?"

"It's not why you're here at midnight."

Raffner's initial silence confirmed Gail's suspicion. "Well," Susan admitted, "I have been approached with something I think you'll find interesting."

"Like a snake in the grass?"

She made a face, which Gail could not have seen. "I hope not. I'm seeing this as a good thing."

Gail twisted in her chair and faced Susan's profile, attracted by something in the tone of her voice — a form of powerfully suppressed excitement that she'd heard only on rare occasions. "You have my interest, Senator."

Susan turned toward her, the lights outside gleaming in her eyes. "Catamount Industrial," she said. "You know about them?"

"Of course. Vermont's own fairy tale." Gail reacted slightly scornfully. "The exception that proved the rule. The founder started out as a tinkerer, began with . . . what was it? Surplus machine tools after the bottom fell out in places like Springfield? He traded that into equipment to run everything from stone quarries to ski slope operations, then branched out into farm machinery, agriculture, banking, God knows what else, before selling out to the second-

or third-biggest agri-corporation in the country for . . . whatever . . . a zillion dollars? I miss anything?"

Susan had been nodding in agreement throughout. "Harold LeMieur," she confirmed. "On the financial high end of the national food chain, born and bred in good-old-Vermont, although he hasn't lived here in decades."

"And who's had nothing to do with us, either, if memory serves," Gail concluded dismissively. "Which is one reason I was told not to waste my time hitting him up for support. Not to mention that he's a right-wing poster child."

Susan was laughing by now. "That's the man."

Gail smiled, caught by Susan's mood. "So, why're we talking about him?"

"Because," Susan said almost gleefully, "if this works out, it'll be the exact opposite of George Bush's 'Hell of a job, Brownie' boner following Katrina. I've been contacted by LeMieur's people, who say he's interested in working with you in creating what they're calling a para-FEMA."

Gail held up her hand. "He's not one of ours, Susan."

"That's the point," Raffner exclaimed. "He wants to do this for Vermont, not us,

172

and he's willing to work with whoever to get it done, even a bunch of liberal wackos. Which is the best part of it, you see? If it works, it'll undermine the whole right–left paradigm we've been fighting for years."

Gail scratched her head. "It doesn't make sense," she said. "What does LeMieur get out of it? He's never done anything that wasn't to his own advantage."

"That's what I asked," Susan argued. "And they said that's exactly why — as he's aged, he's become haunted by his own ogre image. Like what happened to John D. Rockefeller when he got old. He started donating money, handing out dimes to kids, and conning people into thinking he'd become a nice, doddering, generous old man. Totally bogus, of course, but what do we care if you get to stand up at the end of the day and say that under your administration, even the likes of Irene can be tamed through bipartisan cooperation?"

Gail laughed and took another sip of her wine. "Okay," she then said. "Assuming this isn't a total crock to make us look like fools, what's he mean by para-FEMA?"

"In short? His organization would operate as a super-low-interest bank, paralleling FEMA. Applicants to the U.S. government would get whatever money FEMA doles out, then Catamount would show up and handle what fell through the cracks or came up short. It would function as a safety net for people FEMA didn't completely take care of, or who didn't qualify in the first place for some reason."

"They'd be loans?" Gail asked suspiciously.

"Structured as such for those who could afford them. Otherwise, they'd be grants. It would work on a case-by-case basis."

Gail resumed staring out the window, deep in thought. It was a political reality that garbage strikes and snowstorms got politicians thrown out of office — or tropical storms. Her poll numbers had begun high, based on her covering the state like a wet sheet and showing up wherever there was a TV camera. But people standing next to the wreckage of their town and homes were beginning to complain about the lack of money, the slowness of road and bridge repair, and how she'd been acting to set things right.

Political storm clouds were gathering. And certainly, the essence of what Susan had just outlined seemed like a sudden shaft of sunlight.

"Is LeMieur open to sharing the stage?" she asked slowly. "If I used his offer to get places like IBM or Ben and Jerry's or C and S to chip in as well, would that be a deal-breaker?"

Susan remained undaunted. "I wanted to know the same thing. They made it clear that he'd like special mention for starting things rolling, but after that, sure. He'd let whoever pulled out a checkbook step on-stage with him."

Gail shook her head. "And he's ready to act now? Immediately?"

"That's what they told me," Susan assured her. "Of course, none of it can happen if the state drags its feet. It's not like Catamount could simply set up shop independently. All sorts of special allowances are going to have to be cranked out to make it legal. And you'll have to be out front through it all, goading, leading, blackmailing — whatever it takes to make it happen."

"Right, right," Gail replied, and faced her mentor one last time. "Okay, Susan. Call them back and take the next step, but on tiptoes. Word of this gets out prematurely, we'll have so much shit on our shoes, we won't be able to move. What you've brought me is right up there with jumping out of an airplane and only hoping you've got a parachute." She slid halfway out of her chair to put her face inches from Raffner's. "We are fucked if this fails," she said.

Susan smiled, if grimly. "It won't, Gail. This is how people like us get things done. Boldly, not stupidly. I will shepherd this like it was my firstborn."

Gail smiled suddenly and kissed Raffner's cheek quickly. "Go get 'em, girl. I'll be holding my breath."

There was a pecking order of residences at The Woods of Windsor, starting with quarter-million-dollar efficiencies with no view, and culminating with segregated duplexes built apart from the madding crowd, lined up on a ridge overlooking the fields and hills of Vermont's horse country. Surprisingly to Joe, the late Gorden Marshall's apartment was not among the latter. The place that Sergeant Carrier led them to was fancy and spacious, but located alongside a string of similar apartments on the top floor of one of the complex's larger buildings. Either Marshall's resources had their limits, or his Vermont-born sense of decorum had overruled them.

To give Carrier credit, he'd positioned a single officer at the door, and made sure that, unlike himself, he was in plainclothes. Of course, he was also young, fit, uncomfortable in a tie, and sporting a high-and-tight haircut. He had "cop" stamped all over him. But the effort had been made, and Joe mentioned it as they approached, complimenting his counterpart.

Carrier merely jutted his chin down the long hallway, to where an elderly man had just rounded the corner. "You'll be eating those words in thirty seconds," he said dourly. "That's one of the board members. You'll love him."

Joe was already watching the grim expression approaching them, imagining it atop a younger man in a suit, fifteen years earlier, striding toward some stockholders' meeting with fire in his belly.

"Swell," he said gently as the three cops came to a halt at the door.

The old bulldog stopped three feet shy of them and took them in with a withering glare. Joe noticed a small glob of humanizing spittle parked on his lip, along with the fact that his morning's shave had been a little haphazard. The last few years had been taking a toll.

"Who's in charge here?" he asked without preamble.

Carrier looked to Joe and made a small hand gesture of introduction.

Joe nodded and said, "Guess that's me. Special Agent Joe Gunther, of the Vermont

Bureau of Investigation. This is Special Agent Spinney. I think you know Sergeant Carrier." He took in the young man by the door and added, "And this is one of his colleagues, whom —"

But at that point, the retired captain of industry had reached his fill. "I don't care about that. I want to know what the hell is going on."

"Sure," Joe said pleasantly. "And you are?"

"Graham Dee," the man answered. "I represent the board."

"They sent you?" Joe asked.

Dee's eyes narrowed. "I'm acting on their behalf."

Joe pulled out his notepad and clicked his pen, preparing to write. "So therefore an official representative? You're speaking for them?"

Dee's face flushed angrily. "That has nothing to do with the price of eggs," he snarled. "I demand to know what's going on."

"As well you should," Joe agreed pleasantly, closing his pad. "I tell you what. In the interests of efficiency, and since we've just spent a fair amount of time bringing Hannah Eastridge up to speed, I recommend you speak with her first. That way, we'll all be on the same page when we compare notes later."

Ignoring the rest of Dee's bluster, Joe motioned to the young officer, who quickly opened the door so they could file in. Dee made to follow them, but Joe turned on the threshold, the edge of the door in his hand. "Mr. Dee, until we clear the scene, I'm afraid this apartment will have to stay closed to the public. I look forward to chatting later."

With that, he shut the door, cutting Dee off in mid-sentence.

Carrier had a wide smile on his face. "Nice, Agent Gunther."

Joe laughed. "Joe. And I'm sure that'll cost me a pound of flesh later." He looked beyond their tightly packed huddle. They were standing in a kitchenette that led into a spacious, sun-filled living room.

"Sergeant," he began, "you know some of the players around here, like the charming Mr. Dee. What can you tell us so we'll get out of your hair as soon as possible?"

Carrier smiled slightly at the acknowledgments. "My name's Rick, and to be honest, I'm just as happy you guys are here. I hate dealing with these people." Without stepping into the living room, he began pointing out what features of the apartment they could see. This wasn't an official crime scene — yet — and the police guard had been put in place after several people came and went, no doubt tracking minute traces of evidence in and out, but Carrier had gotten the message nevertheless: Treat this as a secure area until informed otherwise.

"Like you probably heard," he said, "Marshall missed his morning get-together with some pals. One of them phoned, got no answer, tried the door, found it locked, and called for help. That's one thing you can say about this outfit — they take care of their own. Internal EMS responded from downstairs — no ambulance or 911 call — and they declared him dead right here. They wrapped him up, stripped the bed, transported him downstairs, locked the door again, and called the family. The doc who runs the medical wing said it was a natural, filled out the death certificate, and until you guys called us, we had no clue what might have happened."

"But you've got one now," Joe suggested.

"Not really," Carrier countered. "We got what I just told you. And I gotta say, I don't see much to this." He waved an arm before them. "I mean, look at it. The guy was found in bed, no signs of disruption, the door was locked, and not a mark on him, unless you found something."

He looked at Joe expectantly, who confessed, "Not yet. The autopsy might."

"Plus," Carrier went on, "from what I was told, he was a medical time bomb — bad heart, bad lungs, used a walker, was on all sorts of meds. One of the nurses I'm friendly with even said they were trying to get him moved permanently to the medical wing 'cause they knew he'd only be getting worse."

He left it at that, lapsing into silence.

Joe took advantage to suggest, "Let's take a quick look."

Carrier bowed slightly. "Be my guest. Try not to get lost."

It was a telling comment. The small apartment was composed of an office, a bedroom, the room before them, and two bathrooms. That was it.

Still, Joe couldn't shake that he was here for a reason. Slipping on one of the latex gloves he kept in his pocket, he used his right hand to ease open a filing cabinet drawer in the office. The drawer had been rigged with metal rails, designed to support hook-equipped files that could be shoved back and forth to allow easy access. As the drawer yawned open, Joe saw that the files had been pushed forcefully apart, creating a large and empty space in the middle.

181

It was an obvious indication of something having been removed.

He checked the tabs of the files before and after the wide gap. All the *C*'s were missing. A glance through the remaining records showed nothing beyond bills, receipts, and assorted documents of no apparent relevance.

A cursory examination of the rest of the apartment revealed nothing out of place, and seemingly, nothing more that had been removed.

He retreated to the entryway, stripping off his glove.

"Find anything?" Carrier asked him.

"Not that jumps out," he said cautiously. "We'll seal the place for now, conduct a proper search when we have a bigger time window."

Carrier was not impressed. "Why're you so interested in this? I don't get it. You sure you're not keeping something in your back pocket?"

Joe barely smiled. "Don't I wish."

CHAPTER ELEVEN

Sammie stopped what she was doing in the kitchen, hearing Emma squealing happily in the front room. She moved quietly down the hallway to watch Willy from the doorway. He was lying on his back, holding the tiny child overhead, cupped in his right hand — her chubby arms and legs thrashing like a turtle's seeking traction. He was lowering her as he might an exercise weight, until they were touching nose to nose, and then catapulting her back up into the air, to her repeated delight.

Willy, his self-preservative instincts never at rest, addressed Sammie without looking at her, despite the fact that she'd not made a noise. "You laying bets she's gonna throw up on me?"

Sammie laughed. "God, I hope not." She entered the room and settled into a rocking chair as Willy continued his play. For her part, she hadn't even heard him enter the house. Only Emma's giggles had informed her. But that was nothing unusual. She was living with a ghost in some ways — a man so bolted down and private, half the time he seemed to wish he'd been born invisible.

He wasn't entirely alone there. She'd known that feeling when she was younger, coming from a home with no love, functioning in a male-dominated profession, and having an attraction for losers when it came to past companionship. She'd had times when even her own company seemed too much to bear.

No longer, though. Of that, she was increasingly sure. Willy may have been everyone's favorite choice for relational disaster of the year, but he'd proved her faith in him to be sound and justified. And Emma was Exhibit A.

Emma's responses began to wane, so her father settled her onto his chest, where she happily lay drooling onto his shirt and playing with his chin.

"Just got back from the land of the one-string banjo players," Willy announced.

"Interviewing more Rozanskis?" she asked.

"A couple," he agreed. "I met two others, too, but I can't say I interviewed 'em. They are a tight-lipped bunch."

"You find out anything new?"

"Hardly. Confirmed that Bud and Dreama had three kids, Nate, Herb, and Eileen, and that Nate hasn't been heard from in forever . . . and, of course, they all thought Herb was six feet under."

"Where's Eileen?"

From his position on the floor, his face appeared upside down to her, making his smile appear all the more clownish. "Ah!" he said. "Great minds think alike. Yeah, I'm guessing she's my next stop. Not much to be gained messing around with the people she dumped — probably because of their crummy conversational skills. Stamford," he added. "To answer your question." He frowned. "Almost in Massachusetts and as isolated as what she left."

Sam rose from the rocker and stretched out on the floor beside them, so that their three heads were less than a foot apart. Emma gurgled happily with her mother's arrival.

"How 'bout you?" Willy asked, touching her hair with his fingertips. "What've you been up to?"

Her eyes widened slightly in alarm at that. "What time is it?"

He told her without checking his watch — another trick he'd perfected over the years.

"We have a staff meeting with Joe in thirty minutes," she said, immediately interpreting his reaction. "And I asked if Emma could come along. No sweat."

Willy smiled and addressed his daughter. "Hey, Junior G-girl. Wanna take a meeting with the big cheese?"

Joe smiled broadly as Sam, Willy, and Emma entered the office. Every time he saw them, this unlikeliest of families gave him pleasure, both because of how much he liked and admired the individuals within it, and because of how it contrasted with the domestic car crashes he and other cops witnessed every day.

"Hi, there," he greeted them. "Sorry for the short notice, but happy it forced you to bring in the young inheritor." He walked up to them and stuck his face into Emma's, as most adults do, as if babies were the short-sighted geriatrics some of them resembled.

"How are you, sweetheart?" he asked in a near whisper.

Emma reached out and swiped at his nose, her expression serious with intent.

Despite his propensity for delivering acerbic one-liners, especially at sentimental moments, Willy merely looked on benignly.

Joe broke away so they could settle in, and

resumed his greeting. "Anyhow, Lester's wife was asking for photos of him, to remember what he looked like, so we came back for a quick visit. I thought it might be good to throw in a meeting, as well, to see where we all stood."

"That's why we have phones and e-mail, boss," Willy told him.

Joe ignored him. "You getting anywhere on Rozanski?" he asked instead.

"Slowly," Willy said. "It's basically a double missing persons case, involving Herb and his brother, Nate. Next stop is to interview the sister in Stamford. How you doin' with Barber?"

"About the same," Joe admitted. "Only, when we went to interview Carolyn's sister, she had Alzheimer's and couldn't talk to us. Her son didn't have much, either, but at least he gave us an album with a newspaper clipping showing Carolyn with the same politician named Gorden Marshall that Sam discovered had died overnight."

There was silence in the room for the couple of seconds that it took Willy to grasp that this was beyond a simple catch-up meeting. "Killed?" he asked, realizing he'd never gotten an answer from Sammie about what she'd been doing.

"They're claiming natural causes," Joe

explained. "But we've sent him up for an autopsy with the local SA's help."

"I found out a little about Carolyn," Sam volunteered. "According to what I could locate, she worked for the legislative counsel in the statehouse, I guess typing up bills. Wasn't married, no kids, didn't own a house, made probably five grand a year. There's a ton that's not on computers from back then, so that's a disadvantage."

Her expression showed how badly she felt that she couldn't rattle off a detailed and revealing biography on command. Sammie openly regarded Joe as a quasi–father figure, since their history stretched back to when she was on patrol and he headed the detective squad downstairs. To have so little to report made her feel like a failure.

But Joe simply shrugged. "Just a twenty-something office girl," he said. "Socially invisible. God only knows what kind of shark pool that was back then."

Lester feigned surprise. "Really? In little old Vermont?"

Joe smiled at him. "Ancient history now, but the legislators and their hangers-on used to drink like fish and act like sailors on leave. If you were a girl and valued your job, you either joined them or got out of town after hours."

"That what you think was behind the 'Governor-for-a-Day'?" asked Sammie.

"I have nothing to go on," Joe conceded. "I'm just saying that the culture was different and that young women like Carolyn Barber were advised to watch their backs."

" 'Governor-for-a-Day' seems to have been a flash in the pan," Lester added. "You think that was because it was just a cover-up for a little hanky-panky?"

"Maybe," Joe agreed. "The Republicans were on the verge of losing power. The plan was probably a way to make them look friendlier to the electorate. I think that was the rumor. But there's no saying that something darker wasn't also at work."

"Does that make Marshall the guy who was doin' her?" Willy asked. "Pretty convenient that he died now — *if* it was of natural causes."

"Yeah," Sammie chimed in. "And not so convenient if someone headed us off at the pass."

"That scenario would mean," Lester suggested, "that Marshall was not the guy doin' her, but maybe the guy who knew that guy."

"Eloquent," Willy sneered.

"Duh . . . ," Lester responded.

Joe cut them off. "Which means we better put Marshall under the proverbial magnifying lens, starting with the contents of his apartment, which we left under guard and seal, thanks to the converted Sergeant Carrier. Carolyn may have been invisible, but Marshall sure as hell made a wake in those days. Pro tem in the senate, head of several key committees. We ought to be able to find someone willing and able to rat him out."

"I don't know, boss," Willy said doubtfully. "Sounding a little harsh with the attitude there."

Sammie used her sweetest voice. "Don't worry, honey-bunny. He could never challenge the King."

The medical examiner's office in Vermont had enjoyed a reasonably progressive ride into modernity over the years, thanks to a combination of well-intentioned people and a lack of attention from the rest of the world. It was currently housed in the bowels of the mazelike Fletcher Allen Health Care Center in Burlington, which itself had been remodeled into something between the world's largest Rubik's Cube and a nonfunctioning Transformer action toy. Still, the so-called OCME — for Office of the Chief Medical Examiner — while tricky to locate, had blossomed into a lean, efficient, quiet organization overseeing why and how the residents of Vermont died.

It was run — and had been for decades — by Beverly Hillstrom, a tall, slender, strikingly attractive blonde whom Joe had known, trusted, and collaborated with since his early days as an investigator. That shared high regard had extended to the physical — just once, years ago — when they'd spent the night together. That encounter, to their mutual relief, had only strengthened the fondness between them and reinforced the sense that they were friends first and foremost.

Amusingly to Joe, however — whose job relied on picking up on life's small, telling details — there had been one noticeable change that marked this very private evolution in his relationship with Hillstrom. In the past, she had referred to him — as she did all police officers — by his rank and last name. That had undergone an improvement.

"Joe," she said, greeting him with a hug in the hallway beyond the reception room. "It's good to see you. When I saw Mr. Marshall arrive, I was hoping that you'd be close on his heels."

Joe laughed, as much at her greeting as in his own continued enjoyment of her perfect syntax. She was one of the best-spoken people he'd ever met.

He gave her an appraising look. "You found something?" he asked.

She squeezed his arm. "I haven't even looked." She led him down the hallway as she spoke further. "He is laid out and waiting for us, however, and he has been washed and had his blood drawn. So, if you care to change into a pair of scrubs, you know where to find me for the next phase."

He stepped into the tight-fitting locker room, at the rear of the equally small office area, changed out of his street clothes, and proceeded down a separate corridor to a wide door at the end. Beyond that he found Hillstrom in the spacious, modern autopsy room — complete with skylight — spreading out what she needed to examine a stark and naked Gorden Marshall.

She looked up as he entered. "I take it the two of you have met?" she asked.

"We have," he answered, approaching the steel table and looking down at the corpulent ex-senator.

"And Todd?" She gestured to a gowned and masked man who walked in from the refrigerated sample storage room, off to the side.

Joe and the all-but-completely disguised diener nodded greetings to each other. The diener in an autopsy suite was like the bouncer at a well-run bar — he did the heavy lifting, to be sure, but was also attuned to everything that occurred around him, in particular the pathologist's expectations and needs. The average autopsy could take several hours and involved quite a bit of effort, especially with a man the size of Mr. Marshall.

"A well-wined-and-dined individual," Hillstrom commented, back to sorting out her tools. "Who, on paper at least, paid the predictable price for most of his earthly vices."

"Meaning high cholesterol?" Joe asked.

"Oh, much more than that," she said. "We just received his medical record from The Woods. He was being treated for hypertension, cholesterol, diabetes, liver disease, cardiac problems, and deep vein thrombosis, among other things. He was also addicted to tobacco and alcohol. I'm not at all surprised that his personal physician was ready to sign him off as a natural. The miracle here is that he lasted so long."

"You think I'm on a wild-goose chase," Joe allowed.

She looked up again, her eyes wide this time. "Good Lord, no. I would never presume such a thing." She reached out with a

193

gloved hand and gently stroked Marshall's considerable belly. "We'll let Mr. Marshall tell us what he knows before we get into that conversation."

Joe had attended many an autopsy. More, in fact, than were called for by his job. For years now, a police liaison had been assigned to the OCME, specifically to communicate with law enforcement, obviating the need for any officer to actually attend an autopsy as part of his or her investigation. That had been common practice in the old days, back when Joe had made it part of his routine, but he was one of the few who — albeit occasionally — still liked to witness the process. Watching the contents of a body being meticulously analyzed was not unlike carefully searching a house, after all. Each and every component had the potential of telling a tale of interest. The trick was in knowing what you were looking for.

That had marked the foundation of Joe's and Beverly's friendship: this passion for clinical scrutiny, not to mention the emotionally charged satisfaction of being on the hunt for clues.

In this case, however, the hunt did not need to extend to Gorden Marshall's organs, or the inside of his skull. It turned out to be surprisingly easier and more readily available than that.

The beginning of any proper autopsy amounted to simply studying the body in detail, including photographing it up close like a mapmaker documenting the lay of the land. As was her routine, therefore, following this, Hillstrom moved to the man's mouth, gently eased his lips apart, and exposed his teeth and gums.

"Ah," she then said.

Joe had learned enough of her ways to immediately sidle up alongside her, so that they looked as if they were praying over Marshall's head. "What?" he asked, peering down.

She had peeled Marshall's upper lip completely back. "The *frenulum labii superioris* has been stressed," she said, virtually to herself.

"Of course it has," he agreed in a similar tone.

She turned her head slightly to catch his eye, their noses almost touching. "Okay. I get it," she said, and pointed to what she meant. "The frenulum is that fragile stretch of skin connecting the lip to the gum. You can feel your own with your tongue right now. You have an upper frenulum and a lower one."

Joe did as instructed and felt the tiny tautness where she'd advised it would be. "Always wondered what that was there for."

"To help us here and now," she answered simply. "You see where it appears reddened and slightly torn?"

He did, although it didn't leap out at him.

"And here," she continued. "You can see what appear to be slight impressions across the surface of the lip's inner aspect."

"Okay," Joe said in a neutral tone.

"It could be argued," Beverly said, leaving her hands in place but stepping back so that Todd could move in and take photographs of the site, "that such damage can result only if pressure is applied to this area just before death — at least damage with this type of coloring and degree of inflammation."

Joe understood where she was headed. "He was smothered?"

She raised her eyebrows, as she often did when he stretched a finding of hers to satisfy his needs. "This is consistent with that mechanism. Pressure is applied over the mouth — say, of a sleeping man, given that he was dressed in pajamas and found in bed and his apartment not disrupted — resulting in the interior surface of the lip being crushed against the teeth.

"But —" She raised the index finger of

her free hand. "— the victim awakens as his oxygen needs reach criticality, and he begins to struggle." She shook her head violently from side to side. "Making his head toss back and forth. That action, combined with the pressure on his mouth, stresses the frenulum, often damaging it, as it did here."

She backed away as Todd finished. "It's not a given that a suffocation always results in such a finding, any more than it is that the hyoid bone is crushed in a hanging or that petechiae have to result from strangulation. But if you find what we did here, the question has to be: How did those injuries get there otherwise?"

Joe was nodding, pleased with his instinct to have sent Marshall here in the first place. "But there must be other findings you can use to back that up, now that you know what to look for? Brain or blood tests?"

She gave him a sad expression. "Not necessarily. If this is a suffocation, that may be it, especially if his heart went into atrial fib quickly. But I do have an ancillary notion. Given that Mr. Marshall was an alcoholic, he may have been drinking before going to bed. That might — and I stress 'might' — have impaired him enough to explain why the frenular damage is as slight as it is. Because this —" And she tapped the man's lip with her gloved finger — "is relatively subtle."

"You're thinking he may not have put up much of a fight," Joe suggested.

"Something else supports that theory," she answered indirectly. "The responding personnel at The Woods routinely document their actions. It's part of their corporate protocol, and one that I greatly appreciate. They faxed me that report, and there is specific mention of the decedent's being supine, in bed, with his arms under the covers. To me, that either indicates that they were pinned in place while he was being suffocated — possibly by an accomplice — or that the attack was sudden and lethal enough that his own enfeebled constitution simply collapsed under the strain."

"How was his pillow situated?" Joe asked.

"There were two of them. His head was resting on one. The other was found on the floor beside the bed."

Joe's cell phone began to vibrate where he'd clipped it to the waistband of his scrubs. He checked the caller's ID. It was Sammie, who knew where he was, what he was doing, and that he'd be poorly disposed to being disturbed for anything shy of an emergency.

He looked up at Beverly. "I better take

this," he said apologetically, as she was already encouraging him to do so with a hand gesture.

"Joe," he answered.

"Sorry," Sam began, "but I knew you'd want to know this right off. There was a fire at the house where you and Les went to see Barb Barber and her son, in Shelburne. They're both dead."

"Arson?" he asked.

"Don't know yet. I just got it."

"Okay. I'll head there right now. Thanks."

He snapped the phone closed and looked up at Beverly. "It appears you're about to get two more customers. House fire in Shelburne."

She gave him a world-weary smile and said, "It was nice seeing you again, Joe. Try to fit in dinner next time." She nodded toward Marshall. "I'll send you my findings on him as quickly as I can."

"Thanks, Beverly," he replied, already retreating toward the door. He stopped there to cast her a more measured look, and added, "And I'd enjoy dinner very much."

CHAPTER TWELVE

Hillside Terrace this time was a far cry from the near-empty street that Joe and Les encountered on the night they'd met William Friel and his mother. Despite the time taken for the news of the fire to reach police channels, for Sammie to contact Joe, and for him to leave Burlington and reach the center of Shelburne Village, the street was still jammed with fire department apparatus, pickup trucks, and police cruisers, along with coils of fire hose as crisscrossed as a plate of spaghetti.

He settled for a space by the curb two blocks away and walked to where a group of men stood across from the charred remains of the modest home Joe had barely left. Clouds of steam and smoke drifted into the afternoon sky from a blackened pyre of collapsed wall studs and roofing material. The air was thick with an eye-watering pungency and the sounds of radio chatter and idling diesel engines.

Joe approached a firefighter dressed in the white helmet and coat of an officer, pulling out his credentials as he drew near. He waited for the man to stop talking into his portable radio, aware of the others in the group all staring at him, and showed them his badge.

"Chief?"

The man's eyes traveled from badge to face. "Yeah?"

"Joe Gunther. Sorry to bug you when you're knee deep, but the people living here are part of an investigation I'm running."

"Guess that makes you out of luck, then. They didn't make it."

Joe pocketed his shield. "So I heard. Anything you can tell me?"

The chief shook his head. "VSP arson guy is on his way. You'd do better to talk to him." He pretended to see something in the distance, invisible to the rest of them, and abruptly said, "I gotta go."

He shouldered through two people opposite and went diagonally across the street without another word.

An awkward silence among the others ended with one of them saying, "He doesn't like cops."

Joe merely nodded at that. "Any of you

know anything?"

"Yeah," the same one said. "The call came in about ninety minutes ago. I was on the first truck. Place was fully involved, right through the roof, like it had been cooking for hours. Hadn't been, though, not according to the neighbors. It just looked that way."

"Why would that be?" Joe asked them all.

"Looked like a gas fire to me," another of them said. "Fast and hot. Plus, it was an older building, like a match head."

"Anyone see anything suspicious beforehand?"

A third man answered, "I work part-time for the PD here, and volunteer for the fire department," he added, explaining his being in turnout gear. "Our people asked up and down the street, but nobody saw anything out of place. No strange cars or people hanging around. We asked if there'd been any comings or goings to the house. Did you come with a real tall, skinny guy when you did your interview a while ago?"

"Yeah."

"You were seen, then, but nobody else. These people apparently didn't socialize much."

"Did you know them?" Joe asked, taking them all in. "Any of you?"

They shook their heads as a group.

"Where were they taken?" he then asked.

"To Burlington for autopsies," the cop said.

Joe glanced across at the remains of the house. "How was this called in?"

"One of the neighbors. It was real sudden, according to her. One minute, everything was fine; the next, it's like a firebomb."

"That's why I'm thinking gas," the first man said confidently.

"It was gas," Jonathon Michael said flatly.

It was a few hours later. Joe had set up quarters in the corner of a normally closed Shelburne coffee shop that had kept a side door unlocked and a couple of lights on, just for the personnel who were still stuck at the fire scene one block over. The shop's owner lived upstairs, had once been a volunteer firefighter, and was predisposed to lending a hand.

"Accident or arson?" Joe asked.

The two of them were nursing mugs of coffee. Michael had also located a sandwich that he was largely ignoring. They'd known each other for more years than either could recall, and had developed a trust that they now took for granted. Michael was with the Vermont State Police, as he had been for his entire career. He was now chief of their arson division, but still regularly came out on assignment to keep his hand in.

"Hard to tell," he said, then taking a bite of the sandwich. He continued speaking as he chewed. "If it was arson, it was well done. The house was old and cheaply built, central heating and cooking were supplied by the propane tanks to the left of the bulkhead door."

Jonathon swallowed before resuming. "What happens is, there's a leak, usually at a juncture. If it's somewhere like in a kitchen or bathroom, people usually smell it before it becomes explosive. But most of those lines run where you can't see them. From what I could piece together, this one was in the basement, not far from the water pump. If someone suggested that the cellar filled with gas just before the pump went on, creating a small spark, I wouldn't call them a liar."

"Is that what you're saying?" Joe asked pointedly.

"Not in so many words," Jonathon replied. "I'm leaning toward 'Undetermined — Accidental,' since I don't have anything telling me otherwise. It did originate in the basement, and I'm pretty comfortable with the water pump scenario."

"But," Joe suggested leadingly.

"Two things," Jonathon explained. "First is that it actually takes a lot of gas to blow up a building like what witnesses described. That tells me that the whole place should have smelled of the stuff, which begs the question of why the occupants — or at least Friel — didn't react somehow. The second thing, which might tie in to the first, is that we found the bulkhead door unlocked. Could somebody have slipped downstairs from the outside and caused the leak — and just let dumb luck and circumstance supply the rest? Sure. The woman never left the house, from what I was told, and except for maybe groceries or post office runs, her son was pretty much a hermit. If I'd wanted them dead, I would've been happy to bide my time. The fewer alterations a bad guy makes to a scene, the harder it'll be for someone like me to discover them later. Of course, that still doesn't explain why Mr. Friel didn't react to the odor.

"Keep in mind," Jonathon added, "there was another bedroom set up down there. It's hard to tell if that's where Friel slept or if it was just a guest room, but it suggests the possibility that something might've been done to keep him from sounding the alert."

"Was that where his body was found?"

"Nope," he said. "I'm just saying that someone apparently lived in the basement, at least some of the time. I have nothing telling me that a linkage exists between that — or any of my ideas — and what actually happened."

Joe pushed at his mug with his finger, thinking back. "We went into one bedroom, on the first floor, that clearly belonged to his mom, and there was at least one other. But I have no idea where he slept. I didn't have any reason to look."

Jonathon remained silent.

"Are you totally done with your investigation?" Joe asked him.

"With the physical stuff, yup. I've got the usual odds and ends to deliver to the crime lab. But assuming they either come up blank or deliver their own version of 'Undetermined,' then I will be done unless you tell me otherwise." He took a swig of coffee and eyed Joe carefully. "*Are* you telling me otherwise?"

Joe sighed, thinking of how similar this conversation was to the one he'd just had with Hillstrom. "No," he said sadly.

It was almost midnight by the time Joe got back behind his steering wheel and did a U-turn in a now dark and deserted Hillside

Terrace. He was therefore surprised and touched with a sense of foreboding when his phone began vibrating. He pulled over by the curb once more and held it up to his ear.

"Gunther."

He recognized the soft laughter on the other end. "My, you are official sounding. How was your fire?"

Joe matched her tone. "You ought to know, Beverly. The two victims should be in your cooler by now."

"Oh, they are," Hillstrom said. "Dispatch informed me a couple of hours ago. I spoke to my investigator at the scene. You two must have just missed each other."

"Yeah," Joe told her. "I got there right afterwards. You talk to him?"

"He didn't have much to tell," she told him. "The police were saying at that point that there was nothing particularly suspicious about it. Did you find otherwise?"

"Not by talking to the arson investigator, I didn't," Joe said. "But I don't like this any more than I liked Gorden Marshall's death." He asked suddenly, "Not to get off topic, but what're you still doing up, and how did you know to call me now? I just got in my car."

She laughed. "Part calculation, part dumb

luck. I knew where you were, and I knew the duration of the average arson investigation, having attended a few in my time. After that, I just guessed."

"Well, you did well. I'm just pulling onto Route 7. I figured I'd grab a room somewhere and maybe drop by your office again tomorrow morning, assuming these two will be on your to-do list."

There was a moment before she said, "I live just north of Shelburne, Joe, and I have more guest beds than I know what to do with. Have you had anything to eat yet?"

"No," he admitted before adding, "But I don't want to impose, Beverly. It's awfully late."

"Which is why I make the offer," she said. "I'll have a bowl of soup ready for you." She gave him directions.

It was a large house, and an expensive one, balanced right on the shore of Lake Champlain. Hillstrom was married to an A-list lawyer and had two grown daughters. The home spoke of the reasonable rewards that two hardworking, successful people could expect after several decades of concentrated labor.

Of course, Joe was a hard worker, too, and had been pretty successful by most people's standards, but he lived in a rental attached to the back of a Victorian pile on a busy street in Brattleboro.

By contrast, this place was a mansion.

He killed the engine in the turnaround before the three-car garage and stepped out into the cool night air. The stars stood out with electrical fierceness, horizon to horizon, their complete and mesmerizing silence offset by the sound of the soft lapping of waves upon the nearby shoreline, just out of sight.

"Soothing, isn't it?" Beverly's voice said from behind him.

He turned to see her coming across the lawn from around the corner of the building, where it fronted a view of the lake's expanse of light-absorbing blackness. The distant glow of Burlington's cityscape marked the lower edge of the sky's stippled sheet of stars.

She was wearing a form-flattering, full-length dressing robe, drawn in at the waist with a soft, thick belt. Her hair was loose around her shoulders and she looked, even in the near dark, comfortable and relaxed. Instinctively, without thought, Joe stepped over to her and gave her a hug, which she returned with a kiss to his cheek.

"You must be bushed," she said, slipping

her arm around his waist and escorting him across the grass, from whence she'd appeared.

They rounded the corner to a wooden deck, one foot up from the lawn and running the length of a row of French doors, all facing the water.

He stopped on the deck and faced the view, his arm now draped across her shoulders. "How did you hold up against Irene?" he asked. "It doesn't look bad, but then again, it's the middle of the night."

She laughed. "That would help, but there's actually nothing to disguise. You folks got the worst of it, in the south. Of course, we're also a good twenty feet above the waterline, which has proved a godsend more than once. Quite a few people closer to the city were inundated, from what I heard." She paused, reflecting, "Terrible storm. Such a shame."

He couldn't argue the point, but it did make him ponder aloud, "Quirky, too, in some ways."

She looked up at him. "Oh?"

"Yeah. I heard how you sent a bunch of your people to Rochester, where the river had eroded the edge of the cemetery and swept a few dozen gravesites downriver."

"That poor town," she said. "As if the

flooding wasn't bad enough, they had to contend with that. We're doing our best to help out, but it'll take weeks and weeks . . . and even then, who knows if we'll be able to find everybody."

"I had a similar thing happen in my neck of the woods," Joe told her, "in style if not substance, at least, since it only involved one grave. But the coffin was filled with rocks. There was no body."

She pulled away slightly to face him, her eyes wide. "You're joking."

"No. That's what I meant by quirky. If it hadn't been for the same kind of mishap that devastated Rochester, we never would've known that somebody'd pulled a fast one years back."

She stepped over to one of the French doors, opening it and ushering him into the house. "That's incredible. I hadn't heard a peep in the news. We better get some soup into you. I set it up in the kitchen."

He followed her as she walked through the living room and dining area without turning on any lights, the stars through the bank of windows bright enough to guide them. "I'm impressed the media missed it," he said. "Guess they have enough to keep them busy."

The kitchen, which they reached through

a swinging door, was softly lighted, lined in dark wood, and had an island in its midst, adorned with a single place setting, facing a back-equipped barstool.

Hillstrom patted the stool and ordered, "Sit," before crossing to a yacht-sized stove and removing a simmering pot from the burner. "Nothing fancy," she warned him. "I hope you like chicken noodle."

"My favorite as a kid," he said, settling in. "That and a glass of milk, if you've got some."

She brought him a steaming bowl and a piece of bread, and poured him some milk before sitting catty-corner to him at the counter.

"You're not having anything?" he asked.

She smiled and got back to her feet. "You talked me into it. A glass of wine."

She crossed to the gleaming fridge and extracted an open bottle, from which she poured two inches into a glass before rejoining him.

"Don't overdo it," he kidded her.

"I rarely do," she said, and took a small sip.

He, too, sampled his soup, instantly recognizing it as being far from the canned variety he was used to at home. "Delicious."

"Leftovers," she said. "You got lucky. One

of my daughters was home over the weekend, so I actually cooked. I like putting
them into shock every once in a while."

"Daniel's not a cook?" he asked.

She watched him spoon another mouthful
before answering, almost shyly, "Daniel's
not anything anymore. We were divorced
last year."

"Oh," he said neutrally.

She smiled sadly at the response. "Yes.
Awkward, isn't it? Do you say you're sorry?
Happy? Nice weather we're having?"

He reached out and laid a hand on hers,
knowing very well that she and Daniel had
been having their struggles, largely due to
his philandering. "Well, I hope in the end
that it's good news, but it is too bad, what
with the kids and all. There's that sense of a
broken dream."

She nodded. "Too true. I guess I knew it
was inevitable, what with his wandering eye.
I thought it was over between us back when
you and I spent the night together. He'd
even moved out. But he seemed so contrite,
so eager to set things right. And he succeeded for a time. I'll give him that." She
lapsed into a brief silence before concluding, "But it just wasn't in the cards. Too
many available temptations for a man of his
disposition."

She squeezed his hand back and then reached for his empty bowl. "More?"

"No, thanks. I'm all set. That was perfect."

She left the bowl alone and cupped her chin in her hand, watching him. "How about you, Joe? Did you ever find anyone after Lyn died?"

"No. My latest theory is that all that pretty much threw a switch in my head. I lost my wife, Ellen, to cancer, years ago. Gail and I broke up after God knows how many years; then Lyn. I'm not getting any younger, and to be honest, the idea of finding someone and starting that nonsense all over again is kind of exhausting."

She laughed. "I hear my younger colleagues going on about their love lives, and I couldn't be happier not to have anything to do with any of it."

She rose and cleared his place. He helped, and they stood side-by-side at the sink, rinsing everything off and putting it into the washer.

"Still," she commented, bumping him with her shoulder. "It's hard to completely deny some of the fringe benefits."

It was his turn to laugh. "I do get your point," he agreed.

She rinsed out the sink and stepped back, drying her hands on a towel. "Okay, you look done in. Follow me upstairs and I'll show you where you'll probably catch all of four hours of sleep, knowing you."

She led the way out of the kitchen and preceded him up a broad set of stairs. He couldn't — and didn't — deny himself the attractive view of her taking the steps ahead of him, thinking back to their last conversation. He had liked this woman from the first day they met, which was saying something, since he'd thoroughly irritated her at the time. And he'd certainly held stirring memories of their one night together ever since.

She took him down a hallway to a door near the end, and introduced him to a spacious guest room with its own private bath, showed him the towels and where the light switches and alarm clock were, and made it clear that she'd completely understand if he wanted to leave early the next day — and to just use the same door they'd entered by.

After the tour, they came to the room's door, and she easily and comfortably put her arms around him and gave him a hug. He moved his hands across her back, enjoying the discovery that she was naked under her robe.

Nevertheless, she pulled away with one last smile and another kiss on the cheek, and bade him good night.

He watched her retreat down the hall to her own room, before closing his door reluctantly, mildly rebuking himself for not having at least made an effort to act on his desire. He suspected that she'd been open to encouragement, and he found himself as disappointed in letting her down as in not having benefited himself.

But he was tired, which he finally acknowledged after stripping off his clothes and slipping between her fresh, clean-smelling sheets, enjoying the caress of them on his skin as he snapped off the light and watched the glimmering from the stars slowly take over the darkened room.

It was by this twilight that he then saw his door reopen, and Beverly, still in her robe, enter like a ghost.

He slid up onto his pillow and watched her approach. Standing by his bedside, she smiled down and said in a near whisper. "I don't want this night to end like that. It's not why I called you."

She undid her belt and dropped the robe from her shoulders.

He peeled back his bedcovers and held out his hand in welcome.

CHAPTER THIRTEEN

Gail Zigman looked up as Robert Perkins, her Chief-of-Staff, entered her office. "Shut the door, Rob."

Surprised, he did so, before settling into a chair facing her desk. The governor made a big deal about her "door never being closed," and worked to make the cliché a fact.

"You have a cell phone on you?" she asked, quickly signing a document she'd been reading as he entered.

He pulled it out of his pocket. "Sure." Of course he had it, he thought. For him, it was like oxygen for a man with emphysema. He was constantly kidded for his dependence on the thing.

"Turn it off. The whole device; not just the ringer."

"Off?" he asked, the phone in midair. "Like off-off?"

She put down her pen and narrowed her

eyes slightly as she focused on him. She didn't speak.

Embarrassed, he turned the phone off and dropped it back into his pocket.

"It's a potential listening device," she explained, "if you believe the latest paranoia, which in this case, I'm inclined to do."

"Okay," he said cautiously.

She leaned forward and pressed the intercom button on her phone and said, "Julie? No calls till I buzz you back, okay? And I mean it. No knocks on the door. Nothing."

"Yes, Governor," came the disembodied reply.

Gail fixed her attention on Perkins. "I'm about to tell you something that cannot leave this room. It can't even be whispered to your pet parakeet. Is that very clear?"

"Very," he said, his brain working hard by now. The entire office had been laboring around the clock, trying to keep ahead of the post-Irene demands and complaints — mostly aimed at bureaucratic red tape and slow action in general — but there'd been nothing demanding of such CIA-style twitchiness.

"Do you know of Harold LeMieur?"

"Sure," he said immediately, caught unaware twice over. "Catamount Industrial. Lots of money. Likes to play kingmaker with people we don't like."

"Let's start with that," Gail suggested. "Tell me how he operates."

Perkins frowned — the closed door and dead cell phone making less and less sense. This was Wikipedia-level information. "Pretty straightforward. He's out front with his beliefs, and backs his kind of candidates by paying either directly or through a PAC. By definition, he's not much of an influence in Vermont, since even our right-wingers see him as an extremist. There were a couple of folks a few years back who approached him for money, when the Take Back Vermont movement was gaining yardage, and he was happy to oblige. But that was about it. He doesn't care about us, anyhow. Plays for bigger stakes, like governorships or congressional races in the rest of the country, and the occasional presidential hopeful. I always got the feeling that ever since he left Vermont, he's been happy to not even think about us."

"Does he have people here?" she asked.

"Sure. Sheldon Scott. Runs a lobbying firm in town for conservative causes. He and LeMieur go back to the beginning. I think they grew up together, somewhere in Franklin County, so Harold makes sure Sheldon's well cared for. LeMieur's big on loyalty —

219

blood brother stuff. He has an inner circle like Howard Hughes used to have, and Sheldon's near the top."

Gail nodded. This, in part, was why she had Rob Perkins as her CoS, as the jargon had it. He knew everyone. "Can you get to him?" she asked.

"As in . . ." He left the implication dangling.

She smiled without humor. "No. I don't do underhanded, as you very well know. I meant, can you arrange to have a private conversation with the man?"

"Sheldon?" Perkins asked, once again pondering the reasons for her paranoia. "Sure," he said. "We know each other. I can walk into his office. I wouldn't recommend it, though — not given that you're my boss now. Too many tongues would start wagging."

Gail hesitated, glancing out the window, and Perkins recognized that she was about to broach the Big Subject. He liked Gail Zigman, which was why he'd accepted her job offer. But he hadn't voted for her in the primary. She'd struck him as too much the populist, an idealist who thought a democracy could actually be run by the people, for the people, instead of by bureaucrats, politicians, and moneyed special interests.

Perkins was a practical, practiced swimmer of political waters. He'd worked for other governors and had grown used to the bad taste that resulted from making accommodations with the wrong people for the right reasons. When Zigman had approached him to be her Chief of Staff, he initially rejected the notion.

But then he'd rethought his prejudice. Was it so unbelievable that a neophyte like her could govern a state? Especially one as predisposed to such a fantasy as Vermont? She had won the election by openly defying the guardians of the status quo, including the state's three Washington, D.C., delegates, who'd made only a grudging show of support after the primary. Succeeding against that opposition alone had been unprecedented.

In the end, Rob had said yes, if only to be part of what his heart and mind imagined would be a short-lived experiment — despite his hopes that it last far longer.

Those reservations made Rob Perkins perhaps the most effective of Gail's allies — the thoughtful, cautious supporter, versus one of her ardent, damn-the-torpedoes fans.

Gail sat back in her chair and looked at him with a grim expression. "Let me ask you something before I go on," she said.

"Shoot."

"How're we doing? Honestly, with no smoke and flattery."

He smiled, given his ruminations. "About fifty-fifty," he answered her. "You're getting high marks for being everywhere at once. That's good. They like seeing you with mud on your shoes, in the middle of the night, lending a hand. Dropping the borrowed National Guard helicopter was a good move. People were grousing about that. What's pulling us down now is that we're playing second fiddle to the U.S. government — represented by FEMA, fairly or not — and, to a lesser extent, organizations like the Guard, the Red Cross, and the Salvation Army. Compared to them, we're looking ineffectual, even with most legislators rallying behind you. As usual, it's things like road and bridge repairs that're catching the media's eye, and there, it sort of hangs on the political leanings of the editor. Some of them are giving you credit; others aren't. And most of that goes back to how you won the election. There are a bunch of professional backroom people with their noses out of joint because of you."

"How might I have handled this crisis better?" she asked.

He waggled his head back and forth,

thinking of how best to present his thoughts. He wasn't beholden to her, and that was his value. They each knew that. But he also wasn't in the business of discussing fantasies.

"You personally?" he finally answered. "I don't think you could have. Others would have gone first to the fat cats, in Vermont and outside, for money and political muscle. They also would've enlisted our two senators and the congressman for their clout. But that's not your style, and you don't have access to those people. I mean, Vermont's DC-Three will do their thing, but not for you. They have to run again, too. And when they begin to bring in the money, you're not going to be invited to the press conferences. It'll be carefully done. It won't be a direct slap in the face. But you won't be in the photo ops. You dissed them pretty harshly when you ran."

To his surprise, his words seemed to be making her feel better. She nodded slowly and said, "I may have come up with a solution for most of that."

He didn't bother hiding his surprise, which made her smile and quickly add, "It's early yet. That's why I asked to see you and why all the secrecy. A mouse squeaks in the statehouse basement at eleven fifty-nine, it's

223

all the talk at lunch. We all know that. But I've been approached with a proposal that might address your concerns, without my administration having to lower its standards in the process."

Perkins didn't like her almost prideful choice of words, but was caught by their implication.

"Who approached you?" he asked, recalling how the conversation had begun. "Not LeMieur?"

"Indirectly," she told him. "Through Susan Raffner."

"Raffner?" he asked, more startled still. He knew of Raffner's importance to Gail, but approaching a governor with a quiet deal through a state senator was a new curveball to him.

And not one he liked. It was too odd, too irregular even for these rebels. Plus, LeMieur was the antithesis of a rebel. Why would he have chosen such a line of communication?

Gail appeared unconcerned. "Yes," she said. "Susan came by my place last night. Said she'd been asked to be a conduit by LeMieur, who'd obviously done his homework about how best to reach me. Turns out he's getting sentimental in his old age, and wants to do something for the state that gave him his start. In condensed form, he wants to use his billions to set up a parallel FEMA in the state, supported by the legislature and me, to directly address the very hiccups you were telling me about when we started this conversation. It would not be competition. From what Susan told me, it would be more like supplemental insurance."

She removed a single sheet of paper from her desk and slid it over to him. "I wrote down what she told me, so that you could think about it and so I wouldn't forget anything. You'll see that I didn't use names in that document, nor did I sign it. I've told you enough that you can fill in the blanks."

He held it up. "I can keep this?"

"Yes, but read it now, in case you have any immediate questions."

He smiled thinly. "Oh, I think that's a guarantee."

A silence settled on the office as he analyzed the proposal that Susan Raffner had outlined to Gail. He read it twice before placing it faceup on his lap.

He countermanded his teeming objections by asking, "What would you like me to do?"

"What do you think, for starters?"

"I'm very suspicious," he answered. "But you probably already know that."

"I counted on it. You're not alone. That's why we're talking."

Perkins nodded. "Okay."

"In answer to your question," Gail continued, "I'd like you to contact Sheldon Scott and arrange a meeting, as soon as you can. He's not the one who approached Susan, so this would be a second foray into the Le-Mieur camp, coming from our direction and using different people. What I want to know from him speaks for itself."

"In other words, is this legit?" Perkins suggested.

"Exactly. The best one to answer that will be LeMieur himself, of course, but at this stage, I just want to make sure this isn't some huge con job that somebody totally unrelated to LeMieur might be pulling on Susan. And — through her — the rest of us. It wouldn't be the first time a cat's-paw was used underhandedly. Let's find out if this is for real."

Robert Perkins picked up the sheet of paper again and glanced at it, although he was no longer absorbing a single word. Having processed his own concerns about this risky offer, he couldn't deny the elegance of the governor's request. If he sat down with Scott and began a generalized conversation, it would take three sentences for him to

discover if this offer was coming from Le-
Mieur or not. It wouldn't reveal what con-
niving might be behind it, but at least it
would shine a light on the real cast of
characters. It would be a start, along the
lines of "know thine enemy."

He stood up, folding the piece of paper
and slipping it into his jacket pocket. "You
got it, Governor. I'll put out a feeler and
report back, ASAP."

She smiled at him. "Thanks, Rob. And the
fact that you don't like it gives me comfort."

He nodded and left her office, lost in
thought about this potential maze of mir-
rors, occurring amid a natural disaster, in a
time of statewide financial instability and
need. He knew politicians well. They reacted to events — sometimes wisely; often
impulsively. The smart ones knew that when
they were feeling comfortable, it usually
meant that they hadn't received the latest
memo.

Rob Perkins couldn't help wondering
what kind of memo he'd be delivering at
their next meeting. And he still didn't know
if his largely untested boss — while clearly
and demonstrably smart — was in fact
savvy, or had just been lucky so far.

Lester Spinney stood on the threshold

between Gorden Marshall's kitchen and his living room, as Joe had done a few days earlier. He was alone, Joe being up near Burlington, still chasing after the possible arson. Sam and Willy were down south — he on the Rozanski disappearance, she manning the fort in Brattleboro and helping to coordinate statewide resumption of day-to-day operations. The Vermont Bureau of Investigation was back up and running, now that the several flooded regional offices had been either cleaned up or transplanted, but Joe had felt that they should stick with what they'd begun, and let the other squads catch their collective breath. Normally, the Brattleboro branch wouldn't have been so spread out, but that was part of how the VBI functioned — unhampered by local boundaries, and not necessarily tied to working with local police. The autonomy and responsibility that the organization gave its agents — all veterans of other agencies — had been one of the primary attractions for Lester when he'd signed up. Today's assignment was a prime example of that. Joe had asked him to find out what he could from Marshall's apartment, before it was returned to The Woods of Windsor and the inevitable next tenant.

Lester flexed his fingers inside his latex

gloves and crossed into the bedroom. Most departments had either a specialized crime scene unit or called upon the state's mobile forensic team to assist. The VBI could and often did do likewise. But this was a crime scene in the minds of but a few, and calling for the techs would have been difficult to justify. Lester knew, therefore, that he was less in pursuit of scientific forensic evidence, and more here to absorb a sense of the man who'd once called the place home.

That and maybe find out what had happened during the last hours of his life.

The stripped bed had been neatly covered with a coverlet. Instinctively, Lester dropped to the floor and laid his cheek against the carpeting, studying its nap between the door and the bed to check for the signs of a vacuum cleaner's back-and-forth furrows. But it appeared as if they'd only addressed the bed following the removal of Marshall's body. Les would have to double-check with Hannah Eastridge that such was standard protocol at The Woods, but he didn't doubt it. His wife, Sue, had once worked at a far-less-upscale nursing home near Springfield, but she'd commented on how, even there, the staff was attentive to neatening up after a resident's death, in part to make it easier on the family who'd come in later to remove personal effects. These places were production lines of sorts, after all — it wasn't good for business to let a bed stay empty for long.

While he was on his hands and knees, Lester crawled along the floor, small flashlight in hand, sweeping his eyes to and fro, looking for any dropped or forgotten object that might prove useful. But the cleaning crew that came by weekly — and which Lester had already been told had last visited five days earlier — was apparently thorough. Aside from a single lost ballpoint pen that he found under the dresser, there was nothing.

Starting with the dresser, however, Les began working methodically from top drawer to bottom. He found a man's jewelry box in the upper right-hand drawer alongside two watches, a Cross pencil, a plastic container of collar stays, and a stack of folded handkerchiefs. He slid the box to the fore, opened it, and discovered a jumbled assortment of cuff links, rings, association pins, and tie clips.

Grunting quietly, he turned to retrieve the camera that he'd placed on the floor by the bedroom door, and found himself staring at a man in a dark blue custodian's uniform with a woman's stocking pulled over his face. In the instant that it took him to register this, the man smacked him on the side of the head with something hard.

Lester felt his knees give out as he flinched against the explosive pain. He heard more than saw the shape of the man retreat, and lashed out to stop him, his hand flailing in the empty air.

"Stop," he heard himself say, or thought he said, as he struggled in vain to stand, propping instead against the dresser. There was something happening in the room — what, he couldn't tell — distinguished by a shadow falling across him, followed by the sound of running feet and the slamming of a distant door, which he knew to be the apartment's entrance.

He finally lurched to his feet, smacking his shoulder against the open dresser drawer, and fell toward the bedpost, trying to reach the door while hanging on like the passenger of a ship about to capsize. He kept shaking his head, hoping to clear his vision.

His balance and eyesight improving, Les picked up speed as he cut through the kitchenette and tore open the front door. He ran out into the hallway, just in time to see the last of his assailant rounding a far corner.

"Jesus," he muttered, touching his temple,

and took off in pursuit, quickly glancing at his hand. There was some blood, but not much, which he took as a good sign. Running, he reached for his cell phone and auto-dialed the VBI dispatch number.

"This is Spinney," he panted to the operator. "I'm in foot pursuit of a male inside The Woods of Windsor. Do you have my location?"

"Yes, sir," she said, almost disturbingly calm. "Your GPS is coming through clear. Can you give me a description?"

"Male. Five-ten. Slim build. Dark blue maintenance uniform. Call Sergeant Carrier of the local PD and send backup."

"Yes, sir."

He reached the end of the hallway, recovered enough that anger had replaced astonishment. There was another corridor ahead — empty — with an EXIT sign above a door about halfway down. Reaching it quickly and yanking it open, he heard footsteps pounding down the stairs below him.

He exchanged his phone for his gun and took the steps four at a time, swinging from the steel tubular railing and kicking off the walls at each turn to give himself extra thrust. Below, he heard the bang of a fire door, suggesting that the man ahead had reached the outdoors and a broader choice of escape routes.

"Come on, come on," he chanted to himself, hoping no misstep would result in a broken leg.

He reached the bottom and stopped abruptly at the door, listening intently over his own breathing. He was suddenly conscious of the possible consequences of crashing through that door — and maybe meeting a man with a gun.

He took two deep breaths, seized the door's panic bar, and pushed slightly, keeping his body alongside the metal frame to one side.

It turned out to have been the wrong time for caution. When he finally exited the building, there was nobody in sight.

"Damn," he said, and broke back into a run, heading toward the nearest parking area.

Coming over the top of the slope separating the building from the lot, however, the only signs of life visible were two cruisers with their lights flashing, entering from the highway at speed and splitting up to cover as much of the parking area as possible.

There were only a few empty cars scattered about, and nothing to be seen of a man on foot.

Lester stood panting on the crest of the

233

small hill, his hands on his hips, scanning all that he could see for any motion, while four uniformed officers left their vehicles and spread out.

Spinney recognized Rick Carrier. "You see anyone driving away when you entered?" he shouted down to him.

Carrier shook his head and began walking uphill to meet him.

Lester checked the side of his head again, his adrenaline ebbing and his knees getting wobbly. He sat down on the close-cropped grass, pulling out his phone to issue an alert for an anonymous man of unremarkable stature wearing a maintenance uniform.

Right, he thought, as he pushed the CALL button. Good luck with that.

CHAPTER FOURTEEN

Stamford, Vermont, was one of the state's original settlements, chartered in 1753, a fact about which Willy Kunkle couldn't have cared less. One tidbit that he had picked up, though — in a state he found otherwise way too interested in its own history — concerned a Stamford man supposedly named Allen who'd hidden in a cave atop a mountain now named in his honor, in order to avoid fighting in the Revolutionary War. Willy liked the story in particular, since Vermonters so regularly touted Ethan Allen for his bravery as the head of the Green Mountain Boys.

Willy wondered — families being the curious things they often were — if the two men were related.

It wasn't an entirely random thought. He was driving down Route 8, off the tapered southern end of the Green Mountains, along Stamford's strung-out bottomland between the Hoosac and Taconic Ranges, in order to interview Eileen Rozanski Ranslow — the sister of the man whose only monument nowadays was a coffin full of rocks. Given his research to date, Willy had become convinced that the Rozanskis were another clan with a story they'd deemed worth hiding.

He slowed his car to note the addresses passing by. Years ago, the state-stipulated 911 regulation that all houses should be clearly numbered had for some reason been decreed voluntary. As a result, all too few of them were.

Happily, the Ranslows had heeded the rule, which Willy hoped was a good sign. If they were compliant enough to make that effort, who knew if they might not be willing to speak with the likes of him?

The house was set back from the road, clad in white clapboards, and about a hundred years old. Willy pulled into the gravel driveway, killed his engine, and in one fluid movement, swung out of the car, noticing the by-now routine detail of how the front yard's grass had acquired a coat of plant-smothering river mud. He was longing for the first full day in which the subject of Irene — or any evidence of her destruction — wouldn't come up in conversation.

Which was clearly going to be a long time from now. Luckily for the Ranslows, though, at first glance, it didn't seem as if they'd lost more than their lawn.

The front door opened as he approached the house, and a small, somewhat squared-off woman wearing glasses and holding a dish towel stood before him with a questioning look.

"May I help you?" she asked.

"Mrs. Ranslow?" he replied, pulling out his credentials. "I'm Special Agent Kunkle, of the Vermont Bureau of Investigation. I hope I haven't caught you at a bad time."

She allowed the faintest of smiles as she said, "I don't know. Are you about to make it a bad time?"

He laughed, taking note of how carefully she was watching him. "I hope not. I wanted to ask you a few questions about your brother Herb."

She nodded several times. "Ah. I was wondering when somebody would come by."

He kept smiling. "Well, I guess that's me. Seems like you know what got me here."

"The graveyard thing," she confirmed. "Sure."

"Right," he confirmed, again struck by her self-constraint. "Could I come in?"

Instead of answering, she stepped aside to allow him passage.

The house reminded him of a thousand others he'd entered — furnished with hand-me-downs and Walmart sets, the walls bare aside from some family photos, the requisite huge flat-screen TV reducing the living room to a single function. It was at once neat enough and messy enough to support a family that — as Willy had researched — consisted of this woman, her truck driver husband, and their two teenage sons.

She led him into the living room, where the set was on but muted, pantomiming the world beyond like the flashing scenery outside a train window.

Eileen Ranslow did not offer Willy any amenities, nor the usual apologies for the home's appearance. Preceding him, she sat on the edge of an upright chair facing the couch, the dish towel still in her hands, and waited for him to choose a seat.

He took the couch opposite.

"What do you want to know?" she asked him.

He took his cue on how to proceed from her — straight down the line, but with enough Big Brother to encourage her to be open from the start. "Are we alone?" he asked.

"Yes."

"Hank and Ted are where?" he inquired, using her sons' names.

It worked. She hesitated and the hands holding the towel moved closer together. "They're at school, at a work detail to help clean up after Irene."

"And Phillip? Making deliveries?"

"Trying to," she said.

"You've lived here about twenty years. Is that correct?"

"Twenty-one."

"And you're the only member of your immediate family, aside from your brother Nate, to have moved away from where you grew up."

Her mouth tightened a fraction before she answered, "If you know this stuff, why're you asking me?"

He fixed her with a severe look. "My information may not be accurate. Please answer the question, Mrs. Ranslow."

"Yes, then."

"Yes, what?"

"Yes, I'm the only one except Nate."

"You don't keep in touch with folks back home?"

"Not much."

"Not much, or not at all?"

Another small flare crossed her features.

"Is there something wrong with that?"

He stayed silent, watching her.

"Not at all," she said, her eyes dropping to the towel, which she draped across her left knee.

"Why is that?"

"Family stuff. I made a new life here."

"You have a falling out?"

She seemed to consider that before replying, "I wanted to see other places."

"What did you do between leaving home and settling here?" he pressed, having been told by others that she'd left home shortly after Herb's supposed funeral and her other brother's disappearing altogether.

"I drifted around," she said vaguely.

"You got arrested a couple of times," Willy reminded her. "Disturbing the peace, drunk and disorderly. What was going on?"

"I was unhappy. I was young." She sat forward for emphasis. "I thought you wanted to talk about Herb."

"Where is Nate now?" Willy asked, ignoring her.

"I don't know. Maybe he's dead." Her voice had picked up an edge.

"Like Herb?" Willy suggested leadingly.

She became silent. Willy rose and circled the cluttered coffee table to sit beside her on a matching chair, a foot away. She shifted defensively but stayed put, at the same time staring at his inert left arm.

"I was shot in the line of duty," he explained, his voice softer and confiding. "Years ago. I know what it's like to be in a tough place. I kept my job because people stuck up for me."

"I'm sorry," she murmured.

"I'm going to take a wild guess, Eileen, but I think *you're* in a tough place. Something happened twenty-seven years ago that tore up your family, probably playing a part in why your mom died of a broken heart."

At the allusion to Dreama Rozanski, her daughter's eyes welled with tears, which she didn't bother wiping away.

"How long did your dad live?" Willy asked softly. "After whatever happened with Herb?"

"A few years," she said dully.

Finally, he got to his reason for being here. "Tell me about that, Eileen — what happened to Herb?"

She sighed and said, almost inaudibly, "He got caught up in the sawmill."

"Did you see it happen?"

She shook her head.

"Were you there, at home?"

"Mom was. I was at a friend's house."

"How did you find out?" he asked.

241

"They told me when I got home."

"Did you see your brother?"

"Which one?" she asked, which he thought interesting.

"Let's start with Herb."

"No. They said it was too bloody."

"So where was he? Where'd they put him?"

"In a closed box. It was the coffin later."

"How 'bout the sawmill? Did you go in there?"

"Later, I did," she admitted, and shivered. "It was horrible. Blood all over."

"Okay," Willy said. "What about Nate? Where was he in all this?"

"He was there."

"At home? At the mill, working with them?"

"The mill." Her words had become so soft that he placed his head inches from her mouth.

"What did they say happened?"

"An accident. Herb got pulled into the saw."

"Is that likely? Some mills are more dangerous than others."

"I wouldn't know."

"Describe the mill to me."

She tilted her head back, as if interpreting an image off where the wall met the ceiling.

"Open sides. Lots of those pulley things. My dad had to put his truck near one wall to drive everything."

"There was more than just the saw, then?"

"There was a big saw. That's where it happened. But there were other machines, too. It was super noisy."

"What happened to it afterwards?" Willy asked. "When I was there, it had been burned down as a fire department exercise."

"Nothing," she said. "Nobody ever went in it again."

"Tell me about Nate, Eileen. How did he take this?"

"He left. The next day."

"Was there a fight?"

"No," she said with more strength, but her eyes wandered to the floor. "The next morning, he was just gone."

"What did your parents say or do about that?"

"Nothing," she repeated. "They just kind of retreated into themselves."

Willy pressed her. "I think you're leaving something out about Nate. Tell me."

"He looked awful."

"How?"

"He was cut and bruised and maybe some of his fingers were broken."

"From what?" Willy asked. "A fight?"

"I don't know."

"Do you think maybe he fought with Herb?"

"Maybe."

"In the mill?"

"I don't know."

Willy reached out and touched her hand. "Eileen, this is important. Do you think they had a fight, and that's what sent Herb into the saw blade?"

She nodded without comment.

Willy nodded and mentally reviewed everything she'd told him. "On the day of the accident," he began, "how did your father handle the authorities? He couldn't just bury Herb and have done with it."

"The sheriff came over after I got home. They talked. I watched them through the kitchen window. It was open."

"The sheriff saw the body?"

"He saw the box," she countered. "He wanted to open it, but my dad got mad — said he knew his own son, and could tell a dead man from a live one."

Willy let out a small, contemptuous puff of air. "And the sheriff bought it," he stated.

"The box wasn't opened up," she replied as an answer.

Willy waited before asking, "What really happened to Herb?"

She gave a half shrug. "I guess he didn't die."

"Where did the blood come from?"

"It was his. He was really hurt. I mean, he must've been. He just didn't die. Whose blood could it've been?"

"People have told me they think this whole thing killed your parents," Willy told her, moving on.

Her voice shrank down once more. "I guess."

"Eileen," he said, matching her tone. "I think you knew about all this when I walked up to your door. I know the price this has taken on you, on your family. But I've also got to know the details. I'm sorry."

"Why?" she challenged him, staring at him, her cheeks coursed with tears. "What does it matter now?"

"You know what keeping it a secret has cost you," he explained. "How could my uncovering the truth be any worse?"

To her silence, he continued, "How many years have you had this bottled up? How many times have you wished you could be honest with your sons? What stories have you made up about your childhood, knowing they were the sort of lies you tell your kids never to tell? You know in your heart this has got to stop."

Speechless, she barely nodded in agreement.

"Tell me what you know," he almost whispered.

"I have Nate's phone number," she admitted at last. "Or the store he lives near. He's pretty much a hermit."

Willy kept any satisfaction out of his voice. "When did you two last talk?"

"Maybe a year ago."

"So he knows nothing about the grave being exposed?"

"Not from me."

"Where's that store located?" he asked.

"Below West Glover, sort of between Hardwick and Barton."

That put it in the state's Northeast Kingdom — a place, like Stamford, not heavily populated. But unlike here, famous for the way it defended its isolation. It was custom-made for someone wanting to fade from view.

He touched her wrist. "Thank you, Eileen. I'll let you know how it goes. But you know the favor I need to ask now, don't you?"

"Don't warn him?" she asked.

"Exactly. Or all of this — and the trust you've just put in me — will be for nothing. With any luck, I'll be the one who might get you all talking again."

She barely nodded her acknowledgment.

"One last thing," he mentioned as he rose to leave. "Have you kept in touch with Herb? Do you know where he is now?"

"No," she said, looking up at him. "I thought he was dead until they told me about the empty grave."

Willy had to take her at face value there, but he didn't like it.

Joe cocked his head to one side and gave Lester an admiring look.

"Spare me," his colleague moaned. "I asked them not to do it."

"Shave half your head to apply a little bandage?" Joe asked him, crossing the room and giving Spinney's wife a hug. "Why wouldn't they?" he finished, speaking over her shoulder. "They knew you were a cop, didn't they?"

Sue quickly turned, her arm still around Joe's waist, and spoke before her husband could respond. "He's kidding. The doc explained they had to get in there and check you out. Look on the bright side, honey — we can always shave the other side and turn you into a cool dude. Your son would love it."

Lester gave her a lopsided smile. "It's an idea."

Joe sat by his hospital bed as Sue left the room to get them coffee. Sergeant Carrier had called an ambulance after seeing Spinney's injury, and they'd transported Les to what the MedEvac chopper pilots nicknamed the Emerald City — the Dartmouth-Hitchcock Medical Center — a vast green and white boxy sprawl tucked in among New Hampshire's wooded hills. Fortunately, Lester proved to have a hard head.

"I heard the description you gave of the man who whacked you," Joe told him. "Anything to add?"

"Only that he must've had a key," Les said. "I locked the door behind me, so I wouldn't get disturbed by the crotchety old guy who yelled at you that first day."

"Mr. Dee," Joe recalled. "Wasn't there a guard at the door?"

"Not when I got there. I asked Carrier about that afterwards, and he admitted they dropped the ball. I doubt that'll happen again. Anyhow, I was checking out the dresser, as part of a general search, thought I'd found something that needed documenting, and turned to reach for my camera when — standing right behind me — there he was. Split second later, he beaned me and took off."

"What did he hit you with?"

248

Lester smiled weakly. "Something hard. He was wearing a stocking over his head — like in a bank robbery comedy."

"White guy?" Joe asked.

"Ecru," Lester countered.

Joe gave him a look. "You *did* get hit on the head."

"Something else," Les added. "When I went after him, kind of seeing double, I thought he might be carrying something, but maybe it was whatever he used to smack me."

His boss stared off toward the far corner of the room, deep in thought. "How long had you been there, grand total?"

"Not long. I started in the bedroom. Maybe fifteen minutes. I checked the floor and under the furniture; the obvious surfaces. I had just begun on the dresser when he showed up."

Joe nodded absentmindedly before asking, "What had caught your eye, that you were reaching for the camera?"

"Marshall had a jewelry box — cuff links, tie pins, junk like that. Some of it looked commemorative — stuff you get for being an Elk or a Shriner. I was gonna take a picture of it so I could ask somebody what was what later on."

Joe's attention sharpened. "What else was

in that drawer?"

"Handkerchiefs, a couple of watches. I forget what else. Why?"

"I went to the apartment afterwards," Joe explained. "To see if I could get an angle on your guy. The drawer was still open. There was no jewelry box."

Lester stared at him. "Big as a book, maybe, but square?"

Joe suggested, "Could be what he was carrying when you chased him."

Les looked chagrined. "I can't believe I was staring right at it. Damn. Two more minutes and I would've had it documented. Who the hell's gonna tell us what I was looking at?"

"Maybe his daughter, Michelle," Joe suggested. "How old do you think Mr. Ecru was?" he asked, changing subjects.

"Not a resident," Lester answered quickly. "He was a jackrabbit — kind of ran like one, too, a little weird — and dressed like a maintenance guy. I never got to ask Carrier . . . or maybe I did. I don't remember, but did they see anyone leaving the complex?"

Joe shook his head. "No, which doesn't tell us much. If he was ballsy enough to sneak up behind you, he could've hung around the parking lot long enough to drive out with the flow of traffic later. It doesn't mean he works there or is a relative."

"He did have a key, though," Lester reminded him.

"True," Joe agreed. "We'll look into that. But why was he there? Was it the box?"

Les volunteered, "If he was the same guy who smothered Marshall, maybe he forgot it when he cleaned out the filing cabinet."

"Big risk to come back for it," Joe mused. In the silence that followed, he added, "But at least it tells us something."

"Like?" Lester asked.

"Well," Joe answered. "I don't know about you, but I'm officially comfortable calling Marshall's death suspicious. Your little run-in with Stocking Mask gives us more freedom to pull off the gloves."

CHAPTER FIFTEEN

Joe found the place without much trouble, beyond South Woodstock, along Route 106. A huge barn with smaller offspring, several fenced-in pastures and exercise rings, and lots of open, empty space, thickly buttered — as was the current norm — with a smooth, gray coating of what Joe had come to call "flood mud." The solid muck was interspersed with deep ragged fissures and fingerling ravines, carved and salted with white stones, and decorated with garnishes of uprooted trees, a tossed-aside pickup truck, and scattered pieces of broken barn and shattered fencing, among other wreckage.

It was raining ineffectually now, ironically without great effect, making the sky match the earth, and prohibiting any action by the heavy earthmovers and other equipment Joe could see strategically spread across the visible acreage, in preparation for rebuilding the facility, virtually from scratch.

This was wealthy horse country — reportedly, one of the most densely horse-populated regions in the United States, which Joe found hard to believe, especially now, as he pulled into the deserted parking area and took in the surrounding devastation. Specifically, this was the Green Mountain Horse Association, the center of the area's equine culture. Since the 1920s, Joe had learned earlier, the GMHA had grown to become the go-to place for riders of all stripes, appealing to everyone from back-country trail ramblers in jeans to folks in hard hats, cutaways, glossy boots, and a fondness for dressage.

But it was all a post-combat battlefield now, littered, gouged, battered, and abandoned. He was here — suitably or not, he didn't know — to meet Michelle Mahoney, the late state senator's heir.

It had struck Joe as interesting, however, that when Hannah Eastridge had told him of Michelle's arrival from Connecticut, she'd added that his best bet for meeting her was to head straight to GMHA. It seemed that Michelle's primary devotion in Vermont, at least lately, had not been her father, but her investment in — and love for — horses.

He wasn't about to be the judge of that. At least not yet. From the little his team had pulled together concerning the late senator, his daughter may have been well advised to prefer animals.

He crossed the lot toward a low-slung, ranch-style building with a shingle hanging out front and entered an informal reception area with a computer-equipped desk and nobody tending it. He heard voices in the back and took his cue from the relaxed look of the place to follow wherever his ears led him.

That was a small, cluttered office in the back containing two athletically trim middle-aged women with sensible haircuts. They were wearing the kind of minimal jewelry that speaks of the wealthy's flair for everyday baubles whose trade-in value might purchase a good used car.

The one at the desk looked up as he appeared at the edge of the door.

"Yes?" she asked.

"Sorry to interrupt," he said. "I was told I might find Michelle Mahoney here."

Her guest chimed in — tellingly, he thought — with, "Who are you?"

He smiled thinly, his guess all but confirmed, and entered introducing himself, "Joe Gunther. Vermont Bureau of Investigation. I'm here about your father."

The desk owner was already rising. "Michelle," she said. "Use the room. I have to talk with Jimmy anyhow. Take all the time you need."

Without waiting for a response, and not receiving one from Michelle in any case, she squeezed by Joe and closed the door behind her.

Joe stood where he was, impressed at the smoothness of the transition. He had clearly just brushed by someone keenly attuned to the ways of the privileged.

He gestured at the door. "Sorry about that. There was no one in reception."

"There often isn't," Mahoney said, watching him with her hands folded. She was wearing jeans and a T-shirt, but — as with the jewelry — of high if muted quality. "Especially lately."

Joe nodded politely. "Right. Looks like the place really got hammered. Too bad."

Her face was a mask of polite reserve. "Yes. No flood insurance, either, which is why I'm here. Who knew that our tiny, picture postcard creek would turn into the Mississippi?"

"A lot of people are saying that," he said. "Did you have horses here at the time?"

"No," she replied. "But I do have five, and

they usually spend a large part of the summer here, so it was just dumb luck none of them were. You, of course, probably know all that."

He tilted his head. "Pardon?"

"That I have horses, live in Connecticut, work as a lawyer, and came here first before checking on my father. You knew where to find me, after all."

Joe considered arguing against his omniscience, but then thought better of it. Instead, he opened a folding chair leaning against the wall and sat down. In fact, he had no idea where Gorden Marshall's body had ended up, except that Beverly Hillstrom had released it to a funeral home. Nor had he known of Michelle's fondness for horses before now.

"We are interested in your father's death," he stated.

Her demeanor was unchanged. "So I understand. Why? I thought he died of natural causes. That's what his physician told me on the phone. He's a little miffed at you, by the way."

Joe shrugged. "It happens. Gorden Marshall was a prominent man. It makes sense to dot the *i*'s and cross the *t*'s when someone like him dies."

She gave him a long, level look before say-

256

ing, "No, it doesn't."

He raised an eyebrow at her, privately impressed. She was, of course, perfectly correct. "Oh?"

"It makes people think you're hiding something, which you are."

He didn't respond.

"What did you say your name was?" she asked.

"Gunther. Joe Gunther."

"Well, Joe Gunther," she explained. "My father was a selfish, narcissistic, mean-hearted son of a bitch. But he taught me two things: One, never get married, because one half of every marriage — regardless of who it is — will end up with the shit end of the stick. Two, everybody's got an angle and/or an ax to grind — at the very least. The first I learned by seeing how he treated my mother. The second I picked up trailing along behind him and conducting post-evisceration interviews with all the people he gutted on his way to the top. Being his only child and a girl, I was groomed to be his aide until I finally woke up. I learned to hate him and respect his wisdom." She paused before concluding, "So what are you up to?"

Joe took a risk. "I think your father was murdered."

She took her eyes off him long enough to stare thoughtfully into the middle distance. Then she commanded, "Explain."

Joe didn't overdo it. "It's a small forensic finding," he said. "But in addition to it, today, one of my men was put in the hospital by somebody removing something from your father's room. We don't know what, exactly."

She shook her head slightly. "One of the other asylum inmates?" she asked.

He smiled. "The Woods? Your opinion or his?"

Her eyes widened. "His? Good lord, no. You don't know of his involvement with that place?"

Joe hesitated.

"He all but created it," she finished. "Put money into it, rounded up backers, helped fill it with cronies — him and a bunch of rich pals. Mostly, he used his influence to get it through the regulatory bear traps. They figured that instead of losing their money to an old folks' home, they should get other people to pay for their living in one — and a luxury one, at that. Sweet revenge straight to the grave. It was the last laugh, as far as he was concerned, although I don't think he figured on getting murdered."

Especially if you're the one who had him done in, Joe thought, at once admiring her steadiness and wondering what fueled it.

"Did you?" he asked.

"Figure on my father getting killed?" she asked, as if the question were purely philosophical. "I asked myself that years ago, when he was doing his best to piss people off. But now? As a crotchety old man? Not unless the cleaning lady did it, or somebody else who had to deal with him daily."

"Not the ideal tenant?" Joe asked.

Michelle Mahoney got up and crossed to the window of the GMHA director's office. She stood there, looking out onto the rain-slicked, deserted wasteland.

"I love this place," she finally said, turning to face him. "I've been coming here since I was a young girl. The people are generous, kind, friendly, enthusiastic, and — believe it or not — from every walk of life. You'd think they'd all be like me. Entitled rich bitches with no husbands or children. But they aren't. They just love horses. Some of them are certifiable, just like everywhere. They talk to the horses like they were babies and carry on like lunatics. You'll see some of them not eat so their animals can have food — they push themselves to the edge financially, and then go to pieces when reality hits and they have to sell the horse or can't afford the vet bills."

She left the window and waved toward a collection of framed photographs on the wall, all of people posing with their mounts in one configuration or another. "But that's a tiny minority," she continued. "The rest of them are salt of the earth, even the rich ones. They don't mind being peed on or shoveling horseshit, or pitching in when all hell breaks loose." She gestured back toward the scene outside. "You saw what happened here. This place has some sixty-five acres, one hundred and sixty-five permanent stalls, six barns. Hell, even the dirt has to be imported so it's the right consistency for competition. And it's all been decimated. Wiped out. No insurance to speak of. Not a huge amount of reserve capital."

She sat back down, leaning forward to sell her point, her face at last animated. "So why the sob story? Because it's not one. How long has it been since the storm? And already, money and manpower have been pouring in. This is a confirmation of love and dedication — of belief in an ideal."

She indicated the empty desk. "That's what I was talking to Judy about. We're having to manage this like the Normandy invasion. We've had so many offers of help, we can't keep them straight." She reached out and grabbed his wrist. "These people give a damn, because it's more than horses or competitions or winning events or strutting around in thousand-dollar outfits or driving up in trucks that cost more than your house. It's about getting rid of all that crap and taking care of the basics: a horse to ride and a fellow human to rely on — the same as it was with the Plains Indians or Genghis Khan and his bunch."

She stopped abruptly and sat back, crossing her arms and legs and giving Joe the stony look she'd delivered when he entered. "It's not about screwing people just for the fun of it."

Joe let a moment's decompression pass before suggesting, "Like your father did?"

"I thought he was a monster," she said plainly. "But he was just a guy like so many others — into politics and power and money and landing the deal. I am the direct beneficiary of all that bloodshed — well educated and rolling in dough — and that's why I'm here, doing my best to put this seemingly self-indulgent playground back together. Because it's got the values and the caring and the vitality and the honesty that my father and his friends touted but subverted for their entire adult lives."

Joe cupped his chin in his hand and smiled at her. "Wow."

She surprised him then by smiling broadly and looking embarrassed. "I'm sorry. The double whammy of this place being wiped out and my father dying . . . And now you're telling me he was killed."

"I don't actually have proof of that, Ms. Mahoney," he said. "And I told it to you because tongues are already starting to wag. You had a right to know."

"Plus," she added, "you wanted to find out if I'd done it."

"Did you?" he asked.

She looked at him contemplatively, "No. I considered it when I was a teenager. Not very realistically, but still. He was such an arrogant bastard, treating my mom like he did and walking around like God's gift. But, to be honest, now that he's dead — especially if you're right about how — it's more of a pain than anything else. I'd just as soon he'd died of having no heart. Now there's guaranteed to be a stink." She shook her head. "He would have loved that."

Joe considered what she'd told him — and how — and was left with a grudging respect. He didn't think that he could ever truly like Michelle Mahoney as a person. There was too much anger and privilege combined, despite her obvious appreciation for the simpler, kinder aspects of life. But he liked her mettle, and her willingness to appraise herself honestly.

He was also thinking that she might be a good source of information.

"You mentioned," he began, "that he helped create The Woods. You also suggested that my colleague was mugged by one of 'the inmates,' as you put it. Could you flesh that out for me?"

"The first part is easy," she said. "Gorden spent most of his political career catering to the rich and powerful. He was Old School with a vengeance — the very politician that everyone thought died with Boss Tweed and James Curley. People forget what Vermont used to be like before World War Two — ultraconservative, hyper-parochial, provincial, and isolationist. There are plenty of reasons that there's not more industry or big business in this state, but some of the major ones stem from the old-timers wanting nothing to do with the outside world. You could argue that quite a few of today's tree-huggers toe the same line, despite their 'think global' bullshit."

Joe watched her speaking, her words at such contrast with her Greenwich, Connecticut, look. She'd referred to shadowing her father down the corridors of power. She'd obviously been one hell of a student — stimulated, according to her, by her disgust with what she was witnessing.

"When the inevitable came crashing in on them," she continued, "when the war cracked the shell and allowed young men to escape and restless veterans to return — and Vietnam then made a lie of so much that we'd taken for granted — people like my father saw a chance to cash in like never before. There was a sudden chasm between the horrified old conservatives and the dope-smoking, commune-living, back-to-nature bunch. The shift from Republicans to Democrats in the '60s was less uniform or universal than people remember today, and for opportunists like dear old Dad, it meant that some Republicans became pragmatic — if they couldn't have the state-house, they would control the money that was coming in at last with the postwar tourist boom. They slipped into that gap between paying lip service to the wide-eyed, crunchy-granola newbies, and doing deals with the hard-eyed capitalists who were figuring out how to make a buck in this new reality. Old Gorden — bless his cynical little heart — took the money from one side, finessed the idealists on the other with carefully crafted legislation, and made out like a pirate. There was no good cause that he wouldn't embrace, and no cash deal that he wouldn't consider.

"Long story short," she concluded, "even before his drinking and bad habits took their toll, he'd been looking at 'the plight of the elderly' and saying all the right things in committees and on the stump — while greasing the skids to turn The Woods into a viable project. Old IOUs got called in, from politicians and millionaires alike, and a bunch of seemingly minor and even unrelated bills slid through the legislative process until the first silver shovel hit the dirt at the groundbreaking."

Michelle Mahoney sighed and delivered her punch line: "The Woods of Windsor is what it is, Mr. Gunther — a retirement home for people rich enough to pay the entry fee; but it's also a snake pit of a few bastards like my father who may look like their fellow residents, but who are in fact unrecognized and untraceable founders and beneficiaries of a highly lucrative business venture. And that," she said, "is why I said what I did about the inmates. There are secrets galore at that place, and I wouldn't doubt that in the minds of a few of those old coots, some of those secrets are worth killing for."

By now, Joe could no longer resist betraying a bit of his ignorance about her background. "What kind of lawyer are you, Ms. Mahoney?"

The smile she gave him was wry and self-deprecating. "Corporate, Mr. Gunther. The apple fell close to the tree."

"I don't know," he complimented her. "It doesn't sound like your father was blessed with your integrity."

"Why did you want to know?" she asked.

"I don't usually get such an organized and clearly delivered summation."

"You're being polite," she said. "My colleagues tell me I'm a bully and a bore."

"You may be the first," he agreed in part. "I don't know about that. But you certainly aren't the second. Have you been to your father's apartment since he died?"

"No," she replied. "Why?"

"Before I answer that," he said, "I'm wondering if you were ever there."

Her face expressed surprise. "Of course I was. I dropped by every time I came here. I didn't like him, but he was my father, and he's all I have, or *had* left."

"How old were you when your mom died?" Joe asked.

"Eleven," she replied softly. "She was a

poor, hapless, bullied creature, but a good heart. I don't think she ever knew what to do with me, but she did try — I'll give her that. That's why I took her last name when I reached majority."

Joe nodded and moved on. "The reason I asked if you'd ever been to your dad's apartment is because I'm hoping you'll go there with me and tell me if you think anything's missing or different from what you're used to."

"You want to find out what was stolen when your cop got mugged."

Joe didn't want to prejudice her beforehand. "In part, maybe. Would you be willing?"

She answered by standing, flattening the front of her jeans with her hands. "Let's go. I can finish with Judy later."

The drive took under twenty minutes, and they went in separate cars, Mahoney predictably navigating a high-end Lexus SUV. At the apartment, Joe was at first disappointed to find that his request for a guard on the door had gone ignored — until he used the key and discovered one of Carrier's men inside.

He laughed at him. "Don't tell me," he said. "Let me guess."

"What?" the man answered.

"Rick parked you inside to spare you from Graham Dee."

The cop smiled. "Don't think I don't appreciate it."

"So you've met the man."

"Oh, yeah. He tags us every time we roll into the parking lot. Quite the unit."

Joe stood aside and introduced Michelle Mahoney. After arranging for a time to return, the cop left them to get some air and a coffee.

Michelle stood looking around. "Kind of funny," she said quietly.

"What?"

"It's over," she said. "It didn't really strike me till now, but seeing this, and smelling him in the air . . ." She left the sentence dangling.

Joe was struck by the same realization — that her matter-of-factness had overshadowed what had actually befallen her. She was an only orphan, and was now confronted with having to forage through her father's belongings, deal with funeral homes and lawyers, all while confronting a lifetime of complicated, not-so-fond memories.

"Would you like to do this later?" Joe asked. "There's no rush."

That was all she needed. She faced him, her eyes shining but dry. "Of course there

268

is. You have a man wounded and a homicide to solve. What would you like me to do?"

He took her through the apartment, room by room, asking her to stop and consider each view as they came upon it. He asked her about furniture moved, pictures missing, objects disturbed, files gone astray. They wound up before the dresser, where he pulled open the drawer and asked her to check its contents. Sadly but not surprisingly, she merely gave him a blank look.

"You think I know what was in my father's sock drawer?"

He indicated the space before her. "It's not socks, for one thing. Take a look."

Amused, she did as he'd asked, even poking her finger in among the odds and ends. "Okay," she then announced.

"Did he have a jewelry box?" he asked her. "With cuff links, tie tacks, things like that?"

Her brow furrowed slightly. "I think my mom gave him one. He used to scatter those things across the top here." She patted the dresser's flat surface, which was clear aside from a decorative lamp. She added, "Where we used to live. It drove her a little crazy. She was kind of a neatnik."

In the end, she fell short of being the oracle he'd hoped for, including about the contents of the stolen box. She did tell him of a politically oriented photograph that was missing from the office wall, and that the telephone must have been voided of messages by someone not her father — she claimed he would never have done that, since he'd habitually used the answering machine as a form of to-do file, stacking up to twenty messages there on a regular basis.

"Do you remember who was in the photograph?" Joe asked, standing before the spot it had occupied, as if willing its ghost to reappear.

She stood beside him. "It was a group shot, with my father. The governor at the time may have been in it. But there were others — men and women, both. I just don't know who. Not sure if I ever did, to be honest."

"You say, 'at the time.' So it was old?"

She considered the question before responding, "It looked old — black-and-white, a little contrasty because of the flash. I'd say a half century, more or less. It was back when my father was at his peak. He looked very pleased with himself."

"You ever see a copy of it elsewhere?" Joe asked hopefully. "In a newspaper, maybe?"

But she announced what he didn't want to hear. "Nope. That might've been it. Probably gone for good now."

Joe had brought along a file of documents related to the case. He fetched it from the kitchen counter and extracted a copy of the photograph that he and Lester had found in Barb Barber's album in Shelburne, of Carolyn and Michelle's father facing the cameras during the Governor-for-a-Day event.

He laid it on Gorden's desk. "This the missing picture?"

She barely glanced at it. "No. As I said, it was a group shot."

Disappointed, he picked it up and handed it to her for closer scrutiny. "That is your father, though, correct?"

"Oh yes," she said, taking the copy. "And this was around the same time. That girl may have even been in the other picture." She waved it gently in the air, adding, "But this isn't it."

"Did you ever hear your father refer to anyone named Carolyn Barber?" Joe asked.

"Never," she said.

"Or hear him mention an event from about that time, called Governor-for-a-Day?"

Again, she couldn't help him. "No," she said. "Sounds pretty silly."

He took the picture back. "Yeah. I thought so, too. Once."

Chapter Sixteen

Rob stepped off the elevator on the third floor and looked around. He'd been to Sheldon Scott's office building before, but only at ground level, where the conference rooms and reception staff were located. He knew that the firm owned the entire building — it was that kind of operation — but he'd gotten the clear impression that people sharing his political philosophy weren't likely to be invited upstairs.

That had always been the projected image of Scott & Company, as the business was officially called. From the formidable turn-of-the-century building to the formal dress code adhered to by everyone down to the lowest-ranked employee, the place smacked of a generally anachronistic attitude — displaying the sensitivity of an upper-crust manor in a land of tepees and yurts.

Not that Montpelier was lacking in monumental architecture — or suits, dresses, and business attire. It was the state capital, after all, even if that state was small and rural. Still, for all the effort exerted in the form of gold domes and urban "power-wear," Perkins had nevertheless spotted a Vermont Supreme Court justice wearing clogs under his robes.

"Mr. Perkins?"

He turned to find a young woman, immaculate from toe to head, standing in an unmarked entrance halfway down the otherwise empty mahogany-paneled hallway.

"Mr. Scott will see you in here."

Perkins approached and followed her into the room she'd appeared from. Having entered, however, he heard the door closed behind him and found himself alone in one of the largest offices he'd ever visited — as big as the entire end of the building, with towering windows on three of its fifteen-foot walls. He was instantly reminded of the set for *My Fair Lady.*

"Rob. How nice to see you."

He glanced about, unable to locate the source of the voice.

"Hi, Mr. Scott," he said nevertheless, the man's age advantage earning him the title — a reflection of Rob's traditional upbringing.

"Up here," replied the disembodied voice,

273

drawing Perkins's attention to the two-story, balcony-equipped bookshelves directly behind him. He walked farther into the room and turned to look up at his host.

Sheldon Scott, in pinstripe suit, red tie, French cuffs, and trademark thick mane of snow-white hair, smiled down on him like the cross between a TV evangelist and an emperor of Rome. Perkins half expected to receive an imperial thumbs-down as a tiger was set free from under the truck-sized desk near the far wall.

Instead, Scott walked the length of the balcony and nimbly descended a wrought-iron spiral staircase, emerging from it with manicured hand extended.

"How long's it been?" he asked.

"Nine months," Rob answered, having checked the fact in his calendar before coming here. "The Cross-Border Conference reception at the Hilton."

"Really?" Scott gestured for him to proceed to the other end of the room, where a cluster of leather armchairs was gathered before a cavernous fireplace. The walls at this end were adorned with books as well, but allowed, too, for a scattering of carefully framed photographs — each of them featuring Sheldon Scott with some conservative luminary, dating back to Richard Nixon and

Barry Goldwater. A large shot of Scott and then Senate President Pro Tem Gorden Marshall caught Perkins's eye, if only because of an article in the morning paper stating that Marshall had died at his retirement home in eastern Vermont.

"Then we're overdue for a catch-up," Scott was saying. "Would you like anything to drink?"

"No, thank you. I'm all set."

Scott waved him to one of the chairs and settled down himself, crossing his legs and shooting his cuffs with the grace of a seasoned actor. Perkins had long considered that one of the weapons in this man's arsenal was this almost theatrical aristocratic bearing. For a country that had violently broken from a monarchy, the United States had, in Rob's opinion, forever-after harbored a longing for royalty, which the likes of Sheldon Scott exploited to the hilt.

"Having a good time working for the governor?" Scott asked airily, as if making conversation.

"An excellent time."

The older man nodded thoughtfully. "This storm has certainly added to your headaches, though. Terrible thing."

"We're managing," Perkins said cryptically.

"So, what brings you to see me?" Scott asked his guest with an expansive gesture of hands, apparently tiring of a game of manners that clearly had no traction.

Rob had expected this opening gambit, and so didn't hesitate to respond, "You wouldn't be seeing me in your inner sanctum if you didn't already know. For that matter, one could say that you indirectly asked to see *me*. So why don't we start there? Why am I here, Mr. Scott?"

The lobbyist gave him an avuncular smile as he lamented, "Ah, Rob. I love it. How I wish our politics were more compatible. I would hire you in a New York minute."

Perkins made no comment.

Scott steepled his fingers before his lower lip, allowing Rob to see that his gold cuff links were stamped with something suspiciously reminiscent of the presidential seal. "All right. Since the topic of Irene has already been broached, let's talk about that. It is hardly my own opinion that Governor Zigman is taking a beating because of FEMA, among other things — deservedly or not. Can we agree on that?"

"I will agree that people have their facts wrong and are blaming us and FEMA for their problems," Rob said cautiously.

"Ah, ha," Scott responded, one finger in

the air. "Still, that suggests that a little help proffered in that area might be seen as a real advantage."

"Depending on the ins and outs attached to that help, sure," Rob agreed. "What are we talking about, exactly?"

"Philosophically?" Scott immediately evaded. "Let's call it the common man's readiest complaint: I need money and I want it now." He laughed at his own wit. "That's their frustration in a nutshell, is it not? Vermonters think FEMA has the cash, and they want it faster than it's being produced. Already, the papers are filling with nightmare stories about the size and complexity of the government's aid applications. All the more poignant with the first twinge of fall in the air."

Again, Rob kept silent.

"The proposal I'm imagining," Scott continued, "would result in a noncompetitive, legislatively backed, but privately funded program that would effectively address those delays and the overall cash availability surrounding the present situation."

Perkins couldn't resist smiling at the careful phrasing — each word chosen for its apparent precision and its vagueness.

He responded in kind. "Well, of course you know that the governor's office can't speak for the legislature."

Scott laughed artificially, making Rob wonder how it was that so many people fell for this man's supposed charms. "Oh, come, come, Rob. We Republicans are barely allowed access to that building. Between the Democrats, the Libertarians, and the Progressives, I'm half surprised Gail Zigman hasn't been proclaimed governor-for-life."

"And yet she hasn't been," Rob said, "which leaves us with an old-fashioned democracy, as clunky as that can be. Which also, by the way, includes FEMA itself. I imagine they'll be fascinated to hear of this project, and more than happy to withdraw their own money if Vermont comes up with a benevolent billionaire to replace them." He seemed to ponder the thought of that possibility, and then asked, "Putting that aside for the time being, where are you proposing the money come from?"

Scott raised his eyebrows. "Was Susan Raffner that poor a messenger that she didn't tell you?"

"I'm just asking for confirmation," Rob said stiffly, beginning to thoroughly dislike the roundabout, quasi-devious, pie-in-the-sky nature of the conversation. He was feeling himself increasingly among the shoals.

"Who did she say was offering his generosity?" Scott asked innocently.

Rob sighed. "Harold LeMieur."

Scott spread his hands wide. "Well, then — there you are."

Perkins frowned. "Are you his official representative with this proposal?"

"I represent Harold on all his affairs in Vermont, and many others elsewhere."

Rob held up a hand, as if in protest, struggling to remember that he was here on assignment, and not to air his own opinions. "I get that. Look. Don't get me wrong. We like the sound of this. It would be good for us, reflect well on LeMieur, and help the entire state get past this mess far more quickly — *if,*" he emphasized, "we're all very clear on who's offering what and how. To be perfectly honest, Mr. Scott, there is nothing in Mr. LeMieur's past that would make me believe he's being genuine with this offer. It just stretches credibility."

Scott was nodding sympathetically. "Totally understandable. You merely repeated what I said when I first heard of this, Rob. There is a factor here, however, that you're unaware of, and I think it may help to change your mind — Harold is not in the best of health."

Rob's mouth fell open, as much stunned by the message as by its manipulative undertone — assuming it was true. "He's dying?" he blurted out.

"He's not well, and you know how sentimental people can get, especially if they've lived a long and full life and feel that they need to give back before it's too late."

"You're telling me *that's* what this is?" Rob asked. "A dying man's guilt trip?"

Scott's polite smile froze. "That's a bit harsh. He is my dearest friend. But it may be one way of looking at it, from your perspective. I see it in a more sentimental light — a man lending a hand to his birth state in its time of greatest need."

Perkins couldn't sit still anymore, he was feeling so uncomfortable with the various covert possibilities — most of them bad. He rose from the clinging embrace of the large chair and crossed to a window to stare sightlessly out onto the Montpelier traffic below. Sheldon Scott let him take his time quietly.

Eventually, Perkins turned and faced the owner of this elaborate scheme. "Mr. Scott," he said. "I'll have to get back to you on this. The ramifications, the logistics, the sheer number of players that would have to sign on to make it happen are staggering, not to mention that the need for money and action is right now — today."

Scott nodded sagely and seemed to carefully consider what Perkins had said before replying, "Of course you're right, Rob. I had mentioned all of this to Harold. It does seem as if we may have knocked on the wrong door. Your mention of FEMA's possible response to this philanthropic gesture makes me think that we should perhaps speak to Vermont's Washington delegation. They are, after all, right there at the seat of power, even controlling FEMA's purse strings. This entire matter may in fact be more than a mere governor can address."

Rob Perkins stared at the man in wonder and horror, fully realizing with that last pitch the true nature of the trap that had begun with Susan Raffner and ended with him. He felt light-headed and slightly nauseated as he heard himself say, "I've got to go. We'll be back in touch soon," while feeling like a man who'd just told his own firing squad that he would in fact enjoy the short-lived respite of a last cigarette.

Sheldon Scott didn't protest, nor rise to see him out. Instead, as if by magic — and reeking of prearranged orchestration — the far door opened and the same tailored woman appeared to usher Perkins from the room. As he passed her by, Rob made a conscious effort to memorize her features, suspecting that he'd see her again, most likely as a witness to his having met with her boss in a clandestine, closed-door setting, no doubt to be portrayed in the worst of all lights.

"Hey," Joe said into the phone.

Beverly Hillstrom chuckled on the other end — a side of her that he had rarely glimpsed. "Hey, yourself. Are you calling about your two burned special deliveries from Shelburne?"

He let out a laugh, startled by the phrasing. "Not actually. I really just wanted to hear your voice."

"Ahh," she let out slowly. "Now, that's very nice. How are you feeling, Joe?"

"Truthfully?" he replied. "Very happy. The whole state is under three feet of silt, you're buried in bodies, and I have an asylum escapee wandering loose, an old folks' home straight out of Agatha Christie, and somebody who's missing his coffin, but I feel as if something fundamental has just slipped into its proper place. I'd like to thank you for that. How 'bout you? Is that way more than you wanted to hear?"

"It's pure music, Joe. I'm very happy about what's happening."

"I'm sorry I had to leave so early," he said. "All this stuff —"

She cut him off. "If you start apologizing for that, then I'll have to join in, and there will never be an end to it. A pinkie swear, Special Agent-in-Charge Joe Gunther: Never let that be a problem. Okay?"

"Okay."

"Would you like to hear about your two cremated bodies? It's preliminary, but it's fine with me if it's acceptable to you."

He wasn't about to turn her down. "Absolutely, Doctor. Proceed."

"The female — Barbara Barber — clearly died of smoke inhalation, and her body was then consumed by the fire. From the report and photographs I received, I have no problem with the police suggestion that she died sitting in her wheelchair. William Friel, however, is a little more problematic, in that I found no signs of the same COD. His throat and lungs were clear of the soot I found in his mother, and his carbon dioxide level was within normal limits. His body did suffer extensively from the fire, making some of this hypothesis only approximately accurate, but right now, I'm thinking that in his particular microenvironment during the conflagration, Mr. Friel died of inhaling super-heated air — a flash fire — rather than of any products of combustion, such as smoke. In some cases, I can find perhaps a cardiac event to explain findings like these, but Mr. Friel appears to have had a perfectly normal middle-aged anatomy. He didn't even have much alcohol in his system, which is something else I look for, especially in house fires."

"And naturally, you didn't find a bullet," Joe said.

"Nor a bashed-in skull, nor a ligature around his neck," she agreed. "As always, the toxicology screen will be coming back in a few weeks and may have something not readily apparent today, but right now, I'm afraid I'm going to have to label this one the same way I did Mr. Marshall."

"Undetermined," Joe concluded.

"Sadly, yes," she concurred. "There is a lingering question deserving of further analysis, however," she added hopefully.

"Oh?"

"It's not much. But, again, it's among the details I search for in cases like this. I always ask myself, 'Why didn't they get out?' That's usually answered by circumstances, as with Ms. Barber, who couldn't move from her wheelchair, or by things like alcohol, drugs, or pre-conflagration death or disability. But as far as we know, Mr. Friel suffered from none of those. So, why did he stay in the building? It had to have been reeking of gas, given the way it went up."

Joe was nodding at the phone in agreement, enjoying in part how the back-and-forth between them — always a natural part of their friendship — felt only enhanced by their personal relationship having reached a new level. It served him as a tiny confirmation of the good feeling he'd been carrying around all day.

"Have you considered suicide?" Hillstrom asked suddenly.

"What?"

"It's not unheard of. You feel your world is at a dead end, you're caring for someone whose suffering is only going to worsen . . ." She left the rest of her sentence unfinished.

Instinctively, he rejected the idea, but he recognized her scientific process. And he'd been to the house. It wasn't a stretch to superimpose her scenario onto the life of William Friel.

Still, considering their other death of interest — and Beverly's similarly unsatisfactory finding — it was unlikely that Friel, with his roundabout connection to Gorden Marshall, should all of a sudden choose this moment to park himself and his mother with Marshall at the morgue.

Somebody lethal was controlling events here, from deep within the shadows, and as

285

far as Joe knew, the only likely victim left —
with direct ties to all three deaths — was
Barb's demented sister, wandering around
on the loose. They'd circulated the "Be on
the Lookout" press release, and it had been
getting coverage in the media, but the state
remained semi-crippled and distracted by
the storm's aftereffects, and Joe was suspicious of the publicity's true impact.

"Thanks, Beverly," he told Hillstrom.
"You've left me thinking, as usual."

"Coming back north soon?" she inquired
seductively.

"Count on it," he replied.

Joe had been crossing the manicured lawn
of The Woods during his call to Beverly, and
now entered the main building to locate
Sam — whom he'd asked to join him here,
prepared for a long stay — and Lester,
recently discharged from the hospital and
cleared for light duty.

He found them setting up in a small
conference room in the office suite where
they'd first met Hannah Eastridge.

"Hillstrom have anything?" Sam asked as
he entered, knowing that Joe had been calling the medical examiner — although
ignorant of their enhanced relationship.

"Another undetermined," he said. "Who-

286

ever's doing this is either very careful or really lucky. There was no smoke in Friel's lungs, though, which certainly implies he was dead before the fire reached him."

"Same for the mom?" Lester asked.

"No. With her, it looks like straight cause-and-effect. Makes sense — he was the one who needed to be taken out before the house could be rigged."

"Which, of course," Sam added, still arranging pads and recording equipment on the table, "is another unproven theory."

"You not liking the arson/homicide premise?" Joe asked, his tone suggesting that he was open to suggestion.

She looked up startled, ever the loyalist. "No, no. I was just saying."

"Point taken," he told them. "But it can't hurt to proceed on that theory until a better one comes up."

"Works for me," she stressed again.

"How do you want to do this, boss?" Lester asked, waving his hand across the table.

Joe sat on a chair against the wall, to keep out of the way. "We have a vague sense of who some of Marshall's friends were in this place. So we should start by interviewing them, one by one, while at the same time drilling down for more names. The man was a community leader, so he was on committees, advisory groups, and what have you. He was also a covert Woods founder, according to his daughter, and tied in to a bunch who're probably less easy to identify, for obvious reasons. But they're no doubt old Vermont politicos and/or financial types." He mused, "If we actually do get the goods on some of them, we might be able to use that as leverage. If nothing else, it would be fun to blow the whistle on 'em to the IRS."

Spinney laughed at the notion.

"The other thing to chase down," Joe resumed, "would be Marshall's phone records. Plus, the usual canvass details like neighbors, friends, et cetera. His daughter might be helpful with some of that, but not much. She kept her distance. Oh, and interview the waiters from the dining room — they see stuff nobody ever thinks to ask them about. Could be that one of them saw the old boy schmoozing with someone we're not supposed to know."

Joe rose and moved to the door. "This is gonna take some time." He cast a look at Sammie. "How's Willy doing with Rozanski? He interruptable? There's no question now that this case is the bigger deal — and you could stand the help."

Sam gave him a smile. "But you wanted to test the water with me first before you called him up?"

"Something like that. Also, if he's about to close it, he might as well be given a little rope."

"I don't know, boss," she said honestly. "This one's become personal, somehow. You know how he gets with those."

They all knew that. "Where is he?" Joe asked, also aware that Willy wouldn't have logged his whereabouts with Dispatch or anywhere else, as each of them was supposed to.

"Northeast Kingdom," she said. "That's all I know. Something about having found a family member who lives in the boonies."

Joe considered that, during which Spinney spoke up, "I don't mind cutting him a little slack. God knows, we'll be here for a few days."

Joe stepped into the doorway and nodded. "Okay — a couple of days. Then I'll yank his leash."

CHAPTER SEVENTEEN

Willy killed his engine within sight of the
cabin. It was in a clearing, deep in the
woods, at the end of a rarely traveled, weed-
choked track. There was no vehicle to be
seen, but the garden was well tended, the
woodpile large and ready for the coming
fall and winter. A few articles of clothing
hung listlessly on a rope between two trees
off to the side, in the afternoon sun. To
Willy, it was symbolic of a life stripped
down, its momentum as arrested and pre-
served as if held in solitary confinement.

Defying unwritten protocol, Willy didn't
wait for a reaction from inside the cabin,
but immediately exited the car, stood before
it to be clearly visible, and held his badge
up high.

In response, the rough wooden door
opened to reveal a thin, balding man with a
long gray beard, dressed in a flannel shirt
and a pair of bibbed overalls. He reminded

Willy more of some touristy calendar art than a sample of the local culture.

"Nate Rozanski?" he called out.

The man didn't move at first, as if frozen by the greeting, before his shoulders slumped and he answered quietly, "I figured you'd show up sooner or later."

Willy approached. "For twenty-seven years?" he asked.

Rozanski watched him, his face somber and defeated.

Willy stuck his hand out in greeting, a gesture he generally avoided. Rozanski's grip was soft and powerless — offered half-heartedly.

"I didn't come to cause you trouble, Nate," Willy told him. "Not necessarily. But you know why I'm here. I need to hear what happened."

"I killed my brother," Rozanski said without preamble.

Willy nodded, having suspected that interpretation. "Can we sit?" he asked, gesturing toward the door.

Nate led the way, taking Willy into a single room with a bed in one corner, a small table in the middle, and a large homebuilt bookcase lining one wall, filled with cans and boxes of food and two small piles of neatly folded clothes. In another corner was a woodstove with a cook top and a couple of pans. There were no decorations on the walls, and only the one window facing the front. There was no plumbing or electricity to be seen. Willy reassessed his image of a self-made prison cell and now saw the place more as a monastic retreat of penance.

He crossed to the table, pulled out the one chair, and waited for Nate to find his own spot to settle, which became the edge of the bed. Given the size of the cabin, that still put him pretty nearby.

"Tell me what happened," Willy instructed him.

"I told you," was the murmured reply.

"You're going to have to do better than that, Nate. I drove a long way."

Nate's voice was slow and awkward, as if lack of use had atrophied its muscles. "I put him into the saw."

"Accidentally or on purpose?"

"On purpose."

Willy coaxed him along. "Did you plan it out, or was it a spur-of-the-moment thing?"

"We fought."

"What about?"

Nate silently stared at his gnarly, inter-meshed hands, dangling between his knees.

"A woman?" Willy prompted.

Rozanski let out a short noise that Willy

interpreted as a chopped-off laugh.

"That funny?"

Nate shook his head once, but then said, "Kinda."

Willy didn't hesitate. "A man?"

Nate looked up, his impassive face as close to startled as seemed possible, given his range of expressions.

Willy pushed on. "Your brother was gay?"

Rozanski scowled. "I hate that word."

"You hate them, too?" Willy shot back.

Slowly, Nate covered his face with his hands. "I didn't know," he said, barely whispering.

"Didn't know what?"

"I didn't understand."

He seemed blocked, so Willy tried redirecting him. "Take me back, Nate, to before that happened. Tell me about your family."

"There's nothing left," he said.

"Your sister, Eileen, would be sad to hear that."

That prompted another reaction as Nate dropped his hands — a slight smile. "I guess so."

"She still loves you," Willy said. "That's why she keeps in touch."

"She's a good girl."

"What was it like — you, Eileen, Herb, and your parents?"

Nate's gaze drifted to the worn wooden floorboards between them when he spoke. "Nuthin' special. Same as all families."

"Most family members don't kill each other."

That didn't jar him. "You asked about before."

"I did. Still, call me crazy, but it sure sounds like there were tensions."

Nate glanced up. "You're a wiseass."

"Never heard that one before," Willy deadpanned. "Talk to me about the family."

A flicker of irritation crossed Nate's face. "We just lived in the same house."

That sounded familiar to Willy. He could have made the same claim. "Nobody got along?"

"Not particularly."

" 'Cept maybe with Eileen?"

"Right."

Willy sighed. "You really want me to drag this out of you? I can do that. You already told me you killed Herb. What's the big deal if you didn't like Mommy and Daddy, for Christ's sake? Spit it out, Nate. Get this shit out. How many years you been waiting for this?"

"It's hard."

Willy leaned close in. *"Hard?"* he almost yelled. "Herb had it hard, dipwad. You *killed* that sorry fucker, Nate. *That's* hard. You're just wallowing in it."

Nate's face had reddened, his hands clenched, and his shoulders hunched tight.

Willy poked him in the arm, and Rozanski recoiled. "Come on, Nate. Let's hear what you got. You been practicing for decades, getting this confession down. Well, it's showtime. The audience is getting restless. Tell me about the family Rozanski. What the hell happened that all that anger finally blew a gasket?"

Nate was beginning to fidget on the edge of the bed, as if he might leap to his feet and lash out.

That's when Willy abruptly shifted gears and laid a fraternal hand on his knee. "Nate," he said softly. "Nate. Look at me."

The other man blinked a couple of times and stared at him.

"It's over, man," Willy counseled him. "All the waiting, all the buildup, all the self-hate. Don't think about it anymore. Just talk. Listen to the questions and tell me the answers. One at a time, one after another. Okay?"

Nate bobbed his head silently.

"What was your mom like? Dreama?"

"Yeah."

"She wear the pants in the family? Roll

over and play dead? Something in between?"

"She rolled over."

"Outstanding. That's good," Willy praised him. "Was that with your father or all of you?"

"Just Bud."

"You called your dad by his first name. That's unusual. What was he like?"

"A son of a bitch."

"Good. He beat you guys up?"

"Yeah."

"He do anything to Eileen?"

Nate's eyes narrowed. "You mean kinky?"

"Sure."

"No," he said emphatically. "He just hit her, like the rest of us."

"What about Herb? More? Less? How did he treat Herb?"

"It changed."

"From when he was little?"

Rozanski nodded.

"Started gentle and got rough?"

"Yeah."

"Why?"

"Herb was soft."

"And stayed soft?"

"Yeah."

"And you didn't like that, either. Is that correct?"

"He was like a girl."

"Like Eileen?"

"Yeah."

"And so what worked for Bud worked for you. Is that the way it was, Nate? Did you let Bud set the example? Maybe to get on his good side? You and Bud against the world?"

Nate murmured, "I guess."

"Did it work?"

He shook his head.

" 'Cause you and Bud were different, weren't you? He hit Herb for one reason and you hit him for another. Am I right?"

"Yeah."

"And then one day, there you are, in the sawmill. Was it the three of you, or just you and your brother?"

"Dad came in right at the end."

"Dad?" Willy echoed. "He was Dad then, wasn't he? Or that's what you wanted him to be. Your dad; your friend; the source of love you thought every family had but yours. Did Herb get all of that, and you got nothing, even with all the beating?"

Nate stayed silent.

"Come on," Willy urged him. "Tell me you didn't feel Herb got what you didn't. Eileen, too, except she was a girl, so that was all right. Weren't you pissed at Herb, Nate? Till he pushed you over the edge?"

297

Nate rubbed his forehead until it reddened. "I pushed him," he mouthed.

"Into the saw blade or over the edge?"

"What's the difference?"

"How did you push him over the edge?" Willy pressed.

"I accused him."

"Of being gay . . ." Willy quickly self-corrected, "Of being a faggot?" he suggested. "A queer? What did you do, Nate?"

Nate surprised him then by looking up, befuddled. "I don't remember."

Willy sharpened his voice. "Cut the crap. What does that mean?"

"I mean what started it. We were working the job — what Bud had told us to do — and Herb said something. I don't know what it was. All these years, I've tried to remember. I just blew up. Started yelling. I grabbed him. . . ." His voice trailed off.

"You threw him into the saw," Willy suggested.

"Dad walked in right then," Nate finished. "Herb was screaming. Blood was everywhere. Bud didn't care about any of it. He just started beating on me."

Willy frowned. "What about Herb?"

Nate shook his head. "He got himself off the saw, I guess. I didn't see it. Maybe he didn't. I was covering my head, trying to get away. Bud had a two-by-four. I finally blacked out."

Willy kept to what Nate believed to be true. "But Herb was dead?"

Nate stared at him. "Of course he was dead. I killed him."

"But you didn't see him."

"Bud put him in a coffin, for God's sake."

"But you didn't see him," Willy repeated.

Nate's voice dropped as he said weakly, "The sheriff came."

"And he didn't see him, either." Willy leaned in to ask, "Did the sheriff see you, with all your cuts and bruises from Bud?"

"No," Nate admitted. "I was told to stay away."

"What happened between Bud and the sheriff?"

"I heard they met in the mill. That's where Bud put the coffin — a box, really. The sheriff drove up, talked with Bud awhile, and he drove off. That was it."

"What about your mom?" Willy asked. "What was she doing through all this?"

"I don't know. When I woke up, after the beating, he sent me to get fixed up by her. She did it, but never said a word, and a day later, he threw me out. I never saw her again."

"Where was Eileen?"

"She came home right after the fight, but I don't know where she was when the sheriff came. I saw her for a couple of minutes when I was leaving the next day. She didn't have a clue. Nobody told her nuthin'. She just looked stunned."

"You keep in touch, though. She told me," Willy said.

"Yeah, sometimes." Nate's tone was wistful. "She had it rough, being alone all of a sudden, with Bud and Dreama ending up the way they did. Her whole world blew up when she wasn't looking. I'm glad she found Phil."

"Ranslow?"

"Yeah. He sounds all right for her."

"When was the last time you and Eileen talked?" Willy asked, remembering what she'd answered.

"I don't know," Nate said. "A year, maybe? I'm too embarrassed to say much, so I leave it to her to find me."

Willy stood up and paced the floor, an impulse that took him all of two steps. "How'd you end up here?"

"I got a job logging, after I left home," Nate explained. "The Kingdom seemed like a good fit. One of the landowners let me build this place. In exchange, I keep an eye out. There's nothing to see, though."

"How long you been here?"

"Over twenty years."

"How do you keep alive?" Willy pointed at the stocked cans and boxes.

"I trade stuff," he said. "Animal furs. I still work the woodlot. It doesn't take much."

Willy turned to face him directly. "I have to tell you something, Nate."

His host stayed seated but straightened slightly, triggered by Willy's tone. "Okay."

"The recent flooding eroded part of the cemetery where your brother was buried. Herb's coffin was exposed. There was nobody in it. Just a bunch of rocks."

Nate blinked. "What?"

"Herb's coffin doesn't have anybody in it, Nate," Willy tried again. "Could be he's still alive."

"Herb?" Nate sounded as if he was barely awake.

"I probably shouldn't tell you this," Willy said, "but you already sentenced yourself to a twenty-year-plus prison term. Your dad may have lied about Herb dying. That's why he wouldn't open the box when the sheriff came. As far as I can tell, nobody ever saw Herb after the accident."

Nate was slowly absorbing it all. "Why?" he managed to say.

Willy gave a shrug. "Who knows? Bud had poisoned you against your brother, although not in so many words. He couldn't believe you took it to the point where you threw him into the saw, so now it was up to Bud to take revenge. He covered his own guilt by making you feel like you'd killed Herb."

"That doesn't make sense," Nate said wonderingly.

"Humans usually don't," Willy answered. "For all I know, maybe the whole parenting thing just fell in on him, and he took this way to clean out the stable except for Eileen, who might've struck him differently because she's a girl."

He sat back down, still speaking. "Nate, I'm not a shrink. I have no clue what drove him to do what he did, or even what happened to Herb in the long run. For all I know, he died two weeks after. But I think Bud buried a box of rocks in part to put everything behind him, and then let it eat him up until it killed him, right after it had done the same to Dreama. From what I know of human nature, your whole family was fucked up beyond repair and did everything wrong to set things right. But like I said, nobody pays me for counseling."

Nate didn't react. He just sat where he was and stared at his guest as if he'd been

302

beamed down into his chair from a flying saucer.

"You say you killed your brother," Willy forged ahead. "I have zero proof of that — no body, no witnesses, no evidence, no crime scene. You guys had a fight, Herb got injured, your dad beat the snot out of you, and then — probably — he covered up by inventing a story, burying the rocks, and throwing his two sons out the door."

At that, Nate's expression seemed to awaken, but Willy cut him off before he could speak. "I know, I know, I can't prove any of it. But Eileen stayed home, and she never saw Herb again, thinking he was in the box. You and I know he wasn't, so where was he? Bud chucked *you* out 'cause of what you did. You say he wasn't too thrilled with Herb — either because of his sexual orientation or just because your old man was as mean as cat shit — so maybe he threw him out, too."

Willy abruptly stopped and fixed Nate with a look, making him squirm.

"What?" Nate finally said in a small voice.

"Who was your doctor when you were all living together?"

"We didn't go to a doctor much."

"Good for you," Willy said impatiently. "If you'd been the one who got caught up in a saw blade, who would your father have taken you to? Especially if he'd wanted to avoid a hospital."

"Dr. Racque, I guess."

"Racque?" Willy repeated. "You're kidding. He live north of Townshend, in Windham County?"

Nate shrugged. "I don't know."

"Thomas Racque? *R-a-c-q-u-e?*"

Nate scratched his temple. "I guess. It looked French."

Willy nodded, pleased. He knew old Doc Racque. Long retired but still alive. He'd actually walked away from the profession after one disagreement too many with the medical bureaucracy, choosing to manage his woodlot and tend to his garden. Willy had dealt with him over twenty years ago on a case, also involving a trauma that should have been reported to the authorities. Thomas Racque was ill-inclined to play by the rules.

Willy had taken an instant liking to him.

"I have nothing saying Herb Rozanski's dead," Willy reported. "Much less murdered."

Joe awkwardly shifted his cell phone against his cheek and ear to hear more clearly. He'd once taken the ergonomics of old-fashioned phones for granted. Never again. "Based on what?" he asked.

Willy did his own readjusting, only in his case, it was Emma's access to her mother's bottled breast milk that he was struggling with.

"I interviewed the old family doctor — a retired old coot I know named Racque. Bud took Herb to him after he finished beating Nate half to death. Herb's arm had taken the brunt of the saw blade, and Racque sewed it back together."

"There any records of this?" Joe asked. He was driving west through the early darkness from a day at The Woods, where he'd been helping Sam and Lester prepare to interview all residents with any ties to Gorden Marshall.

"That was the whole point," Willy said contemptuously. "Bud wanted it under the radar and Racque was happy to oblige. Not that Racque thought it was that big a deal. It wasn't like Bud came to him and said, 'Hey, one son tried to murder the other; patch him up.' Racque thought it was an accident, and neither Bud nor Herb said anything different."

"So why the subterfuge with the box of rocks?" Joe asked.

"I met with Nate Rozanski today, too,"

Willy said. "Up in the middle of Lockjaw, Vermont, in the Kingdom. He thought he'd killed Herb, till I told him otherwise. After he gave me Racque's name, we got to talking more easily, and I asked him the same question. He's a little dim — been living like a hermit too long, for one thing — but he told me Bud said something along the lines of, 'You're dead to me now; both of you are.' I think Bud got to have his cake and eat it, too. He screwed Nate by making him think he'd killed his brother, on one hand, and I bet he convinced Herb that the fake funeral was to protect the kid's back, while sending a not-too-subtle message that a queer son was not welcome at home.

"Herb may have been gay, which his old man hated. But if I'm right, Bud got to throw each of them out as embarrassments in one fell swoop, and kept the daughter until she jumped ship on her own. Father-of-the-year material, he was not."

"So you're done?" Joe asked reasonably. " 'Cause we could do with some help up here."

Willy demurred. "I think I have a line on Herb. Should be quick, though."

The favor was implied, and Joe was struck by the way it had been phrased. Willy was not taken to asking for permission. He kept to himself, didn't reveal case details, and delivered results like some TV cowboy from the '50s. Joe occasionally fantasized that had it been feasible, Willy would have slung some of his bad guys over a saddle before bringing them in for questioning.

"You all right with this?" Joe asked. "Is there something else bugging you?"

"You want me to do a half-assed job?" Willy challenged him, his attitude surfacing.

"Just make it short," Joe told him. "You can give me the details later." He hung up before Willy did the honors.

Willy smiled at the phone before putting it down and readjusting the bottle, watching his daughter's contented face as she worked her cheek muscles rhythmically.

"Hey, daughter," he said in a near whisper, his face inches from her downy hair. "I may not be father of the year, either, but you will never not be the love of my life, no matter how screwy I get."

Joe reached Burlington at a little after seven, and knew without thinking which of Beverly's two primary addresses — home or office — to visit first.

Sure enough, after letting himself into the medical examiner's office via the coded keypad on the employees' entrance, he wandered through the quiet, tenebrous suite, enjoying the stillness here as he did in his own office in Brattleboro, until he reached her corner enclave, which predictably was filled with light.

He paused at the doorjamb and made a slight brushing noise with his shoe, enough to draw her attention without startling her.

She looked up from her desk, a quizzical expression immediately yielding to happiness.

"Joe," she said, smiling and rising to circle the desk. "God, what a sight at the end of the day."

She'd exchanged her standard scrubs for a summer dress with buttons running down the front, the bottom few of which she'd left open, for freedom of movement and style — of which he thought she had plenty.

Abandoning the reserve she wore along with her uniform, she looped her arms around his neck and kissed him long and passionately as he ran his hands along her back and below, inventorying what she was wearing underneath the thin fabric.

"Good Lord," she said finally, pulling away just enough to speak. "I do like what is developing here."

He laughed, kissed her again, and leaned slightly to one side to swing her door closed, his other hand gathering up the hem of her dress. "You mind?" he asked.

She kissed his earlobe, reached out as his fingertips touched her naked thigh, and snapped the lock shut on the door. "This is a first I've been dreaming about for years."

CHAPTER EIGHTEEN

Rob Perkins entered Gail Zigman's office and this time closed her door himself. He sat heavily in the chair opposite her and said, "We've just been royally fucked."

Gail removed her reading glasses and stared at him. "What?"

"Sheldon Scott," he reminded her in a dull monotone. "You sent me to meet with him. Turned out to be a classic bait and switch. If this goes the way I think, I will take full responsibility, say I acted unilaterally, and resign. I don't know if that'll be enough, but it can't hurt, and I deserve it anyhow for not having advised you better. For what it's worth, from the bottom of my heart, I apologize, Governor. You should have been better served."

Gail was openmouthed. "Rob, what the hell are you talking about? What happened?"

Perkins took a breath and tried again. "I'm

sorry. It was just so boneheaded. So amateurish — exactly what they were expecting from a bunch of tree-huggers. I feel like an idiot. My own arrogance made me careless."

Gail quietly slapped the top of her desk a couple of times. "Rob. Enough. You can beat yourself up later. Tell me what you're talking about."

"I went to see Scott, as we discussed, at his office. Only it wasn't at his office. It was upstairs."

"What's that mean?"

"In the Monday-morning quarterbacking coming next, it'll mean I was there for a secret meeting with the Dark Side — if you're on the left — or that the Zigman administration was being offered holy insight and guidance by the Yoda of politics, if you're on the right."

Gail nodded silently, preparing for what was coming.

"Scott has a room to make Jay Gatsby drool, all lined with books and photographs of him and the conservative glitterati. I'd never been there before, and I should've smelled a rat right off, but instead, I just wandered in — witnessed by some photogenic female flunky who no doubt will have a memory like an elephant's."

"Okay," Gail prompted him gently.

"Anyhow, he never actually said that Le-Mieur put a deal on the table, at least not like what Raffner outlined. Instead, he danced around, referencing LeMieur, avoiding any details, and babbling about how dear Harold is getting old and sentimental, wants to give back to his state, and is at death's door — which I don't believe for a second. Basically, it was contrived to make me suggest — very reasonably, of course — that the plan we heard from Raffner would be a bear to put in place in a timely fashion, that FEMA would probably freak out, and that I'd have to report back to you in any case — all of which I said right on cue. What it amounted to was a gigantic stall, designed to interest us, but without enough details to make it actionable."

Gail didn't respond, still waiting for the punch line.

"Then he stuck his fangs in," Rob went on. "Like a fucking cobra. Oozing sympathy, he immediately said — if not in these words — that this was clearly above the pay scale of a mere governor, and that the DC-Three should be the ones to handle it. It was put way smoother than that, of course, but that was the gist of it."

"He's telling us to fuck off and he's pitching it to our Washington delegation?" Gail asked, baffled. "After he initiated contact?"

"It won't be that simple," Perkins replied, not helping to enlighten her. "Or that clear. The punch line, Governor, is that he played us — or me — like patsies."

He rose to his feet and began pacing the width of the room, still speaking. "Everything we did seemed completely rational and aboveboard — that's key to any good con. A rich guy approaches through a trusted intermediary, offering financial aid in a time of public need. What do you do? You respond by meeting with his people and asking for details."

He stopped to address her directly. "But the fix is in from the start. 'Cause it has nothing to do with money. It has to do with politics. I will guarantee you that Scott's people are reaching out right now to the DC-Three — or, better still, did before our meeting — either telling them that LeMieur has made us an altruistic offer we can't handle, or that we approached him in desperation because we don't know what we're doing, can't figure out how to work with FEMA, and are running out of ideas."

Gail blurted out, "But the entire Washington delegation is Democratic, as is the president. What credibility does Scott have, or LeMieur, or any of their pals?"

313

Rob's sorrowful smile confirmed what she already knew. "That's the whole point, Governor," he said. "You got elected by thumbing your nose at the Democratic machine, including the D.C. contingent. You and Raffner, both. It was a populist fluke; a heady exception to the rule — typical of what can happen in Vermont. But the basics in this state are the same as everywhere else: Money talks, and money talks best to politicians."

He sat back down. "The capitalists and the DC-Three were blindsided by your election, but when Scott and LeMieur approach them with this fantasy, a number of irresistible possibilities are going to crop up." He held up a finger. "One, the Holy Trinity will peg this as a far-right capitalist attempt to take a slap at FEMA, them, and the president, and they'll hold you accountable for having set it in motion." A second finger went up. "Two, that reaction will justify Scott and company going into a rant and rave about how big government liberals are standing between the little people and an ailing rich guy's philanthropy." With the third finger, he concluded, "And three, after the conservatives have used your own party to crucify you, each camp will fuel the fire of public opinion by portraying you as an incompetent neophyte who's been caught playing out of her league. At which point — given voter fickleness — anything'll be possible, come the next election."

He paused just enough to take a breath and added, "Which is why I'm perfectly willing to take the bullet and say it was my idea to approach Scott in the first place, without your knowledge."

Gail was angrily shaking her head. "Out of the question. I won't let you do it. This is not a done deal. I will not be outmaneuvered by a bunch of political barracudas. We stuck it to 'em when we won the election; we'll stick it to 'em on this, too."

Perkins didn't respond. He was distracted by whether she was referring to Scott and his cronies — or to the leaders of her own party.

Joe Gunther rubbed his eyes.

"Am I boring you?" the old man inquired shrilly. "I don't want to put you to sleep just because I'm trying to save this institution from shutting down."

Joe blinked at Graham Dee and answered, "No, sir. You are giving me a headache; not putting me to sleep."

"Well, pardon the hell out of me."

Joe addressed the utterly useless assistant

315

director of The Woods of Windsor, "Mr. Whitby. I agreed to meet with you and Mr. Dee out of courtesy. I have done so now for an hour and have run out of time and patience. It has been made crystal clear to me that the board, personified by Mr. Dee, is unhappy with our line of inquiry —"

"Unhappy is hardly the word," Dee began again, before Joe cut him off.

"Be quiet, Dee. Enough is enough. I have listened to you politely. Now you get to do the same. If you interrupt me again, I'm leaving. Do not think for one second that I'm not aware that you asked for this get-together exactly when Hannah Eastridge was called out of town." He held up his hand to shut down Whitby's protest. "I don't want to hear it. I also want no part of your insider politics. A crime has been committed at this facility. We are being unobtrusive, polite, efficient, and working almost around the clock, given the schedules of the staff and residents. If you push me any harder with your complaints, I will fill this place with cops, pull off the gloves, and really give you something to bitch about. And if you're worried now about bad publicity and losing new applicants — as Mr. Dee has stated several times — then you are on a slippery slope of your own making, gentlemen, not mine."

Joe rose and headed for the door of Whitby's office, stopping there to conclude, "This is an official police investigation. Consult your lawyer about what it means to interfere with it."

With that, he walked out and closed the door behind him, finally releasing the smile he'd been suppressing while watching Dee's face change color throughout his speech.

He found Sammie in the break room adjacent to where they'd been conducting most of their interviews.

"Got an aspirin?" he asked her as she was fixing a cup of coffee.

"George Whitby?" she asked, not looking up. "I saw you go into his office."

"Whitby and Graham Dee. Apparently, we're ending the world as they know it, putting anyone and everyone under hot lamps and beating them with hoses."

She dug around in her bag and handed him a small bottle and a glass of water from the sink beside her. "God, if they only knew."

"Meaning what?" he asked, taking a couple of pills.

"Meaning ninety percent of the people we've interviewed so far are loving this.

317

Most of them disliked Marshall, so the gloves are off there, but they dish dirt on each other like nobody's business. It's all Les and I can do to keep them on track. If we weren't so interested in a silly murder of someone nobody liked anyhow — to quote one of them — we'd have a full caseload of extramarital affairs, food thieves from the dining room, old lechers putting their hands where they don't belong, and a closet full of scofflaws, cheats, tightwads, and tax dodgers. This is like *Peyton Place* meets *Dallas*."

She took a sip of her fresh coffee and raised her eyes at him. "And sex. You should hear about it."

He smiled at her. "Meaning I should sign up?"

She looked startled and then embarrassed. "Oh, boss."

He quickly reassured her. "Down, girl. Just kidding. Is Lester with one of them now?"

"Yeah. I was waiting for my next one to show up, so I thought I'd grab a cup."

"Great. Do you have time to give me a quick breakdown of where we are?"

They'd been given two interview rooms, access to the break room, and a back office they were using for a temporary squad room, to which only they and Hannah Eastridge held the key. Sam now led him there and briefed him on their progress, showing him a chart on the wall listing everyone of interest and how each related to one or more of the others, complete with photographs when available.

Gorden Marshall appeared all alone, near the top, marking the apex of a galaxy of residents, along with a few outsiders Joe recognized, like Michelle Mahoney. Above Gorden's name was a small cluster of outsiders, including the last Republican governor and other illustrious Vermont politicians and financiers from the past half century. Among those was one of the richest men in the country.

"He knew Harold LeMieur?" he asked Sam.

"Best buddies, from what we've been told. Harold's influence and money helped get Gorden where he got."

Joe walked up to the small photograph tacked to the end of the line drawn from Marshall's name to LeMieur's. It had been taken at a dinner and featured several men sitting at a long table, wearing tuxedos.

"Who's the Silver Fox?" he asked, tapping on the picture. "Next to LeMieur."

Sam squinted slightly. "Oh — Sheldon

319

Scott. The biggest conservative lobbyist in Vermont, which means he spends a lot of time out of state, where the right-wing oxygen makes him happier. He and Le-Mieur are joined at the hip."

She sat down at the table in the room's center and opened a master file. "Okay, this is what we have so far, which isn't much."

Although she and Lester had been conducting interviews for only a couple of days, they had made remarkable headway. One advantage was the locale — they didn't often have the luxury of an entire community being under one roof. For another, its population didn't wander much or far — thus, while the interview schedule had accommodated the odd meeting or bridge game or doctor's visit, by and large, it had functioned like an assembly line.

Sam, in her typically energized style, slid the file of accumulated interviews over to him, rose to her feet again, and stood beside the chart, in order to guide her boss through their discoveries to date.

"We decided to break the whole into categories, given the total number of people, versus just the ones who had anything to do with Gorden Marshall, which turns out to have been quite a few."

She tapped her finger on one group of

names. "These are people who knew him before he came here to live — fellow politicians, businessmen, lobbyists, and the like. Over ninety percent of them are men, but most of them have spouses or companions, which doubles the interview number for us, since we don't want to miss any potential pillow talk."

She continued in this vein, guiding him through her atlas of possible players, segregated into groups and subgroups like offshoots of an animal species. In the end, she stepped back to encompass the overall effort, and concluded, "The interconnecting lines tell us who's sleeping with whom — whether married or not — who had what kind of relationship with Marshall, and in what context, and who we think is most likely to have had a financial tie to him. In general, the guys have been pretty tight-mouthed, and the spousal/companion route has been a gold mine. The ladies are very happy to throw dirt at each other and the guys, both. But it's early yet."

Sammie shook her head. "Sad to admit, the whole deal isn't much different from what we're used to in the streets. These people just bathe more often."

"Amazing work," Joe complimented her. "Have you been able to figure out how many you have left to interview?"

"Not yet. Everyone we talk to adds some-body we didn't know about. Of course, many of those are duds — or too polite to talk freely — but a few have told us quite a bit. We've got a ton of homework left to do, and then we have to go over it again to make sure we've caught all the connective tissue."

Joe was flipping through the cover sheets, nodding. "Okay. I'm assuming you've found nothing so far fingering whoever killed him. We don't want to lose sight of why we're here."

"No," she admitted.

"You have a chance to check Marshall's phone records?"

"Yeah. We were hopeful when Michelle told you about the answering machine be-ing empty when it shouldn't have been, but so far, we found nothing surprising or unusual in the numbers he called." She waved her hand at the board with all the names. "Whoever left an incriminating mes-sage must've been one of these — blended right in. We did apply extra pressure on whoever we found in the phone record, but so far, nobody's standing out."

She sat back in her chair and let her hands drop to her lap. "Really frustrating, to be honest. To have so many suspects and none of them measuring up."

Joe closed the file. "Just have to keep digging. Any word from Willy?"

"He was at home last night with Emma. We're switching off tonight so he can go to Burlington. After that, he'll probably join us here."

"He and I talked about that. He said he wanted to finish up on the Rozanski thing, even though he has it on good authority that Herb's still alive."

Sam looked thoughtful. "Yeah, he mentioned it."

"And?"

She sounded quizzical. "I'm not sure. There's something going on with him and this case. He should have wrapped it up fast, and it's not really his kind of thing. But he's been talking about it, which he also doesn't do, and he's been super attentive to Emma since it started."

She smiled at that. "Not that I'm complaining. Don't get me wrong. He's a great dad and really helpful with watching her and all. But it's like he's going through something private that Emma alone can make better. Only since Rozanski."

Joe stood up. "You know all the devils he lugs around inside. He probably fell over something that hit home. That's why I cut him some slack. He actually asked me permission. That's a first."

Sam laughed, despite her concern. "Yeah. The boy's going off the tracks. Next thing, he'll stop kicking dogs and torturing suspects."

Joe joined her. "Naaaah." He checked his watch. "Speaking of which, why don't you head off home early and let me take over your interviews. I should've been on them sooner anyhow, so this'll give me an opportunity to get my feet wet."

Sam didn't need to hear the offer twice. "Thanks, Joe. I really appreciate it."

Willy closed the door of his car and looked up at the address number opposite. He was in Burlington's North End, on a block of nondescript, largely windowless buildings — warehouses and small wholesalers clinging to solvency like shipwreck survivors to flotsam.

He checked the location against the scrap of paper in his hand, crossed the street, and cautiously twisted the knob of the unmarked door in the cinder block wall before him.

He entered a shabby, poorly lighted office with three desks, two of them piled high with old catalogs and computer printouts. Seated before the third was a slender man, before the screen of a dusty, battle-scarred computer monitor covered with columned figures.

He turned at Willy's appearance, his face registering surprise. "Whoa," he said. "I'm sorry. We're not really open. I mean, not to the public. This isn't a business — not retail, anyway."

"Herb Rozanski?" Willy asked.

The man froze and the color drained from his face.

"I'm sorry?" he asked in a whisper.

"It's not what you call yourself now — Jon Fox; very Hollywood, by the way — but you're Herb Rozanski." Willy extracted his badge and displayed it.

The man swallowed hard. "Not actually. No, I'm not."

"You changed it legally. I get it," Willy said conversationally. "I might've done the same. Are we alone here?"

Rozanski pushed away from his desk and stood up, his right arm hanging limply by his side. "Yes. I'm the bookkeeper. The owner, he . . . he doesn't come by much."

Willy pointed at the arm, smiling slightly. "Saw blade. Mine was a bullet. But neither was an accident." He patted his left shoulder. "We're sort of mirror images." He waved casually at Rozanski and urged, "Sit,

sit. I'm not here to upset your applecart, Herb. Eileen says hi, by the way."

"Eileen? You spoke to her?"

"Yup," Willy confirmed, pulling another chair over and settling down, thereby encouraging Herb to do the same. "How do you think I found you?"

"She told you?" He was stunned.

Willy crossed his legs. "What do you think? That you're John Dillinger? You're a dead man. Nobody's looking for you. Probably nobody cared when you disappeared. You've been living a paranoid fantasy for decades now, looking over your shoulder for no good reason."

Herb's mouth tightened. "What do you want?"

"Don't blame Eileen," Willy continued, ignoring the question. "She's never told anybody else, and not just because they didn't ask. She's good people, and except for Nate, you're all she has left." Willy smiled. "And Nate's a basket case. Living in the woods for over twenty years hasn't done him any good at all."

Herb stared at him. "You talked to Nate?"

"That's how I convinced Eileen to open up about you — took me a home visit and two follow-up phone calls to get her there. She's very protective of you. I would've talked to Bud and Dreama, too, if they'd been available. You probably don't know this, Herb, what with all the fuss and bother over Irene, but your coffin came up full of rocks. After all this time, you're officially out of the closet, so to speak."

"What?"

"Storm water eroded the cemetery, exposed the coffin you were supposed to be in. Imagine how people felt."

Herb stared at him, speechless.

Willy grunted. "You're right. They didn't feel anything."

"Why're you here?" Herb asked, reacting to Willy's tone.

Willy gave him a hard look. "Good question. What've you done since you limped off into the wilderness?"

"What do you care?"

Willy's relaxed posture didn't change. "Don't give me 'tude, bro. I've wasted a lot of time hunting you down. This is when it better count for something."

Rozanski scowled. "What?"

"Tell me what you've been up to."

Herb was visibly thrown off. "I don't know. I moved here, to melt into someone else, mostly. I did odd jobs — whatever I could with one arm. Then I found this place."

"That's it? No family? No love life? What do you do when you're off the clock?"

Herb took in his murky surroundings. "I don't . . ."

"Hey," Willy suggested. "Gay guys can have a life, in this town, especially."

Herb refocused on him. "You know that?"

"Isn't that why Nate tossed you onto the saw blade?"

He hesitated before answering. "In part."

"The other part being what you and Nate each wanted out of your piece-of-shit old man."

"He took care of me," Herb said stubbornly.

"Tell me how," Willy challenged him.

"That whole thing with the empty coffin; throwing Nate out; taking me to Doc Racque to be patched up."

"And then throwing you out, too, because he couldn't live with the embarrassment of his own screwup."

"What screwup? He wasn't the one who cut me up."

"Wasn't he?" Willy asked. "Didn't he force the two of you to compete for his attention, whatever that was worth? Didn't he peg you as gay, maybe even before you did, and start driving that wedge between you and Nate? He fucked you up, good and proper, and then tossed the two of you out so he could play the martyr. Your fight with Nate was like manna from heaven. There was no reason for Bud to fake your death, except that it let him cut bait and forget about you *and* your brother."

"No."

"Your mom knew it," Willy persisted. "That's what killed her. Your father was a narcissistic bully, Herb — his way or the highway. And when he was faced with his own failures, he just slammed the door on them. You and Nate and Eileen, too, to a lesser degree — you were all three told to just figure it out on your own. Only Nate went into the woods to live like a hermit, but isn't that what you all did, in the end?"

Tears were running down Herb's cheeks. He rubbed them away with the heel of his one hand. "Why're you doing this?" he asked.

" 'Cause I'm pissed off, is why," Willy said, leaning forward and grabbing Herb's hand in his own and holding it up between them. " 'Cause of this and what it represents. You think you're the only one with a sob story? Stand in line."

Herb pulled away and glared at him. "*That's* what this is? Suck-it-up time? What a crock. You swagger in here with your crippled arm and brag about how quote-unquote people like us should just shrug off the past and get on with it? 'Gay guys can have a life'? What the fuck do you know about being gay? You clearly aren't."

It was a watershed moment for Willy — who knew too well that he was in the midst of transition. The old Willy would have kept the battle going, challenging this man for each foot of advantage. But that's not why he was here — not in whole. Part of him was angry and frustrated. But not at Herb Rozanski.

Willy sat back, relieved by Rozanski's outburst. He stated quietly, "No, I'm not. I've got other labels. I suppose everybody does, somehow or another, real or made up. I have a boss who can figure out shit like that. But me, I just get mad, and I get alone, and then I turn into a black hole."

To Herb's credit, he smiled, and said, "I know the feeling."

Willy nodded and stood up, moving toward the door. He opened it partway before looking back. "Jon Fox? Reach out to Eileen. She misses you. You could get to know her kids. And what the hell? Maybe Nate, too. He's changed, and could really stand some help. I always thought other people were

around to mess me up. I was totally wrong.
Don't make the same mistake."

CHAPTER NINETEEN

Joe looked up at the knock on the door-frame. The interview room was open, allowing him to see a slim, attractive, gray-haired woman, probably in her seventies, standing tentatively on the threshold.

"Hi," he said, rising and coming around the table.

"I was told that someone wanted to talk to me about Gorden," the woman said.

Joe escorted her to the chair facing his. "Yes. Thanks so much for coming. My name is Joe Gunther. I'm a policeman. Are you Nancy Kelley?"

"Yes, that's right," she said, sitting down as he returned to his seat. He'd been handling Sammie's scheduled interviews for several hours by now, making this number four. It had not been a productive evening so far, whittling down his expectations.

"Again," Joe began, "I appreciate your being here. I know it's not what you had planned —"

"Oh, no," she interrupted happily. "You people are all the talk. I'm delighted to be included."

"Great," he said without enthusiasm. "Well, then, as you probably already know, we're looking into Gorden Marshall's death —"

"Was he really murdered?" she cut in again.

Joe held up his hand. "Let's not jump the gun. First things, first."

She laughed. "Ah. You didn't answer. That means yes."

Joe smiled indulgently. "Very good. You've been watching your TV shows. Actually, we don't know that for a fact. It may turn out he died of natural causes. That's why all the interviews."

She looked slightly disappointed. "Oh."

Joe opened his notepad to a fresh page and cued his voice recorder. "I tape all these conversations so that there's no confusion later on," he explained. "Do I have your permission to do so now?"

"Of course," she said. "This is quite exciting."

"Outstanding," he muttered, quickly reviewing a few notes from Sammie's overview file. "Do you prefer to be called Mrs.

Kelley, or Nancy?"

"You can call me Nancy."

"And you swear under penalty of law that everything you'll be telling me today will be the truth to the best of your knowledge?"

"Oh, yes."

"Great. I understand that you are the widow of Jeremy Kelley, is that correct?"

"Yes. Jerry and I were married for fifty-one years."

Joe smiled. "Congratulations. Sounds like you two had a good time."

"It had its moments," she said cheerfully.

He looked up from the page he'd been writing on, caught by the phrase. Her face appeared as upbeat and slightly vague as before, but he sensed a look in her eyes that suggested he might have finally ended up with someone with a tale to tell.

"Mr. Kelley was a colleague of Marshall's, back in the day. Is that correct?"

She nodded. "Oh, yes, thick as thieves."

"He was also a state senator?"

"Not at first, but he became one. He was a representative for four terms before he ran for the senate seat. Won on his first try. He was always very proud of that."

"I can imagine. Is that when he and Marshall got together?"

"After Jerry won the senate? No, no.

They'd been working together before then. It wasn't like it is now, with everyone staying in their own corners, calling each other names."

"They socialized?" Joe asked conversationally. "I'd heard about that."

"Oh, yes." She smiled.

"Dinners at each other's houses; things like that?" he pressed, knowing very well that the socializing was often of a rougher nature, and often exclusive of spouses.

She hesitated. "Well, not so much that. They were mostly away from home. You have to remember, before 1965 — when the Supreme Court changed everything — it was 'one town, one rep,' regardless of population density. That made for two hundred forty-six representatives, most of them far from home, and that was before the interstate came in, too, so travel was much more involved."

Joe didn't interrupt, waiting to ask instead, "And where were you at this time? You married Senator Kelley right about then, if I have the dates right. That must've made you a little nervous as a young bride."

Her cheeks darkened a hint. "Jerry was a good man."

"I didn't say he wasn't. He was also a man. How did you two meet up?"

335

It was an obvious enough question, if borderline insulting, but she seemed at a sudden loss for words.

"Where was your hometown?" he asked, hoping that might help.

It did seem easier to answer. "Berlin," she said, with the Vermonter's emphasis on the first syllable.

"A stone's throw from Montpelier," Joe observed, leaving the implication hanging. By now, his interest in Nancy Kelley had sharpened. It was clear to him that she was being coy and evasive at the same time. Why, he wanted to find out.

"Yes," she acknowledged.

"You grew up in Berlin?" he asked pleasantly.

She seemed surprised. "Why, yes. I did."

"Sort of a shame what's happened to it over the years, with all the development," he said. "The hospital first and then the mall. Not that much left of what used to be a small town."

She was surprised. "You know Berlin?"

"Sure."

She frowned and glanced down, adding. "There's nothing left, if you ask me. Everything is new and modern and ugly."

"Well," he philosophized, "being right next to the capital made that pretty much inevitable, don't you think?"

"I suppose."

"And," he added with a friendly smile, "I bet as a teenager, you found Montpelier hard to resist, no? You and your girlfriends?"

She laughed, if a bit sadly. "You could say that."

He made an educated guess. "And that's where you got your first job?"

The humor spread across her face. "My goodness. You are good. How did you know that?"

He waved away the compliment. "Lucky. But that was the funny thing about those days. State government grew like crazy just before that big change in the '60s, when the Democrats began taking over. Did you get one of those government jobs?"

"I did," she admitted. "It was very exciting. There was such energy. Everything was changing, after all those years of . . . well, nothing, really. It was like the whole state suddenly found a heartbeat."

"I like that," he praised her. "What a great image. It must've been intoxicating."

"It was," she agreed.

"Did you make new friends? I mean, it's not like a country girl going to New York or anything, but it still must've been like entering a new world. I'm guessing you moved to Montpelier to live, too?"

She laughed again. "I did. I had a tiny apartment with two other girls."

He joined her encouragingly, "Isn't that great? I know the town pretty well. What was the address?"

Without hesitation, she recited it with a child's reflex, including the apartment number.

He didn't give her the chance to ponder her openness. "Right, right. A short walk to downtown. Not so easy when the snow flies, I bet, but not too bad. It's amazing how little those neighborhoods have changed. Chances are, your place is still housing young people who work for the state. What was your job, by the way?"

She fell into his conversational pattern. "I was a legislative secretary in the statehouse."

"No kidding? Wow. That's right where the action was. Well, it makes perfect sense now how you met your future husband. You practically worked together."

"Hardly," she corrected him. "We girls were invisible. We called ourselves the Boiler Room, just typing all day — endless piles of paperwork."

Joe sympathized. "That's tough. Builds up energy for after hours, though — for everyone, from what I was told. Montpelier was party central. I was living over the mountain back then, and still, I heard stories. People working all day and playing all night."

Her eyes glistening, she admitted, "We had some lively times."

"I heard rumors," he said, "of places just outside town where legislators and lobbyists and bureaucrats and everybody else would all go to drink and have a good time, regardless of their politics or how they'd treated each other on the floor."

"Those were no rumors," she said, looking coquettish. "That's what I meant when I said things had really changed."

Joe nodded in agreement and made his first effort to bring her into the here and now. "I gather several of the folks from those happier days are here at The Woods now."

"A few," she said.

"Like Gorden Marshall?" he asked.

"Well, yes. Of course, among others."

"How are things between you all, given the passage of time, and how things used to be?"

Her forehead wrinkled. "You mean, who killed him?"

He smiled. "We don't know that anyone killed him, Nancy. But since you bring it up, was there anyone who had a bone to pick with him?"

"He wasn't a nice man," she said candidly. "He never was. Still, if someone had wanted to do him harm, it seems to me they would have acted long before now. It's not like he had any power anymore."

"I heard he had something to do with the founding of this place," Joe told her.

She looked at him blankly. "I didn't know that."

"Did you have much to do with him?"

"No," she said. "After Jerry died, I almost never spoke to him."

Joe again scanned the fact sheet that Sam had prepared.

"Did you ever know Carolyn Barber?" he asked.

She paled abruptly and seemed ready to fall back into her chair, her other hand reaching to her forehead.

"Are you okay?" he asked, half rising. "Can I get you anything?"

"No, no. Please. Stay seated. It's nothing. It just surprised me. I mean that name —"

"Barber's?" he asked.

She seemed to be trying to gather her wits, and with some degree of calculation.

"It's just been so many years," she finally uttered.

He frowned at the unlikely explanation. The BOL featuring Carolyn's disappearance had gotten good coverage in the news, even with the ramped-up competition from Irene.

"Carolyn's gone missing," he explained. "It's been in the news. She was a resident at the state hospital and wandered away during the flooding. I'm surprised you didn't hear about it."

Kelley looked confused — but more, he thought again, by what she should say, rather than by what he was telling her.

"I don't read the news — or listen to it," she said. "It's too depressing. Carolyn's gone?"

Joe wasn't buying it. "Yeah," he confirmed. "Like a leaf in the wind. Did you know she was at the state hospital, in Waterbury?"

"Poor soul," she said sadly.

He moved along. "The reason I asked about Carolyn is because I ran across a mention that she was named Governor-for-a-Day, a long time ago, back when Marshall was at the peak of his power. No one seems to remember the details behind it. Supposedly, it was some weird publicity stunt."

Nancy Kelley had transformed completely. Her shoulders were hunched, her hands clasped in her lap, her head bowed, and her eyes downcast.

"It was more than that," she said — so

341

quietly, he wondered if the recorder had picked it up. Instinctively, he moved it closer to her.

"Tell me about it," he urged.

She looked up almost shyly, her age-creased face suddenly etched with anguish. "Why do you want to know?"

Joe took a stab at correctly interpreting her body language. "I want to see if I can help her. I think she's in trouble. Did you know her well?"

She nodded without comment, and admitted, "She was one of my roommates."

"In Montpelier?" he asked, amazed by his good luck.

"Yes."

"This is great news. We've been searching all over for her, hoping she was okay. Have you heard from her?"

She looked up at him as if responding to an electrical shock. "Me? Why would she call me?"

Joe tilted his head ambiguously. "I don't know. Why not? You were friends once. It's not that strange."

Her ready denial spoke of her rising anxiety. "No. I haven't spoken to her in over half a century."

"Ever since she was committed?" he pursued.

"I knew nothing about that," Kelley said with a catch to her voice. "Last I saw her, she'd *been* heartbroken, but she was happy."

"In my experience," Joe quickly followed up, "it takes someone else to break your heart."

A silence stretched between them, and Joe realized that Kelley was quietly crying, her tears striking the backs of her hands, which remained unmoving in her lap, still tightly interlinked.

"Tell me, Nancy," he urged her. "What happened?"

"She got pregnant," was the answer.

"Do you know by whom?" he asked after another long silence.

He could see only the top of her gray head as she said, "No. She never said. And then she went away."

"Did she have the baby?"

"I don't know."

Joe thought for a couple of seconds. "But you were roommates," he commented. "You must have known who she was dating at the time. Girls talk about that kind of thing, don't they?"

Her crying worsened, to the point where she began wiping her eyes and nose on her sleeve. Joe looked around, saw where Sam

343

had placed a napkin on the counter behind him, beside an empty coffee cup, and brought it to Kelley, kneeling beside her chair in the process.

He rubbed her frail shoulder as she put the napkin to use. "Tell me what happened," he repeated.

"She was raped," she whispered.

"Who did it?" he asked.

Her whole body shuddered. "She said there were too many to know."

Her weeping was uncontrollable by now. Under normal circumstances, given her age and the fact that he had nothing on her legally, Joe would have suggested bringing the conversation to an end.

But he wasn't so inclined. The absence of Carolyn Barber had been gnawing at him since he'd found her single footprint in Irene's muddy track. He'd had a foreboding then, similar to discovering that a small child had wandered off into a life-threatening environment. The complete absence of Carolyn Barber ever since had seemed proof of her demise, and hearing what Kelley had just told him only drove the sensation home — along with the dread that her end had not come accidentally. Now he had to consider that her killer might have been after her for a very long time.

Of course, he was sure of none of it, except that the only lead he'd found was sitting beside him right now.

He continued to rub Kelley's shoulder as he asked, "She was raped by several men at once?"

She nodded silently, still sobbing.

"How do you know this?"

"She told me."

"When did it happen?"

She didn't answer at first.

"Back when you two were going to those parties?"

She nodded again.

"When you met Jerry," he suggested more than asked.

She doubled over in response, as her crying turned to keening and her body began to shake.

Relentless, he rose behind her and began massaging her shoulders, murmuring, "It's okay, Nancy, get it out. It's been tearing at you for decades. Get it out. It's okay."

She finally calmed enough that he returned to her side, kneeling again, and said, "Tell me about you and Jerry and the parties, Nancy. And Carolyn."

Taking a deep breath, she straightened slightly, her face damp and her clothes stained with tears. "You were right," she said. "They were a regular thing, and Carolyn and I and some other girls were there a lot. It was new and fun and exciting. These were the most important people we knew. We ate well and drank like fish and even made some money, which meant something in those days." She faced him pleadingly to add, "And Jerry and I really did fall in love. That was real."

"I'm sure it was," Joe soothed her. "Look at how long you stayed together."

"Right," she said. "That's right."

"So, what happened to Carolyn?"

"I don't know, exactly. It was a big night. A crazy night. A major bill had gone through or something. It's been too many years, and so much was happening back then. But everybody showed up — lobbyists and legislators and staffers. You name it, they were there. There was a river of alcohol and girls we didn't even know . . ." She paused before finishing, "Things got carried away, even for us."

"Do you have any idea what happened?" Joe asked.

"No," she said. "We got separated. I only found her afterwards, in one of the bedrooms — this was at a hotel outside town. It's gone now. She was a wreck, only partly conscious, her clothes were a mess — what there were of them. She didn't remember much of anything."

"What did you do?"

"Put her back together as best I could and took her home. Two months later, she told me she was pregnant."

"Did she know who the father was?"

"No. She said she passed out entirely during the rape at one point. She had no idea how many there'd been."

Joe moved to sit on the edge of the table, still within reach. "I need to ask you some more questions, Nancy, as you can guess. But can I get you a glass of water or something before we continue? Or would you like to take a small break — maybe visit the ladies' room?"

Nancy dabbed at her eyes one last time with the damp napkin and sat straight up. "No. I'm fine. It's hard, but I'd like to get it finished with, if you don't mind."

"Of course," he said. "I want to ask you about what happened afterwards, but before we move on, I need to go over a couple of things about these parties."

She took a deep sigh. "All right."

"You made it sound like they happened all the time — or at least frequently. But surely what happened to Carolyn wasn't part of the norm, was it? Word would've leaked out."

"There were two types of party," she explained. "I should have gone into that. I was too upset. I'm sorry. There were the regular ones — with drinking and dancing and maybe a little hanky-panky between consenting adults — they happened often, mostly on weekends, involved all sorts of people, and weren't really organized."

She stopped to concentrate. "And then there was another type," she continued, "that involved a special bunch of men. I heard them call themselves the Catamount Cavaliers once, although when I brought it up, I was told to keep my mouth shut, or else. I'd come across a pin — like something you'd wear on your lapel — that had a gold *CC* mounted on it. Very fancy. And I asked what it was for."

"Who did you ask?" Joe wanted to know.

"Oh, it doesn't matter," she said. "He's long dead, and I only knew him by his first name anyhow. He told me they were like the Hellfire Club, of Ben Franklin's day, when he lived in England for a while. I didn't really understand what he was talking about, but I knew it had to do with sex. And that it was super secretive. I was told in no uncertain terms never to say a word about any of it, and I never did — until now."

"Do you know how it was organized?" Joe pursued. "Who its members were?"

"I don't know about the first, but the members were supposedly very influential — businessmen, politicians. I never knew. Any dealings that we girls ever had with them were under special circumstances, and the lights were either always out, or we had blindfolds on."

Joe was having a hard time imagining all this. Human debauchery was no stranger to him — not after so many years on the job — but this was still Vermont, and while he'd always assumed that some human misbehavior made it into the state to a degree, something like an organized men's sex club would have been a stretch.

Apparently not.

"How big was this group?" he asked.

"Not big. I always thought the pins and whatever else they did were just to make them feel special. The funny thing was that their parties and the regular ones sometimes happened at the same time in the same place, like when Carolyn was raped. We'd all go to what we thought was a typical blowout, but we'd never know when some of us might be invited upstairs to entertain the Cavaliers. It only happened once in a while. It wasn't the norm. I can't even swear that's what happened that weekend, with Carolyn. But I did find her in one of the upstairs rooms, which is what made me think the Cavaliers had something to do with it."

Joe was scratching his head. "A gang rape in the same hotel while the party was going on?" he summarized.

She repeated, "I told you things got out of hand. The Cavaliers seemed harmless till then — group sex with hoods and costumes and stuff that usually made us girls laugh. What happened to Carolyn only happened that once, that I know of. I think it really scared them. I know I was never invited to any of their parties after that, and I don't know anyone else who was, either."

Joe pondered what she'd told him while gazing at her in wonder — this small, slim, gray-haired lady with slightly gnarled hands and sensible shoes. He was trying his best not to imagine her in the situations that she'd so frankly detailed, while at the same time recalling what Sammie had told him about some of the shenanigans that regularly took place at The Woods.

"Okay," he said. "Let's move on a bit. What happened to Carolyn after she told you she was pregnant?"

Kelley raised her eyes to him. "That's the crazy thing — she made it sound like the most wonderful thing in the world. Carolyn came home one night, waving a wad of money and laughing, saying that her ship had come in and that they were going to do the right thing and take care of her and the baby from now on. She started packing right then and there. That was right after the whole Governor-for-a-Day hubbub, when she made the papers and was squired around like a celebrity."

"Who did she mean by 'they'?" Joe asked.

"She wouldn't tell me. Said that was the deal. If she identified them, everything went up in smoke. If you ask me, everything went up in smoke anyhow, because I never heard from her again."

"She packed up that night and disappeared?" Joe asked.

"Pretty much. It actually took a couple of days, but that was it."

"Did she talk any more about it during those two days? Anything that might help?"

She shook her head. "I asked, but she kept her mouth shut, even once accusing me, 'You want to ruin everything?' like this was some great move up for her."

"How about Jerry?" Joe persisted. "You

and he must've talked about this."

"We did," she conceded. "Especially after Carolyn's big day in the news. But he was as clueless as I was."

"But he was one of the Cavaliers, wasn't he?"

"Not Jerry," she said quickly, her face reddening, which made Joe suspicious.

"What about the baby?" he asked, letting it go. She'd been helpful so far, and he hadn't been gentle on her. He was willing not to challenge her devotion to Jerry.

But she couldn't help him. "The baby — as far as we knew — vanished with Carolyn," she said. "It was like a beam from outer space came down and took her away."

Joe let out a sigh. "It's an amazing story. I'm glad you got out of it with a happy ending, to be truthful."

"I know," she admitted. "You can be so stupid when you're young. Good thing I was lucky."

"What about your life afterwards?" Joe asked, looking to end their conversation on an up note.

"Jerry and I married. That whole world changed anyway. Vermont sort of joined the twentieth century, and everybody started acting more responsibly." She paused to stare into the middle distance before concluding, "Those were incredible times."

"I'm thinking Carolyn might agree with you," Joe said, adding, "She had a sister, didn't she?"

"Yes. Barb."

"Did you know her at all?"

Nancy frowned slightly. "No. We met once, but that was it. They weren't close."

Joe thought back to his conversation with William Friel, on the same topic. "Really?" he said. "I was told otherwise."

"Barb was very judgmental. She didn't approve of Carolyn's lifestyle."

"So the break occurred because Carolyn moved to Montpelier?" Joe suggested.

"If there was a break," Kelley said. "I didn't know them before. I thought they always hated each other."

Joe nodded sympathetically, imagining the older, plainer, less playful sister feeling left on the fringes of Carolyn's supposed happiness. "How 'bout afterwards?" he asked. "After the pregnancy. Do you know how Barb was then?"

"No. The one time I saw her was when Carolyn moved in with me. I always guessed she'd have an I-told-you-so attitude, though. She struck me as the jealous type. That's one of the reasons I was happy about Carolyn hitting it rich at the end."

Joe felt bad about having shattered such a cheerful image. But it also triggered one last inquiry. "I'm going to ask you a final question, Mrs. Kelley, and I want to stress to you that if you answer yes, you'll be in no trouble. I just need to know: Has Carolyn been in touch with you recently?"

She fixed him with her eyes and answered, "No. The last time I saw her could have been her last day on Earth. The break was that complete."

Joe nodded slowly. "I have a feeling she wouldn't argue with you there," he said.

CHAPTER TWENTY

Dave Spinney was almost as tall as his father, having reached his later teens, and liked to walk alongside him more in public than he'd used to, especially in Springfield, where they'd lived his whole life. Back when he was a kid, with his old man younger and more full of fire — and a trooper for the Vermont State Police — it hadn't been much fun. Dave's friends steered clear of him whenever father and son appeared together, and Lester made comments anyhow, if he recognized any of them from a distance — referring to whatever trouble they might have gotten into, or just avoided, or the company they were keeping.

That had been a real drag. Worse than having a dad who was school principal.

But now that Lester had been with the VBI for several years, fewer people knew him, he didn't chase after them in a cruiser anymore, and — his son could grudgingly admit — Dave had also grown up considerably. Especially after Lester had risked his job to save Dave's butt when the latter had gotten tangled up with a bunch all destined for jail.

That had been a confusing time, a chance to make some hard choices, and an opportunity to recognize his parents in a more mature light — with their fears, their vulnerabilities, and their love for him and his sister clear to see. He wasn't happy that he'd gone through it, but he was pleased with the end results — enough to have announced an interest in joining the state police in a couple of years.

They were at the local supermarket, doing the weekly grocery shopping, which Dave's mom often couldn't do because of her hours at the hospital.

That was fine with the men, since they had their own style and taste in food, with which Sue didn't argue.

"You having any more headaches, Dad?" Dave asked as they walked behind their cart.

"From when that guy bonked me?" Lester asked. "No. That only lasted a couple of days. I'm good now. I can't deny that I'm happier running interviews for a while, though. I tried jogging this morning and could still feel where he hit me." He tapped his head, now sporting a recruit's high-and-tight haircut to balance out the tonsorial damage left behind by the ER nurses. "Good thing it's not a vital organ, huh?"

He poked his son in the shoulder, grabbed a loaf of bread as they walked by the bakery section, and tossed it to Dave like an underhanded football. Dave snatched it out of the air and diverted it into the cart as they laughed.

"Ice cream?" Lester asked as they neared the end of the aisle.

"Cherry Garcia," Dave answered without pause.

They rounded the corner and aimed for a row of glass-fronted freezers when a young man appeared out of the end of an adjacent aisle, carrying a six-pack of beer.

Lester took no particular notice of him, until he saw him freeze in midstep and stare, as if caught in a searchlight at night. Instinctively, Les also stopped, reaching out to grab Dave by the back of his shirt.

Dave twisted, smiling, to ask what was up, while the young man dropped the six-pack on the floor with a dull thud and took off running in the opposite direction.

That did it. Lester, having not recognized the man's face, definitely remembered his awkward running style. This was the guy who'd smacked him on the head.

"Son of a bitch," he muttered, "it's him," and took off in pursuit.

Dave didn't hesitate. He followed his father, abandoning their groceries as they all headed for the broad bank of doors beyond the checkout counters.

"POLICE," Lester called out. *"Stop."*

Lester glanced over his shoulder. "Stay back, Dave. I want you safe. Phone 911. Officer in pursuit."

Dave dropped out of his father's peripheral vision while staying in the chase and pulling out his cell to make the call.

One by one, they dodged and weaved through the thin crowd, bursting out into the parking lot like successive coins shot from a slot machine.

The supermarket was located on the edge of downtown Springfield, in a shopping plaza built on a small peninsula, bounded on three sides by the Black River. A major roadway capped it across the top. Aside from an access drive to the road, far from the store's entrance, there was a single narrow pedestrian bridge spanning the water between the plaza and an old mill site.

This is where the runner headed.

Lester knew this part of town from driving around in search of a parking place.

Dave, on the other hand, had hung out here as a kid every Saturday night with friends. He knew it as he did his own living room. Instinctively, therefore, with no word to his father, he split off at an angle, using his youth, his long legs, and the lay of the land to best advantage, and went to cut off their prey from reaching the footbridge.

Their target saw him coming — as did Lester, whose caution shifted to pride at the sight — and veered off toward an awkward juncture at the edge of the plaza, where the river, the road's embankment, and a row of tangled trees all met up in an ignored and jumbled eyesore behind another building.

"Stop where you are," Les repeated, now panting with exertion. *"Police."*

Of course the other man didn't stop, and, judging the underbrush near the trees to be impenetrable, he plunged down the embankment through a tangle of storm rubbish and mud, toward the water.

"Damn," Lester swore under his breath as he and David followed suit.

Fortunately, they were spared anything beyond wet and muddy feet, as the guy before them slid on the loose talus of river rocks and went sprawling into a filthy mixture of water, mud, and urban trash that swirled lazily in a small eddy. Without comment, Lester and David each took hold of a leg and dragged their prize back to dry land, where — finally defeated — he just lay on the ground, looking up at them.

Expressing himself via gesture only — still gasping for air — Les reached out, smiling broadly, and slapped his son on the back.

"At the grocery store?" Joe asked, incredulous.

"It happens," Lester told him. "It's not that big a state. His name is Travis Reynolds. I ran his criminal record. Typical stuff — nothing over the top. He's a bad boy heading for worse. I have him locked up at the Springfield PD right now. Thought you might like talking with him."

Joe was back home in Brattleboro and checked his watch instinctively, not that he had anywhere else to go, or anything else to do just then. "You think he'll play?" he asked.

"I think he might with you," Les told him truthfully. "If you were introduced as the big boss holding a deal in his hand. I've let him know that we could lock him up for a very long time on what he did to me. He has no clue I couldn't pick him out of a lineup if you paid me."

"Sold," Joe said. "I'll be there in half an hour."

Springfield was less than forty miles north of Brattleboro, one among a scattering of industrial-era towns lining the shores of the Connecticut River — all once reliant and dependent on the water as a power source and a conduit to urban centers like Hartford and beyond, and now largely left to their own wits, surviving in a very post-industrial world.

As if reflecting this downturn, Joe's journey was thin on traffic and shrouded in darkness, in contrast to similar trips that he'd taken into Massachusetts and beyond, where signs of commerce and manufacturing burned late into the night. It was Vermont's particular burden to be the envy of its powerhouse neighbors — whose residents flocked to relax in its pastoral spaces — while it aspired to acquire at least a fragment of their capitalist musculature.

A burden that had been thrown even more into contrast by its beauty being devastated by Irene.

Springfield itself, however, had suffered little. A community founded on the force of its river, which carved through the heart of downtown, it had long ago harnessed, dammed, and confined the water's force between fortified embankments — and thus escaped most of the storm's rage this time. As Joe pulled into the police department's parking lot, the town looked much as it always had.

This was more than Joe could say for Lester Spinney, who greeted him in the lobby looking like a slime-fouled clam digger from the knees down. Behind him, Joe also noticed the poster telling of Carolyn's having gone missing, prominently displayed on the public bulletin board.

"I take it he ran," Joe suggested.

"You take it right," Lester confirmed, gesturing toward an inner door. "This way."

They located Travis Reynolds in a small windowless room, sitting on a steel chair at a bolted-down table, with one wrist handcuffed to a large ring mounted in concrete beside him. His entire body looked like Lester's shoes.

"Hey, Travis," Joe said cheerfully, entering the room alone and shutting the door with a theatrical clang.

"I'm Joe Gunther, second-in-command of the VBI," he said as he sat opposite the encrusted young man and began methodically laying out a pad, pencil, and a voice recorder. "Heard you've had better days, is that right?"

Travis made to ignore him until, startlingly, Joe half rose from his seat, leaned into his face, and shouted from inches away, *"Is that right?"*

Travis pulled back, his eyes round. "What the fuck, man?"

Joe followed, resting his hands on the tabletop to loom over him. He kept his voice loud. *"What the fuck?* Is that what you just asked me, Travis? *What the fuck?* Really? Is that what you're offering? *Answer me."*

Travis was pressed against his chair back, his chin tucked in, his cuffed hand pulling on the ring. His voice was plaintive and whiny. "Are you crazy? What do you want?"

Joe sat back down and looked at him pleasantly, his voice back to normal. "I want you to be very practical, Travis," he said. "I want you to think about what's best for you when you talk to me."

"I don't have to talk to you," Travis replied, but his voice lacked conviction.

"Oh, Travis," Joe said. "Do you want to take that chance? I mean, you're the one who put a cop in the hospital. Not something the state's attorney or any judge is going to like." He stopped, as if in thought, before continuing, "Let's see . . . what are you? A two-time loser? Damn. Not a great bargaining position. You never know, of course. You might get lucky and duck the hangman. It happens. Once in a blue moon."

Travis stared at him, clearly flummoxed by what he was hearing. In fact, he wasn't a two-time loser, nor was he facing any hangman, metaphorically or otherwise. Judges tended to belittle assaults on police officers, even with the additional charges Reynolds was facing.

"Travis?" Joe asked, his voice growing rich with warning. "I'm not a patient man, and I am seriously pissed off at you."

Travis swallowed, once. "What d'you want?" he asked quietly.

"To balance the books," Joe told him. "You tell me everything that got you in this jam, and I'll see what I can do to cut you some slack with the state's attorney."

Travis made a face. "You'd make my putting your cop in the hospital go away? I really believe that."

"Okay," Joe said, counting off the charges. "Aggravated assault, assault on a police officer, breaking and entering, theft, evading arrest, failure to obey a police officer . . ." He looked up. "That's just off the top of my head. I got more to play with, and I won't take any of it off the table unless you give me something. How good that is dictates how much I take off. Your choice."

Reynolds stared at him, but without defiance this time.

"No tricks," Joe said. "You do the math. This is a straight-up deal, 'cause I know you have something to give me."

Still, the young man resisted.

"Tell you what," Joe went on. "I'll add murder to the list for good measure, since you're the only guy we have for that, too."

"What?" Travis exclaimed. "I didn't murder nobody."

"Why do you think everybody's so interested in that fancy apartment?" Joe asked. "The old-timer who lived there was killed, Travis. Now, I don't know if you did that or not, but do you really want me to think you have something to hide?"

Joe slapped his hand loudly on the tabletop, making Travis jump in his chair.

"Now's the time to talk," Joe yelled.

"I didn't kill nobody," Travis said quickly. "It was just a grab job."

Joe smiled supportively, his voice again conversational. "Something you were paid for?"

"Yeah."

"Who paid you?"

"Some guy. I don't know his name."

"Tell me about that."

Travis pressed his lips together briefly, and then began his confession. "I got a call, like out of the blue. This guy said he heard I do odd jobs, and did I want to pick up five hundred bucks."

"He say how he heard of you?" Joe asked.

He shook his head. "And I didn't ask. What do I care?"

"Of course," Joe agreed.

"Anyhow, I said cool, and he tells me to go to the old folks' home, to go behind a Dumpster near the back, and find a cardboard box with a uniform in it and a key."

"How were you going to get paid?"

Travis tapped his temple with his finger. "Right, right. There was an envelope, too, with half the money in it." He laughed suddenly. "And I mean it," he added. "It was cut in half. Five one hundreds, cut in two. A note said I'd get the other half afterward."

"You keep the note?" Joe asked.

"Huh? No. Why?"

"How 'bout the money?"

Travis smiled. "Hey, man. Like that was a long time ago. That's long gone."

Joe nodded, resigned. "What else did the note say?"

"Told me to go to one of the apartments — gave me the number — told me to use

366

the key, and told me to do stuff.''

Joe merely raised his eyebrows in inquiry.

"Right," Travis repeated. "Let's see. There was a photograph in one room I was supposed to take. He told me to erase the answering machine. And there was a box in the dresser, in the bedroom, with a pin or something in it I was supposed to grab. That's where I bumped into your cop."

"How about some files, from out of the desk?" Joe asked, caught by the omission.

Travis looked at him. "Oh yeah. I forgot. Them, too, but they were already missing. It was just those three things."

"You're saying you were already in the apartment when the police officer entered?" Joe asked.

Travis registered surprise. "Oh, yeah. Scared the shit outta me. I was in the office, doin' the picture and the phone, and I heard him come in. I thought for sure he'd find me, but then he went the other direction."

"Why didn't you leave then?" Joe asked.

"And miss out on the five hundred?" Travis protested. "I don't think so."

"You knew he was a cop?"

"Oh, sure," Travis replied without thought. "You know, he had the camera case. Plus, he looked like one."

Joe moved on. "What did you do then?"

"Snuck up behind him and whacked him."

"With what?"

"I don't know. Some heavy statuelike thing I grabbed off the hallway table when I went in. I put it back when I ran out with the box."

Joe shook his head despite himself, thinking of the multiple errors. No one had even glanced at the marble figurine still sitting on the side table, not thinking that Reynolds might have done something so spontaneous to begin with, and so orderly afterwards. And he could hardly believe that Lester hadn't double-checked the apartment — except that it was all too human a mistake.

"You grabbed the whole box?" he sought to confirm.

"After that, I did, sure," Travis admitted. "I wasn't about to hang around with him on the floor."

"Yeah," Joe concurred. "But what exactly had the man told you to take?"

"A pin. A round one, like they wear on a lapel. You know, like those little American flags politicians have. But it was dark purple and had two gold letter *C*'s on it."

"He tell you what they stood for?"

"The *C-C*?" Travis asked. "Nope — no clue. But I found it in the box later, after I

368

got away."

"What about the picture?" Joe asked. "You said he wanted that, too."

"Yeah. I grabbed it," he said. "It was pretty small. Not much to look at."

"Describe it."

Reynolds shrugged. "Like I said, small. Black-and-white. The frame was kinda cheap. It was just a group of people."

"Recognize anyone?"

"Nah."

"Tell me about it," Joe urged him.

He looked faintly irritated. "I don't know — bunch of old people. Well, old people now, I guess. It was an old picture — the clothes, the hair — you could tell."

"How many?"

"Five, maybe?" he answered. "Men and women. It wasn't great. Looked like a party snapshot to me. They were drinking, lifting their glasses. That kinda stuff."

Joe stood up. "Hang on a sec."

He stepped outside to retrieve his case, which he brought back with him, sitting down to rummage through several folders he had within it. He extracted a single photograph and laid it before Travis.

"This one of the people?" he asked, pointing to a copy of the picture of Marshall posing alongside Carolyn Barber in the

Governor-for-a-Day shot.

"That's two of them," Travis confirmed.

"You're sure?" Joe asked.

"Yup. I remember her 'cause she was pretty, even for an old picture, and him because there were other shots of him around the room."

"And there were two or three others?"

"Yeah. At least one more woman — not much to look at — and a couple of dudes. So, yeah — I guess that does make three. I wouldn't know the other ones, though. Like I said. I just noticed these two 'cause of what I said — they kinda caught my eye."

"Like you said," Joe echoed quietly. He replaced the photograph thoughtfully. "Go back to the files that were missing. What were you told to steal, had they been there?"

"Everything in the *C* section. I didn't like that part, since I didn't have anything to carry them in, so I was just as happy they were missing."

"Tell me what happened after you lost the cop who was running after you," Joe said.

"I went back to the Dumpster and picked up the rest of the money."

Joe straightened. "It was already there? The missing halves?"

"Yup. Just like he said. I left the picture, the clothes, and the box — after I looked into it to make sure the pin was there, which it was."

"Then what?"

"Then I walked outta there," Travis said.

"You didn't drive there in the first place?"

"Nah. That's not how I work. Never leave the car near the hit — that's what I say. Makes for a slower getaway, but a cleaner one. Admit it," he said cheerfully, his eyes bright. "You never would've found me if I hadn't bumped into that cop, right?"

Joe shook his head sadly. "Wrong, genius. We never would've found you if you hadn't taken off. That cop had no idea who you were. It was your running away that he recognized. You forget you had a stocking on when you clubbed him?"

Travis stared. "Oh, shit. You're kidding me. Really?"

"Why were you wearing that anyhow?" Joe asked. "If you didn't expect to meet anybody?"

"It's my trademark," he said. "I never work without it." He sighed and slumped in his chair. "I can't believe I forgot that."

Joe let him stew while he reviewed what they'd discussed. "You said that the man called you," he said then. "How was that? You have a cell phone?"

"Sure. You guys took it when you busted me."

"That a disposable phone or a regular cell?" Joe asked.

"Nah. It's a regular one. I finally splurged."

Joe smiled. That meant that they might be able to trace its incoming calls.

"And he didn't say how he got your name?"

"Nope."

"You have any guesses about that?"

Travis hitched a shoulder. "I know a lotta people. Coulda been anybody."

That, Joe thought, was unfortunately true.

"He didn't introduce himself?"

"Nope."

"How 'bout later?" Joe asked. "After he found out that the files were missing. He must've called you back for an explanation."

"Yeah, he did," Travis said. "But he didn't seem to care once I told him. He just heard what I said and hung up. He sounded funny, but he didn't say any more."

"How do you mean, 'funny'?"

"Different, you know? Like he had a cold or something."

Joe frowned as he considered another possibility. "A cold?" he then asked. "Or maybe wasn't the same guy?"

Travis nodded receptively. "Oh, yeah. That would work. It wasn't a great connection — like a bad cell phone. But sure. It mighta been somebody else. I didn't think of that, 'cause we were talking about the same thing. But that would explain it."

Glad it explained something to you, Joe thought.

He met Lester outside, who immediately said, "I was listening from next door. I've already started the paperwork to get into his phone. Who do you think it'll be?"

Joe shook his head. "Damned if I know at this point. Someone who's clearly hoping to erase the past, along with Carolyn Barber's role in it."

Lester looked at him steadily before he asked, "You think she's dead, don't you?"

Joe's own cell phone went off as he replied, "I wouldn't be surprised. If I were some of these people, I wouldn't want her alive with her name plastered all over the state." He hit the answer button without looking at the screen. "Gunther."

"It's Beverly."

He broke into a broad smile and moved away from his colleague, crossing to an adjacent office. "Hey, there. How're you doing?"

"Actually, pretty well," she answered in her precise language. "I've discovered something I think you'll find valuable."

"Okay," he said. "I'm all ears."

"Following our last conversation," she told him, "I returned to the two house fire victims from Shelburne. I couldn't let it go."

He nodded appreciatively at the phone. "God, you are good."

She responded, "I don't know about that, but I like to be thorough. As you know, I was troubled by my inconclusive findings concerning Mr. Friel. So I tried a few things that lie just a bit outside the protocols."

"Yes . . . ," he encouraged her.

"Well, one of the by-products of the fire was that his heart suffered from charring and shrinkage, as did the rest of his body. I therefore took several of his major organs and analyzed them more carefully, including the heart, which I rehydrated so that it would return — at least in part — to its original dimensions. It was far from perfect, of course, but it was an improvement over what I'd first analyzed."

"You did find that bullet," he stated, now only half joking.

This time, she remained serious. "Not quite. It was a hemorrhagic wound track."

He tightened his grip on the phone. "A

knife wound?"

"More like a skewer," she answered, "as in a shish kebab. I was thinking of an ice pick, except that those have become virtual antiques by now."

"You're sure?" he asked. "I mean, enough that you'll be amending the death certificate?"

"Oh, yes. That's why I wanted to tell you first."

"You are something else, Beverly. Nicely done."

"You're very welcome, Joe. My pleasure."

He snapped the phone shut and returned to where Spinney was filling out paperwork.

"Good news?" Les asked at his boss's expression.

"Depends on who you are, I guess," Joe said. "Hillstrom just figured out that William Friel was stabbed in the heart."

CHAPTER TWENTY-ONE

The entire squad was back in Brattleboro, for their first staff meeting in days. They'd been dropping by individually, to catch up on paperwork and collect messages, but it felt odd to have them all in the same room again.

"It's been a bit of a grind," Joe told them from his spot of preference, sitting on the windowsill. "But we're making headway, and I thought we should compare notes face-to-face. Willy, let's start with you and Rozanski."

"Nothing to tell," Willy reported with predictable brevity.

"Aside from what you will tell us," Joe responded pleasantly and without hesitation.

Willy, feet propped on his desk, sighed. "No runs, no fouls, no errors," he said wearily. "Herb Rozanski is alive and well, if a little mangled, and living under a legal alias in Burlington. He and his brother, Nate — also alive and a hermit in the Kingdom — agree that they had a fight and that their dad covered it up by pretending Herb got killed. Was it against the law? Yeah, but the old man's dead, and nobody gives a damn, so I'm declaring the case closed." He waited for a reaction before adding, "Unless there's an objection."

Everyone knew better, and Joe also knew that Willy's report would be complete and properly filed, if it hadn't been already. Despite his unregimented demeanor, Willy was maniacal about tending to details.

Joe therefore let the subject slide. "Good. Now to the swamp pit that's been swallowing the rest of us. To begin with — right or wrong — we thought we had a missing state hospital patient, an ex-politician dead of natural causes, and two people killed by an accidental house fire in Shelburne. Some of us have been pursuing different aspects of these three cases, but since it's become pretty clear that they're all cross-connected and a whole lot more complicated, I'm thinking that from here on, we better treat everything as a single unit, just to be on the safe side."

He held up the photograph of Carolyn Barber and Gorden Marshall on her big

377

day, decades ago. "This, for instance, shows two of our major players, back in the '60s. There is no way in hell that her disappearance and Marshall's suspected murder don't overlap."

"Like as part of the Catamount Cavaliers?" Willy suggested, adding, "I been reading the reports."

"Perfect example," Joe agreed.

"How solid are we on Marshall being a homicide?" Lester asked. "I know Hillstrom found a stab wound in Friel, but are we still relying on Marshall's damaged upper lip as our only proof of foul play?"

"You got circumstantial stuff, too," Sammie contributed.

Joe pointed to her and nodded. "Right. It's not bulletproof, but somebody made an effort to stop us from reaching back into Marshall's history."

"There's no downside to working him as a homicide," Willy said generally.

"Speaking of Marshall," Joe said. "Did we get anything more out of his phone records?"

"Not much more than what I told you," Lester said. "There was a reporter from the old days who told me they just reminisced. The guy said he was writing a history book and found Marshall to be pretty useless.

And there was a call from an outfit named Scott and Company. Sheldon Scott is a conservative lobbyist who used to be buddy-buddy with Marshall way back when, but from what they told me, it wasn't Scott who phoned."

"Who was it?" Willy asked.

"They didn't know and couldn't track it — or wouldn't — but Scott himself was out of town."

"It still may not be a dead end," Sammie said.

"The phone records?" Joe asked. "Or Scott and Company?"

"Either. The *messages* on his machine were erased. To me, that sounds like it wasn't 'who' that was being covered up, but 'what' that person said."

"What do you think was in the files from Marshall's desk?" Willy asked. "There doesn't seem to have been much follow-up about them."

"Probably related to the Catamount Cavaliers," Joe stated, "but no way of knowing."

"Except," Willy pursued, "that Travis Reynolds said they were already missing, which means they were probably taken at the time Marshall was snuffed. The rest — the picture and the lapel pin and the phone messages — happened later."

"The killer forgot the other stuff?" Lester asked. "Or he was interrupted?"

"Crazier things have happened," Willy answered. "But I'm betting on something else."

"There were two of them," Joe filled in.

Sam and Lester looked back and forth at their colleagues.

"What?" Sammie asked.

"Somebody knocked off Marshall and boosted the file —," Willy began.

"— And somebody else hired Travis to rip off his apartment," Joe finished. "I like it."

"Two separate parties covering their tracks?" Lester asked.

Sam was already nodding in appreciation. "It does work. I mean, it's as good a theory as anything else we got."

"Why, though?" Lester challenged them. "Why kill Marshall, why steal his file, and why would somebody different come back later to steal the other stuff? Pretty unpopular guy."

"Not just that," Joe mused. "But the second party heard about the death almost before Marshall's body started cooling."

"The former Cavaliers," Willy suggested. "Horny old fuckers still covering their asses. He was supposed to have coffee with pals on the morning he turned up dead. Think one or all of them might be old Cavaliers?"

"And, if not," Sam said, "we know how fast news travels in that place."

"It can't be that hard to find out who the Cavaliers were," Lester suggested. "Go back to the archives, find out who was in power, who the local cops were, the hotel owners, all the other players. There'll be others like Nancy Kelley, with stories to tell."

"How 'bout Travis's phone records?" Joe asked then. "We get anything there?"

"We got the numbers," Sam said. "I'm still connecting them to who they belong to. Won't be much longer."

The buzzer went off on Joe's desk phone. He picked it up and answered, "Gunther."

"There's a man down here who'd like to talk to you. Name's Michael Nesbitt."

"Hang on," Joe said. He covered the mouthpiece and asked the group, "Anyone know Michael Nesbitt? He's downstairs. Wants to talk."

He got a universal response of blank stares.

"Send him up."

Minutes later, there was a tentative knock at the door. A small, round, unremarkable man in a baseball cap appeared in their doorway.

"Mr. Nesbitt?" Joe asked. "Come in. What

can we do for you?"

Their guest reached into his pocket and extracted a crumpled piece of paper. "I saw this on a wall," he said, "and thought you'd like to know that I saw this lady. It said to contact you, but my phone's still out, and I don't own a cell, so, since I had to be down here on other business anyhow today, I thought I'd just come over."

Sam, being nearest to him, took the poster from his hand and flattened it on her desk. It was Carolyn Barber's BOL advisory. Sam held it up silently so the rest of them could see what Nesbitt was talking about.

"You saw Carolyn Barber?" Joe asked.

"I gave her a ride," he answered.

"From where?" Willy asked.

"Near Waterbury. I live in Williston — well, a little south of there — and I was heading home in the storm when I saw her by the side of the road. She was a mess, so I stopped to see what I could do."

"This was during Irene?" Lester asked.

"Yeah. I'd been doing some catch-up work on Sunday. I work — well, I *worked* for the state — Natural Resources — and I was heading home, like I said. . . ." He paused and looked around, increasingly at a loss for words.

Joe walked over to him. "Mr. Nesbitt, I'm

sorry. We've been very rude. Have a seat and take a breath. We were just caught off guard by your news. We've been looking for Carolyn for a while." He pulled a guest chair away from the wall and steered Nesbitt into it, asking, "Would you like a cup of coffee?"

Nesbitt sat but waved away the offer. "No thanks. I'm all set."

Joe pulled out another chair and sat near him. "Okay," he resumed. "From the top. The storm was getting bad, you were told to head home, and you saw Carolyn by the side of the road. Is that about it?"

"Right. She was just standing there, soaking wet."

"How was she dressed?"

"A long . . . kind of, I don't know. I guess it was like a robe or a coat of some kind. Not very thick. And she had like a dress underneath it."

Joe tried to interpret the description. "Did it really look like clothing, or was it maybe more like the kind of thing they give you in a hospital? Was it a robe like that?"

"Yeah, yeah. It was. And she didn't have shoes."

"Both shoes were missing?" Lester asked pointedly.

"Yeah. I know that 'cause I commented

on it. I was really worried about her. She was out of it."

"You didn't take her to the hospital?" Willy wanted to know.

Nesbitt faced him with his hands spread out. "I tried. I really did, but she got so worked up, I didn't dare. I didn't want to make her any worse than she was. Plus, she told me where to go."

"Where was that?" Joe asked.

"To her sister's, in Shelburne. That's not that far from me — not when you consider the circumstances. So I was happy to help her out. I mean, I was heading out anyhow, and it felt good to lend her a hand. She was in a bad way."

"How so?" Sam asked. "Cold and wet only, or something else?"

"Oh, no," Nesbitt emphasized. "She was that, sure, but she was like, funny, you know? Talking weird and stuff. It kind of made me nervous at first, when I thought maybe I'd picked up a nut. But she was super nice once the heater kicked in and she knew I was doing what she asked."

"Taking her to her sister's, you mean?"

"Right. After that, she quieted down. I had a blanket in the back seat that I gave her, too, and that helped, I think."

"What did you talk about?" Joe asked.

"I asked her what had happened, and she said she'd been flooded out, which wasn't hard to believe. That's why she wanted to go to her sister's. It wasn't exactly clear with all her muttering. After I saw the poster, I guess I was pretty stupid. She said she was surprised by the rising water, and barely got out with her life." He paused again and added ruefully, "Guess that's what happens when you fill in the blanks on your own. I couldn't have been more wrong."

"Understandable," Joe soothed him. "What else did you two discuss?"

"Not much, to be honest. She fell asleep as soon as the heat got to her. I watched her pretty close at first, 'cause I wanted to make sure she was *only* sleeping. Know what I mean? But she was." He allowed for a small laugh. "I actually felt better when she started snoring a little. That seemed like a good sign."

"How did you know where to go?" Sam asked.

"Oh, I woke her up when I got near to Shelburne. She just pointed the way. She didn't seem totally sure about it, but she got it right in the long run."

"You remember the address?"

"Not exactly, but it was a dead end, parallel to Route 7."

385

"Hillside Terrace?" Lester asked.

"That was it," he said happily.

"And then what?" Joe asked. "Was the sister there?"

"The nephew was. I knocked on the door when we got there, and this guy opened the door. He was really surprised to see us. You could've knocked him over with a feather. He was all pale and at a loss for words. He offered me money, but I said no, that I was happy to help, and that was about it."

"So you never saw the sister?" Joe pursued.

Nesbitt's expression saddened. "I think I did, actually, not that I was introduced. But when the nephew opened the door, I saw an old woman in a wheelchair behind him, just staring at nothing. He saw me looking and just said something like, 'My mom — Alzheimer's' or something really short like that."

"How did you know he was the nephew?" Willy asked.

"He came outside to help me get her out of the car," Nesbitt explained. "Called her 'Aunt Carolyn.'"

"How did she act when he did that?"

"She was still pretty out of it," Nesbitt told them. "She didn't really say anything to him, and he seemed stunned anyhow.

Now that I know more about her from the poster, some of that makes sense. I guess he sure didn't expect to have her show up on his doorstep." Nesbitt looked around at them all before asking, "What was she in the hospital for, anyhow?"

"Mr. Nesbitt," Joe asked instead, "Why did you take all this time to get hold of us? It's been a while."

He raised his eyebrows. "Oh. I been out of state. Like I said, I sort of found myself on involuntary leave — that's the way they put it — so I went south to visit family for a while. Wasn't till I got home yesterday that I saw that poster at the town office, where I was settling a bill. There's no picture, but my eye caught on the name Carolyn. That's what the nephew called her. And then the description on the poster did the rest, mentioning the date and Waterbury and the storm and all the rest. Even down to her outfit. That's when I decided I better get in touch, since I was coming to Brattleboro anyhow."

Joe stood up. "We're glad you did, Mr. Nesbitt."

Lester stood also and took their guest's elbow. "Why don't you follow me next door so I can get this all down as a sworn statement?" he asked. "That way, we'll get the whole process squared away and you can be free of us from now on."

Nesbitt began following him outside, but hesitated at the door to ask, "Is there any reward for what I told you? I'm sorta between a rock and a hard place right now."

"No," Joe told him. "Sorry."

Nesbitt shrugged and left, following Lester.

"Milk of human kindness," Willy said as the door closed.

"Good for us, though," Joe said. "What d'you make of it?"

Willy was first. "Tells me Friel was lying his ass off when you and Spinney dropped by to chat."

Joe nodded, remembering the greeting that he and Lester had received in Shelburne. "Friel asked us to wait at the door, in order to prepare his mother for our coming in — more likely, it was to make sure Carolyn had time to go into her bedroom in the basement."

"It also means Carolyn wasn't so far gone that she didn't know what to do once she got out of the hospital," Sammie added.

"Okay," agreed Joe. "But then what? She escapes; they put her up and keep mum to protect her; then something goes off the tracks."

"Marshall gets killed, for one thing," Willy said.

"Right after it's circulated that Carolyn's on the loose," Sam added.

"But not circulated by us," Lester pointed out. "We took a while with her posters."

"So, by an insider," Sam came back.

"And then, one-two-three," Joe chimed in, "Friel gets stabbed, Barb gets cremated alive, and presumably, Carolyn gets grabbed."

"Or killed," Willy suggested. "No point keeping her alive, and it would probably be easier to kill her before smuggling her out of the house."

Joe recalled something Jonathon Michael had told him; "The bulkhead door was unlocked. Anyone could have gotten in, whenever they chose."

The other two stayed silent, playing out a list of variations in their minds. Joe stood up, pushed the guest chair back against the wall, and reached for his jacket.

"Where ya headed, boss?"

"The scene of the crime."

Sam turned to Willy upon Joe's departure. "That mean anything to you?"

"He has a itch he wants to scratch in private."

She used that to change topics. "You would know about that."

"That a loaded comment?" he asked. "Or just practice?"

She smiled, used to how his inborn paranoia processed things. "Checking your dipstick," she answered him. "You been on some kind of odyssey. I just want to make sure you're okay. That *we're* okay."

Instead of the usual quick one-liner, he kept quiet, which made her rise from her chair and sit on the edge of his desk, where she rested a hand on one of his crossed legs.

"Herb Rozanski?" she asked.

He didn't look at her. "He's got an arm like mine," he said.

"From the saw?"

"Yeah. He got it sewed up, but it never worked again."

"He okay?"

He gestured dismissively, but answered nevertheless, "He's coping. Might as well be hollowed out, though — a living pumpkin. Smile on the outside; nuthin' inside."

She squeezed his leg. "There but for the grace of God? That what you're thinking?"

"Grace of something," he offered. "Don't know about God."

"How 'bout grace of yourself?" she suggested. "Grace of the people that love you?

What's Herb got?"

She'd heard enough about the Rozanski case to know part of what was eating at him. Willy was deemed unapproachable by most people, but to her, he wasn't that complicated. This was a smart man with a big heart that had been stepped on enough to make him angry, suspicious, and in pain. That's how she saw it, all the babble about PTSD and the rest notwithstanding. She'd seen him with their daughter, and had been won over by him herself.

"How'd you leave it with Herb?" she asked, thinking that might have played a role in his present mood.

"Told him to go back to his brother and sister." His voice was so quiet, she barely heard his words.

"You think he will?"

"I doubt it," he admitted candidly. "He's pretty far gone."

"You tell him they'd be open to it?"

His voice rose slightly. "Oh, sure. Mouse fart in a high wind, if you ask me."

"And so there it sits," she mused, hoping to be echoing his thoughts. "Like a ball game suspended in the middle of the last inning."

"Yeah, well . . ." He left it there.

She leaned over and kissed his cheek, and

spoke into his ear. "Unless maybe you get one of them to get in touch."

He straightened in his chair, pulling away from her a bit. "Not my problem, babe. They wanna fuck up their lives, I'm not their nursemaid."

She moved her hand up his thigh, smiling. "You know you want to. You just don't want it to fail. It's already failed. How can your giving it a small push do any damage?"

He looked at her then, his expression critical. "Jesus, listen to you. Mother Frigging Teresa. You'd think you would've learned by now."

She laughed and got up, knowing better than to push. "I had, till I met you. You made me an optimist."

Joe stood beside his car, taking in the neat, square, rubble-filled cellar hole on Hillside Terrace. He was struck by the sad irony that what was once the foundation of a family home had become the custom-made receptacle for its charred remains. There was a discussion about preserving the wreckage as a crime scene, complete with around-the-clock guard, but the consensus had been that it was all too little, too late by now, and that the case against the killer of William Friel and his mother would have to rely on evidence beyond what might be lurking here.

Which is what had lured Joe back. For, while the site had been destroyed — no doubt with the hope of erasing all traces of a crime — that crime had nevertheless taken place. And it was Joe's experience that — as with a lingering odor — the residue of such an event often hovered in place, sometimes to the advantage of those in search of it.

As if on cue, he saw what he was looking for, even sooner than he'd anticipated. There was a movement at one of the windows neighboring the Barber property, indicating — Joe anticipated — the presence of the almost customary neighborhood busybody.

He left his car and crossed the street to knock on the front door.

He didn't get the opportunity. The door opened as he reached the front porch steps.

"Are you from the insurance company?" a woman asked, whose body and hairstyle reminded Joe of a Saint Bernard on its hind legs.

"Police," he countered. "Joe Gunther. And you are?"

She stepped out onto the porch. "Karen Freed. I thought the police were finished here."

They didn't bother shaking hands, having already passed that part.

"Oh, you know," he said lightly. "The usual ton of follow-up paperwork."

"I thought it was a homicide," she said, her voice rising.

He continued up the steps. "What makes you say that?"

Her eyes narrowed craftily. "Okay. I get it. Don't worry about me. I'm going to my grave with all my secrets intact. People know that about me around here."

Joe wasn't quite sure what that meant. He stayed quiet.

"I saw it go up," Freed said. "My house was built the same time as Barb's. If you're telling me that was an accident, I'm selling tomorrow, 'cause it exploded like a bomb."

"And that's why you're thinking homicide," Joe suggested.

She smiled, and for a moment, he thought she added a wink. "That's why *you're* thinking homicide," she said.

He didn't argue. "Okay. You seem to be aware of what happens in the neighborhood, could you tell me what you saw that night?"

"I already told a cop in uniform."

"I'm aware of that," he lied, having relied on Jonathon Michael's narrative, rather than on individual statements. "But sometimes, with the passage of time, memories sharpen."

"It was real sudden," Freed recalled, needing no further prompting. "I was sitting watching TV, and there was a bright flash out the window — and a boom, like an explosion. Shook the house."

"When was this, roughly?"

"Late. About eleven."

She hadn't asked him in, so Joe settled onto the porch's broad wooden railing, enjoying the sun on his back. She remained standing, framed by the open doorway behind her.

"Any comings or goings from there earlier that you noticed?" he asked.

"Earlier that night? Nope."

"How 'bout right after?"

But she rejected that. "There was tons of action after the fire department got here, and that was pretty quick. They were really fast and good, moving cars around and setting everything up, just like on TV. But it was a goner as soon as I saw it through my window. The whole house looked like the mouth of a volcano. That's why I know it's a homicide — that a bomb did 'em in."

"I take it you knew Barb and her son?" Joe asked.

Freed looked disapproving. "Oh, yes."

"That doesn't sound good," he said, lead-ingly.

She pursed her lips. "Very odd people."

"How so?"

"Oh, you know . . ."

Joe didn't let on that he did, remaining silent.

Freed sighed impatiently. "You ever meet them?"

"Once," he admitted. "Of course, that was after she'd been disabled."

She broadened her stance slightly, as if responding to a boat deck's slow roll. "I know it's horrible to say, but that disease was the only thing left that could quiet that woman down."

Even for Joe, who'd heard some pretty harsh things, that was a corker.

"Really?" he said as blandly as he could.

"She was like the Wicked Witch of the West," she explained. "Treated everybody like dirt, no matter what they did. Most negative person I ever met. And the way she talked to *him.* It was terrible."

"Yelled some?" Joe prompted.

"I'll say. He could never do anything right."

Joe tried to be philosophical. "They say that anger and paranoia often run hand in hand with Alzheimer's."

But Karen Freed was having none of it. "Bah. Unless she'd had it for forty years, I wouldn't hide behind that fig leaf. She was just a terrible person. Sometimes, there's no getting around it."

"And yet he stayed with her."

She considered that. "Yes," she agreed. "That confused me, too, at the beginning. But sometimes a man is just too spineless to act in his own best interest. Plus," she added. "It was her house, and as long as he could put up with her, he lived there for free. I bet he used all her money for groceries and the like, too. I never saw him work a lick, so that has to be true."

Joe thought back to something that Beverly had mentioned in passing. "You think he might have killed her and committed suicide?" he asked.

She looked genuinely astonished. "Good Lord. What a thought." She paused. "I suppose it's possible," she added without conviction.

"I'm not saying that's what happened," Joe carefully followed up. "But you knew them better than I."

"Then I'd say no," she replied. "He didn't have it in him. Besides, the smart thing would have been for him to kill her and live happily ever after. Nobody would have been suspicious — a woman in her condition."

Joe reflected on an earlier comment. "Mrs. Freed, you said that when the fire department showed up, they moved some cars. What did you mean by that?" He turned to point across the way. "I see his Chevy right there, and it looks like it got burned pretty badly. Did they move it?"

"No, no," she said. "The other one. Her car. That's the one they moved. It was closer to the house."

Joe was still for a second, trying to process this. "What kind of car?" he asked. "Is it on the block now?"

She moved, marching to the edge of the porch, resting her hands on the rail like Captain Bligh, and scrutinized the street.

"No," she announced. "It's not there. Maybe they towed it. It hadn't been legal for years. It was a Buick Skylark — dark green."

"You remember the plate number?"

She gave him a withering stare. "I don't go around keeping things like that in my head."

"Of course," he said agreeably. "Did you actually see the car being moved? I'm just trying to figure out who drove it."

She tucked in her chin thoughtfully. "No.

398

One minute it was there. The next, it was gone."

"And now that we've been discussing that whole evening, can you recall anything else? Something you saw through one of their windows, maybe? Or something you heard?"

A look of distaste crossed her face. "I'm no Peeping Tom. What do you take me for?"

Joe kept that to himself and thanked her for her time.

CHAPTER TWENTY-TWO

Gail was pacing the floor of her office. Once more, the door was closed, and the only people in attendance were her innermost circle, including, among others, her chief-of-staff, Rob Perkins; her personal assistant, Alice Drim; and — oddly, in Rob's opinion — the head of her security detail, John Carter, who actually worked for the state police.

"You all need to know that a shit storm other than Irene is heading our way," Gail was saying. "Each one of you — press secretary, security, legislative relations, and the rest — will have to keep an eye open. I know Rob is usually the one to break this sort of news, but this is special."

She stopped long enough to face them. "We were recently approached by Sheldon Scott, representing Harold LeMieur, who was supposedly offering an alliance where his money would be used to supplement whatever FEMA didn't cover. In true independent Vermont style, this was to be a practical, homegrown solution to some of the confusion and anger that's beginning to heat up and which made Katrina such a disaster years back."

Rob watched her face like the dispassionate political scientist he tried to be at his best, seeing the stress, the sleeplessness, and even the fear beneath the smooth and cadenced prose.

Of course, he wasn't at his best — he was feeling directly responsible for her awkward position, and as helpless as she to come up with a good solution.

He gave her high marks now, though. She was sounding strong and well organized. Of course, she was also among her most reliable allies.

"Unfortunately," Gail continued, warming up. "It turns out that the entire scheme was a cynical way to make us look bad during the state's time of greatest need. The offer of financial aid was not made in good faith. It was made so that it could then be immediately leaked to the DC-Three through back channels, colored to show us up as gullible fools for even considering it. The Holy Three already don't like us, of course, so they've just issued a press release stating, item by item, that LeMieur doesn't

401

have near the capital available in the first place to have made the offer; this is simply an attempt to make FEMA and the president and Big Government look bad; the GOP is cynically aiming to make hay during a crisis; et cetera, et cetera. You can fill in the blanks.

"What won't be said in so many words," Gail added, "but will be circulated far and wide, is that (*a*) this office didn't share the information about LeMieur's offer with the DC-Three when we first received it; (*b*) we were too desperate, naïve, and inexperienced to see it as the manipulative, crooked deal it is; and (*c*) we were so proud of being independent that we sold short the hard efforts of FEMA, the president, and the Democratic Party during this crisis, just so we could score a political point."

She then admitted tiredly, "You have to hand it to 'em. Scott and his cronies willfully risked looking bad, so that Democrats could end up mauling each other in a blame-game. And of course, they'll hide behind the claim that LeMieur does have enough cash available — since no one can say, one way or the other — and was simply refused out of political spite. A pretty brilliant ploy in a state where the most conservative wing of the Republican Party has

402

little to lose."

Alice Drim raised her hand hesitantly.

"Yes, Alice?" Gail asked, unintentionally sounding like an interrupted schoolmarm.

"What does all this mean to us?"

"It means that if they've done their homework, I may become the first one-term governor in this state since Ray Keyser got booted out by Phil Hoff in the early '60s."

There was an audible shifting of bodies in the room as everyone adapted to her unexpected bluntness.

"I still don't understand," Alice persisted. "We were voted in because of our independence from this kind of trickery. Why wouldn't our bringing it to light simply make it go away?"

Gail smiled sadly. "If it were only that easy."

"You were just supposed to ignore an offer to lighten the burden on all those people out there?" Alice pressed on, her voice rising, gesturing out the window.

Gail quickly agreed with her. "It's an excellent point, and it'll be exactly what we're going to say. Rob and I have been working out the details of our own statement, to be released within the hour." She held up her hands, a preacher at her own hoped-for revival. "Look, folks, I'm not about to lie down and die because of this. I only wanted to tell you about it so you wouldn't be blindsided when you heard it in the news. We've been screwed by some cynical assholes. And just as we taught them how idealism and virtue and independence can win an election, we'll show them how this kind of totally fabricated bullshit can't be pulled on an educated electorate."

Rob Perkins watched Gail's small audience, seeing a rebirth of optimism and determination. He didn't fault any of them for their willingness to fight back. It was Gail's mention of an educated electorate that had him worried. He'd been in the game for a long time, and never once had he been impressed by the clear-thinking and intellectual dispassion of the average voter. They did what they did for the damnedest of reasons, sometimes, but rarely because they'd been moved by a rational, cool-headed explanation of the facts.

He did agree with his governor on one thing, though: It was about to be one hell of a fight.

Joe was on his cell phone as he drove, having already lost his connection twice. Phone carriers protested that the mountains made coverage a bigger-than-average challenge in

Vermont. But Joe knew too well that local resistance to the unsightly towers was as much an obstacle as the topography. And in his old traditionalist's heart — despite inconveniences like the one dogging him now — he couldn't say that he, too, didn't prefer a pristine view over ready access to a phone signal.

He redialed Spinney and picked up where he'd left off. "I didn't get a plate number. The busybody who told me about the car didn't know it. It's got to be the last one Barb Barber had before the Alzheimer's took her off the road. Just have DMV dig it out of their computer files."

"You want that BOL to go out to surrounding states, boss?" Lester asked.

"It can't hurt," Joe said. "But my instinct tells me this car is still in Vermont. I don't know what the hell's going on, but it's personal, and it goes back decades — to when Carolyn Barber was alive and well and in the middle of something I don't think she understood. It's my bet that when Irene knocked out the power at the hospital and allowed Carolyn to wander free, she became the first domino in a line of at least three dead people by now, and maybe more."

"Okay," Lester said. "I'll get this out as soon as we hang up. Before you go, though, we got a hit on Travis Reynolds's cell phone records."

Joe paused to concentrate on passing an eighteen-wheeler, conscious of how talking on a phone undermines a driver's attention. "You find out who hired him to ransack Marshall's apartment?" he asked.

"Indirectly," Lester explained. "The number traced back to a Dolores Oetjen, who lives in Calais, north of Montpelier. She makes no sense to me at all right now — sells real estate, no record, no involvements that I could find with any of our known players — but I definitely want to grill her about this. She's either a wild card bad guy; has a pal who used her phone without her knowledge; or is the patsy of somebody sophisticated enough to have randomly routed a phone call through her number to put us off the scent."

"Sounds like fiction," Joe muttered.

"Still possible, though," Spinney attested, who knew much more about such things than Joe ever wanted to.

"All right," Joe said. "Chase her down. And bring someone with you. I'm getting an increasingly creepy sense about this case."

"Got it, boss. I'll grab Sammie. Willy's gone AWOL again."

Willy pulled over opposite the same address he'd visited earlier, in Burlington's North End.

"You good?" he asked his passenger.

Nate Rozanski didn't answer. He remained slumped in his seat, his hands in his lap, his eyes fixed straight ahead.

"Nate," Willy spoke to him sharply.

He slowly turned his head.

Willy gestured to the warehouse across the street. "The brother you killed is in there. He's alive if not well. He's got a mangled arm like mine. He's alone and cut off and heading nowhere fast, all because of you."

Nate's mouth tightened, and his eyes dropped to the console between them.

Willy smacked him in the chest with the back of his right hand, causing Nate to look up, startled and with a flicker of anger.

"Pissed you off a little there, didn't I?" Willy challenged him. "Good. Fine. Well, turn some of that on yourself, for once. Instead of wallowing in guilt, get mad at yourself; get mad at your loser father; get mad at what you did and start fixing it. How many people have a chance to put things right? For years, you've been holed up with your self-pity for company. Well, guess what, you sorry woodchuck, *you didn't do it.* You fucked up, but you didn't kill him."

He reached out suddenly and cupped Nate by the back of the neck, forcing their faces to be inches apart. "Get your ass in there, Nate. *Fix this,*" he said.

Nate kept the gaze, absorbing the message, and then slowly nodded. "Who are you?" he asked wonderingly.

Willy felt a surge of emotion overtake him, welling up and prickling the backs of his eyes, born of a lifetime of asking himself the same question.

But he wasn't going to let this idiot have the satisfaction.

"I'm the guy who's gonna kill you if you don't get out of my car."

Nate gave him a small smile, and did as he'd been told.

Joe parked before a building that, from the outside, looked like a custom-made incubator for worker dysfunction. It was old, single-story, windowless, and located in a commercial no-man's-land between Montpelier and Barre. It reminded him of a huge grave marker, lying flat on the ground.

He found the front door, looking lost and

hopeless against the blank slab of the wall surrounding it, and entered to discover a receptionist behind a thick, scratched, cloudy Plexiglas partition with a large hole in its middle — through which, Joe thought disjointedly, anyone could have extended a hand holding a gun.

"Joe Gunther to see Jodi Hamer," he announced.

Shortly, a smiling, upbeat woman with a strong handshake greeted him at the lobby's inner door.

"Mr. Gunther? Delighted to meet you. I just got the faxed release document we discussed on the phone. Thank you for doing that. So many other police officers have a tough time understanding our need to cover our butts."

Joe followed her into the building's embrace and down a long, well-lighted corridor. Belying the place's exterior, its residents had worked hard and successfully to brighten up its inner spaces. "Believe me," he told her supportively, "I have been in your shoes. I want to thank you for being clear about what you needed. Did you find what I'm after?"

"Yes," she said happily. "It took a little digging. Right now, because of Irene, we've never been busier in here, duplicating as many records as we can. Our priority, as you can imagine, is to re-create everything lost in the basement of the public safety headquarters — fingerprint files, arrest records, et cetera. State hospital admissions from decades ago were a pretty low priority."

She looked back at him and smiled broadly, adding, "In a way, it's a huge kick for me personally — selfishly speaking. All this justifies the requests we've made for years to back up hard records with digital copies. I can tell you, it's been like pulling teeth sometimes, and the process has been far from perfect, but we've made inroads, and if there's one good thing that'll come of this disaster, I bet it'll be better funding."

She led him through a door and down a claustrophobically narrow aisle of opposing shelves. "Okay, here we are. Hospital admissions around the time you're interested in." She pointed at a nearby table crowned with a mechanical version of a resting pterodactyl. "That's a microfiche reader. Know how it works?"

Joe smiled at her. "That's very sweet. I'm guessing you know damned well I'm probably more comfortable with one of those than with any computer."

She laughed. "Well, I wasn't going to mention it. I'll leave you to it, then. Happy hunting."

It was onerous work. The cardboard boxes containing Hamer's cherished microfiches reflected the era before mental health patients were dumped on to the community, often with the rationalization that they'd become assets to society. What he was poring over was the legacy of the "old days," when people were committed for being eccentric, or offending influential family members — or getting in the way of prominent politicians. There were thousands of entries, loosely organized, haphazardly filed, and all but unreadable without resorting to the cranky, eye-straining reader by Joe's side. Even then, most of the forms were handwritten, and frequently tough to decipher.

Nevertheless, after several hours, he located what he was after — Carolyn Barber's official commitment papers. And with them, something he hadn't been expecting: the name of the person who'd signed them.

CHAPTER TWENTY-THREE

"That it?" Lester asked.

Sam checked her notepad. "Yeah. Not much to it."

In fact, Dolores Oetjen's realty office looked like a private residence with a shingle hanging out front. "Nice place, though," Sam added, almost as an apology.

They got out of the car and looked up and down the street, properly called West County Road. There wasn't much to see, Calais being not much of a metropolis.

"What's with the town's name?" she asked, knowing of Lester's penchant for local history. "I always wondered."

"Rhymes with *palace*," he said. "After the French port city. It's a Revolutionary War thing — everybody was crazy about the French back then. You know, Lafayette and all that. There are several villages within the township. The biggest hoot is that one of them was called Sodom for like a hundred years, 'cause it didn't have a church. Friendly, huh? Love thy neighbor."

Sam looked across the roof of the car at him in surprise. "Still?" she asked.

"Nah. It's Adamant, now. They claim that's because of the stone quarries, but I bet it's because of their thick skin."

In fact, they were in another of those small villages — this one named Maple Corner — which prompted Sam to ask, "Wasn't this where those guys posed nude for a calendar?"

He smiled. "Yup. *The Men of Maple Corner.* Half a million bucks raised for the community center." He indicated with his thumb. "Down there. 'Bout ten years ago. Started a rage of imitators. Crazy like a fox."

They walked up to the modest house and followed instructions to PLEASE COME ON IN.

They found a young woman typing on her computer, seated at an antique desk in a front room arranged to look like an office.

The woman sprang to her feet at their entrance. "Hi," she said cheerily, rounding the corner of the desk and ushering them in. "Welcome. I'm Dolores Oetjen. Glad to meet you."

Sam almost felt sorry for having ignited so much enthusiasm. "Hi, Dolores," she

413

said, shaking hands. "Don't get your hopes up. We're cops, not buyers."

Nice, Lester thought. Too much Willy time.

Dolores's face fell. "Police? What happened?"

Les spoke up. "Absolutely nothing, Ms. Oetjen. We're here for a huge favor, is all. Sorry to have alarmed you. Can we all sit down?"

Put to ease but still confused, Oetjen waved at the chairs facing her desk. "Sure," she said. "How can I help?"

"We're on sort of a hunting expedition," Sam explained, fitting her tone to Lester's. "Much of what we do is chase down leads, just like you see on TV, and one of those leads brought us here."

Oetjen pointed to herself as she sat back down. "To me? What did I do?"

Les allowed for what he hoped was a comforting laugh. "Probably nothing, Dolores. But your phone number popped up on a list of others, and we wanted to ask you about that."

"My number?" she parroted.

Sam allowed for a slight edge to creep into her voice. "Yeah, Dolores. Your number — on the phone of a guy we just put in jail."

Oetjen's mouth opened in surprise.

"What? Who?"

Lester extracted a photograph from his pocket and laid it on her desk. "You ever see him before? His name is Travis Reynolds."

She stared at the picture without touching it, as if it might be electrified. "No," she replied, her voice reflecting her growing concern. "I don't understand. How did he get my number?"

"You phoned him," Sam said bluntly. "You had *his* number."

Oetjen straightened in her chair. "But I don't know him."

Lester leaned forward and tapped his finger on the oversized desk pad calendar she had before her. "That's the date the call was placed from here."

As she had earlier with Travis's photo, Oetjen stared at the calendar. "I don't know," she murmured.

Sam stood for emphasis and leaned on the desk. "Ms. Oetjen, just so you realize, this is a murder investigation. You might want to start getting your head straight here."

"What were you doing that day, Dolores?" Lester asked gently, in classic good cop–bad cop style. "Is it written down there, maybe?"

Oetjen looked up at him. "None of this

makes sense."

"The calendar," Sam said flatly.

The young woman placed her hand to her head and looked around haplessly, saying, "Right, right. I'm sorry. Of course. It's . . . ," before seeing her tablet computer lying off to her right, faceup on the table. "I don't actually use the paper calendar. My mom gave it to me, but I can't carry it around."

She hurriedly brought the tablet to life, smiling reflexively at Lester as Sam rolled her eyes.

"I don't know," Oetjen said, her eyes scanning the screen. "It was a normal workday. I had a couple of appointments . . . one house showing."

Les laid his hand on the desk phone. "Is there cell service from here?" he asked.

"It's not very good," she replied.

"So you usually use this?"

"Yes."

"It looks like a sophisticated phone. Does it record outgoing calls for the previous month, do you think?"

She looked at him. "I don't know. I suppose it does. I've never checked. That would be handy, wouldn't it?"

Sam had heard enough. She walked away and began sightlessly staring at house offerings on a poster across the room.

Lester smiled. "Dolores," he offered, "If you'd allow me, I'd be happy to see if it works."

She waved at the device. "Oh, sure. Be my guest."

Spinney began punching commands into the phone as Sam turned and asked in a more pleasant tone of voice, "How many extensions do you have in the house?"

"Three," was the instant response. "And a cell I keep in my purse for when I'm on the road."

"Les," Sam asked. "Is that unit gonna capture all outgoing calls, or just the ones placed on that unit?"

Lester was their most electronically skilled member, although Willy had made it his mission to catch up.

Les glanced at Oetjen. "You bought the three phones as a package? This looks like one of these sets that can have up to six extensions."

"It is."

"There you have it," he told his colleague. "All calls'll be logged in here. This is like the mother ship."

They watched him as he continued hitting buttons, guided by the small screen mounted into the phone's display.

"Here we go," he finally announced, pulling out his own cell phone and quickly taking a picture of the image on the screen. "At ten forty-three that night, lasting three minutes."

Oetjen half rose in shock to stand and stare at the display. "What? Ten forty-three? Are you sure?"

"Yup." He tapped the source of the information with his fingertip.

She sat back down heavily. "I don't believe it."

Sam quickly returned, circled the desk, and stood with her face inches from Oetjen's. "It wasn't you, was it, Dolores?"

"No," was the barely whispered response.

"So who was it?"

"It must've been Aaron."

"Aaron who?"

"Whitledge."

"He your boyfriend?"

Dolores nodded, qualifying, "Kind of."

"How long have you two been seeing each other?"

"Not long. Six months. Usually only on weekends, but not every one, either."

"Tell us about him," Lester suggested as Sam backed away.

"He's nice," she said vaguely.

"I'm sure he is. How did you meet?"

"At a party." She rubbed her forehead.

"Well, sort of one. It was at a bar, actually. A club, I guess."

"Name?" Sam asked.

"The Four Leaf Clover, in Montpelier."

Sam changed her demeanor, becoming more intimate in her body language, and almost confided her next comment. "You more interested in a commitment than he is?"

Oetjen sighed. "Yeah. As usual."

Lester stayed silent as Sam continued. "He a bit of a player?"

After hesitating, Oetjen murmured, "Guess beggars can't be choosers."

"Tell us about that day," Sam tapped the desk calendar. "What was it like?"

"It was fine. He came up, we had fun, he stayed the night — which he doesn't always do."

"How 'bout at ten forty-three? What were you doing then?"

"I was sleeping," Dolores said, her voice stronger. "I had a sale that day, which is a big deal for me. I'm not doing that well, especially nowadays, and sure as hell not after that stupid storm. So when Aaron came up, we celebrated. I overdid it a little with the wine. By ten o'clock, we'd had dinner, watched a Netflix movie, cuddled a bit. I was wiped."

"But he stayed over?"

"Yes. That's what I said."

"Are you a heavy sleeper, Dolores?" Les asked.

She smiled sheepishly. "I think I am, especially if I've been drinking."

"So Aaron could've used the phone without your knowing it?"

"I suppose," she said. "I don't know why, though."

"What do you know about him?" Sam asked. "Where's he work, for example?"

"Montpelier. I think for state government."

"You think?"

She flushed. "He said he wasn't really free to talk about it. That his boss had him do special things sometimes that he couldn't discuss."

Lester almost laughed. "Like he was a secret agent?"

Dolores looked embarrassed. "I know. I know. It seemed kinda dumb to me, too, but then I thought maybe he was covering for being a file clerk or something. I liked him. He was nice to me. And so what if he wasn't into commitment or anything long-term? He made me feel special, and I started thinking that was good enough."

"Did you ever go to his house?" Sam

420

asked. "Or did he always come here?"

"No, we spent the night at his place a couple of times. Mostly, he wanted to get away from Montpelier. It was a cool apartment, though. I liked going there. It was a converted loft or something, overlooking the main drag — State Street. Not big, but nice, with big windows."

Lester handed over his notepad, open to a blank page. "Write down the address."

"And add whatever phone numbers you have for him," Sam requested.

Oetjen did as requested, asking as she wrote, "Is he in trouble now? You said you were looking into a murder."

Les made a point of laughing. "Good Lord, no. We're not looking at him. We just want to see how he connects to this other guy, and even *he's* not the one we're after. This is like looking at a bunch of pick-up sticks, and figuring out which one fell first."

"That being said," Sam added grimly, folding the sheet of paper and placing it into her pocket, "We don't want you calling Aaron after we leave. You do that, we'll know about it, and we'll be back to talk about the price of hindering a police investigation. Do you understand that?"

Oetjen nodded.

Sam leaned onto the desk again. "I didn't

421

hear you."

"I understand," Oetjen said meekly.

Back in the car fifteen minutes later — and after borrowing a photo of Oetjen and Whitledge posing before the statehouse — Sam turned to her partner and asked, "How much you wanna bet she's on the phone right now?"

Lester laughed. "You and Willy really are a match made in heaven."

Joe was on the interstate when his cell phone went off. Someone had asked him once what he looked forward to the most when he retired. He'd reached into his pocket, extracted the cell, and answered, "Turning this damn thing off, once and forever."

But right now, as usual, he pulled it out and answered, "Gunther."

"Hi. It's me."

Despite his eagerness to reach his destination, he pulled over to the side of the interstate.

"Hey, there, Governor. How're you doing? I've been hearing the news reports. I can't quite figure it all out, but it sounds like you have your hands full, as if Irene wasn't enough."

Gail Zigman sounded tense and exhausted. "Tell me about it. Imagine trying to make political hay while the whole state is hurting. These damn people are like maggots, I swear to God."

What Joe had been hearing, of course, was far from anything that simple or clear, running the gamut from a political ambush to a prime example of neophyte arrogance and inexperience, combined.

"I am sorry," he said, hoping to steer clear of a lengthy debate. As a couple, they'd been compatible on some levels, and less so on others, making many of their friends wonder how they'd stayed together as long as they had. One of their points of divergence had been Gail's tendency to see issues in starker shades of black-and-white than he.

"I thought about calling you," he added. "But with all this, I didn't want to get in the way. I know you've become the proverbial one-armed paperhanger."

"Oh, Joe," she said sadly. "You should know you can always call. I would never be too tired or too busy to talk. You've always been my safe haven."

Thinking back, he considered that "often" might have been more accurate than "always." But he appreciated the sentiment, and felt all the more generous in light of what he and Beverly had reignited.

"I guess the bottom line," he offered, "is that the governorship is a long way from the Brattleboro selectboard."

"Well, yes and no," she half agreed. "Some of the brains are as small, but you're right about the numbers being bigger. Speaking of which," she segued, "what do you know about a guy named Sheldon Scott?"

Joe was silent, grateful to have pulled off the road. Scott, of course, had surfaced in the past history of the late Gorden Marshall.

"He's a lobbyist, isn't he?" he asked non-committally.

"He's a right-wing, flesh-eating barracuda is more like it," she responded. "He's the son of a bitch behind the mess that's making Irene look like a summer shower."

Joe frowned. Even at her most stressed, Gail rarely gave in to such narcissistic language. He'd been hearing of a few thousand people who might have argued with her about the relative impacts between Irene's devastation and Scott's political shenanigans.

"You really are feeling the heat on this, aren't you?" he asked. "I don't think many of us on the outside are getting the full story."

"You probably never will, Joe," she said.

"I'll be a one-term wonder because of this prick, and he'll slink back into the slime. Nobody will ever hear about all the back-room knife-wielding that went into this. It has nothing to do with the people or the state or doing what's best for the poor bastards whose houses went downriver. This is about power, and men, and the good ol' boy system — alive and well, even in this socialist Nirvana."

Joe pulled in his chin at the vitriol, and tried to introduce a little levity. "Hey, don't hold back. Tell me what you think."

She tried to play along. "Never can and always will, Joe. Someday, you'll be arresting me for sedition or something."

He laughed. "That *can't* be against the law in Vermont."

"Well, this crap should be," she countered darkly, adding, "So, what do you know about Scott?"

"Just what I told you, and it sounds like considerably less than what you already know."

"I need more," she said bluntly.

He didn't respond, holding the phone to his ear and staring out at the traffic as if in suspended animation. In all their time together — through her brief stint as a deputy state's attorney, her years as a selectman, even during her recovery from being raped, Gail had never asked him to break the law on her behalf.

Until she'd run for executive office, when she'd asked him for something inappropriate concerning the previous governor. That, Joe had refused to do.

Now she was on the brink of doing it again.

"Have you thought through what I think you're about to ask?" he asked her.

"You getting technical on me?" she shot back.

"I'm remembering my oath of office," he said carefully.

But not carefully enough.

"Meaning I've forgotten mine?" she asked sharply.

"No. Meaning that you're under a huge amount of pressure and you need all the help you can get."

"Which you won't give me."

"Which you don't want," he argued levelly. "Gail, you will always have a piece of my heart. You know that. But you don't want to do this."

She didn't respond.

"Ask me for something I can grant," he said, "and it's yours. That's probably why you called in the first place. You just got a little blurry 'cause we're friends. Don't worry about it."

In the persistent silence, he added, "Look, I realize I don't know all the details, and that it's probably complicated as hell, but I bet you can beat it if you bring it to the people who voted you in. You were the one who told the wheeler-dealers and the politicos to take a hike, and it got you elected. *That's* your strength, not playing their game on their terms."

"I know how to politick, Joe. You stick to catching bad guys."

He quieted, letting the frustrated egotism of her comment linger between them.

"I'm sorry. I gotta go," she finally said. "I didn't mean to jam you up. Take care."

The phone went dead.

CHAPTER TWENTY-FOUR

The Pierson Library in Shelburne is tacked on to the old town hall, which looks, from Route 7, like something close to Thomas Jefferson's heart as an architect. The actual library, however, is in the modern ex-town offices and police station to the rear, and coincidentally shares a large parking lot with the same fire department that responded to the Barber residence a couple of blocks to the south.

It was here that Joe Gunther was headed when he'd spoken with Gail — direct from his scrutiny of the old Vermont State Hospital admission forms — and here that he hoped an old-fashioned piece of pure, unadulterated inspiration might bear fruit.

He introduced himself at the front desk and asked for the reference librarian.

He was met by an amused response. "I'm afraid we're not that big or fancy. There are only six of us here, including the director.

Maybe you should talk with her first."

He was escorted to the office of a lively middle-aged woman with long red hair, who greeted him with a surprisingly firm grip.

"How may we help you?" she asked after introductions were made and the circulation assistant had left.

Joe looked a little self-conscious. "This is a long shot, in more ways than one," he admitted. "But if somebody were to walk in here asking how to find a historic local celebrity — maybe an old politician who was famous back when — what might you tell them?"

The director smiled as she said, "It's all about the Internet nowadays. I'd steer them to Elizabeth, our new technical services person."

"She here today?"

"She's here every day. She's become our most crucial employee, complete with a master's degree in the subject. Would you like me to introduce you?"

She led him to another part of the library, suitably equipped with several computer stations, and to the desk of a young woman with an infectious smile and bright, intelligent eyes.

"Elizabeth? Special Agent Joe Gunther, of the VBI."

The librarian's face lit up. "Am I supposed to call you a G-man? It qualifies, even if it's state government."

Joe laughed. "Oh, Lord — please don't. People are confused enough about who we are."

"You're the result of political expediency," she said, shaking hands. "But I think it's a great idea, and I hear good things about what you do."

He was impressed. "I think I've come to the right person," he told her boss. "Thanks so much."

"How can I help you?" Elizabeth asked as the director walked away.

Joe repeated his earlier question, adding, "The reason I ask is that I'm hoping you helped an elderly woman a while back, who clearly had no idea what the Internet was, or probably even how to operate a computer."

Elizabeth looked astonished. "Wow. You really are a G-man. How did you know that? That's like a perfect description."

Joe allowed himself a moment's elation. Once in a while, he thought, things actually could come together.

"Did she give a name?" he asked.

There, Elizabeth was less helpful, however. "No, and we usually don't ask. It goes with the whole confidentiality thing. She was really nice, though."

"What did she want to know?"

Elizabeth rose from her desk and walked over to one of the computer stations. "She had heard about computers. Just never operated one. And while her typing was wicked rusty, I could tell she'd been trained. She put her hands on the keyboard like an old pro, sort of instinctively."

"Did she mention who she was looking for?"

She shook her head. "I asked her, in order to demonstrate how Google works, or one of the other search engines we use, but she was clearly not willing to talk about it, and I didn't push."

"Right," he murmured. "The confidentiality thing."

"You got it. So, after about twenty minutes of instruction, I let her be, and she hammered away right here for an hour or so. Never asked for any more help, either, which is unusual."

"She take notes or print anything out?" Joe asked.

"Oh yeah," Elizabeth recalled. "I forgot. She asked for a pad, so I guess she did take notes."

Joe glanced at the blank computer screen,

addressing it as he spoke to her. "I don't suppose this has something like a history file or something — that would tell me what she looked up."

Elizabeth laughed outright. "Oh. Big no-no in the librarian world. If it did have such a record, you'd have to get a search warrant or something before I'd open it for you, but I can spare you the effort anyhow — I wipe the memories clean at closing, every day. There's nothing to look for."

Joe nodded appreciatively. "I can see why your director spoke so highly of you. Can you tell me what this lady looked like, at least?"

She considered that before responding, "Sure. Small — under five-five — and kind of thin and wiry. White hair, nice eyes — blue — and really strong hands. She shook mine when she left, and I was really surprised. I thought her clothes were funny, though," she threw in as an afterthought.

"How — funny?"

"Like they were the wrong size — bought for someone taller and bigger."

Joe nodded, all suspicions confirmed. "And maybe a bit old-fashioned?"

Again, Elizabeth's face showed her delight. "Yeah. Exactly."

"How did she seem mentally?" Joe asked.

She reflected, as was her habit, it seemed, before answering, "Not a hundred percent. And it wasn't just being old. I get a lot of that around here, so I'm used to it. But there was something else. I didn't get to talk with her much, like I said, but I sensed something off, somehow."

"Had you ever seen her before?" he asked suddenly.

"Nope. 'Fraid not."

"Did she make any reference to anyone local? Or say where she was staying?"

"Just that she was from out of town, not a library member, and wondered if it was okay to use the computers, which of course it was."

"Anything you can add I might've missed?"

But she shook her head again. "I'm not super good at stuff like that. I stood next to her, so I got the height and general shape, and the eye color, but other than that, she just looked like an old lady. No horns or beard or anything."

Joe laughed, startled. "Right. I'll keep that in mind."

He was back on the road, heading southeast, his head full of what he'd learned at the Shelburne library, and of how it interconnected with his other recent discoveries. This part of a case — in the lucky situations where it applied — was like the adrenaline rush he'd once felt as a teenage athlete, with the winning goal within his grasp. Earlier frustrations or fatigue seemed to vaporize, replaced by a sense of certainty so sure, it almost overwhelmed any realistically remaining doubt.

And yet, a small part of him felt hollow and oddly aching — a compartment in his brain not normally alive at a time like this. But he felt it nevertheless, and yielded to its need of a little nurturing.

Overriding his own sense of caution — yet again — he pulled out his cell phone while still driving.

"Hello?" came the hesitant response. "Joe? Is everything okay?"

He wasn't used to Beverly sounding tentative. "Sure. I catch you at a bad time?" he asked.

Her voice lightened immediately. "No. Not at all. I was just thrown off — the private line combined with the odd background noise. I guess it worried me for a moment."

"I'm on the road," he explained. "Just wanted to say hi. Absolutely nothing else."

He heard the warmth in her response.

"Joe, there never needs to be anything else. I love it that you gave in to impulse. You are okay, though?"

He smiled, that compartment in his brain back in balance. "I am way better than okay, Beverly. Thank you."

Les and Sam were parked across the street from Aaron Whitledge's address in Montpelier, with a good view of the very windows that Dolores Oetjen had described, overlooking the downtown bustle. They had gone upstairs upon arrival and pounded on his door — along with those of several of his neighbors — but not surprisingly, everyone was out, presumably at work. In a town like Vermont's state capital — the smallest such entity in the United States — employment was high, most often related to either insurance or government.

Unfortunately, at this point, they still didn't know who wrote Aaron Whitledge's paycheck. Les had called in for a Spillman computer check, and found little beside a couple of old speeding tickets, and they hadn't heard back from the fusion center, which generally produced a more comprehensive portrait of any citizen, but took longer to deliver.

But it was late in the day, past most

435

people's working hours, and they were hoping they'd get lucky with a man who might prefer to return home before heading out to dinner or the party circuit.

Sam's cell phone buzzed, displaying a picture of Emma on its screen. She retrieved it from the dashboard and read the caller's name before raising her eyebrows at her partner.

"Hey, boss," she answered, putting the phone on speaker.

"What's your location?" Joe asked in a tinny voice.

"Downtown Mount-Peculiar. We think we located the guy who phoned Travis and maybe hired him. We're sitting on his apartment right now."

"I'm a few minutes out," he told her. "I'll hook up with you there. What's the address?"

Sam gave it to him and asked, "How 'bout you? Been busy?"

"Yeah — if I have this right, Carolyn Barber is alive and well, driving her sister's old car and wearing her borrowed clothes. And I'm starting to get the distinct sensation — based mostly on my gut — that she's reeaally angry."

Sam stared sightlessly out the window ahead of her. "Are you saying what I think you are?"

"Well," he said. "It's a process of elimination, combined with human nature, but of the people we know who've been murdered so far — Marshall and Friel and Barb Barber — all of them have Carolyn in common, and all of them did her dirt, except maybe Friel."

"Barb?" Sam asked, surprised. "I thought they just didn't get along."

"You could say that," Joe agreed. "I found Carolyn's commitment papers earlier today, signed by her sister nine months after Carolyn announced to her roommate that she was pregnant."

"Ouch," Sammie said, instinctively thinking of her own child.

"What happened to the baby?" she asked.

"I have no idea, but I'd love to get my hands on Barb's financial records for that time, to see if Carolyn's commitment coincided with any money changing hands."

"Damn," Lester said. "That's harsh."

"Maybe," Joe agreed. "But why else would she have done it? If the father was a bigwig, with a reputation to protect, there would have been good reason to make such a deal, especially with no love lost between the sisters in the first place."

"But why didn't Carolyn say anything?"

Sam protested.

"From everything we've heard," Joe said, "Carolyn was a walking zombie when she was at the hospital, which is definitely not the description I got from the Shelburne librarian I just interviewed. Could be that Carolyn was kept artificially demented all these years. That would take a pharmacologist or someone to say with any credibility, but I can imagine a woman in that situation — madder than hell but locked in suspended animation — really blowing a gasket if she somehow got lucky enough to break free."

"How did she locate Marshall and get a key to his apartment?" Lester challenged him.

"I think she found him through the Internet," Joe replied. "And as far as access goes, *we* found out Nancy Kelley and she knew each other. Could be Carolyn got hold of somebody else at The Woods and finagled a way to get a key. Either that or Kelley's holding back. We can squeeze her later and maybe find out."

To the silence he received from his colleagues, he added, "I don't have all the answers, guys, and I'm not sure I'm right about any of it. It just fits. Finding that baby's birth certificate wouldn't hurt, though."

Lester had been looking out the side window at the entrance to Whitledge's building, and now interrupted, "Oh, oh. Folks? Hate to break this up, but our mark just came home."

"You go ahead," Joe told them. "I won't be long."

As it turned out, they all met Aaron Whitledge at about the same time. Checking his mailbox in the lobby, he was joined by a downstairs neighbor, and escorted her to her door on the second floor, loitering to chat as Les and Sam kept out of sight.

The two cops were therefore still introducing themselves at Whitledge's apartment on the top floor when Joe came climbing up the stairs to join them.

Whitledge — young, slim, well dressed, and haughty in expression — looked surprised at Joe's arrival.

"Three of you?" he said. "What is this?"

"Maybe the most important conversation of your life," Joe said as he stepped onto the landing, despite not fully knowing who this man was.

Sam, however, picked up on the line. "Invite us in, Mr. Whitledge, so we can read you your future."

Whitledge demurred, placing his hand

439

protectively against the doorjamb. "Do I need a lawyer?"

"Not as far as we're concerned," Sam continued, taking the lead. "It depends entirely on you."

She left it at that, allowing a telling silence to settle. Whitledge looked from one of them to the other and finally dropped his arm and backed up, still holding his mail in the other hand.

"Might as well find out what the hell's going on," he said, half to himself.

They were in a large room — with Oetjen's big front windows — that served as living room and kitchen, combined. It was airy, nicely appointed, but not pretentious, although Sammie wondered how Oetjen could ever have taken her boyfriend for an embarrassed file clerk. These were clearly richer digs than that.

Whitledge dumped his mail on a coffee table and nodded toward some armchairs and a sofa. "Sit," he said, choosing a chair for himself. Joe considered the body language and interpreted a man working very hard to appear unconcerned.

Sam apparently came to the same conclusion and walked over to stand close to their host, forcing him to look awkwardly up at her.

"Just for the record, you are Aaron Whitledge?"

He shifted slightly in his seat. "Yes."

Lester and Joe, also still standing, spread out to either side of her, a couple of paces back.

"And you are romantically involved with Dolores Oetjen?" she continued.

His voice betrayed his confusion. "Yes."

"Who is your employer, Mr. Whitledge?"

"Sheldon Scott and Company."

Joe kept silent, although startled by the name coming up twice in the same afternoon.

"What do they do?" Sam asked.

"We're a lobbying firm."

"And your job description there?"

He hesitated for a fraction of a second. "I'm a sort of gofer. A special projects guy."

"What kinds of projects are those?"

Joe could tell the younger man was still inside his comfort zone. "They vary in scope and complexity. Sometimes, it's research; other times, it's just acting as a glorified messenger boy. It's like the title indicates — a jack of all trades."

"That's interesting, Jack," Sam challenged him dismissively. "But even more interesting is that you seem to have no curiosity about my bringing up your girlfriend. Don't you like her?"

Whitledge crossed his arms and legs. "Sure I do. Sweet kid."

"Who happens to be your exact age, correct?"

"Okay," he said uncomfortably.

"But still no 'Oh, is she all right?' Or, 'Did anything happen to poor Dolores?' " Sam pressed. "What's wrong, Mr. Whitledge? There something about her you don't want us to know?"

"No," he protested loudly, and used that to struggle to his feet, trying to avoid bumping into Sam in the process. He spoke as he moved toward one of the windows, where she immediately followed him. "What're you saying? Did something happen to her?"

Sammie again crowded his personal space. "Not a thing, Aaron. Did you do something to her?"

"Of course not. You were the one saying that. I don't understand this. What have I done?"

"We actually know what you've done, Aaron, and how you set up that sweet kid, as you call her, to take the fall for it. Who do you report to directly, Aaron?"

Joe answered that. "We know that, too. It's the boss himself."

Whitledge's quick flicker of the eyes

betrayed his fear. "I answer to whoever gives me the assignment."

"Which in this case was Sheldon Scott," Joe persisted.

"Was it your idea or Scott's to use Dolores's phone?" Lester asked, adding to the chorus.

Whitledge opened his mouth and then shut it again.

"Who is Travis Reynolds?" Sam demanded, closing in so that their bodies were almost touching.

Whitledge pressed his back against the window frame. "Who?"

"The man you called at ten forty-three on the night you made sure Dolores got good and drunk and was passed out in her bed. That Travis Reynolds."

"I don't know who you're talking about." But the voice was sulky now, having lost its edge.

"The man you ordered to enter Gorden Marshall's apartment," Joe reminded him.

"The same Gorden Marshall," Sam picked up, "who was murdered the day before."

"Did you order that done, too?" Lester asked. "Or did you do it yourself, as a special project?"

Whitledge's mouth dropped open. "What? Hell no. What're you talking about?"

443

"We're talking about who all this leads back to, Aa-ron," Sam said loudly, drawing out his name.

"You actually think you're the only one who knows how to stab someone in the back?" Joe asked. "You haven't figured out that Sheldon Scott was doing this sort of thing before you were even born?"

"That's where he's put you, Aaron," Sam picked up. "You're the meat on the end of the hook, custom-made to satisfy our appetite. How do you think we found you?"

Joe approached in turn, speaking in a softer, paternal tone, "Now's your chance to wake up and make it stop. Tell us the truth. You have your whole life ahead of you. Or your whole life to throw away."

"And I'll guarantee you one thing," Sam threw in. "Sheldon Scott won't give a rat's ass what happens to you, so be careful about thinking how any loyalty will be repaid."

Whitledge made to speak, but Joe cut him off. "Aaron. You've probably seen on TV where the cops and the suspects sound like they're playing verbal chess. That's not what's going on here. We're not make-believe. We're conducting a murder investigation. You're our primary suspect because of the phone call you made to Travis. You either tell us who wound you up and pointed you in the right direction, or we call it quits, throw the book at you, and go home." He put his face an inch away from Whitledge's and slowly asked, "Do you understand what I just said?"

The young man swallowed and nodded. "Yes, sir."

Joe stayed where he was. "Did you kill Gorden Marshall?"

"No, sir."

"Did you call Travis Reynolds from Dolores's phone?"

Aaron paused just long enough for Sam to snarl, "Careful."

"Yes," he admitted.

"And on whose orders did you make that call?" Joe asked.

"Mr. Scott's," Aaron said softly.

Joe and Sam stepped back. She caught Whitledge by the elbow and brought him back to his chair. Only this time, they all joined him, suddenly looking like a group of friends — where everyone but Aaron was wearing a gun.

"Okay," Joe said, his voice still supportive and coaxing. "Take us from the top. When did Scott first contact you about all this?"

"I don't remember the day exactly," Aaron readily replied, looking relieved. "But it was after Marshall died." He sat forward abruptly to add, "And I didn't know anything about any murder. I was told he'd died, of old age or something — I don't know."

"That's fine. Keep going," Joe urged him.

"Anyhow, Mr. Scott brought me into his room upstairs, where he has his private talks — that's what we all call them. So I knew right off something was up."

"You'd never been asked there before?" Lester asked.

Aaron looked embarrassed. "No. I let people think so because it makes me sound important. But this was the first time I've been asked to do anything like this."

"Thanks for being straight with us, Aaron," Joe complimented him, as if rewarding a pet. "What next?"

"It was pretty straightforward. He gave me Travis's number and told me to tell him to go into Marshall's apartment and remove that stuff."

"What stuff, exactly?"

"A framed photograph, some files, and a pin from a jewelry box. He was really specific describing them and where they were. And he told me to make sure the phone's message machine was erased."

"Details, Aaron," Joe said. "What photograph? Which files?"

"A framed black-and-white shot, about five by seven," he said. "Showing a bunch of people holding glasses and toasting the photographer. And everything out of the *C* file — he didn't tell me exactly what — said just to make sure everything was grabbed. And the pin was dark purple, with two gold *C*'s engraved on it. He showed me one that looked just like it."

"He explain its meaning?"

"No. I'm sorry, but maybe it tied into what was in the *C* files."

"Let's talk about Travis," Joe said, recalling what Reynolds had told him earlier. "How was he supposed to get in?"

"There would be a box behind a Dumpster at the old folks' home where Marshall lived," Aaron explained. "A key would be inside, along with a maintenance man's uniform and some money — or *half* the money, that's right. I forgot. Travis was supposed to return the stolen things and the uniform to the same place, and the rest of the money would be there, waiting for him."

"Meaning you had a confederate?"

"Yeah, but I don't know anything about him. I asked Mr. Scott about that when he assigned this to me, and he said something like, 'Not your concern.' I got the message."

"What if something went wrong?" Joe

asked. "Like Travis grabbed the wrong picture or something? What were you supposed to do then?"

Aaron looked at him, mystified. "I don't know. Did something go wrong?"

"I'm asking, 'if,' Aaron."

"I don't know," he repeated. "That's all he told me. I made the phone call like I was told. Mr. Scott had told me to use a cold phone — that was the phrase he used, which is what made me think of Dolores's instead of my cell or something — and that's what I did. That was the end of it."

"But you reported back to Scott?" Joe wanted to know.

"Oh, yeah."

"And he was satisfied?"

Aaron nodded. "As far as I know. He didn't say otherwise. He did tell me that under no circumstances was I ever to mention this to anybody, including him — that he'd make it worth my while. So that was it, as far as I was concerned. Until today," he added in a lowered voice.

"Did Scott say anything about the files?"

"No."

"Did you ever call Travis back?"

He shook his head, leading Joe to suspect that Scott's was the second phone call Travis had mentioned — the one he assumed

448

Aaron had made after catching a cold.

"Had you ever worked with Travis before?" Lester asked, to confirm Aaron's earlier statement.

"No."

"Aaron," Joe asked him, "did you ever wonder what it was Scott got you involved in? What this was all about?"

Whitledge shrugged. "Skeletons in the closet. That's what I figured. It's what all these politicians worry about. I figured it was to avoid bad publicity. I had no clue it had anything to do with murder."

"You know where Scott lives?" Joe asked him.

"Sure," he said, and quickly gave the address. "We're invited there every December, for the Christmas party. It's huge."

Joe stood up, prompting the rest of them to do likewise. He walked up to Aaron and took his hand in his, as if to wish him farewell. But he didn't let go as he emphasized, "Aaron, same rules apply with us as they did with Scott. Not a word about this conversation till I get back in touch. There's one additional incentive to keep your mouth shut, though. You know what that is?"

Whitledge looked confused. "No."

"If you do think you might win points by talking to your boss, keep in mind what he has to lose — and what he might be willing to do to anyone he sees as a snitch."

The young man swallowed and remained silent. Joe let his hand drop. "We'll be back in touch soon to wrap this up. Enjoy your evening."

Outside on the sidewalk, Sam faced Joe to ask, "What was that? Don't we want to buckle him up and start building a case against Scott?"

"One of the reasons I was heading in this direction when you two were parked across the street," Joe explained, "is that I think Sheldon Scott has bigger worries than Aaron Whitledge right now."

CHAPTER TWENTY-FIVE

Sheldon Scott lived in a mansion, east of
downtown Montpelier, with a sweeping
view of the valley below — made all the
more spectacular at this time of day by a
crimson setting sun coloring the Winooski's
waters like a spilled ribbon of red paint.

The driveway was marked by pretentious
twin granite pillars and — some twenty feet
down the broad gravel path — by something
that made Joe swear as he steered around it.
It was an older model, dark green Buick
Skylark.

"What?" Lester asked.

Sam answered, "That's Barb Barber's old
car. The one Joe thinks was stolen by her
sister."

Joe picked up speed, skidding around the
several curves leading up to the house, and
spitting stones onto the neighboring grass.
"I'm too late," he said grimly.

"You think she went after Scott?" Sam asked.

"I do," he said, fighting the steering wheel. "And Marshall and Friel and Barb. We've been seeing her as a victim through all this. I'm not saying she's not that —" He paused to slam on the brakes before the huge building.

"But she could be our killer, too," Sam finished for him as they piled out of the car.

They stared up at the building quickly, gauging their approach.

"Call for backup," Joe ordered, circling to the car's trunk and extracting three ballistic vests and the one shotgun he kept back there. "We can't wait for them, but I want 'em on the way."

Still attaching his Velcro straps, he ran up the broad stone steps to the carved double doors of the main entrance and laid his hand on the handle. It yielded, and the door opened a crack.

He charged the shotgun's chamber as his colleagues pulled out their handguns. "Okay," he said, "Exigent circumstances. We're going in, but no fanfare. Fast and low."

He swung open the door and swept in, cutting to the left as Lester and Sam followed suit like parachutists leaping from a plane.

They found themselves in a large, front lobby, facing an ostentatious curved staircase ahead and a row of doors down both side walls, all dominated from above by a chandelier better suited to a European castle.

There wasn't a sound or a movement aside from their own.

Joe gestured to them to spread out and check the doors as he approached the staircase walking backwards, his weapon at the ready, his eyes fixed on the second-floor balcony that was half hidden by the chandelier — an ideal nest for a shooter anticipating their entry.

But he saw no one.

"Joe," came Sammie's voice, echoing off the towering walls and marble floor.

He left the stairs for the door she'd opened to enter the library, which turned out to occupy most of the house's left wing, and which — unbeknownst to any of them — resembled Scott's office in Montpelier.

Lester joined him to see Sam standing near the center of the room, before an elaborate antique wingback chair.

Sitting there comfortably, with a surprised look on his face, was Sheldon Scott.

"He dead?" Joe asked, thinking — in one of those disconnected moments that challenge one's sense of proportion — that Gail's current woes were going to be considerably lessened by this development. She was still facing a storm of her own — no doubt about it — but with Scott's demise, its primary driving force had been suddenly removed.

"Yeah."

"You're sure?"

"No carotid," she answered. "He's still warm, but I know dead."

Joe could attest to that. He turned to Lester, who anticipated him by reaching for his cell phone and saying, "Upgrade the BOL on Carolyn and get a full homicide response on this, including the crime lab."

Joe nodded, adding to them both, "And let's make sure the house is clear. Right now. We can come back here once we're sure we're alone."

They quickly made a tactical sweep of the entire building, ending up in the four-car garage, where they discovered a vehicle missing and one of the doors wide open. A phone call to VBI Dispatch revealed that Scott had four cars registered to him; the missing one was added to the alert.

Minutes later, they were back at the

library door. "Did you see what did him in?" Joe asked of Sammie.

"Small puncture wound over the heart," she replied. "But smaller than a bullet, and no gunshot residue. That seemed to be it."

Joe recalled Beverly's finding with William Friel. "Like an ice-pick?"

"That would fit."

They stayed where they were, not wanting to further contaminate a crime scene. Sammie added, pointing, "The pillow on the chair opposite him looked depressed, unlike any of the others. Like somebody had been sitting on it."

Joe nodded, mostly to himself, and turned to face the front entrance across the lobby. "So maybe she knocks on the door, he opens up, they begin to talk and he brings her in here. They sit, she hears all she needs to, and she sticks him."

The three of them retreated to the foot of the stairs, hearing sirens approaching from afar. "God only knows where Carolyn is now," Joe said, "but I bet she's not moving too fast, given how long it's been since she drove regularly. Maybe we'll get lucky."

Sam sighed, "Let's hope somebody gets her before she does any more damage. She's doubling the state's homicide rate."

■ ■ ■ ■

They didn't find Carolyn Barber. They located Sheldon Scott's BMW, abandoned in a nearby grocery store parking lot and covered with Carolyn's fingerprints, but of her, they found no further trace.

They did discover the stolen photograph from Gorden Marshall's apartment — along with the key and the uniform that Travis Reynolds had used to infiltrate The Woods. They were in Scott's office, off his upstairs bedroom, lumped together in a pile. There was no *CC* lapel pin, however, and no files — which were now presumed to have been stolen by Carolyn for their contents on the same day that she smothered an alcoholically impaired Gorden Marshall. Intriguingly to Joe, a single thumbprint of Carolyn's was lifted from the photograph's glass, as if she'd held it contemplatively after stabbing Sheldon downstairs. That discovery made him think as well that she'd possibly removed the purple and gold Catamount Cavaliers memento, perhaps as an ironic souvenir. If that was true — and since she remained unaccounted for — Joe couldn't help considering that she might have more ex-Cavaliers on her list of men to kill.

Indeed, that possibility had led to a thorough and ongoing effort to identify who might be left among Scott and Marshall's fellow club members.

Fueling the concern about Carolyn's motivation, a search of Scott's home uncovered a trove of Cavalier artifacts in a large wall safe, along with hundreds of unrelated confidential files. There was only one pin — probably Scott's own — but many letters, more vintage photos of people in high spirits, and other documents attesting to the faux-formal nature of the organization's genesis, complete with a salacious but official-looking framed listing of "Rules of Mis-Behaviour," handwritten in mock Old English style.

Finally, in what amounted to a pathetic footnote, there was a memo in Scott's hand, informing Marshall to play along with Carolyn's demand for money and to be named Governor-for-a-Day, complete with attending pomp and ceremony — part of her price for keeping her pregnancy quiet. Then, as inevitable and as cold as revenge can be, there were copies of adoption documents, legally rendering a female infant over to the care of Mr. and Mrs. Gorden Marshall, and a copy of the same commitment papers that Joe had read earlier in the state hospital archives, dated the same year, along with hand-lettered notes indicating the establishment of a mood-altering regimen that was to be perpetually — and illegally — maintained to keep Carolyn Barber in a state of permanent stupor.

Sheldon Scott had clearly been a man to keep track of his favors to others.

Joe was organizing his paperwork several nights later, closing out as much of the case as possible, and repeatedly reminded of its cost in human misery — not unlike that of Tropical Storm Irene. He kept wondering how and if Carolyn could have possibly survived, assuming that recent events hadn't already taken their toll, sweeping her away like so much trash in a flood. She was no youngster, after all, and by now had no family, no resources, and — as far as they'd been able to determine — nowhere to go.

Her prior missing person notices had all been taken down, replaced by wanted posters and, sadly, more sensationalist media coverage than she ever received when she was simply presumed missing.

His desk phone rang, as if responding to his ruminations.

"Gunther," he answered.

"Agent Gunther, this is Michelle Mahoney, Gorden Marshall's daughter?"

"Of course, Ms. Mahoney. What can I do for you?"

"It's probably nothing," she said. "But I was putting the final touches on moving my father's junk out so they can sell his apartment. I found something I thought you should know about, just in case it's helpful. Are you able to meet with me right now? I'm on the interstate, heading south, near Brattleboro. I think that's where you work, no? I am sorry for the short notice, but —"

"Absolutely," Joe interrupted her. "I'm still at the office. Would you like to come straight here? It's not far from exit two."

"That would be great," she said, her gratitude plain. "Just give me directions."

He heard her approaching down the hallway, less than fifteen minutes later, and went out to usher her in. She was elegantly dressed, as usual, in the casual country look that places like Orvis and J. Crew idealize, and he offered her Sammie's office chair.

"What's on your mind?" he asked.

"I found something a little disturbing," she told him. "This morning, as I was making one last check around."

"Okay," he replied leadingly.

"There's not that much left," she went on. "All the walls are stripped, and half the furniture is gone. So the place is pretty much empty."

He remained silent, sensing her difficulty in wording what came next.

She touched her hair absentmindedly. "Well," she admitted. "It's left me for a loop, to be honest. I came into the apartment and found something in the middle of the floor, placed on top of a handwritten note."

"The apartment wasn't locked?" Joe asked, his interest sharpened.

"No. I didn't see the point. Plus, the movers don't have a key." She reached into her handbag and extracted a small item that she held out for him to examine.

He extended his open hand and received a dark purple lapel pin, engraved with twin golden capital letter *C*'s.

"Ah," he said, surprised.

"You recognize it?" she asked.

"Yes. I do."

"This was with it," she added, going back into the purse.

She handed over a small piece of paper, on which was written, *I have always loved you*. It was signed, *Mom*.

Joe looked up to see tears brimming in Michelle Mahoney's eyes.

"I don't understand," she said simply.

He pulled his own chair over so that they were sitting almost knee to knee in the semi-darkened office.

"I think I do," he said. "Let me tell you what I can about your real mother."

EPILOGUE

Paul Canfield read the article slowly and carefully, as if watching for any movement among the words before him. He was a deer hunter by passion — or had been before old age had brought that and much more to an end. Trophies in the form of antlers, mounted heads, and celebratory photographs by the dozen adorned his log home outside of Bradford, Vermont. The entire place had a distinctly male feeling to it — he lived alone, having been married three times to women who'd found his company quickly objectionable. He also had three children, whose names he knew, if little else. Sharing space, or anything else, had never been his strong suit.

Canfield had been a man in a hurry for most of his life, given to the pursuit of advancement and reward, and not so interested in the care and nurturing of his fellow human beings. A smart man, most colleagues and acquaintances had to concede, but rarely a kind one.

He dropped the newspaper onto his reading table and watched the portrait on its front page become haloed by the circle of light under the lamp. SCOTT INVESTIGATION CONTINUES, the headline read, with a smaller subhead underneath it admitting, "Police releasing few statements."

No kidding, Canfield thought. You can't release what you don't have. The cops had said that they had several good leads about who'd killed Sheldon Scott, but they refused to give up names. That seemed telling to Canfield. They were stuck.

He frowned at Scott's photograph. It was a glamor shot, clearly circulated by his office, which was apparently running smoothly following his death. He looked dashing and incisive, his white mane offset by black eyebrows and a piercing look. Canfield assumed the whole thing had been touched up in the darkroom — or whatever they used nowadays — but he had to admit that he hadn't seen Scott in years.

He was glad the man was dead, though; gladder still that he'd been murdered. Even a man as hard as Paul Canfield had found this former comrade-in-arms to be a heartless, manipulative bastard.

Not that he hadn't done good work. Or hadn't made them all a pile of money. Canfield would give him that much. The son of a bitch could work the system — he and his sugar daddy Harold LeMieur. Talk about having friends in the right places.

Canfield placed his hands on the arms of his chair and painfully struggled to stand, pausing at the end of the process to take a breath. He'd read about Marshall dying days ago — admittedly from natural causes, according to the one early report that he'd read. Now it was Scott's turn.

Canfield shuffled over to the bookcase beside his fireplace and stood before an elaborately framed glass box sitting on a shelf at eye level. He turned on the special light switch on its side, filling its interior with an attractive golden glow.

There they all were — youthful, vibrant, full of vitality and promise. The young bucks of the party's conservative wing, complete with glasses raised. Less ideologues than opportunists, this particular group had used the cause as a cloak to pad their pockets and quench their appetites. The Catamount Cavaliers — the elite of the elite, as they'd seen themselves.

He scanned the several photographs surrounding the dark purple lapel pin that he'd had mounted in the middle of the box, right over a copy of the group's tongue-in-cheek rules. He studied Scott's face, Marshall's, his own, and the others'. Three of the four pictures featured women, their gaiety touched — he thought now — with perhaps a hint of apprehension.

They'd had good reason for that, he reminisced. People would have a fit today, if they knew what the Cavaliers had been all about. He smiled at the memories that brought to mind.

The doorbell rang, straightening his back and creating a scowl.

At this hour?

He turned away from the display and headed slowly for the cabin's entrance, turning on the porch light as he opened the door.

Before him stood a slight, white-haired woman, younger than he by a few years, with an embarrassed smile on her face.

"I'm so sorry to bother you," she said. "But my car stopped running, a mile down the road. I don't know why. I was so happy I saw your light through the woods. . . ."

She left the thought unfinished, no doubt expecting Canfield to follow up with an invitation for her to at least use his phone to call for help.

But he didn't, true to nature. He just stood there, watching her face, his forehead furrowed.

"Could I come in?" she asked. "I don't have a cell, and I ought to call a wrecker or someone."

Reluctantly, he stepped back and widened the door, asking, "Do I know you?"

She looked up and smiled as she entered.